# Children of the Revolution

## BOOK 3 IN THE WESTWARD SAGAS

# Children of the Revolution

## BOOK 3 IN THE WESTWARD SAGAS

### David Bowles

Children of the Revolution: Book 3 in the Westward Sagas

Plum Creek Press, Inc.®
15610 Henderson Pass, #701561
San Antonio, Texas 78270-1561
210-490-9955
210-403-9072 FAX
www.westwardsagas.com
info@westwardsagas.com

ISBN 10—Print: 0977748472
ISBN 13—Print: 978-0-9777484-7-1

ISBN 10—E-Book: 0977748480
ISBN 13—E-Book: 978-0-9777484-8-8


Cover Art: Aundrea Hernandez
Author Photo: Lilian Foreman
Editors: Lillie Ammann, Jan McClintock

# Dedication

Laura Lee Sankey Pursell

*One of the Angels of Radam Lane*

1949–2012

# Preface

*Children of the Revolution: Book 3 in the Westward Sagas* is the story of patriots Adam and Elizabeth Mitchell's progeny. Their six oldest were not only children of the American Revolution, but survived the bloody Battle of Guilford Courthouse, fought on the family farm March 15, 1781. This book is not about war, but how it affected the children who became *America's First Generation*.

I have written the Westward Sagas Series as historical fiction, based on actual events in history. Vital statistics are based on extensive research and known facts, including the Family Bible started by Adam Mitchell ten years before the signing of The Declaration of Independence. Where sufficient historical records are available I used that data; where it wasn't, I created it in a believable way that I hope you find entertaining.

Geographical locations are accurate with the exception of Limestone, Tennessee which wasn't created until after the railroad came. The previous names Freedom and Klepper's Depot have been forgotten except by a few. The importance of the area, home to Samuel Doak, his Salem Church and Washington College is too significant to chance confusion. Likewise, Johnson City, Tennessee is not mentioned as it didn't exist during this period. The Knob Creek Community is in present day Johnson City.

The personas of Peggy, the protagonist, and her siblings were created by me. Even though they lived hundreds of years before me, I know them well. I hope you enjoy the story of America's first generation.

# Acknowledgements

The Westward Sagas continues in *Children of the Revolution*, the third book in the series. I have dedicated this book to my dear friend, Laura Lee Sankey Pursell, who encouraged me to write.

Many have helped to bring this epic story to publication, foremost my daughter, Sherri Williams, who took the reins of the family business several years ago to allow me time to research and write the hundred-year odyssey of our family. I see in her many of the strengths of our ancestors. My well-organized administrative assistant, Holly Langford, handles the everyday stuff of a writer's assistant—copy editing, coordinating travel, scheduling, keeping me organized and writing—not an easy task.

My cousin Ann Winkler Hinrichs, a Mitchell family genealogist, has provided many useful documents that have helped me better understand our early ancestors and the role each played in Colonial Times. Cousin Diane Bland, also a dedicated genealogist, has provided much information on the Rebeckah and Thomas W. Smith family, who will be the real-life characters in book four, about expansion of the west.

Photographer Lilian Foreman took the authors photo and graphic artist Aundrea Hernandez again produced an outstanding book cover.

My editor Lillie Ammann and her assistant Jan McClintock did an excellent job of editing and formatting this book for print and e-book distribution.

From across the pond, Berry Brothers and Rudd, Plymouth Gin Distillers, and Rules Restaurant all provided important documentation and gave permission to mention their company names. The Grandfather Mountain Stewardship Foundation in North Carolina cheerfully assisted us with details of their mountain.

Advance readers who read a very rough first draft of *The Children of the Revolution* are: Bill Willis, Bonnie Disney, Carole Cordova, Katherine Goodloe, Dorothy Breezee, Paul Ruckman, Sue Carter, and Betty Jane Hylton. They did an excellent job and many of their suggestions were incorporated into this book.

# Chapter One
## Return to Guilford

The weary horsemen rode hunkered down in the saddle as they climbed the Deep Gap Trail of Grandfather Mountain. Snow blew into their faces, turning eyebrows and other facial hair into curly little icicles. The men weren't dressed for such extreme cold this late in the spring. They chose this route because, under normal conditions, going over the mountain was faster than going around the mountain along the river trail. Mother Nature's surprise obscured the panoramic view of the Watauga Valley and the town of Boone below in the distance. Adam's grown sons had often heard their father describe the view from the top of "ole Grandfather."

Adam hollered over the shrieking wind. "Robert, you best take the lead now—your eyesight is much better than mine. Everyone into single file."

The drifts of snow now came halfway up to the horse's knees. The two short-legged pack donkeys tethered to the last horse sensed their precarious predicament. They struggled and pulled back on the reins as John, the youngest Mitchell on the trip, tried to coax the stubborn animals forward, knowing that the donkeys had ample reason to resist.

"We best stop," Robert, the oldest of Adam's sons, yelled back. "I can't see the trail any longer. We could wander off a cliff."

Adam pulled on the reins to stop his horse. "I know you're right, but we could freeze to death on this mountain."

1

William, the middle son, agreed. "We best take our chances on the mountain."

Adam shouted over the howling wind. "I'm sorry I brought you over the mountain rather than going through the valley." He shook his head. "Had no idea this spring storm was coming."

Robert looked at his brothers before he spoke. "We know, Father."

"You did what you thought was best at the time." Jimmy Witherspoon yelled to be heard over the howling wind.

Adam dismounted. "Best make some type of shelter."

They found a heavy thicket where a herd of deer had taken refuge from the storm. Their approach startled the deer, and they scattered. The heat of the bodies of the creatures that had been lying there caused a smoky steam to rise.

Jimmy knelt to feel the warmth by holding a bare hand over the exposed dry ground. He looked up at his companions and smiled. "I think we should take advantage of the dry gound"

The men placed a heavy oilcloth tarp on the ground to sit on and used the rest of the tarps carried by the donkeys to create a makeshift shelter. They huddled beneath the tarps in a circle, clutching the bulky material the best they could to prevent it from blowing away. Their backs were up against one another to preserve body heat. Each spread his bedroll over the front of his body—shoulders to feet. The scant fire was too small and too far away to provide warmth, but it would deter the predators that roamed the mountain. Snow drifts piled up against the tarps, forming a wall that would help protect their bodies against the whistling wind.

Jimmy removed a small, leather-bound Bible from his satchel and clutched it reverently to his chest. The Bible had been a gift to the minister from members of the Hebron Presbyterian Church. "Will you pray with me?"

They prayed, and Jimmy recited Psalm 23 from memory as it was too dark to read from the Bible. They found comfort in the Scripture and Jimmy's prayers.

They knew someone must stay awake if they were to survive. They told stories and jokes far into the night, trying not to succumb to unconsciousness and sure death.

Adam volunteered to stay awake so the others could get some rest. He reminded himself of many dangerous experiences they had survived and prayed they would get through this situation. He and Elizabeth were fortunate that all their children survived to adulthood, except for baby Joseph, who had been taken in his sleep by a bolt of lightning. *God must have needed him for an angel.*

As he slept, Robert began to shake and utter the strange sounds that his father and brothers had heard many times before.

"Please, don't bring any more bodies. No more, please," Robert pleaded in his sleep.

Adam leaned over and spoke softly to his son. "It's all right, Robert. It's just a bad dream that will go away when you wake up." He sighed, knowing that Robert's nightmares would never go away, nor would his.

Before dawn, the wind began to die. Adam could see stars and a waning crescent moon through a small hole in the tarp over his head. The moonlight gave the new fallen snow that covered the mountain a bluish tint. Grandfather Mountain was known for its snow-covered cap into the summer, but a blizzard this late in the year was unusual. Adam leaned over and placed a hand on the clergyman's knee to wake him. "You did good, Jimmy. Our prayers have been answered."

Jimmy tried not to reveal that he had fallen asleep. "That's g-g-ood."

"At daylight, we're getting off this mountain and on to Guilford Courthouse," Adam said.

Jimmy yawned. "It's now called Martinsville."

"I know, but it will always be Guilford Courthouse to me."

Robert stretched and rubbed his eyes with gloved hands. "Sounds like a strange name for a town."

Adam shrugged. "Never was a town, just a few farmhouses near the courthouse of Guilford County. For lack of a better name, we just called the community Guilford Courthouse. I believe it was our neighbor, Francis McNairy, who first called it that."

Robert said, "I went to school with his son John."

"That's right. Matter of fact, Francis and John both witnessed the sale of Mother's farm to Mr. Hamilton."

John wrinkled his forehead, "I don't understand why someone would give back land that they paid you good money for."

"From his correspondence, it seems the responsibility of protecting hallowed ground was more than Mr. Hamilton could endure," Adam said.

His sons became very quiet, each in their own thoughts of that dreadful March day when their home was destroyed by the British and their lives altered forever. Jimmy had often heard the stories and shuddered at the thought of what the family had endured during the battle. Not only was he their minister, but he had also attended Samuel Doak's Salem Church and school with Adam Mitchell's sons. Now he was assisting Peggy, the eldest Mitchell daughter, to teach at the Hebron School.

After a short silence, the men started to move. Once out from under the smelly oilcloth, they could see the sun slowly rising over a few dwellings in the far distance.

Adam pointed. "That's smoke billowing from fireplaces in Boone. Boys, get a good look at it—you dang near gave your lives to see it."

"Is Boone in North Carolina or Tennessee?" John asked as he rolled his bedroll.

"Don't know for sure." Adam shook his head. "It was North Carolina when ole Daniel Boone first settled it, but it's so close to the boundary of three states it could be anyone's guess. Might even be Virginia."

They fed the animals cracked corn. The men gnawed on deer jerky and didn't bother to build a fire. They just wanted to get off the mountain.

The snow had stopped, but the ground was covered with drifts of white powder—knee-high in places. Leading the horses, the men trudged down the northeast side of the mountain, a descent that would take most of the day.

***

Half-frozen and wearing wet clothes, the men stopped at the only inn along the road.

"Welcome to the Boone Inn, gentlemen." A little man of no more than five feet spoke with a British accent. "I'm Jonathan Wilkes, the proprietor. What can I do for you?" he asked, looking nervously at the gun-toting mountain men. Then he relaxed when he saw Jimmy's collar and the Bible he cradled.

"We need to warm up, eat a good meal, feed our animals, and get some rest," Adam said.

"I have a large room upstairs with a fireplace that the five of you can share. Three can sleep on the rope bed, which has a fine feather mattress, and two can roll out bedrolls on the floor."

"Sounds good, don't you think?" Adam looked at his traveling companions, who eagerly nodded their approval. "We'll take it."

Opening the door to the room for his boarders, the innkeeper asked, "Where are you from?"

Adam answered, "From Knob Creek, north of Jonesborough."

Mr. Wilkes led them to the barn. Once the horses and mules were cared for and the men had eaten a warm meal, they retired to their room.

The roaring fire in the large, limestone fireplace warmed their bodies and dried the heavy linsey-woolsey clothing hung about the room.

At breakfast the next morning, Mr. Wilkes asked, "What brings you this far from Knob Creek?"

"Headed to Guilford Courthouse on business," Adam said.

The young innkeeper appeared to be about the same age as Robert, who was twenty-seven. Mr. Wilkes said he was a newcomer to the mountains, having recently moved from New York to buy the inn from the previous owner.

He stood only a few inches from Adam. "Must be important business," Wilkes said, peering inquisitively into Adam's eyes.

"Yes, it is."

The innkeeper leaned closer to hear more, as if he expected Adam to whisper a secret into his ear. Adam ignored Mr. Wilkes' question and leaned back away from him.

"Were your parents loyalists?" Adam asked.

"They were neutral," Mr. Wilkes snapped. "Would you like more biscuits?" He held out the breadbasket toward Adam.

Adam grabbed the breadbasket and slammed it on the table. "They had to be either Tories or Patriots. Only Quakers were neutral. With your inn serving whisky, I don't think you would be of that sect."

The other four men looked at their elder, surprised at his sudden anger toward this little man.

"I was just a child during the Revolution. My parents always told me they didn't get involved in the war." Wilkes picked up the breadbasket and turned away to offer biscuits to the other men.

Adam jumped up from his chair and shouted, "How could your family not be involved in the Revolutionary War?"

The innkeeper remained silent, looking down at the dusty buffalo hide that covered his hard-packed dirt floor, obviously uncomfortable with Adam's outburst.

"Adam, the war is over," Jimmy said. "We won our freedom. What difference does it make?"

Adam's face turned red. He glared at Jimmy, then at his sons, then at the innkeeper. Shaking his head, he stormed toward the door without his coat. At the door, he turned back and took a deep breath. "I best check on the horses. You need to gather your belongings."

John followed his father. "Let me help you."

Jimmy said, "I have never seen or heard Adam Mitchell speak to anyone like that, Mr. Wilkes."

"Me, neither," Robert said.

"Sounds very bitter about a war that his side won." Mr. Wilkes picked up Adam's plate.

Jimmy took a deep breath. "Yes, but that war cost him everything he had."

Robert's and William's thoughts drifted for a moment back inside the spring house when they were young boys listening to the cries of the wounded in their cornfields.

John followed Adam into the stable adjacent to the inn. "What happened in there? I've never seen you so angry at anyone."

"His accent and his looks reminded me of the British guard who taunted me and the other Guilford Militiamen in the pigpen where we were kept prisoner after the battle."

"He reminds you of someone who mistreated you?" John asked.

"Yes." Adam looked down at the ground. "But, more than that, I dread seeing the farm fields that your grandfather and I cleared, knowing that all those bodies are buried in what was our farm."

"I understand, and I think my brothers and I feel the same." John put an arm on his father's shoulder. He looked into Adam's blue eyes and saw a small tear from a man who seldom showed any emotion.

"I just don't know if I can oversee the land from so far away."

"Don't you think Reverend Caldwell would help? He lives nearby."

"I know he would if he could, but he and Rachel are both getting old." Adam took a deep breath.

John said, "You have sons who will follow your wishes."

"That's right!" William said as he entered the stable.

Adam smiled at his sons. "I know, but you boys are all getting married and soon will have your own families to care for."

"Father, we're family. We'll do what needs to be done," William said.

When the reverend and Robert came in, Adam said, "Get your horses saddled. I'll pay our board and apologize to Mr. Wilkes."

***

The sun shone brightly without a cloud in the sky. The travelers rode hard to make up for the time they had lost in the snowstorm. As they approached a fork in the road, they reined in their horses.

"Things are beginning to look familiar," John said.

William pointed straight ahead. "I remember that fork."

"I think we've made it, boys." Adam spurred his horse forward.

When the others caught up to Adam, they found him on his knees in front of a small rock structure embedded in the side of the creek. Adam gently caressed the rocks he and his father had laboriously stacked so many years ago to make a cool place for the family to store dairy products and eggs.

Adam looked around the tiny space. "This is what's left of the spring house."

"It's amazing that it's still standing," Robert said.

"If the British army couldn't destroy it, nothing else could," Adam said.

John and William stood up in their stirrups to look down into the roofless shell of the spring house from the top of the creek bank.

John looked around and spoke. "It seemed much larger when I was a child."

"Of course, everything seems larger when you're a child," William said.

John shook his head and mumbled, "I don't even want to think about it."

Adam and Robert stepped into the ruins, followed by Jimmy.

Jimmy looked at Adam, and then around at the tiny space. "You mean this is where Mother Mitchell, Elizabeth, and the children hid during the battle?" The stories Peggy told him were beginning to make sense. He visualized them inside with the door shut, thousands of soldiers going at one another, guns and cannons blazing amidst the clang of swords and bayonets.

Adam and his sons didn't say a word, but all nodded their heads to acknowledge the question.

Adam led his horse a short distance up a small knoll. The boys followed, leading their horses and the pack animals to the spot where their home had once stood. It also was in shambles, another victim of the horrific fight that had taken place here.

Standing in front of where the front porch had been, no one said a word. They just gazed at what had been their home. Suddenly a mongrel bitch came charging out from under the remains of the porch. The yellowish dog stopped three yards in front of the men and growled menacingly, the hair on her back standing up straight. She appeared to be nursing.

"She has a pack of pups under there that she's protecting." Adam approached her slowly, holding out a piece of deer jerky. "Here, old girl, take this."

"Careful," Robert said.

"She's starved from nursing her litter." Adam reached out further to her.

The excited dog wouldn't take the jerky from his hand, so he tossed it in front of her. She grabbed it and scurried back under the rubble. As soon as her head disappeared from the men's sight, they heard sounds of movement and a babble of yelps.

"Hear the pups?" Adam asked.

"Sure do," John answered.

Adam looked around the area and then at his sons. "What do we have that would fill her stomach?"

John reached for his rifle. "I'll go shoot a rabbit before it gets dark."

"Good idea. We can camp here by the ruins tonight and give the old girl some human company, whether she wants it or not," Adam said.

The men worked together to build a fire and create a shelter with the tarps. They would be in Guilford County several nights, and Adam remembered the frequent spring rains of the Piedmont.

A gunshot rang out. Everyone jumped.

Adam took a deep breath. "Sounds like John hit something."

"Hope it's a big one." Robert patted his stomach. "That ole mamma dog isn't the only one who's hungry."

"Me, too," William said.

Jimmy said, "You won't have to wait long. I hear John coming now."

"That's the biggest rabbit I ever saw!" exclaimed William as he pulled the large deer carcass off John's horse.

"I came up on a rabbit, and just as I was about to fire, this deer came out of the timber. I only had one shot, so I took the best one."

Adam patted his son on the back. "Good job. We can feed the mongrel and still have meat for us."

"You sure do worry about that dog." Robert helped William hang the deer spread-eagle in an elm tree to bleed out before butchering.

"She reminds me of Lulubelle. She's the same color but a different body shape." Adam sighed deeply, remembering the death of the family dog the previous summer. "I sure miss Lulubelle. Wonder how this dog ended up here at our old home?"

"This is for her." John pitched a handful of innards under the rubble of the house.

"Did you see how fast she wolfed that up?" Robert asked.

The reverend leaned down to look under the house. "She's pretty weak—couldn't catch a mouse in her condition."

After a hearty meal of venison, cornbread, and red beans, the men laid out their bedrolls and were just about asleep when a raspy voice cried out of the darkness. "Adam, is that you?"

John and William instinctively reached for their guns.

"I'm Adam Mitchell. Who goes there?"

The voice, sounding like that of an old man, answered, "Adam, it's Trapper John come back to haunt you."

Adam strained his eyes, trying to make out the features of the strange-looking man through the billowing smoke of the campfire. The man held a long shepherd's crook. He wore a full-length cloth robe tied at the waist, and his belongings were strapped to his back. The center of his head was bald. His thin, shaggy, gray hair and long, gray beard had only a few thin streaks of dark hair. "Is it really you, Trapper?"

The men met halfway and embraced in a bear hug so intense they almost fell in the campfire. Robert, William, and John jumped up and joined in the welcoming celebration as Jimmy enjoyed watching the reunion of old friends. "Which one of you young 'uns is Robert?" Trapper asked.

"That would be me."

"Can't believe you're all growed up. Do you remember me carrying you in a papoose as I plowed your father's fields?" Trapper asked.

"I don't remember that, but I remember you coming to our house for breakfast."

Trapper looked at the other three young men, "You must be . . . "

"I'm William, the next oldest—exactly four years younger than Robert."

Trapper looked at the two other men and turned to one of them, "I think I see a family resemblance. You must be John."

"That's right, the third son."

"Well, then, who is this fellow smiling like a possum?"

Adam said, "Trapper, meet Reverend James Witherspoon, our pastor. We call him Jimmy."

Trapper grinned, showing only a few teeth. "You Mitchell boys getting into so much trouble you have to bring your preacher with you all the way from Knob Creek?"

"Reverend Witherspoon came along in hopes of meeting Reverend Caldwell and Rachel," Adam said.

"I'm honored to meet a man of the cloth. I know Reverend and Missus Caldwell are excited about seeing Adam and the boys. I'm sure he'd want to meet you." Trapper bowed his head.

"The honor is mine," Jimmy said.

"Have you eaten? We have lots of stewed venison left." Adam pointed to the pot sitting beside the campfire.

Trapper stepped closer. "You know, I wouldn't turn down something to eat."

The men gathered around the campfire and watched as Trapper gulped down three big bowls of venison stew and the remaining cornbread. They put a pot of coffee on the fire for what would be a long night of catching up between old friends.

"Can I get you anything else?" Adam asked.

"Jist another cup of that coffee, if you please. Widow Jessop doesn't keep any at home. She thinks it's bad for me." Trapper shook his head. "After all the rotgut whisky I drunk, what difference does it make? I sure miss a good cup of campfire coffee now and then."

"How did you know I was here?" Adam asked.

"Mr. Hamilton told me you would be here by the first day of May. Course, I can't read or write, so I don't know what day that would be. I guess he got tired of me asking every day when you would be here. So he told me in three sunrises you'd be here. This morning was three sunrises since he told me that."

"Then you can count," Adam said.

"I can't count much, but I can get to three. So I went to the courthouse this morning, and Mr. Hamilton said you wrote that you would be here today. He seemed put out that you weren't here. I told him that if you said you was gonna to be here, you'd be here—and here you are!"

"We planned on being here sooner, but we got caught on Grandfather Mountain in a snowstorm," Adam said.

"This late in the spring?"

"Yes sir, it was some blizzard. Thought we were going to freeze to death." Adam made a brushing motion with his hand as if to wipe away that thought. "Now I have to know how you escaped the Hessian soldiers when they captured me. For all these years, until I got John Hamilton's letter, I thought you were dead. Tell me what happened."

Trapper chuckled. "Once those Hessians broke through the front line of the Guilford County Militia near Hoskins Farm, everything happened so fast." Trapper took a sip of coffee.

Adam said, "Yes, it did."

"I followed you up a cliff jist behind you a little ways. As I got to the top, I seen they had you. No sooner than I seen you, the ground underneath me gave way, and I was jist swallowed up."

"Swallowed up?" Adam asked.

Trapper looked down, "I felt so bad I couldn't protect you like I promised your mother I would."

"There were too many of them; there was nothing you could have done," Adam said. "How did the earth just swallow you up?"

"The bank of the creek gave way under my weight. I fell backward into the dry creek bed, and the cliff jist caved in on top of me. As luck would have it, my face fell next to a big fallen timber. An opening under that log gave me jist a crack to see and breathe. I laid there on my face for a long time. That dirt was so heavy, it felt like it was crushing my bones."

The listening men looked at each other with expressions of horror.

"I thought I was dead, and then I heard the voice of a sweet old lady—reminded me of your mother. All I could see was her shoes in the creek bed jist a few feet from my face. I begged her to please help me. She couldn't figure out where I was, and I couldn't tell her because I didn't know. She got some men, and later on they tole me they dug all day and night to get to me. I was pretty far gone by the time they got me out. Miz Jessop was the lady what found me; she took me home and cared for me until I got better. It took quite a while, though."

"The cliff caved in and the soil covered you up. That makes sense." Adam nodded. "For nearly sixteen years, I didn't know what happened to you. I'm so glad you're alive."

Everyone just sat there without speaking or moving as they contemplated Trapper's story.

Jimmy broke the silence. "Praise God!"

Trapper looked at Jimmy, his brow furrowed. "What do that mean? The Quakers say that all the time, but it was Miz Jessop what saved me. Just like that momma bear did when I was jist a baby. God weren't there, neither."

"I understand, Trapper, that you haven't been churched." Jimmy attempted to explain. "Trust me,

Trapper. God has a plan for you, and He had a hand in saving your life by sending you the help that you needed, whether it was in the form of Mrs. Jessop or the momma bear."

The minister had heard the stories of Trapper John and how he claimed to have been cared for by a mother bear when his widowed father died in the woods with Trapper in a papoose on his back. The Indians who found him with the bear confirmed this story, and Adam had seen the scars on his neck where the bear carried him by the scruff of the neck, as she would her cub.

"That's some story to live to tell about," John said.

Trapper nodded. "I hear Mr. Hamilton wants to give your mother's farm back."

"That's why I'm here. I'm trying to figure out why." Adam looked at his friend for an answer.

"He told folks that he keeps seeing the ghost of your mother. Says she's come back as a dog and guards what's left of the home and won't let nobody near it."

About that time the yellow momma dog came out from under her hiding place.

William pointed. "You mean her?"

"That's her. Don't let her bite me." Trapper started backing away in fear.

"She won't hurt you, Trapper." John reached to give the animal some more venison.

Trapper stopped but continued to eye the dog. "She's run off everybody that comes here. That ole dog ran me all the way up New Garden Road last time I was here."

"She was just protecting her pups." Adam handed Trapper a chunk of venison. "Pitch her a piece of meat, and she'll be your friend forever."

Trapper timidly tossed the venison toward the dog.

"Mr. Hamilton thinks this dog is my dead mother?" Adam asked.

"He says that dog told him not to never let anybody disturb the resting place of the brave men that are buried here."

"Come on. Be serious." Adam pointed at the canine. "That dog talked to John Hamilton?"

Trapper nodded. "That's what I heard." Adam gazed at the pitiful-looking, old dog with its tail between its legs and shook his head. "He thinks my mother has come back as this dog?"

Trapper leaned back, his bushy eyebrows raised toward his balding head, making his dark eyes seem larger than they were. "That's what they says."

The men all had a good laugh.

"Well, Mother, if that's you in that bag of bones, I guess we better start feeding you a little better."

Adam held a piece of the fresh-cut venison in his palm. The dog approached with her tail out from between her hind legs.

Trapper took a couple of steps backward. "Careful."

"My mother wouldn't bite the hand that feeds her." Adam let the dog take the morsel and then lick the deer blood from his hand.

The dog wagged her tail as Adam stroked the fur on her back. Everyone watched, expecting her to attack.

"You're welcome, Mother." Adam got closer and caressed the dog with both hands. "Should we call her Mother Mitchell?"

Robert looked from the dog to his father. "You're not going to name that dog, are you?"

"If she's going to share our campfire and food, she should have a name."

"If she is Grandmother Mitchell, she should have a Biblical name," William said.

"Why not call her Lulubelle, after our old, faithful dog?" Adam asked.

"Much more appropriate than naming her for Grand-mother." John moved cautiously toward the dog. "Here, Lulubelle." He held out his hand.

The dog sniffed John's hand, and finding nothing to eat, returned to Adam's side.

"I think Adam has a new friend, " Jimmy said.

Adam reached down and gingerly patted the dog's head. Lulubelle got up and went under the porch.

Then Adam turned to Trapper, "Tell me what happened after this Jessop woman found you."

"I don't 'member much till I woke up some days later. I heard lots of people talking in a tongue I never heard before. I kept my mouth shut and jist listened 'cause I didn't know if they was friend or foe, and I didn't know where I was, neither."

"That must have been frightening," Adam said. "Where were you?"

"Turns out, I was at the New Garden Meeting House being tended to by a bunch of German Quakers. They was also caring for some wounded Hessian soldiers and talking in that strange tongue, which I found out was German."

"Then what happened?" Adam asked.

"Miz Jessop thought I was touched in the head for I didn't talk to nobody, but she still decided to take me in. She walked me around her nice little place and showed me how to do the chores, and I started helping her around the farm. She's a widow woman. I been staying with her ever since. Miz Jessop treats me real good, and I try to do right by her. I feed her chickens, herd her sheep, and tend to them at night, and I get to sleep out un-der the stars that way."

Adam laughed as he was reminded of how frightened Trapper John was of the chickens when he helped him on the farm. "So, Trapper, you're a sheepherder now and no longer afraid of chickens?"

"I still don't like chickens, but I like herding sheep. Now tell me what you been doing since the battle."

"Elizabeth and I had six more children—four boys and two girls—after the war. Peggy, the oldest girl, and the reverend here," Adam nodded at Jimmy, "teach at the Hebron School. She's learned the piano and plays for our little church there in Knob Creek."

"Peg is all growed up now and teaching school," Trapper said, shaking his head. "You got a big family."

"She's still not married." Adam looked at Jimmy as if it were his fault.

Jimmy had heard this before. He knew Adam wanted him to marry his oldest daughter, but having known Peggy since childhood, Jimmy knew that the only way that would happen was if Peggy decided they should marry.

Trapper John ignored the looks exchanged between Adam and Jimmy. He continued, "Knob Creek had the best trapping I ever found on either side of the mountain."

"Peggy is buying up all the beaver pelts from around Knob Creek, paying top dollar. She has a buyer from Amsterdam who sails into Philadelphia to pick them up," Adam said.

"Little Peg is a fur trader?" Trapper asked.

"Yes, she is quite a businesswoman, and John is her number one supplier of pelts."

"It sure is difficult bargaining with your own sister," John said.

Jimmy smiled. "It's not easy for anyone to bargain with Peggy."

"She also takes furs as her teaching stipend or for ministering to the sick." Adam said.

"Ministering the sick?" Trapper said.

Adam answered, "Peg has become a pretty good healer—she's delivered most of the babies around Knob Creek."

The brothers and Jimmy lay back on their bedrolls. Robert and William were sound asleep, and John and Jimmy were about to doze off.

Adam pointed to the others. "Looks like the boys have gone to sleep. You're welcome to spread your bedroll here. We can talk more in the morning."

"I'd like that." Trapper rolled out his bedroll close to the campfire.

"Goodnight, Trapper."

"Goodnight, Adam."

Adam was nearly asleep when the dog crawled out from her den. She moved slowly on her belly until she reached the area where her new friends were sleeping, then she curled up at the foot of Adam's bedroll.

\*\*\*

When the sun came up over the tall timbers, Lulubelle woke Adam by licking his face. He thought of the many times as a young boy, back in Pennsylvania, when his mother had awakened him with a good morning kiss.

Trapper smiled as he put more wood on the camp fire. "Looks like Mother Mitchell never left your side last night."

The four pups were frolicking around the camp looking for their mother. The largest one spotted her and tried to get to a nipple, but she resisted.

"She's trying to wean them," Adam said. "They must be about two months old—time they should be eating solid food."

Adam prepared breakfast. The tantalizing smells of biscuits and venison gravy woke William, John, and Jimmy.

"What's cooking?" William asked as he pulled on his buckskin boots.

"Your favorite—biscuits and chopped venison gravy. Will you wake Robert? Daylight is burning. We got business to tend to and people to see."

"Something's wrong with Robert!" Reverend Witherspoon called out as he kneeled beside Robert's bedroll trying to wake him.

Adam handed Trapper John the wooden spoon. "Watch breakfast so it doesn't burn, while I check on Robert. I should have known something was wrong. He wasn't his usual self last night. He was just too quiet."

Trapper moved the large Dutch oven off the hot embers and placed the lid on the simmering gravy. Then he turned his attention to the biscuits in the other Dutch oven, lifting the lid to see if they were ready.

"Robert, can you get up?" Adam felt his son's head.

Robert barely moved his head. In a hoarse voice, he said, "I feel so weak."

"You may have caught a cold during the blizzard on the mountain; you have a fever. I'm going to send for Reverend Caldwell, the best doctor in Guilford County."

Trapper brought a porridge bowl with venison gravy and a biscuit and handed it to Adam. "See if he can take a little breakfast."

Adam managed to feed him a few bites of the gravy-soaked biscuit. The others ate their breakfast as Robert slept.

Adam looked at William. "I know you were only ten when we last lived here. Would you be able to find your way to Dr. Caldwell's home and bring him here?"

"I'm pretty sure I can find him."

"Tell him Robert's in a bad way and to come quickly," Adam said.

Jimmy asked, "Could I go with William?"

"That's a good idea," Adam said. "Be careful."

John volunteered to sit with Robert until the doctor arrived.

Adam and Trapper fed the pups scraps from breakfast, and they ate their first solid meal with relish. The pups' mother sat and watched the men pampering her offspring and seemed relieved that she would no longer be nursing.

Trapper straightened up and rubbed his back. "I need to check on the sheep down in the fields, and then I'll be back."

"That's fine," Adam said. "I need to wash up a bit at the springs before we look up Mr. Hamilton."

Adam could hear sheep's bells ringing and an occasional bleat as he approached the springs that fed the old spring house. Trapper's flock must be nearby. Lulubelle was close behind, following Adam's every move.

Adam opened a small haversack that contained a tiny bar of pine tar soap, a razor, and a small piece of a looking glass. He looked around to make sure no one was there, then looked at Lulubelle. "If you are my mother, then let's have a talk while no one is listening. Talk to me, old girl, as Trapper said you did to John Hamilton."

The dog swished her tail and walked a short distance away to a large tree directly behind and above the crumbling walls of the spring house. The tree had shaded the structure from the sun and hid it from the enemy on the day of the battle. Lulubelle started pawing at the dirt just inches from the trunk of the tree while Adam shaved a week's growth of beard from his face and then washed his body in the cool spring water. As he buttoned up the freshly washed clothes Elizabeth had so neatly packed for him, the dog barked impatiently. Adam realized she wanted him to climb up the creek bank to look at the hole she had dug.

"Well, look here at what you've found." Adam got on his knees to inspect the strange, round object she had uncovered. Coated in red mud, it appeared to be the top of a small human skull. *I can't believe she dug up a soldier's grave.* As he touched it he discovered the round object was metal and much larger than the top that Lulubelle had unearthed. Digging deeper, he dislodged a solid cannon ball about four inches in diameter. *Must have come from one of the British six-pounders during the battle and missed its target, landing so hard it embedded itself in the soft earth of the creek's bank.*

The donkeys began to bray and the horses nickered as Lulubelle ran over the hill to see who was coming. The rider was not a farmer dressed in clothes of linsey-woolsey, but a distinguished-looking gentleman wearing a powdered white wig, attired in a fine suit of tailored clothes. He was a big man, well over six feet tall, with a ruddy face and a well-groomed, gray moustache and green eyes.

The stranger asked, "Are you Adam Mitchell?"

"Yes, I am. Who might you be?"

"Adam, it's me—your old friend John Hamilton."

Adam shook Hamilton's hand. *I don't remember John Hamilton being my friend.* "I'm sorry I didn't recognize you. It's been so long since I last saw you. Nearly fourteen years."

"We have both changed, perhaps for the better—a little older and wiser." Mr. Hamilton tied his horse to a post.

"I'm sorry I couldn't make it for the May session of the court yesterday. We—"

"Your son William told me about your difficulties on Grandfather Mountain. He also said your son Robert is gravely ill. I gave William and your reverend directions to Dr. Caldwell's. They should be here soon."

Mr. Hamilton saw Lulubelle for the first time. He jumped back, respectfully removed his black tri-cornered hat and made a timid attempt to bow toward her, as if she were a lady.

Adam pretended not to notice this strange encounter and stooped to scratch Lulubelle on the head as she sat patiently by his side.

"I see you've met the protector of Guilford Courthouse," Mr. Hamilton said.

"You mean this old mongrel dog?" Adam knelt beside the panting Lulubelle and continued to stroke her fur.

Mr. Hamilton cleared his throat. "Is there anything I can provide you or your sons in the way of comfort while you are here? I have a guest cottage; you needn't stay outdoors."

"Thank you for your kind offer, but we are quite comfortable in our camp. Let's walk over to the lean-to, and you can meet my other sons." Adam picked up the six-pound cannon ball and carried it to their shelter where he laid it gently on the ground.

John looked at the object on the ground. "What's that?"

"My new doorstop." Adam turned to his son. "How is Robert?"

"He hasn't opened his eyes since you left. He just moans like he is in terrible pain, keeps mumbling something about the dead soldiers he buried in the corn-fields." John looked from his father to the visitor and back to his father, waiting for an introduction.

"John, this is Mr. Hamilton, with whom we came to do business."

"Glad to make your acquaintance. I would shake your hand, but I've been tending my sick brother, who is feverish."

"I appreciate your concern for my health." Mr. Hamilton held on to his hat with both hands, being careful not to touch anything or to get too close. "I lost my mother to a cholera epidemic when I was a child so I don't like to take chances."

Adam said, "Why don't we move out under the shade of a tree?"

"Good idea. Does that, err—dog follow you every-where?" Mr. Hamilton nodded toward Adam's new companion, the yellow dog following along beside him.

"She's been by my side since I found her under the porch with her pups."

"Has she . . . " Mr. Hamilton paused, and his face reddened. "Has she said anything?"

"Just barks when she doesn't like something." *He does think this dog can talk.*

Lulubelle looked over the ridge behind what had been the Mitchell home and started to bark.

"She's saying someone is coming down the lane." Adam looked toward the sound of a wagon and team. "I hope it's Dr. Caldwell."

As the rickety old farm wagon got closer, they could see it was Trapper John and a white-haired, matronly-looking woman dressed as if she were going to a church social, white gloves and all.

"Adam, this is Miz Jessop. She's a pretty good healer. I went and fetched her as I thought she might be some comfort to Robert until Dr. Caldwell could get here."

"Glad to meet you, Mrs. Jessop. This is John Hamilton and my son John."

"I met you many years ago when you came to our farm with your father to buy apple trees. Unfortunately, I know Mr. Hamilton, having dealt with him on the estate of my late husband, but I am glad to meet your son John. Now where is your son that's ailing?" Mrs. Jessop cast a disapproving eye toward Mr. Hamilton, walking past him as if he were a pile of horse dung.

Trapper looked like he wanted to speak to Mr. Hamilton, but instead just nodded respectfully. Adam recognized the animosity that Mrs. Jessop held for the county clerk. *Must have been some difficulty settling her husband's estate. Seems like Trapper knows the situation; I'll ask him what caused such ill will when we are alone.*

"Over here." John led the way to where his brother lay.

"Thank goodness you kept him in the shade. Fetch my basket, Mr. John," Mrs. Jessop told Trapper.

"That's what she calls me. Mr. John—jist like Mother Mitchell." Trapper rolled his eyes at the others.

Lulubelle growled and snapped at Trapper, who moved quickly to the open wagon. Avoiding the dog on the way back, he brought the basket to Robert's side. Mrs. Jessop was feeling his head with her ungloved hand.

"Quite a high fever. This boy is very sick and needs lots of fluids. I brought some of my chicken soup, which

I make every Tuesday. Keeps me and Mr. John well. Hopefully, it will cure what's ailing your son." Mrs. Jessop gently lifted the crock of soup from her basket and began slowly spoon-feeding Robert, allowing the rich broth to trickle down his sore throat.

Robert opened his eyes and smiled at Mrs. Jessop. "Grandmother Mitchell."

"They call me Sister Jessop, but I knew your Grandmother Mitchell well."

"I think Robert likes your soup," John said.

Barking, Lulubelle took off to higher ground to check out who else was coming. The donkeys kicked and brayed, the horses shook their heads and whinnied, letting everyone know they were also aware that riders were coming. This time it was William, Jimmy, and Dr. Caldwell.

Dr. Caldwell dismounted and gave Adam a brotherly hug. "I see you have Robert under the very good care of Sister Jessop." He referred to her as Sister Jessop out of respect for her position as one of the few women preachers in the Quaker community.

Sister Jessop moved over to make room for Dr. Caldwell to examine Robert. "Yes, but he needs a real doctor."

Dr. Caldwell thought back to that cold February day, twenty-seven years ago when he delivered Robert, Adam's firstborn. He remembered how hard he tried to save Robert's mother, Jennett, who died from complications of birth three days later.

After giving Robert a thorough examination, the doctor asked, "Sister Jessop, is that your wagon and team under the tree?"

"Yes, it is."

"Can we use it to take Robert to my place? I want him off the ground and in a good feather bed with no chance of him being rained on."

"Certainly, you may use my wagon."

"Thank you." Dr. Caldwell stood and patted her gently on the shoulder.

It was obvious the two clergy had a deep respect for each other, even though their customs varied greatly.

Dr. Caldwell greeted John, Trapper, and Mr. Hamilton, then turned toward Adam. "Robert is very sick. He will need constant care and rest for at least a week, maybe more. He can get that at my home from Rachel and me. With your permission, I would like to move him there."

"Whatever you think is best, Reverend. You are the learned doctor."

"Adam, you and the boys pick him up slow and easy and move him to Sister Jessop's wagon."

"I'll make him a bed." Sister Jessop grabbed up his bed roll and got to the wagon first to make a comfortable place for the men to lay Robert. Trapper John held the team steady as Robert was laid into the wagon bed.

"Make the ride easy on him, Trapper. Sister Jessop, will you sit in the back with Robert and keep giving him water from this canteen?" Dr. Caldwell handed the canteen to Sister Jessop. "I'll be riding behind you, if you need me."

She climbed up on the wagon, with the assistance of Adam and Jimmy.

"The boys and I will be following you as soon as we pack up and break camp." Adam said. "We'll try to catch up with you. If we don't, we will see you at your place."

"I assume our business will have to wait?" Mr. Hamilton asked.

"Let us take care of my son, and then I will find you and we can take care of our business when I know Robert is out of danger." Adam started breaking camp with the help of John, William, and Jimmy.

Adam picked up the cannonball.

"Where did that come from?" William asked.

"Lulubelle dug it up near the big sycamore tree that shades the spring house." Adam hid it under the rubble of the porch.

William pointed to the tree. "That one?"

"Yes, that one. Why do you ask?"

"How did you know it was there?" William asked.

"The dog uncovered it, apparently fired from one of General Cornwallis's cannons that missed its target and it lay buried in the mud all these years."

William stared at the dog. *Could it be possible?* The dog, tilting her head, stared back at William then at Adam.

"That cannonball did not miss its mark—that's what destroyed our home." William said.

"Why do you say that?" Adam said.

"Only two people knew where it was buried, Grandmother Mitchell and me." William glanced at Lulubelle again; she looked at him the same way as before. "Grandmother Mitchell found it inside our house after the battle. It was the mortar that knocked out a big piece of the roof and the front wall. She asked me to bury it under the big sycamore tree behind the spring house. Grandmother said to never tell a soul where it was buried because if the British came back and found it, they could use it to destroy some other patriot's home. I never told anyone—only she and I knew it was buried there."

William and Adam looked at the yellow dog. Then John and Jimmy looked at the cannonball, then at Lulubelle, who was smiling. No one said anything. They just finished gathering their camp for the move to the Caldwell farm.

# Chapter Two

## Confessions

"Lulubelle, I want you to stay here and protect the farm. We've left you a hindquarter of venison, and you have the spring for water. I'll be back to check on you and the pups as soon as I can." Adam looked at the dog, who just sat and turned her head from side to side as he spoke.

"Do you think she understood you?" William asked.

John and Jimmy, already in the saddle ready to ride, chuckled.

"I don't know. Just in case she is Mother, I don't want to have her mad at me for not telling her what's going on." Adam mounted his horse. "Let's get going as daylight is burning."

John and William mimicked their Father, silently mouthing "daylight is burning" together and turning toward Jimmy in doing so. They all knew what he was going to say, having heard him recite his old adage often about getting a move on. All three laughed.

"What's so funny?" Adam asked.

"Nothing," John said.

William said, "Just admiring how well you can still mount up."

The horses cantered down a narrow trail toward the Caldwells' home, located several miles southeast of the battlefield.

After a while, Adam stopped and pointed from a high vantage point and said, "That's the Buffalo Creek Church over in the trees just above the creek, where you boys were baptized by Reverend Caldwell."

29

"I remember Mother saying you helped build that church," William said.

"That's right, and working there with Reverend Caldwell is where I learned the skills of a carpenter."

"You learned that trade from Reverend Caldwell?" Jimmy asked.

"Yes, he was a carpenter before becoming a clergyman." Adam looked at Jimmy. "Don't look so surprised. Jesus started out as a carpenter."

"That's right. Just hadn't thought about a minister of today starting as a carpenter," Jimmy said.

John and William viewed the church back in the woods from at least a mile away.

"It seemed much larger when we lived here," John said.

William shook his head. "I told you everything seemed bigger!"

As they rode, Adam told them about the family members buried in the church yard behind the sanctuary. "I hope to take all of you to see the church and cemetery if we have time. Jennett, Robert's mother and my first wife, is also buried there."

"What happened to her?" John asked.

"Jennett had a difficult time with Robert's birth and she died when he was three days old."

"Is Reverend Caldwell the only doctor in Guilford County?" Jimmy asked.

"That's right." Adam nodded his head. "He tried to save Jennett's life. He did all he could."

"I'm sure he did," Jimmy said.

\*\*\*

"Here we are. John, William, take the horses and mules to the barn. Rachel doesn't like them near the house, especially a bunch of them at once. Makes for a smelly situation on a warm day." Adam handed his horse's reins to William and hurried to the house.

Rachel met Adam at the door and hugged him tightly. "I'm so glad to see you, Adam, and so sorry Robert is sick."

"It's been a long time, Rachel. I've missed you and the reverend so much since leaving Guilford." He kissed her on the cheek. "Elizabeth sends her regards and wanted to come, but she is just not up to such a journey."

"Peggy told me in her letters that her mother has not been well." Rachel led Adam to the room where Robert was.

Reverend Caldwell was on his knees beside the bed, his head bowed in prayer. Robert was on the bed, flat on his back with his eyes closed. His face was as white as the handmade quilt that covered him. Adam gasped, startling the preacher for a moment.

"Come in, Adam."

Approaching the bed slowly, Adam said, "He's so pale. Is he gone?"

"No, he's very much alive," Dr. Caldwell said. "I just bled him. That's why he's so pallid."

"Oh!"

"As a doctor of medicine, I've done all I can. Now I must call on my faith in God to help Robert. Would you like to pray with me?"

"Yes, but let me gather his brothers and Jimmy. I know they'll want to join us." Adam stepped out to find them talking to Rachel and motioned all to come in. They circled the sick bed and joined hands in a unity prayer.

Word spread in the community that Adam and his sons were at the Caldwells' with Robert, who was recovering from a serious illness. Neighbors and church members came, as did many Mitchell family members who still lived in Guilford County. They prayed for his recovery and brought food and comforting words. Their prayers were answered by the end of the week. Robert's fever had gone down, his color began to change for the better, and his voice was coming back.

Adam and Reverend Caldwell were seated in the study that adjoined the room in which Robert was recuperating, discussing his miraculous recovery.

"I think I need to bleed him again and make sure the infection is out of his body."

"Let's not do that," Adam replied.

"But he must be bled," the doctor insisted.

"He's doing so well. Why put him through such agony?"

"If you prefer that I not do a final bleed, then I will honor your wishes." Reverend Caldwell seemed surprised that Adam didn't insist on a final bloodletting as was the usual prescribed treatment for an infection.

"Peggy and Dr. Chester have both stopped the bleeding of their patients and think Dr. Rush's theory of the treatment for infection is in error," Adam said.

"Who is Dr. Chester?"

"For years, Peggy's been the only midwife and healer around Knob Creek. She helped birth most of the babies born in our part of the county. Dr. William Chester came to Jonesborough recently from Lancaster. He was trained by the famous Dr. Benjamin Rush and bled his patients accordingly. He noticed that Peggy didn't bleed her patients and they seemed to do as well as those he bled. They kept accurate patient records, and he is now convinced that Dr. Rush's treatment for infection is flawed."

"Dr. Rush's treatment is flawed?" Reverend Caldwell looked astonished.

"That's what they say."

"As you know, Adam, I was trained in medicine by Dr. Woodside, a medical doctor who was a relative of Rachel's. After he died, I had only his books to rely on. Thank you for sharing this information with me. It's difficult being both a doctor and a clergyman to the congregation. Sometimes I fail, as with Jennett." Reverend Caldwell looked down at the wooden floor.

"Please don't blame yourself for Jennett's death. Everyone knows how hard you worked to save her." Adam placed a comforting hand on the reverend's arm.

"Thank you," he said, looking up at Adam.

"I should thank you, Reverend, for all you and Rachel have done for my family over these many years. Your guidance has always been the keystone of our family's health and faith."

"You're welcome, Adam. Your family's presence is missed here in Guilford." The reverend put his hand on Adam's shoulder and stared into his face. "What is troubling you so, Adam?"

"I miss Guilford and its people. I think often of moving back and with John Hamilton giving us the homestead, we would have property to rebuild on." Adam looked down at the reverend's feet and shook his head. "I don't think that's what Mother would want, and I know that I could never farm the land that holds the remains of so many brave soldiers. Besides, Guilford Courthouse has horrible memories for Elizabeth and the children who witnessed the battle."

"Being on the battlefield was a horrible experience for your family, especially Robert." The reverend's voice broke as he spoke. "I am so sorry for what I did to your Robert." The reverend looked into Adam's eyes.

"You just saved his life!"

Reverend Caldwell stood and looked out the window. Then he turned back to face Adam. "Yes, but when he was fourteen, I took away his boyhood." The minister began to cry. "I made a big mistake. Adam, will you forgive me?"

Adam stood up, looked Reverend Caldwell in the face, and clutched the shoulders of his friend's long-sleeved shirt. Adam was frightened, never having seen David Caldwell so distraught. "Tell me what happened."

"Robert found me at the McNairy house, which I had turned into a temporary infirmary to care for the wounded. He had been searching for you, not knowing you had been captured. Robert told me that he and your mother had looked at every wounded and dead soldier scattered about the battlefield. Tired and with little help, I asked Robert to get a wheelbarrow, and gather and bury the human limbs I had amputated before they putrefied. He obliged me, but I didn't think of the long-term implications of this precious young man taking on such a gruesome chore. During his convalescence the last few days, nightmares came during his fever and I heard his cries of agony. I realized I had scarred him for life during an unthinking moment. I pray you and Robert will forgive me for what I have done." Reverend Caldwell looked into Adam's eyes for the forgiveness he sought.

"Reverend, for many years I have blamed myself for not sending my family away from Guilford Courthouse when I learned the British were coming. Mother and Elizabeth refused to leave the farm. I gave Robert a gun and put him in the spring house with his grandmother, mother, and siblings with instructions to protect them at all cost. A tremendous responsibility for a lad who had just turned fourteen."

The minister put his arms around Adam. "I will never forget how awful war is."

"Nor will I." Adam shook his head defiantly.

They embraced for some time, each lost in their own memories of that fateful day.

Reverend Caldwell pulled away. "Do you intend to take back the farm?"

"That's what I've been wanting to talk to you about."

"Let's take a walk. I want to show you something, and we can discuss your concerns without interruption."

Outside, Reverend Caldwell pointed the way down a well-traveled path. They walked side by side, not saying a word, each waiting for the other to speak. Decades of ministry kept the reverend in control, not uttering a word but watching and listening.

Breaking the silence, Adam said, "May I ask you about the deathbed letter you received from mother? It was delivered by a Lieutenant John Armstrong of the U.S. Army."

"That was in the spring of 1788," Reverend Caldwell remembered.

"Mother died the last week of March, in the eleventh year of Independence."

"I remember like yesterday, that soldier dismounting from his bay mare in front of the house, announcing who he was and that you had sent him. Rachel and I both knew it was bad news. You couldn't have picked a better courier for such a letter, and he was honored to have been chosen to deliver it. He told us Judge McNairy and a young lawyer named Andrew Jackson had introduced you."

Reverend Caldwell yanked open the door of the Log College where he and Rachel taught the young men of Guilford County. "I want to show you where John McNairy sat." He pointed toward a bench near one of the two windows of the log structure. "Your Robert sat next to him. They were the best of friends. Now, John has been appointed a federal judge in Nashville." Reverend Caldwell beamed with pride. "His father told me he'll be paid eight hundred dollars a year."

Adam gestured impatiently. "Tell me about Mother's letter."

"I'm sorry. I get carried away about my pupil's success. I wanted to share the story with you." Reverend Caldwell looked a little embarrassed.

"I understand, but I want to hear about the letter while we have this time together." Adam took a step closer.

"Lieutenant Armstrong was aware from conversations with Judge McNairy that your mother provided shelter and medical attention to the injured soldiers in her corn fields and secured the release of the Guilford County Militiamen whom Cornwallis had captured."

"Did you know Armstrong was sent to Jonesborough by the Secretary of War at the direction of George Washington?" Adam asked.

"You don't say."

"That's what he told me. Seems some in Philadelphia thought Governor John Sevier was cooking up a conspiracy with the British to gain control of the Mississippi River for the State of Franklin," Adam said.

Reverend Caldwell said, "John Sevier would never join the British in any endeavor."

"That's what Armstrong's investigation concluded, but by then the State of Franklin had dissolved and the Franklinites pledged their loyalty to North Carolina and the new nation. Now, Tennessee is the sixteenth state and John Sevier is our Governor." Adam sat down on a school bench and the reverend followed, sitting across from him.

"Armstrong is now second-in-command at the War Department," Reverend Caldwell said. "Word is, President Washington recommended that he become Adams's Secretary of War when Henry Knox steps down."

"I'm impressed by him as was my daughter Peggy. We met the lieutenant by way of introduction from her beau at the time, Andrew Jackson. Andrew and John McNairy both lived with our neighbors the Taylors before moving west to Nashville to set up the court there. Andrew carried Mother's will and recorded it there. Her will was one of the first records ever recorded in Davidson County."

"While Rachel read your mother's letter aloud to me, the lieutenant stood at attention. He was moved by your mother's written words, and I could see his eyes tear up."

"What did the letter say that upset John Hamilton so much that he wants to give the property back to me?" Adam asked.

"You don't know what your mother's letter said? I thought you wrote it for her." The reverend looked surprised.

"No, Elizabeth's father John McMachen wrote the letter and Mother's last will and testament a few days before she died. He was by her side to the end."

"From her letters, I knew your mother and Mr. McMachen were very close. I am surprised they didn't marry, both being without a spouse."

"Mr. Mac proposed, but Mother said she could never marry another man after Father's death. Mr. Mac understood," Adam said.

"Mr. Mac?"

"That's what everyone called him in Washington County, where he was the first county register. They just couldn't get his name right. Some called him McMahon, others McMachen, which is correct, but those that weren't sure just called him Mr. Mac. He liked it, and the family started calling him that."

Reverend Caldwell shifted on the bench. "Now that I know you never saw the letter, I wish I had kept it for you. Mr. Hamilton asked for it as he wanted to explicitly carry out your mother's wishes. I do remember she described vividly the horrific sight of the dead and dying soldiers on her property after the battle—how she ran about looking for you, and not finding you, assumed you were dead."

"What did Mother want Mr. Hamilton to do that has caused him such distress?"

"If I had your mother's letter, I would be glad to share it with you. Mr. Hamilton is no longer a member of my congregation, but we have had many discussions about your mother and her farm. It would not be proper for me to discuss his revelations. I will tell you that on account of his buying the Mitchell farm, he has had a very unusual spiritual awakening. When you talk, I am sure he will tell you about it. I would rather you hear it from him."

Reverend Caldwell opened the schoolhouse door for Adam. They walked the trail from the Caldwell school to the manse on the same path that Reverend and Rachel Caldwell had strolled arm in arm for thirty years.

# Chapter Three

## Relinquishment of the Battlefield

When Reverend Caldwell and Adam returned from their walk and approached the manse, Adam noticed a white horse tied to a rail of the loafing pen attached to the barn.

"That looks like the horse Mr. Hamilton was riding when he came to the farm on Monday," Adam said.

"It is indeed Old Blue."

Adam looked at the horse again. "That's a strange name for a white horse."

"Not really. If you look closely, you'll notice a bluish tint about his coat, especially where the sun rays shine. A strong horse of good stock he is—look at that broad back and those strong legs. It takes a big horse to carry a man the size of Mr. Hamilton or me."

"I assume he came to finish our business," Adam said.

"That may be the reason, but our county clerk has become one of our frequent callers of late, bringing fresh game and farm products to Rachel."

"I thought you said he isn't a member of your congrega-tion."

"Not at this time he isn't." Reverend Caldwell opened the door for Adam.

Mr. Hamilton was in the parlor visiting with Rachel and her guests from Knob Creek.

"Good to see you, Mr. Hamilton," the minister said.

Reverend Caldwell wiped his dusty boots on a small deer skin on the wooden floor just inside the foyer. Rachel wrapped her arms around him, and he gave her a kiss. Adam carefully wiped his boots on the soft deer skin, remembering from his boyhood how Rachel fussed about her wooden floors. For years, the Caldwells, like most of the settlers in the Piedmont area of North Carolina, had nothing but dirt floors in their log dwellings.

Mr. Hamilton nodded to Adam, "Glad to see you under better circumstances than last Monday." He glanced toward the room where Robert convalesced. "The patient looks much better today."

"Mr. Hamilton brought us some plump pheasants this morning; had his slave girl clean and pluck them," Rachel said. "All I have to do is put them in the big skillet with some vegetables for supper tonight."

Reverend Caldwell said, "Well, thank you, Mr. Hamilton. We'll put them to good use."

"I had planned to look you up today, Mr. Hamilton, as Robert is doing much better," Adam said. "Your being here makes it convenient for me. If you have the papers for me to sign, we can complete our business."

"I do and I would like to have the opportunity to discuss this land transaction with you and your sons, in private, if we may."

"That would be good, as I do have some questions," Adam said.

"You must have tea and crumpets first," Rachel said in such a way as no one could refuse.

William mouthed to his brother John so as to not offend their hosts, "Tea and crumpets?"

John shrugged his shoulders to indicate that he didn't know what Rachel was talking about, either.

Adam remembered fondly Rachel's little pastries with her delicious fruit jellies and jams. *I wish my Elizabeth were here to partake of Rachel's hospitality. She would have enjoyed this. I shouldn't forbid Elizabeth to keep tea in the house. It's just that the mention of the word reminds me of the British bastards that destroyed our home. Obviously, the*

*Caldwells have forgiven the Brits enough to drink tea. I don't think I can ever be so benevolent.*

"Come this way." Reverend Caldwell gestured toward a long dining table set with fine china for afternoon tea. The sturdy oak table was adorned with an Irish linen tablecloth laced with intricate little crosses and fishes.

When they were all seated, Reverend Caldwell said, "Let's give thanks."

He gave thanks for Robert's speedy recovery and for the opportunity to see Adam and his sons again. He asked forgiveness for lost souls who were trying to return to the church.

As Rachel poured the hot tea, Reverend Caldwell passed a pewter tray of crumpets. Jimmy gently caressed the tablecloth with the palm of his hand. "How appropriate your tablecloth is, Mrs. Caldwell, with the symbols of Christ woven into it. Did you make this?"

"No, it was a gift from Reverend and Mrs. Annan made by the ladies of the Pine Street Presbyterian Church in Philadelphia as a twenty-fifth wedding anniversary present to us."

"I know Reverend and Mrs. Annan and have been to their home," Jimmy said.

Reverend Caldwell looked up in surprise. "You have?"

"How would you know them?" Rachel's voice and expression showed her excitement.

"I preached to the congregation of the Old Pine Street Church last fall," Jimmy said proudly.

"We went to the opera in Reverend Annan's carriage." William looked at Jimmy, who nodded in agreement.

"Really?" Reverend Caldwell was quite impressed with the young clergyman Adam had brought.

As the host's attention was turned toward Jimmy Witherspoon, Adam leaned toward Mr. Hamilton and whispered, "Now would be a good time to discuss our business."

"Yes, it would." Mr. Hamilton rose from his chair and bowed toward the hosts. "Thank you, Rachel, Reverend, for the refreshments. If you will excuse us, Adam and I still have business to tend."

"Please use my study." Reverend Caldwell gestured toward the room.

Mr. Hamilton looked around the table. "Adam, as we are getting older and must depend on your sons to carry on the perpetuity of this commitment, I would like them to hear what I have to say regarding this matter."

"Robert needs to rest, but William and John can join us." Adam motioned for them to follow him as Mr. Hamilton led the way to the reverend's study.

Adam pointed out the pastor's great literary works, many written in Latin and Greek. "Reverend Caldwell can read and recite from the Latin and Greek books as well as those in the King's English."

The collection of leather-bound books and elegant furnishings in the pastor's study amazed John and William. Adam could remember Reverend Caldwell tutoring him as a young man in this very room, working from these same books. He looked around the room and then at his sons with a proud smile. "It is from this study and Reverend Caldwell's books that I received my education."

Mr. Hamilton sat in Reverend Caldwell's desk chair. Adam and William sat in high back, wooden chairs, made years ago by their host. John stood in the doorway of the study. Mr. Hamilton cleared his throat and shifted in his chair before speaking.

"I know my giving back the Mitchell homestead sounds highly unusual to you. Please understand that it is important that I receive nothing in return, other than your promise to protect it from any use that would disturb the soldiers buried there."

"You want nothing from us?" Adam asked.

"Only that you fulfill your mother's wishes and that you never sell it to anyone who will not follow those wishes."

William and John listened intently to Mr. Hamilton's every word, expecting some strange request.

"You mention often my mother's wishes," Adam said. "Would you explain?"

"What she mentioned in her letter, and what she told me," Mr. Hamilton said.

"You talked to my mother?" Adam stood and looked down at Mr. Hamilton. "I took her over the mountain with the children shortly after the battle. I returned to request a re-grant of the 107 acres, because the original grant had mysteriously disappeared from the courthouse, but my mother did not come back with me."

"I didn't exactly . . . talk . . . to her . . . " Mr. Hamilton stam-mered, his face turning the color of a ripe peach.

Adam sat down again, but his eyes never left Mr. Hamilton's face. "Mother left Guilford County shortly after the battle and never returned. You couldn't have talked to her."

John tilted his head and looked at Mr. Hamilton out of the corner of his eye. "That's right. William and I went with Grandmother when Father took us over the mountain."

"Please hear me out. It is not easy for me to tell this story." Mr. Hamilton again cleared his throat.

"We apologize for interrupting you. Please continue." Adam looked at his sons in a way that warned them not to interrupt again.

"As you know, Adam, I served under Alexander Martin in the war. He is now a U.S. senator and was governor of North Carolina." Mr. Hamilton took a deep breath. "A powerful man, but hated by many—and for good reason."

Adam nodded, "I know about his court-martial and resigning a colonel's commission after Germantown."

"He came back to Guilford County after giving up his military service, started a law practice, and built a home near Salisbury.

Martin practiced law in both Rowan and Guilford Counties. He taught me the law and how to use it for personal gain." Mr. Hamilton shook his head as if to get that thought out of his mind.

"I remember you were the sheriff before the battle," Adam said.

"Martin secured the appointment for me, obliging me to be at his beck and call."

Adam added, "I remember you were popular with the Whigs for confiscating property from the Tories."

"And some patriot's property as well—all by means of deception and fraud, all planned by Martin." Mr. Hamilton looked down at the floor.

"Governor Martin took property from Whigs?"

"Yes, and I helped him," Mr. Hamilton murmured.

John moved from the doorway to sit on the arm of the sturdy chair that William occupied. They listened intently to the confession by this man who had been a sheriff and was now county clerk.

"How?" Adam asked.

"Thomas Henderson was county clerk the year before the battle. Martin was state senator then. The county leaders took lands and private property that belonged to Edmund Fanning—the land adjoining your property. I took two heifers for my part. The others took whatever they wanted."

"Didn't anyone protest?"

"How could they?" Mr. Hamilton raised his head and looked at Adam. "I was the sheriff and the others were all elected officials of the county, all related."

"What did the landowners do after you confiscated their property?"

"They all left, except for your family. When your mother didn't move after your father's death, the plan

44

Alexander Martin had for the valuable land surrounding the new courthouse fell apart."

Adam looked confused. "When I sold the property, you mentioned missing records. I have always wondered how you knew about the records disappearing from the courthouse in Salisbury. Mother and I never told anyone, except Reverend Caldwell."

"I am sorry to say that I was the person that removed them. I hope that you will forgive me."

"You removed them?" Adam and his sons looked at each other, then at Mr. Hamilton.

"I must confess everything to you. Please allow me to finish, and I think you will understand why I must do this. As the clerk of the county, Thomas Henderson was in a much better position to make land acquisitions than I was as the sheriff. We accumulated a great deal of land working together. He was appointed as the new clerk of Rockingham County, which was created out of Guilford County, and I was appointed to the position of Guilford County Clerk. Then we had two counties from which to steal widows' and orphans' lands. As you know, I am still county clerk, a position I would like to retain, if that is possible."

"Why are you telling us this?"

Mr. Hamilton leaned forward. "I must, Adam. Please, hear me out. Your family had moved over the mountain to join Mr. McMachen. General Cornwallis had surrendered at Yorktown. The war was over. Even though significant battles were fought and won in this state, the State Assembly voted against ratification of the national Constitution."

Adam said, "I know about that, and I always wondered why North Carolina voted against ratification."

"The governor and other leaders of the conspiracy were afraid that our land grab scheme would be found out by the new federal government. Many of our constituents suspected us, but with the records of the counties in such shambles, it would be difficult to prove."

*Now things are beginning to make sense,* Adam thought.

"When you started investigating the disappearance of your father's original land grant and applied for a re-grant, I feared I might be caught up in the conspiracy." Mr. Hamilton shrugged his shoulders and turned his palms up. "That's why I paid you three times what the land was worth—to get the matter settled quickly and put a stop to the questions."

"I was satisfied with the price." Adam shifted in his seat.

"You should have been. £158 was exorbitant, but worth it to me if it let me keep doing what I was doing. After you left the county for good, I continued my wicked ways when I knew I could get away with it. Like robbing Widow Churchton of her estate." Mr. Hamilton paused and looked at the floor. "Reverend Caldwell and the elders had suspicions of my misconduct for many years and eventually ousted me from Buffalo Presbyterian Church. It embarrassed my poor wife to the point that she killed herself. My grown children left and no longer communicate with me. The only family I have now are my slaves."

"I am sorry for your loss," Adam said.

Mr. Hamilton nodded his thanks. "I decided to sell your farm with another parcel of land I own near the courthouse to a Virginia plantation owner who wanted land to grow tobacco. I broke the promise I made to you and your mother to never disturb the sacred ground of your fields."

Adam bounded up from his chair. "You didn't!"

"Yes, I did. The wealthy buyer was already en route to Martinsville from Frederick County, Virginia. I was in my parlor, as usual indulging in the elixir of forgetfulness, dreaming about the lucrative land sale that was pending, when I heard riders coming. I thought the riders might be the buyer, but it was Reverend Caldwell and this Army officer."

"Did I hear my name?" Reverend Caldwell stood outside the door.

"Yes, you did, Reverend. Please, come in and join us. I am about to finish my confession and would like you to hear what I have to say," Mr. Hamilton answered.

The minister entered the room. "Are you sure? I know this is difficult for you to do."

"I have done it many times in my head. It is easier now to tell the story."

William and John got up and offered their shared seat to the reverend, and then moved to the doorway. Reverend Caldwell and Adam sat down.

Mr. Hamilton continued, "The reverend and Lieutenant John Armstrong had your mother's deathbed letter and wanted to read it to me, which they did. It was the most eloquent letter I have ever heard or read. Your mother asked the reverend to call on me to thank me personally for being the protector of the battlefield."

"You had already decided to sell the property?" Adam asked.

"Yes. I am not making excuses, but that was before I knew of the letter and her death. After Reverend Caldwell and the lieutenant left, I fell asleep in a drunken stupor. I awoke to find your mother standing at the foot of my bed. She told me that if I didn't cancel my plans to sell the land, she would haunt me for the rest of my life and that I would burn in eternal Hell for my sins."

Adam wrinkled his brow. "What did Mother look like?"

"She looked just like she did the last time I saw her before you moved, but slightly older. There was this glow around her, like a firefly glowing in the dark." Mr. Hamilton shuddered. "She had her say and was gone. Just went through the wall. I was afraid, but I convinced myself it was the whisky causing me to see and hear the ghost of your mother." Mr. Hamilton paused and looked intently at each person in the room.

"I had promised Lieutenant Armstrong I would meet him at the spring house the next day when the sun was high. He wanted me to show him where the mass grave of the soldiers was. I arrived early and watered Old Blue in the creek, then went into the spring house to get myself a cool drink directly from the spring. The door was missing, but it still had enough roof to make shade." Mr. Hamilton lowered his voice. "In the dark corner was a young man in the uniform of a Continental soldier, drawing up a canteen of spring water. He introduced himself as Richard Taliaferro from Surry County. Said he was getting his fallen comrade, Jesse Franklin, some cool spring water. I started to introduce myself. He told me, 'We all know who you are and what you intend to do, Mr. Hamilton.'"

John's and William's eyes opened wider.

"He walked past me and waded across the creek, spooking Old Blue so badly he ran off toward New Garden Road. I followed where the soldier came out of the water on the other side of the creek. There were no footprints on the creek bank." Mr. Hamilton looked at Adam.

*That's some story*, Adam thought.

"Where did your horse go?" John asked.

"Lieutenant Armstrong saw Old Blue hightailing it toward home with an empty saddle. He naturally assumed I had been thrown. After chasing my horse a ways, he grabbed the halter and tethered him to his saddle and came looking for me. Armstrong said he had never seen such a scared horse. I didn't tell him Old Blue saw a ghost."

The brothers looked from Mr. Hamilton to their father and back again.

Mr. Hamilton kept talking. "He asked to see the burial site, which I showed him. The lieutenant drew sketches and made lots of notes in his journal, like he might fight the battle again someday."

"That soldier is a sharp young man." Adam looked at Reverend Caldwell, who nodded in agreement.

Hamilton said, "It was like Lietenant Armstrong knew my plans for the battlefield. He said that two hundred years from now, people would still come from all over to see where these gallant men fought for this sacred piece of ground. He warned me that it would upset the survivors and the ghosts of the men who died here if their resting place were ever disturbed."

Mr. Hamilton paused, shook his head, then looked first at Adam then at John and William. "I wish to be exonerated from this responsibility." He pulled a document out of his coat pocket and handed it to Adam.

The document was already signed by John Hamilton and his signature had been witnessed by John McMurry, County Trustee, on May 1, 1797. It was written in John Hamilton's very distinctive, yet fine penmanship and read exactly as follows:

> *John Hamilton to Adam Mitchell relinquishing of a Deed Registration*
> *I do hereby relinquish all Bargain Seal on purchase between Adam Mitchell and myself in Consequences of the within Described Land and do hereby Revoke Taking Desannul all & Singular the Right & Interrest that I Now have or ever had to the Title or Lands Contained therein by Virtue of Sd Title & this profane meaning of this Certificate is to Recover all Right & Title made to Me by Adam Mitchell in this Title to him and his heirs as although this Title had Never been Made Heretefo my intial and Seal this first Day of May 1797*
>
> *J. Hamilton*
>
> *Test John McMurry*
> *Execution of the above Certificate was Ackd. in open Court*

*Let it be Recorded*
*Test J. Hamilton CC*

"There is no place for me to sign," Adam said.

"That's correct. This is not a buy, sell agreement. It is my relinquishment certificate to you that our previous bill of sale has been canceled by me, the buyer."

Adam looked at the document again, "I have never heard of a certificate of relinquishment."

"Since I was appointed the county clerk, there has never been one filed in Guilford County."

Adam read the document again, turned it over and looked at the blank back, then handed it to John.

"I've never heard of anything like this, either." John examined the document as his father had and passed it on to William.

William looked the paper over and asked, "How do we know this is a legal document since none of us even knows what it is?"

Reverend Caldwell put his hands on his knees and pulled his large frame up into a standing position, stretching and taking the floor at the same time. "Adam, Mr. Hamilton and I have had many discussions on how to handle this matter. He could have sold it back to you for a pittance or signed a quit claim deed signing away any interest in the property. To do a sale or a quit claim would be admitting that he, in fact, did own the property. Adam, I am hesitant to become involved in this matter, but Mr. Hamilton's reason for buying your property had to do with a previous, dishonest indiscretion. He needs to do this in such a way as to say he never owned the 107 acres in the first place, to avoid the possibility of impeachment and criminal prosecution."

"I see," Adam acknowledged. "And if the property is ever misused, it will be because of my actions rather than his."

Both Reverend Caldwell and Mr. Hamilton nodded in agreement.

"What do I need to do?" Adam said.

Mr. Hamilton continued, "Just accept a copy that I have for you and honor your mother's wishes. I would like one of your sons to sign under the county trustee's signature should anyone question this transaction later. As we missed the May session of county court last week, I will not be able to file the certificate for record until the August session of the court."

Adam looked at John and William, "What do you boys think?"

"Sounds to me like what Grandmother Mitchell wants." John looked at William, who nodded in agreement.

"Well, let's do it." Adam handed the document to William for a signature, and everyone shook hands and thanked each other.

Outside the study, Rachel and Jimmy heard the men moving around and talking after they finished their business.

Rachel knocked softly. "May I come in with Reverend Witherspoon?"

"Certainly, my dear," her husband answered.

She came into the study, smiling and her face beaming. "I have a wonderful suggestion that I hope you will all agree to. Tomorrow is Sunday and you, my dear husband, have been so busy you haven't prepared a sermon." She shook her index finger at him teasingly. "It just so happens we have a visiting Presbyterian preacher, a graduate of Washington College, and a relative of Dr. John Witherspoon of Princeton University, who has offered to preach for you tomorrow." She extended her hand toward Jimmy as if she were introducing him for the first time.

"That is a marvelous idea. I know the congregation would love to hear another pastor preach, especially one who has preached to Pine Street Presbyterian in the nation's capitol." Reverend Caldwell looked at Adam. "You had planned on visiting your old church while you are here?"

"With all that has been happening, I forgot tomorrow is the Sabbath. Yes, I would like to attend church and then leave first thing Monday morning, if Robert continues to improve." Adam looked at his sons, who smiled and nodded.

"Good, that's settled. Now, everyone but Jimmy out of the study, as Reverend Witherspoon has to prepare his sermon." Rachel waved them toward the door. Moving into the parlor, Mr. Hamilton looked humbly at Reverend Caldwell. "Would it be proper now for me to attend church services tomorrow as a guest?"

"That would be good, and after church, the elders will meet in session to consider your request for reinstatement and other church matters. I would recommend you be prepared to make a public confession and ask the congregation for forgiveness."

# Chapter Four
## Homeward Bound

Five horsemen rode slowly through the overgrown fields of the battleground toward Huntington Creek. The sun rose in a big orange ball, warming their backs this cool, spring morning. They stopped at a high place known as Lookout Ridge for one last glance at what had once been their home. Looking down on Martinsville, they could see Trapper John watching over Sister Jessop's sheep, just white dots in the lush, green grass. Adam waved goodbye, not expecting a wave in return as his old friend would not be able to see him in the shadows of the tall timbers.

"Lulubelle, come on, girl. Get a move on. We've got a long way to go." Adam turned in the saddle to see if she was following.

He had the pup that looked like her in a gunny sack slung over his shoulder. Jimmy, John, and William each carried a litter mate, their heads out of the sacks, looking wide-eyed at the world. They didn't whine or whimper as their heads bobbed up and down to the cadence of the horses. Robert led the donkeys, who bore the usual food and supplies for a long trip, plus the many gifts from family and friends.

Adam, who was bringing up the rear, hollered for all to hear, "Keep going. I'll catch up with you. I need to check on the momma dog."

Adam found Lulubelle sitting in the middle of the road waiting for him. He dismounted and knelt down beside the sad-looking dog. "What's the matter, old girl?" He patted her head gently. "You don't want to go, do you?"

She looked back down the road toward her home.

"If your mind is made up, I know I can't change it."

She cocked her head to one side then the other, intently staring into Adam's eyes as his mother often did, looking deep into his mind and soul for his thoughts.

"I understand. This is your home. You raised your family here and did a fine job of it." Adam wiped a small tear from his eye with the back of his hand as the dog started to slowly walk away.

She went a few yards, then stopped and looked back at Adam.

"Go on, girl. It's going to be all right. Your pups will have a good home. I'll make sure of that. Go on now." He waved his arms to shoo her on.

She moved down the road a little further, stopped, and turned again.

"Go on home now." He shooed her along with his hands and watched her disappear around a curve in the road. "I'm going to miss you," he whispered.

Jimmy and John came riding back to check on Adam, who was standing in the middle of the trail, holding the reins of his horse and looking back. The pup was still in its gunny sack pouch over his shoulder.

"Where is she?" Jimmy asked.

"Heading back to where she belongs." Adam grabbed the saddle horn with both hands and pulled himself up onto his chestnut mare.

"Did you say goodbye?" John asked.

"I did."

"Was it Grandmother or Lulubelle you said goodbye to?"

"Both." Adam turned his mount toward Tennessee.

John looked at Jimmy and mouthed, "What does that mean?"

Jimmy shrugged.

The horses cantered through Herman Husband's abandoned homestead just west of Horse Pen Creek. Adam told the boys how this neighbor had been involved in the Battle of Alamance, the first skirmish between the Regulators and the Tories. They stopped to let the horses graze. The pups were allowed out of their gunny sacks to run and play and select that perfect little patch of grass.

"They're really too big to carry." Adam watched them play in the lush clover.

"Do you think they'll follow us if we don't carry them?" John said.

"Here, Smoky." Robert offered a piece of jerky to the only male pup from the litter.

John had claimed him and named him Smoky as his fur had the coloring of the mountains back home.

William said, "Let's train him to lead the others, and we won't have to carry them on horseback."

John cut up some jerky, called the pup, and gave him a treat when he came. The dog got the idea pretty fast. The cream-colored female came to John for a treat.

"Looks like our old dog when she was a pup." John handed a piece of the jerky to the puppy. "Remember how she scratched on the schoolhouse door after recess, just when Peggy was starting penmanship class? It was like that dog had a timepiece and could tell time."

William grinned. "The old gal would make her entrance, and the pupils would have a good laugh as she went to her pallet near Peggy's desk and plopped down, usually with a loud sigh."

"The children really miss Lulubelle," Jimmy said.

Adam stepped back toward his horse. "Enough talk about old dogs. Let's get a move on — daylight's a-burning."

The boys laughed.

"What's so funny?"

"You always say that," William said.

"Well, it is. God gives us just so much daylight each day to get things done. If we waste it, that's a sin, isn't it,

Jimmy?" Adam grabbed the reins of his horse and turned her.

"Could be, Adam. I'll have to think about that." Jimmy mounted Star, the horse Peggy had given him on his graduation last year from Washington College.

"Heading home!" William hollered, turning his horse westward.

Three days later, they reached Boone. Pleasant weather allowed the men to camp outdoors rather than staying at the inn.

They sat downwind from the campfire, ready to eat their evening meal as John dished up beans and salt pork from the big pot he had prepared.

Adam took a bite. "Good beans."

"Thanks," John said.

"You're gonna make Mary Ann a good wife," William wisecracked while eating his plate of beans. "That reminds me—you owe me big for posting that bond of marriage for a thousand dollars."

"What's this about a thousand-dollar bond?" Adam looked at his sons through narrowed eyes.

"I signed it in December for John's proposal to Mary Ann Barnes," William answered.

"I only posted a fifty-dollar bond for Robert's marriage bond to Elizabeth Allison. You posted twenty times the required bond?" Adam glared at William.

William stared back at Adam. "It was Peggy's idea to post a large bond. She said it would assure both Mary Ann and her father of how serious John's intentions were, as Mary Ann had another suitor."

"Peggy hatched this scheme for you?" Adam shook his head in disbelief. "That sounds like my Peg."

John said, "She would have put up the bond herself, if women were allowed to post bonds."

"What did Mr. Barnes say when you showed him the bond?" Adam asked.

"He asked, 'Do you have a preacher in mind?' I said, 'Yes.' Then he asked if Sunday, December 17th would be agreeable. I said, 'That's only two weeks away, but I don't know why we couldn't.' Then he says that's the date he and Mrs. Barnes had set for Mary Ann's wedding to her other suitor. The marriage went on as planned, except I was the groom instead of the Hazelwood boy." John couldn't hold a straight face. Now everyone was laughing.

Adam looked at William. "Did you have a thousand dollars?"

"Well, uh, no, but no money changes hands unless John reneges on the marriage."

John nodded in agreement. "It was a surety bond to make sure the groom honored his commitment."

"Why didn't you come to me about it?"

"Didn't want to bother you." John took a deep breath. "And we all knew you wouldn't approve of William posting such a high bond."

"She meant that much to you?" Adam asked.

"Yes, she's everything I ever wanted in a wife."

"William, what would you have done if John had changed his mind?"

"I would have hurt him real bad." William grinned and everyone laughed.

"Well, the plan worked and just in the nick of time, it sounds like. Now I'm going to bed." Adam laughed out loud and laid back on his bedroll using his saddle as a pillow.

The cream-colored pup curled up next to Adam and both were soon asleep. The other travelers, tired from a long day on the trail, followed his lead.

Adam had breakfast cooking early the next morning. The smell of bacon frying and biscuits baking woke the others.

"It's ready." Adam took a sip of camp coffee.

"You're in good spirits," Robert said.

"Ready to get back home to my wife and children," Adam said.

"I'm ready to get back to my bride," Robert said.

"Me too," John said.

Adam filled their plates one after the other. "When you going to make me a grandfather, Robert?"

"I'm working on it."

"You been married for seven months and she's not pregnant."

"She will be soon."

Adam smiled at his son. "That so?"

Robert nodded.

"That would make your mother and me proud." Adam looked at the rest of the group. "Eat your breakfast, boys, and let's hit the trail. If the sun is just right in the afternoon, there's a spot we can see ole Grandfather, whom the mountain was named for."

"Who named it that?" John asked.

"Don't know. It's been Grandfather Mountain since the first time I came over the mountain. Old-timers tell me the Indians called it Tanawha, which means 'fabulous hawk.'" Adam gazed at the panoramic view of the majestic mountains ahead of them.

They made the crest by way of the Deep Gap Trail by noon.

Jimmy slid off his horse and looked up at a high peak. "I see it. I see why they call it that."

"I don't see any old man." William squinted and looked in the same direction as Jimmy.

"He's right there." Jimmy pointed to a high bluff in the distance.

"I see him," Robert said.

Adam stared at the bluff. "I finally see Grandfather, after all these years."

"I don't see what you're talking about," William said.

Jimmy pointed again. "He's there. I see how the mountain got its name."

"Let's go get a better look. Maybe I can see him if I get closer." William looked at Adam for approval.

"Go on," Adam said. "You may never get another chance to see him again."

Jimmy, William, and John started up the trail toward the optical illusion that was created by the bright sun and the rock structure of the mountain. Robert, still weak from his illness, stayed with his father.

Adam watched them for a few seconds before walking toward his horse. "I'm going to take a nap while they're gone."

"That sounds like a good idea." Robert took the saddle off his horse.

Adam removed his saddle, then unburdened the donkeys and hobbled them to graze in the fresh mountain grass. Adam and Robert rested under the shade of a ledge that protruded out of the side of a cliff.

Robert looked around at the shelter that nature had made. "Wish we had this shelter during the storm."

"That would have been nice." Adam lay back with his head on his saddle.

Three of the pups curled up beside Robert; the yellow-haired one lay next to Adam.

Robert lay flat on his back looking up at the stalactites that formed on the ceiling of the cave-like shelter. "What is the day of the month?"

"The eleventh. Why do you ask?"

"I have to sign the indenture for the town lot I bought in Jonesborough on the fifteenth."

"What are you going to do with it?" Adam asked.

"Build Elizabeth and me a home for our family."

"On Main Street with all that wagon traffic heading to Nashville?"

"That's what makes it such a good investment. The Chester Inn is doing so well that Dr. Chester might need some competition someday. That lot would be worth a good penny someday for Jonesborough's next inn."

When he didn't get a response, Robert looked at Adam and realized his father had dozed off. Robert shut his eyes and was soon asleep. After a while, the pups became restless and started to yelp.

"The boys must be coming," Adam mumbled, still half asleep.

The horses snorted loudly and the donkeys brayed that high-pitched sound they made only when scared for their lives. Adam and Robert looked at each other and without saying a word, grabbed their rifles. They knew that something had spooked the animals and they could soon be in a fight for their lives.

A large black bear was tearing at the tarps that covered the provisions on the ground. Robert had a bead on the bear and pulled the hammer back slowly.

Adam reached his arm out near the gun. "Don't shoot."

"That damn bear is going to kill a horse."

"If it was, it would have already attacked. It smells the smoked hams and bacon we're carrying."

The bear stood on its hind legs, at least six feet tall, revealing that it was a boar. He growled and snarled at the men in a menacing manner. They slowly backed toward the covered shelter, worried about the excited pups adding to the bear's agitation.

"I can take him," Robert whispered.

"I know you can." Adam spoke just loud enough for Robert to hear him. "But just let him take a ham or side of bacon, then he'll leave us alone."

The bear went down on all fours, pulled back the tarp with his teeth, grabbed a ham, and sauntered back into the brush to eat it.

"If he comes back, shoot him." Adam moved from animal to animal to settle the horses and donkeys, talking to them softly. When they heard Adam's voice, they began to calm down.

"Easy, Star, easy. Everything is going to be all right." Adam motioned to Robert that the bear was gone.

"Should have let me take him."

"Then what? We would have a five-hundred pound bear to skin, and we don't have the time to deal with it. Now if those boys will come on, we can get off the mountain before dark. Let's get saddled up and be ready to go when they get here."

\*\*\*

The children saw a cloud of trail dust through the open window of the schoolhouse.

Samuel ran to the window. "It's them!"

James and David followed their brother. The children were so excited to see their father that Peggy couldn't control them any longer and dismissed the class. It was Friday afternoon, nearly three weeks since the men had left for North Carolina. Peggy was as anxious as the children to see her father, brothers, and — she had to admit — Jimmy.

The pupils called Jimmy "Reverend Witherspoon." He was their preacher and a teacher at the Hebron Church School that adjoined the complex of log structures on the Mitchell farm.

Thirteen-year-old Jennett rang the school bell, pulling the woven rawhide rope with all the might her skinny little arms could muster. She was excited her father and brothers were home. Ringing the bell alerted the neighbors along Knob Creek that school had let out early.

Peggy hurriedly discarded the ink-filled walnut shells used by the older pupils, then placed the small slate boards of the elementary students on her desk to grade later. Rebeckah, Peggy's fifteen-year-old sister, stood on her tiptoes, erasing the large slate board on the wall behind Peggy's desk.

"I have finished. May I go now?" Rebeckah asked.

"You may, and I will tell Father that your spelling has greatly improved since the last grading was done."

"Thank you, teacher." Rebeckah curtsied and was out the school door running to welcome her father, brothers, and Reverend Witherspoon home.

Peggy's siblings were instructed to call her "teacher" or "Miss Mitchell" in the classroom, like the other students who were not family members.

Peggy stood at the washbowl in the corner of the classroom cleaning the chalk dust from her hands and trying to scrub the indigo ink stains from her long, slender fingers. She primped and fussed with her long hair using the bone-handled mirror and brush set she had purchased last summer in Philadelphia. Smoothing out a few wrinkles from her long, schoolmarm dress that covered everything except the toes of her shoes, she closed the schoolhouse door. *That will have to do.*

Outside, the children were gathered around the travelers. Elizabeth had come out of the nearby house and watched the children welcome their father home.

"Samuel, get your brothers away from the horses before one of them gives a kick," Adam said.

Samuel, who had just turned eleven, grabbed four-year-old Hezekiah by one hand and seven-year-old James by the other.

"Look what I brought home." Adam pulled the cream-colored pup from his gunny sack and held it up for all the children to see.

"Puppy!" Hezekiah screeched in his high-pitched voice.

"No, four puppies!" John held up Smoky.

William and Jimmy pulled the pups they carried from their gunny sacks and showed them off, to the delight and surprise of everyone.

*Another mouth to feed.* Elizabeth looked at the canine from a distance. She didn't want to get attached to another dog as she had Lulubelle, who died last year.

Robert saw his wife's carriage in the barn and looked anxiously around for his bride.

"She is in the house." His mother gestured toward the main house.

"I've got a surprise for her." Robert ran toward the cabin with a small package in his hand.

"She's got a surprise for you." His mother spoke so everyone but Robert could hear.

"What's the surprise?" Adam said.

"You'll have to wait your turn." Elizabeth kissed her husband.

"Rachel made this for you." Adam handed his wife a neatly wrapped package.

Elizabeth opened the package to find a new spring bonnet. "That is so much like Rachel." She tied the bonnet on her head and smiled for Adam.

"I brought you a new door stop. Now we can put that old field stone out in the yard where it belongs." Adam held out his prize for Elizabeth to see.

She cringed. "It's a cannonball."

"How would you know that?"

"One just like it tore our house apart in North Carolina. That's how I know. Where did you find it?"

"It's a long story. I'll tell you about it later."

They heard Robert howling from the house.

Adam jerked his head up. "What in the world?"

"Come see your surprise." Elizabeth grabbed Adam's hand and led him toward the main house.

Knowing the commotion didn't signal disaster or imminent danger, Peggy approached Jimmy and her brothers, who were busy in the barn putting up the tack and currying the horses. "Did you have a good trip?"

"Everything went well, except Robert took sick and a bear tried to eat our horses." Jimmy smiled as he removed his saddle from Star.

Peggy suppressed a sigh when she saw that special smile she so adored. "What happened to Robert?"

"Not sure, but we all got caught in a blizzard on top of the mountain and nearly froze to death." Jimmy placed his saddle on the saddle rail.

Peggy caressed the stallion she had raised from a colt. "A blizzard this late in the year?"

"That's what we thought, but we learned that snow-storms are not uncommon on Grandfather Mountain this time of year." Jimmy poured a bucket of cracked corn in the horse trough for the horses.

"How did Star do going over the mountain?" Peggy rubbed the stallion's well-formed neck.

"He did well—you did a good job of training him."

Screaming and hollering from the main house became loud enough to be heard in the barn.

William looked up from currying his horse. "Sounds like Father."

"You're fixing to be an uncle, as is John." Peggy poked her head around the horse to see her brother's reaction.

"Robert's going to be a father." Jimmy poured another bucket of corn.

Adam came out of the cabin with his arm around his wife, waving his hat in the air. "We're going to be grand-parents."

The ringing of the school bells drew neighbors and family to see what the commotion was about. They surrounded the Mitchell cabin, offering congratulations and welcoming the men home.

"When is Elizabeth due?" Jimmy put down the bucket.

"Early September, best I can tell." Peggy waved at her Father, who waved back.

"Could it be a boy?" Jimmy said.

"She is carrying the baby low, which is a good indication it might be a boy. Why your concern over the gender?"

"Robert said he and Elizabeth were going to name their first child James after me if it's a boy." Jimmy beamed with pride.

"Well it's a fifty-fifty chance it will be a boy." Peggy saw her father coming to help tend to the horses and greeted him with a hug.

John, William, and Jimmy went to the main house to congratulate Robert.

"How's my matchmaking daughter?" asked Adam.

"What do you mean?"

"I heard about your scheme to help John win over the Barnes girl."

"What did you think of it?" Peggy asked.

Adam said, "Well, obviously it worked. It only took two weeks to get her to the altar after her father saw the number of zeros on the marriage bond. Would he have gotten her without your interference?"

"I don't know. John is shy when it comes to such things. He needs to be pushed." Peggy said.

"I have taught my children to read the Bible and adhere to its teachings. There is one passage in the Good Book that I do not agree with and that is, 'The meek shall inherit the earth.'"

"Why, Father?"

"If the men who signed the Declaration of Independence had been meek and not made their demands known to King George, we would still be sipping tea. If John truly wanted to marry Mary Ann, he should have let her know in no uncertain terms his intention."

"Father, you need to tell John, not me."

"Well the same goes for you. If you want to marry Jimmy, you need to tell him."

Peggy's mouth formed a perfect "O." "In good time Father. In good time."

"My dear Peggy, you will soon be twenty-five years old."

"I'm glad you're home. I need to grade today's schoolwork while there's still some daylight. Please excuse me." Peggy hurried off toward the schoolhouse, which also served as her sanctuary when she wished to be alone with her thoughts.

She heard the ringing of the dinner bell, but kept working as night fell on the schoolhouse. She lit a candle and was reading from a Mary Wollstonecraft book when she heard a knock on the door.

"Who's there?"

"It's me, Jimmy. May I come in?" He didn't wait for an answer but entered with a pewter plate filled with food.

"That smells good." She put her book away.

"Your favorite, pulled pork. You were missed at supper. Didn't you hear the bell?" Jimmy sat at his desk next to hers.

"I heard the bell, just wasn't hungry."

"Your mother made a plate for you. I'll leave it with you." Jimmy got up and moved toward the door.

"How are your accommodations?"

"They are sufficient for my needs. William and I get along quite well in the bunk house." Jimmy turned from the door, his hand still on the latch. "Thank you for your concern."

"Come and sit with me while I eat. Then let's go for a walk along the creek."

"I would enjoy that." Jimmy pulled out a stool.

"Tell me about Rachel and Reverend Caldwell."

"They were both so gracious, and Rachel just went on and on about you and how she looks forward to your letters."

"I was nine years old the last time I saw them."

"Did I tell you that I preached at the Buffalo Church?"

"You did? What was your sermon about?" She took a bite of pork.

"Forgiveness."

"Why did you pick forgiveness?"

"It just seemed appropriate, as the session was meeting afterwards to consider reinstating an ousted member."

"Who was it?"

"John Hamilton."

"He must have done something terribly bad." Peggy put her hand on Jimmy's. "I'm proud of you.

Do you realize you have spoken at two of the oldest and most prominent congregations in the Presbytery?"

"If Reverend Balch is not going to be here, I will hold services here in this very room. You will get to hear the sermon I gave at Buffalo Church."

"I look forward to hearing you preach." Peggy took his hand and stood up. "Let's go for that walk."

Peggy blew out the tallow candle on her desk and said, "I don't think we'll be seeing much of Reverend Balch anymore. He is involved in establishing a church and school near his home in Greeneville."

Jimmy lifted up the stuck front door, pushing it out for Peggy.

"I need Father to fix that door," she said.

"What's this about not seeing Hezekiah Balch?" Jimmy asked.

"He preached last Sunday and stayed two nights in anticipation of your return. He wanted to talk with you, but had to get back to Greeneville on business. Seems he has gathered enough financial support to open the college in Greeneville he has been talking about for some time." Peggy stopped and looked at Jimmy. "You understand what this means, don't you?"

"What does it mean?"

"You are now the full-time minister at Hebron." She grabbed both his hands and swung them. "You are excited, aren't you?"

He studied Peggy's face. "What did the elders say?"

"Now they can pay you more than the pittance that you have been receiving, and it solves the Hopkins issue."

"The Hopkins issue?"

"Remember how Reverend Balch changed so after going back east three years ago?"

"I was still in school at Washington College, but I remember Reverend Doak was quite upset with his preaching."

"As were members of Hebron Church, who left to attend Salem Church. Hopefully, they will come back when word is spread that Reverend Balch is gone."

"I am the minister of Hebron Church now?"

"That's right. You've been praying for a church of your own. Now you have one." Peggy said.

"Yes, my prayers have been answered."

They walked along the creek, neither saying a word for several minutes.

Finally, Peggy spoke. "You are happy about this?"

"Yes, it's just happened so fast that I don't feel prepared."

She turned to look Jimmy in the face and took both his hands. "Reverend and Sister Doak saw in you the makings of a great minister when you were just a young boy. They've spent the last ten years grooming you to be a preacher. How can you feel unprepared?"

"I have never felt quite adequate at my calling."

Peggy sat down on the large flat boulder, gently pulling Jimmy with her. "I don't know how you could feel inadequate. I heard you preach to the congregation of the Pine Street Presbyterian Church. You gave an excellent sermon, and they invited you back."

"Peg, I have always been unsure of myself in everything I have been called on to do."

"I know, Jimmy. I remember when you couldn't say hello without stuttering. That's why Reverend Doak had you read the Scripture lesson out loud to the congregation every Sunday. I don't remember you ever stuttering while reading the Scripture. Why didn't you stutter in front of the congregation?"

"I didn't want to fail Reverend Doak or embarrass Mother."

"You were afraid of disappointing your mother?"

"Yes, I want to make her proud of me."

"She will be very proud of you becoming the minister of Hebron Church."

"You think so?"

"Why wouldn't she?"

"My mother is not easily pleased." He frowned, then smiled. "But, I know my brother Thomas will be."

"Thomas is your half-brother?"

"No. Everyone thinks we are, but actually there is no blood relation."

"How can that be?" Peggy had heard this from others but wanted to hear it directly from Jimmy.

"When I was a young lad, mother married a widower, Thomas Smith, who already had a baby boy named after him. I don't remember much about him other than one day, Mr. Smith left and never came back. We never knew what happened to him. So, Mother had me and baby Thomas to take care of. She raised us like brothers, giving Thomas the middle name of Witherspoon so he wouldn't feel like an orphan. Our feelings for each other are no different than any two blood brothers."

Peggy looked up into the cloudless sky. "Your mother raised Thomas like her own child?"

"That she did."

They sat quietly gazing at the reflection of the moon in the water of Knob Creek, each deep in their own thoughts.

Peggy turned to look at Jimmy. "Do you wish to have children?"

"First, I must find a suitable wife."

"Peggy, where are you?" a girl's voice called out in the dark.

"Over here, Jennett."

"Mother needs you. She thinks Hezekiah is running a fever."

Jimmy stood up. "I'll go with you."

"No you don't need to catch a fever. You have a sermon to give come Sunday."

Peggy followed her younger sister up the trail to the main cabin where her parents and the four youngest boys slept.

When she entered, the four-year-old held his hands out for her, as did seven-year-old James.

"He doesn't have a fever." Peggy picked up the smallest child, holding his cheek to hers.

"He felt warm to me and looked flushed in the face. I'm sorry to have bothered you," Elizabeth said.

"Gives me a chance to tuck the babies in."

"I don't know what I would do without you." Elizabeth looked at her oldest daughter.

"Ibby and Rebeckah could do what I do." Peggy tucked Hezekiah in, hugged James, who was curled up on the shared bed, and said goodnight to Samuel and David, who were already asleep in the loft.

Jimmy lay back on the almost-six-foot-square boulder, thinking about his difficult childhood and how hard things had been for his mother. Now he was in a position to help her and Thomas.

He heard something in the water. *Must be that pesky muskrat the boys have been trying to trap.* Then he saw Ibby climb up on the bank, the moonlight glistening off her naked body.

*I shouldn't be seeing this. Does she know I'm here?* He watched as she dried herself and put on a long robe. *She has such a beautiful body, I can't help but stare.*

"God, please forgive me," Jimmy prayed below his breath.

He lay perfectly still on the boulder, waiting, hoping that Ibby had not seen him. He wouldn't move until he was sure she had gone to the cabin she shared with Rebeckah and Jennett. His heart beat fast, burning with a desire he could not remember ever being so intense. This was the first time he had ever seen a completely naked woman. What a beautiful sight it was.

"Jimmy, is that you?" Ibby spoke from behind him.

"Hello, Ibby." He yawned. "I must have fallen asleep stargazing."

"It's a good night for it." Ibby looked up at the stars and sat down on the boulder next to Jimmy.

"I need to turn in. It's been a long day."

"Stay and watch the stars with me," Ibby said. "Look, there is a falling star. It's beautiful. Make a wish."

"A meteor," Jimmy said.

"I would rather think of it as a star, like in the Bible." Ibby turned toward Jimmy and said, "Do you come to the creek often at night?"

He shifted position, moving a bit further away from her. "Occasionally, especially on starry nights like tonight."

"Now that the weather is warmer, I like to come before bedtime for a swim. I sleep much better when I do. You should join me sometime." Ibby leaned against him.

"I don't think that would be a good idea."

"Why? I can't see you if you're in the water. Besides, with all my brothers, I've seen men before."

"I would be embarrassed in the water with a woman."

"We'd be in trouble if fish thought that way." Ibby scooted off the boulder and wiped the dust from her hands. "See you in the morning at breakfast."

Jimmy tried to speak but could manage only an affirmative nod as Ibby turned to walk up the path to her cabin.

# Chapter Five
## Travel Plans

Elizabeth rang the dinner bell later than usual for breakfast. It was Saturday, with no school or church, so the family could have a leisurely meal.

Peggy, Ibby, and Rebeckah were busy helping their mother cook for the thirteen residents of the Mitchell farm. Jimmy took his place next to Peggy's seat at the long sideboard. Ibby sat across the narrow table board. She looked at Jimmy, but he looked away, avoiding her stare. When Ibby offered biscuits across the table, he had to look at her to accept them. As he did, Jimmy was captivated by her beautiful smile and facial features.

"Thank you." Jimmy cleared his throat, hoping no one noticed his rough voice. *Why am I just now seeing her beauty? Is she aware I saw her naked last night on the creek bank?*

"We saw grandfather on the mountain," William announced to everyone at the table. "Didn't we, Jimmy?"

Lost in his thoughts of Ibby, Jimmy didn't respond.

"Jimmy, William asked you a question." Peggy looked at him with raised eyebrows.

"I'm sorry, William. What did you say?"

"Tell them about the image of grandfather on the mountain."

"It was like Adam said. It looked like a grandfather to me."

"Kind of like me," Adam joked, reminding everyone again that he would soon be a grandfather.

Everyone laughed except Jimmy, who was lost in his own thoughts.

Peggy turned to Adam. "Tell us about your journey."

"Father has told us. If you would have come for supper last night, you'd have heard all about the trip," Ibby snapped.

"Excuse me for asking," Peggy snapped back.

Their father looked from Peggy to Ibby and back again. "It was a good trip."

William laughed. "Grandmother Mitchell is back as a dog."

Peggy looked to her father for an explanation.

"I'll tell you about it later. Pay no attention to your brother."

When she saw she wasn't going to get an answer, Peggy said, "I plan to take my pelts to Philadelphia much earlier this year."

"When do you plan to leave?" Elizabeth asked.

"As soon as my preparations are complete, hopefully by the end of the month."

Elizabeth wrinkled her forehead. "What about school?"

"Now that Jimmy is back, he and Ibby can finish up the school year."

"Why the sudden urgency?" Adam asked.

"Last year, I got lucky when Captain McDuffy purchased my pelts so late," Peggy said. "Ships sailing from Europe set off during May and arrive in Philadelphia by the middle of June. The more buyers, the more offers— just simple business."

Adam beamed a smile at his daughter. "Sounds like you've thought it out quite well."

"I have."

"Who are you taking with you?" Adam asked.

"Me!" Jennett raised her hand and waved it for attention but was ignored.

"I'm hiring Jake Thompson with his wagon and team, and I'll ride Mr. Jackson."

No one spoke for several long seconds.

Adam looked down at the table. "You're so much like your Grandmother Mitchell."

"I don't want Peggy to go without family," Elizabeth said.

"With Robert and John tending their own crops, Father will need every hand in the fields to get the corn harvested," Peggy said. "Mr. Thompson makes the trip regularly, and the wagon trail is safer now."

Adam nodded. "You have it so well planned. How could I disapprove?"

"Father, I wasn't asking for approval."

"Oh." Adam looked hurt after the curt remark.

The family sat quietly, then James, who had crawled under the table to Peggy said, "I wanna go wiff you."

Everyone laughed.

Peggy picked James up and cradled him on her lap. "I'll miss you, too, but you must attend school and learn to read and write."

"How long will you be in Philadelphia?" Elizabeth asked.

"I'll try to be home before the baby is born."

"Good. I know that Robert and Elizabeth will want you here." Elizabeth stood up and started to clear the table.

Hezekiah climbed up on Peggy's lap with his brother. "I'll clean up for you, Mother." Peggy started to lift James off her lap.

"Stay where you are and give your brothers some attention. Ibby and Rebeckah will help me."

Jennett glared at Peggy. "You took Ibby and Rebeckah last year and promised you'd take me next."

"You have school. Make good grades, and I'll take you next time." Peggy caressed her sister's long, braided auburn hair, wiping a tear that rolled down her check.

Jennett sniffed and ducked her head.

"I'll be going to town shortly." Peggy lifted Jennett's chin. "Would you like to go with me? Mr. Deaderick will give you some candy."

Jennett nodded and put an arm around Peggy's neck. "Can we ride in your new buggy?"

On the ride to town in the carriage, Jennett said, "It sure is a smoother ride than Father's wagon."

"Springs!" Peggy said.

"What springs?" Jennett looked around. "I don't see any springs."

"Springs under the carriage are what make the ride smoother. Wagons don't have that comfort. I'll have Jake show you how they work when we get to the livery stable."

Standing in the doors of the stable, Jake Thompson saw Peggy coming in the carriage he had sold her—a neat little buggy for two that had belonged to David Deaderick, Jonesborough's first merchant.

Jake removed his hat and bowed. "What brings the Mitchell ladies to town today?"

"I've got business with Sara," Peggy said. "Then with you."

"Do I need to put my trading britches on? You beat me up real bad on that carriage you're riding in."

Jennett laughed. She enjoyed watching Peggy trade barbs with men.

"Would you please show Jennett how the springs work while I check on your wife and the baby?"

Jake helped Peggy and Jennett down from the carriage.

His wife Sara came out of the door of the living quarters, which had previously been a tack room., She cradled her newborn and said, "Welcome, Peggy. This must be your sister—she looks so much like you. "

"Sara, this is my youngest sister, Jennett."

Sara looked at the two sisters. "I know I've seen you at church before. It's a pleasure to meet Peggy's sister."

Peggy said, "Let's go inside. I want to see how you and the baby are doing since I delivered that precious girl. Might as well check on the boys too."

"I'll take care of your horse and buggy," Jake said.

Jennett said, "I like the carriage, Mr. Thompson."

"It's much lighter than a wagon." Jake pointed to the undercarriage of the buggy. "See those springs? That's what absorbs the bumps in the road and makes for less stress on the carriage and the passengers."

They led the horse and buggy into the big barn, where Jake watered and fed the horse rolled oats.

Sara opened the door to the living quarters. Although she had made the area comfortable for the family, it still smelled like a stable.

Peggy followed Sara into the room. "Sara, I want Jake to take me and my pelts to Philadelphia. Do you have any problems with that?"

"I would if it was any other woman than you. When you leaving?"

"Soon as I can get my lot of furs and pelts ready." Peggy took the baby and laid her on the bed. "Get your clothes off so I can take a look at you."

"I was hoping to go with you, to see Philadelphia again while it is still the nation's capital." Sara hung her dress on a wall peg and sat on the bed to watch Peggy examine the baby.

"Not with an infant. It's just too long a trip, and the boys are doing so well they shouldn't miss school." Peggy laid the baby in the cradle, and looked into Sara's ear.

"Who's going to teach school?"

"The reverend, Ibby, and Rebeckah."

"Your sisters not going this time?"

"Just me this year." Peggy looked down Sara's throat. "You sure you're comfortable with Jake and me going alone?" She motioned for Sara to lie back on the bed.

"With you, at least I know Jake will be taken good care of, if he took sick." After she completed her exam, Peggy said, "You both are doing well, except for the rash on the baby's behind. I'll leave you some ointment for that. If either of you or the boys take sick while I'm gone, I want you to see Dr. Chester."

Sara pulled her dress over her head. "I don't know about that. I don't feel comfortable with a man doctor looking at me."

"You have got to get over that—most doctors are men."

"But I'd rather you take care of us." Sara finished buttoning her long dress up.

"I will, but if I'm not here and you get sick, you need to see Dr. Chester. Now, where are those boys of yours?"

"They're down on the creek." Sara opened the door and looked down on Little Limestone Creek, which ran through the center of Jonesborough.

"I hope you don't let them play in that filthy water," Peggy said.

"I try to keep them away from the creek, but it's like keeping a bear out of a pot of honey." She turned back to face Peggy.

"I know, but you must. There are too many people dumping their bed pans in it. It's best the boys stay out of the creek."

"I'll try."

"I'm going to talk to Jake about when we can leave." Peggy stepped out of the living quarters.

Jake asked, "When you want to leave?"

"Sooner the better." Peggy looked toward the creek.

"Next week?" Jake suggested.

"Tuesday morning?" Peggy looked at Jake.

"That's good." Jake nodded.

"Be at my place at first light. Come, Jennett, let's see what Mr. Deaderick has that we can't do without."

Jake watched Peggy and Jennett hurry down the street, then turned to Sara, who was standing in the doorway holding the baby. "I've never seen Peggy when she wasn't in a hurry."

The bell over the door rang as the Mitchell ladies entered Mr. Deaderick's store.

"How are the two prettiest girls in Jonesborough doing today?" Mr. Deaderick asked.

Peggy nodded a greeting and said, "We both have a sweet tooth and would like to taste some of your delicious treats."

"I received some twisted licorice from a Philadelphia confectionary that you might like. Let me treat you to a sample." Mr. Deaderick cut two small pieces, placed them on a piece of butcher paper, and handed them to Peggy and Jennett.

"Thank you, Mr. Deaderick," Jennett said.

Peggy smiled her thanks. "Have you taken in any more pelts since we spoke last?"

"I've taken in a few silver bellies."

"Silver belly?" Jennett squinched her nose.

"That's what the fur traders call the gray beavers that are trapped around these parts. Their belly shines like silver in the sunlight. Bring a good price—don't they, Peggy?"

"Yes, they do. Will you tell the trappers I'll be leaving next week and need their pelts by Saturday if they want me to buy them this year?"

"I'll tell those I see."

"That would be appreciated. Now, I'll need eighteen wheels of your licorices."

"I think that's about all I have. I should have ordered more."

"Jennett, why don't you wait for the candy while I have a word with Dr. Chester at the inn? I'll be back for you soon," Peggy said.

She found Dr. Chester sitting on the front porch of his inn, watching the comings and goings on Main Street.

"Surprised you aren't with a patient." Peggy sat in the empty chair next to the doctor.

"Seems everyone is well in Jonesborough. How's everyone at Knob Creek?"

Peggy reached into her bag and retrieved some papers. "I want to leave these with you. They are notes I have made on every patient I've seen recently. I'm leaving for a long trip and don't know when I'll return. I'll inform the family and congregation at tomorrow's church service and advise them to call on you for their future medical needs."

Dr. Chester looked over his eyeglasses at her. "You sound as if you're not coming back."

"I will, but not for a while. My sisters Ibby and Rebeckah are older and with Jimmy now the pastor of Hebron, I can take a much-needed holiday—something I've always wanted to do. I may even travel to Europe."

"I so envy you. I wish I had gone to Europe when I was young. Will you write me and tell me about your adventures?"

Peggy turned sideways to face him. "Only if you promise to not tell a soul until after I've sailed. I don't want my family to know of my plans."

"Is everything all right at home?"

"Everything is fine. I will need you to check on the family and let me know how they're doing."

Dr. Chester leaned forward. "You must tell them, Peggy."

"I will in time. If they knew of my plans, they would beg me not to go, and I wouldn't. I'll write them just before I sail. Can I count on you to keep my secret?"

"Of course you can."

Peggy leaned over and kissed the doctor on the cheek and gave him a hug. "Take care of yourself."

Peggy rushed off toward Deaderick's to pick up her order and fetch Jennett, who was being entertained by the shopkeeper's tales.

At the Thompson place, Nick and John were playing stickball in front of the stables. Nick nodded. John said, "Good morning Miss Mitchell and Jennett."

"It's afternoon now, but thank you. Would you like to try some licorice candy?"

The boys nodded. She broke off a small piece of licorice for each boy.

"Thank you," John said. Again, Nick nodded.

"You're welcome. Now, I want to take a good look at you boys. Let's go inside."

Peggy knocked, and Sara, who was nursing the baby, invited them in. Peggy saw ugly boils on both of the boy's legs.

"They both have infected boils on their legs and buttocks. Use that sulfur ointment on the sores and keep the boys out of that creek."

John said, "We like to play in the creek." Nick nodded in agreement.

"Did you like the candy?" Peggy asked.

"Yes, teacher." As usual, John spoke and his brother nodded.

"If you promise me that you'll never go into the water of Little Limestone Creek again, I'll give you each a wheel of licorice."

John said, "I promise." Nick nodded.

"Nick, I want to hear you say it."

"I promise," Nick said as he nodded again.

Peggy looked down at Nick. "Why do you let John talk for you all the time?"

"We always say the same thing. I'd just be repeating what John says." Nick shrugged his thin shoulders.

"Just say ditto, like teacher taught us." Jennett made ditto marks in the air with her fingers.

"I like that," John said.

Nick nodded and said, "Ditto."

"Goodbye, Sara. Will I see you at services tomorrow?"

"Yes. Looking forward to hearing Jimmy preach."

"Goodbye, boys."

"Goodbye Miss Mitchell," John said. "Thank you for the candy."

"Ditto," Nick said with a nod.

Peggy smiled. "I think we should call you Ditto instead of Nick."

Everyone had a good laugh. Then Peggy and Jennett walked out to find Jake with the horse and buggy waiting for them.

# Chapter Six
## Farewell

Peggy said her goodbyes to the family at breakfast. Jake Thompson waited by the wagon as she bade her pupils farewell. She was close to them, having assisted in the birth of most of the children whom she taught. Peggy stood erect and spoke firmly, reminding the students that in the few weeks remaining of the school year she expected nothing but their best efforts in the classroom.

"You should respect Ibby and Rebeckah as your teachers, and honor Reverend Witherspoon as you do in church. Remember, he knows where I keep the willow switch," Peggy joked.

Afraid to show any emotion, she reached for the door and looked back one last time. "Goodbye."

Jake assisted her onto her horse. She waved at the children as they called out to her.

"Goodbye, Miss Mitchell."

"We'll miss you!"

"Come home soon!"

Jake drove the wagon, which was pulled by a team of four Morgan horses, with an extra horse tethered behind the wagon. Peggy led the way as if she were racing the devil. They chewed on deer jerky and biscuits as they rode. They hoped to make it across the shallows of the Watauga River and camp on the other side before dark. That would be a distance of nearly thirty miles, a good start on the six-hundred-mile journey. Fortunately, the spring rains had been sparse, which left the river much lower than usual and made for an easy crossing.

"Peggy, you just about wore my team out today." Jake sprawled out on his bedroll, trying to keep the weight off his aching buttocks.

"Better get used to it." Peggy removed the cast iron lid from the Dutch oven.

"You ride like you're running from the law."

"The sooner I get those pelts to Philadelphia, the better my chances of getting a fair price." Peggy coughed and fanned the smoke from the fire away from her face with one hand while stirring the salt pork and gravy with the other.

"You got a good price last year, and it was much later." Jake shifted on the bedroll.

"I just got lucky. Things are not so good in England." Peggy put the lid back on the bubbling pot.

"How would you know that?"

"I read the *Philadelphia Gazette* every week," Peggy answered.

Jake lowered his head and looked downward. "Oh."

Peggy realized Jake was uncomfortable talking about reading as he had never learned to read or write.

"Why are things different this year?" Jake asked.

"It is a financial issue, brought on by the Bank of England concerning the conversion of bank notes for gold. I have read much about it and still don't understand it." Peggy shook her head.

"Sure wish I had gone to school and learned to read. It's embarrassing that my boy's know their ABC's and I don't. Thank you for teaching them what they know."

"Thank you, Jake. It means a great deal hearing you say that. Your Nick and John make teaching worthwhile. Those two are always coming up with something."

"I need to check on the horses." Jake stood up and stretched his long body before sauntering over to where the horses were hobbled for the night.

"Don't take too long. Nothing is worse than cold biscuits and gravy."

After eating, Peggy made her bed upwind from the wagonload of foul-smelling pelts. She gazed at the stars and thought of places like Paris and London—places she had only read about but was determined to visit.

The smell of coffee and biscuits woke Peggy from a dream of faraway places to the reality of the mountain wilderness.

"Good morning." Jake bent over the campfire for the coffee pot.

Peggy stretched her arms and yawned. "The coffee smells good."

"Hope you like it strong," Jake said as he handed her a cup.

Peggy nodded her approval. "I learned to drink coffee from my father, who likes strong, black coffee."

"It's about fifteen miles to the Holston River. If all goes well, we can get across it before dark."

"We did twice that distance yesterday," Peggy said.

"I know, but I won't push my team that hard again."

"You're right." Peggy nodded. "We rode hard yesterday. I'll tie Mr. Jackson behind the wagon and ride with you, giving him a rest."

"I'd enjoy your company." Jake looked at Peggy and asked, "Why did you name your horse Mr. Jackson?"

"You never heard that story? Everyone in Jonesborough knows it." Peggy laughed.

"Well, I don't know it."

"Tennessee's Attorney General, Andrew Jackson, on his first trip back to Jonesborough for court session, stabled his stallion at Daniel's." She laughed. "I had left my mare with Daniel for shoeing. The mare came in heat, and somehow the stallion that Mr. Jackson was so proud of ended up in my mare's pen."

"Bet he wasn't happy about that."

"No, he certainly wasn't," Peggy said. "When Andrew saw his stallion topping my mare, he was furious and demanded a stud fee from Daniel. Daniel told Andrew that the mare was mine and he should take it up with me. Andrew never said a word to me about the incident. I received a beautiful foal without paying Mr. Jackson his customary fee." Peggy laughed. "That's why I named the horse Mr. Jackson."

"You mean Senator Andrew Jackson?"

"That's him," Peggy said.

"Why didn't he confront you about it?" Jake asked.

"That's what makes it funny. You wouldn't have any way of knowing, but he experienced my wrath many years ago and didn't want to encounter it again." Peggy laughed, remembering how surprised her suitor had been when she spurned his courtship.

"Well, whatever happened, you ended up with a fine horse."

They harnessed the team and started down the Wilderness Road that went north then east to Abingdon, Virginia. Peggy and Jake stopped near a rippling creek to give the horses water and a chance to graze on the lush grass. The travelers took refuge from the midday sun under a large hickory tree above the creek bank.

Peggy looked at Jake. "Would you really like to learn to read and write?"

"I'd give anything to be able to read a book to my children or write a letter to my wife someday."

Peggy pulled a small two-sided slate board out of her saddle bag and handed it to Jake. "See the letters on the back of the slate board?"

"Letters?"

"That's right—letters of the alphabet. Those twenty-six letters are the building blocks of a word. Once you know and can make the letters, you can make words, then sentences."

"Sentences?" Jake looked puzzled.

"For now, we are going to learn the alphabet. Don't worry about anything else," Peggy said.

As they harnessed the team again, Peggy recited the alphabet to Jake, three letters at a time. By the time they reached the Holston River, he had all the letters memorized.

As they forded the river, Jake recited the letters of the alphabet perfectly.

Peggy smiled at her pupil. "You've done a good job of reciting the alphabetical order of the letters. That is the first step to learning to read and write."

"Thank you for teaching me the alphabet, Peggy."

"You're a good student. You learn fast." Peggy held out a piece of chalk and the slate board. "Give me the reins."

Jake handed her the reins and took the slate and chalk.

Peggy wrinkled her brow. "With the wagon bouncing like it is, it will be difficult, but try to copy the letters one at a time, until you can make them all."

After working on the letters of the alphabet most of the afternoon, Jake said, "We should reach Abingdon soon. Let me take the reins from you."

"My pleasure." Peggy handed him the reins and took the writing implements.

"Do you want to stay at the inn?"

"If Mr. McDonald has a room—if not, we can camp near Wolf Hills." Peggy gave a little sigh. "I'm in hopes he has a room. A warm bath would be nice."

Jake coaxed the team up a steep hill with a teamster's demanding voice and a sharp whistle.

"I see you know the road. That hill is why you took the reins."

"The road is good from here to Abingdon." Jake shook the reins, and the team stepped up the pace to a smooth canter. Twenty-four hooves pounding the hard-packed dirt of the trail sounded like music to Peggy's ears. She loved the sound of a fast-moving team of horses.

Jake pulled the wagon and team up in front of the Abingdon Inn. Out came Joshua Coffee, not looking anything like the pig herder they had encountered on the trail last year.

Joshua said, "Welcome to the Abingdon Inn, Miss Mitchell. Good to see you again, Mr. Thompson. It's been a while since you've been through."

"First freight I've had moving east in some time. Seems everything is going west these days," Jake answered.

"Would you have a room and can I get a hot bath, please, Mr. Coffee?" Peggy asked.

"Yes, Miss Mitchell, you can have your choice of rooms tonight."

"I'll take the one that's the farthest from the stables." Peggy fanned the air as two of the horses relieved themselves. "I'm tired of smelling horses."

Jake laughed. "Give me the room over the stables. I'll feel right at home."

Joshua looked from Peggy to Jake.

Peggy said, "To understand the joke, you have to know that Jake lives inside the Jonesborough Stables."

Joshua nodded and motioned them toward the door. "Please go on in. I'll take care of your team and wagon. Molly will be down to fix you something to eat."

"No hurry on the food," Peggy said. "I'm most anxious to get my bath."

A pretty young Negro girl and Molly, the daughter of Mr. McDonald, the Inn's owner, brought in the long coffin-shaped tub for Peggy's bath. Peggy had attended the wedding when Molly had married Sheriff Robert Preston last year under the oak tree behind the inn.

Molly, a voluptuous, freckled-faced redhead, dropped the tub a few inches from the floor and screamed in delight when she saw Peggy. "It's you, Peggy Mitchell! I'm so glad to see you again. Josh just said our guest was a 'Miss Mitchell.' He should have told me it was you."

Peggy stepped around the tub and hugged Molly. "How are you?"

"I just had a baby last month. We named her after you and your grandmother."

"You call her Peggy?"

"We call her Margaret, your given name."

"I am honored." Peggy held Molly's stout shoulders and looked into her hazel eyes.

"If it wasn't for your Grandmother Margaret saving Robert's life after the battle and then your saving him from infection last year, I wouldn't have a husband and our little Margaret would never have been born." Molly smiled at Peggy.

Peggy gave her friend another big hug. "Where is the baby?"

"She and her brother, Robert Jr., are with my mother. Their father has gone to Philadelphia to solicit for a war pension as a wounded soldier from the war."

"How is his health?" Peggy asked.

Molly frowned and shrugged. "He has a great deal of pain."

"I know, and the pain will never get any better." Peggy looked at the young Negro girl.

"Peggy, this is Fanny, our new house girl. She'll fill your tub with warm water." Molly pointed at a nearby shelf. "There's an assortment of scented soaps. I like the lavender. Now, you have a good soak and relax while I fix a special supper for you. I'll be in the kitchen. Fanny will stay and attend to your every need."

"Thank you, Molly . . . Fanny."

Peggy recalled how comfortable the long tub was. The family tub was too short to stretch her long legs in. She slid into the tub and submerged all but her head. *Someday, I'll have a long tub like this for bathing.* Fanny poured in another pot of warm water, and Peggy relaxed in the soothing water until it cooled.

Peggy dressed in a white muslin dress, put her long auburn hair up in a loose bun and went down for dinner. She entered the dining room to find Mr. and Mrs. McDonald, baby Margaret, Robert Jr., and Molly waiting for her. Mrs. McDonald handed the baby to Peggy, who cradled the infant in her arms and pranced around the dining room like she was dancing. Everyone laughed and enjoyed seeing Peggy's reaction to her namesake.

"What's happening?" Jake came into the room and looked around at the commotion.

"This is Margaret Preston, named for me." Peggy's face lit up with pride.

Jake admired the baby. "Your name is Peggy."

"The family has always called me Peggy, but I was named for my Grandmother Mitchell, who lived with us. Two Margarets in one house could cause confusion. Same goes for my sister, Ibby, who was named after our mother, Elizabeth.

"Peggy and Ibby are nicknames, like Ditto," Jake said.

"That's right, like your son Ditto." Peggy laughed and told the McDonalds how the boy acquired his nickname.

Joshua and Fanny began to bring in the food and place it on the long, walnut table. Mr. McDonald asked everyone to be seated. He said grace, and they all ate together, family style.

"When do you think the sheriff will be back?" Peggy looked at Molly.

Molly looked down at her plate and squirmed in her chair. "You never know when that husband of mine will be home."

Mr. McDonald frowned, then looked at Molly with a sad smile.

Noticing that talk about Sheriff Preston seemed to make Molly and her father uncomfortable, Peggy changed the subject. "How is business at the inn, Mr. McDonald?"

The tenseness in their host's manner eased. "The inn is doing well, thanks to improved roads and regular stage-coach runs. As you can see, when the stage is not here, we have no business, except a few locals that frequent our bar. When the central government is moved to Washington, our little inn will be a busy place."

"When will that be?" Peggy asked.

Mr. McDonald beamed. "Officially in the year 1800, but some offices are already moving as the buildings are finished."

"Sounds like a great opportunity for a teamster." Peggy looked at Jake.

"I hadn't thought about that. All those government goods will need to be moved from Philadelphia to Washington."

"If you're thinking about hauling for the government, you best get a move on as the transition is already underway," Mr. McDonald said.

Jake said, "Thanks for telling me."

"You'll be able to find out in Philadelphia who to contact. I'll help you." Peggy said.

Jake nodded, but his brow was furrowed. Peggy knew he was concerned about not being able to read and write.

Mr. and Mrs. McDonald and the children went to their quarters, and Jake excused himself to check on the horses. Fanny cleared the table, leaving Molly and Peggy alone for the first time.

Peggy slid into the chair opposite Molly. "What's wrong?"

Molly looked up at Peggy, took a deep breath, then looked back down at the table. "I'm worried about Robert. When he's home, he's drunk. When he sobers up, he always has somewhere to go and stays away for weeks sometimes. He gets mad if I try to talk to him about his drinking or where he has been."

Peggy reached across the table to hold Molly's calloused hands.

"Sometimes, I don't think he cares about me or the children." Molly sniffed back tears.

"I'm sure he does." Peggy moved around the table, put both arms around Molly, and just held her. "War sometimes does strange things to a man."

Fanny came into the room. "Is there anything else you need me for?"

"No." Molly shook her head.

"Goodnight then, Mrs. Preston, Miss Mitchell." Fanny bowed her head and shut the door behind her.

Peggy sat with Molly while she had a good cry, then Peggy retired to her room. She lay on the featherbed with the wooden shutters swung open to the clear, crisp night. The glow of a full moon illuminated the room, and a cool breeze blew through the room. She fell into a tranquil slumber, thinking of poor Molly and feeling glad that she hadn't married the sheriff.

***

The same moon glowed over the pond on Knob Creek where Ibby had just waded into the cool water. She swam up to the big rock on the bank and made a big splash with her hand. The splash soaked Jimmy, who lay on his back gazing at the stars.

Ibby laughed and pointed. "You might as well come in. You're already wet."

"I will if you turn away."

He undressed and tossed his pants and shirt onto a nearby mountain laurel bush.

Ibby looked over her shoulder to make sure Jimmy was watching as she swam to the other side of the pond. He followed her as she went under the water. When he came up for air, treading water, Ibby was nowhere to be seen. He called for her, and she came up out of the water from behind and pushed him under with both hands.

Jimmy grabbed at her, forgetting for a moment that she was unclothed. His hand touched her naked legs, and Jimmy panicked. He swallowed a considerable amount of water, which strangled him. He made it to the rock, coughing and hacking.

"Jimmy, are you going to be all right?"

"I'll be fine—just give me a minute." Jimmy clung to the rock and tried to catch his breath.

"I'm sorry. I wasn't trying to drown you."

Jimmy stared out across the creek. "Please look the other way, Ibby, while I get out of the water."

Ibby swam back to where she got in the pond. Jimmy pulled himself up on the giant rock and sat with bended knees, trying to hide his arousal. He didn't understand the new and disturbing feelings that engulfed him. He thought, *I am a mature man—a minister, no less. Why am I feeling so confused?*

Ibby pulled a long sleeping gown over her body and came to where he sat. "Are you afraid of all women or just me?"

Jimmy shifted backwards a little and refused to look at her. "I shouldn't be here with you. You're just seventeen."

"Peggy was just sixteen when she was courted by Andrew Jackson."

"But he was properly courting her as her beau. They weren't swimming in the creek at night, just the two of them. This just doesn't seem right."

"You do realize that I'm closer to your age than Peg is?" Ibby turned and walked briskly up the path to her sleeping quarters, disappointed the night had not gone according to her plan.

# Chapter Seven
## Wilderness Trail

Peggy and Jake said goodbye to the McDonald family at breakfast. Molly packed them a whole smoked pork shoulder and a basket of johnnycakes to eat on the trail. They planned to make it to Wytheville, Virginia, and camp near the river crossing before dark.

Joshua held the lead horse of the team by its harness, while Jake helped Peggy into the wagon.

She took the reins and looked at Jake. "I'll drive, as you have homework to do."

He nodded, and both waved goodbye to their friends. They headed north up Abingdon's Main Street, which would become the Wilderness Trail outside of town.

"Jake, did you know today is the last day in the month of May?"

"It is?"

"May is the only month of the year spelled with only three letters. I'm going to teach you how to spell and write the month of May." Peggy shook the reins and the well-trained team responded, stepping into an easy canter.

Jake smiled and pulled the slate board and a piece of chalk out of his haversack. "I'm ready."

"The month of May is a homonym, meaning it is a word that has several different meanings." Peggy explained the different usages for the word.

Jake wrote the word over and over on the slate board as Peggy drove the team, stopping occasionally to help him make a letter or answer a question.

The day passed quickly as both teacher and student concentrated on Jake learning to read and write. That evening, they made camp near the river, hobbling the horses to graze the river bank.

They gathered driftwood along the riverbank for their campfire. Peggy found a patch of greens to eat with the smoked pork shoulder.

A wagon heading west approached their camp as the fire began to burn.

"Mind if we camp near you?" the man driving the wagon asked.

"You're welcome to camp here if you wish," Jake answered.

"Much obliged."

Two women and a boy climbed out of the overloaded wagon.

Jake acknowledged them with a nod, then turned back to the white-haired man with matching beard. "My name is Jake, and this is Miss Mitchell."

"Glad to meet you, Mr. Mitchell."

"No, I am Jake Thompson, and this is *Miss* Peggy Mitchell. We are not married, least not to each other—just traveling together."

The younger woman put her hand over her mouth, and the older woman looked from Jake to Peggy. Jake was oblivious to what his comment suggested. Though she was embarrassed, Peggy would wait for an opportunity to explain their relationship.

"My name is Douglas Aiken." The man motioned to the rest of the group. "My wife, Ann, my mother, Lee, and my son, Caleb."

"Glad to meet you." Jake offered his hand to Mr. Aiken and shook firmly.

"Been here long?" Mr. Aiken asked.

"We're just making camp for the night on our way to Philadelphia. Where you going?" Jake said.

"We're headed for Kentucky to meet up with my sister, Toni. The whole family's moving there from Lancaster."

Peggy put a couple of pieces of wood on the fire. "Would you all join us for dinner? We have a smoked pork shoulder and greens—more than the two of us could ever eat."

"Our cornbread and a big pot of red beans are already cooked," the elder Mrs. Aiken said.

"We can put together a potluck supper like we do at church," Peggy said.

"Where do you attend church?"

Peggy answered, "I'm the school mistress at the Hebron Church School, and I play the piano during church services."

The Aiken women, looking relieved to learn that this unmarried couple traveling together was churched, got the pot of beans out of their wagon. The new friends enjoyed a hearty meal.

After supper, Mr. Aiken sent Caleb to their wagon. The boy returned with two dulcimers and a lap harp.

"For your generosity of sharing the fine vittles, we'd like to make music for you."

Mr. Aiken handed the lap harp to his mother. He and his boy tuned their instruments and started to play popular songs like "Blind Mary," "Douglas Tragedy," "Am I Born to Die," and "Over the River Charlie." Soon everyone was singing and having a good time.

Music brought a welcome respite from the boredom of the long journey. When the embers of the campfire ceased to glow, the happy sojourners bid one another adieu.

*** 

Rebeckah and Jennett were helping Ibby clean up the kitchen after the evening meal and the usual Wednesday night Bible study. Jimmy had excused himself for his customary stroll along the creek. Adam and Elizabeth had retired early after putting Hezekiah and James to bed in the loft.

Rebeckah washed the last piece of pewter ware in a large cypress tub and handed it to Ibby. "I know what you're trying to do, and I don't like it." Rebeckah wiped her wet hands on her apron.

"Me, neither." Jennett brought the cast iron pot from the fireplace and handed the heavy cooking vessel to Rebeckah to be washed last.

"What are you talking about?" Ibby stood on her toes to put the plates in the plate rail above the fireplace.

Rebeckah said, "You're trying to steal Jimmy's affections."

"You can't steal anyone's affections." Ibby looked at her sisters and rolled her eyes.

"Can, too!" Jennett made an ugly face.

"Hush! You'll wake Mother, Father, and the boys." Ibby brought her index finger to her lower lip. "Let's take this conversation outside."

The sisters hurried through the chores in silence and hung their aprons on a kitchen peg. Ibby led the way from the cabin to the barn with Rebeckah and Jennett following close behind. The chickens cackled, letting it be known that they didn't like being disturbed after going to roost. The family milk cow swished her tail and mooed as the hens scurried about the barn.

Ibby faced her sisters with her hands on her hips. "Just what do you mean, saying I'm trying to steal Jimmy's affections?"

"Since Peg left, you've been flirting with Jimmy in class. Whispering in his ear, passing him notes," Rebeckah said.

"We saw you in the pond with him last night." Jennett mimicked Ibby with her hands on her own hips. "Naked!"

"You were watching us! How dare you spy on me?" Ibby shook her head and stormed out of the barn.

The chickens scattered as both sisters followed right behind her.

She stopped, turned around, and looked down at her younger sisters. "Why are you following me?"

"We want to talk to you about your behavior," Rebeckah said. "What you're doing is shameful."

"Shameful? Rebeckah, you're only fifteen and Jennett is a year younger. How would my little sisters know what is right for me?"

Rebeckah took a deep breath. "Your actions are shaming the family."

"Shaming the family?"

"Yes, shaming the family. You're openly flirting with Peggy's beau."

"That's not right, Ibby, and you know it!" Jennett faced her older sister with her arms folded across her chest.

Ibby moved away from her sisters as if she were going to leave, and then turned and came toward them. She stopped only a few inches from Rebeckah and glared into her face.

"Whoever told you Jimmy was Peggy's beau?" Ibby demanded.

"Everyone knows that Father and Reverend Doak intend for them to someday marry," Rebeckah said.

"Have you ever heard Jimmy or Peggy say they had plans to marry and have children?" Ibby asked.

"No," Rebeckah said. "But everyone knows they will someday."

"Have you ever seen Peggy express any intimacy toward Jimmy?" Ibby asked.

"She can't—he's our pastor," Jennett said.

Ibby shook her head and flailed her arms, exasperated at her sisters' naivety.

"Yes, he is our pastor, teacher, and a good family friend to all of us, but Jimmy and Peggy will never marry."

"Why would you say that?" Rebeckah asked.

Ibby inhaled, then exhaled, before answering. "Because there is no intimacy. Have either of you ever seen them hug or kiss?"

Rebeckah and Jennett looked at each other with matching wrinkled brows.

"There can be no love where there is no intimacy," Ibby said.

Rebeckah and Jennett stared at their sister in silence.

"I love Jimmy, and I intend to tell him how I feel."

Rebeckah asked, "When will you tell him?"

"When the time is right." Ibby said.

"How will you know the time is right?" Jennett asked.

"I'll just know."

***

Two days after leaving Abingdon, Peggy and Jake made it to Ingles Ferry. The fast-growing settlement on the banks of the New River had been named for William and Mary Ingles who established a ferry and trading post.

This marked the east end of the Wilderness Road. Beyond the Roanoke River the trail was called the Great Wagon Road to Philadelphia.

As Peggy looked around inside the store, she noticed a sign that read "No Pelts Taken—Cash or Whisky Only." She queried the shopkeeper, "Can I ask you why you aren't trading for pelts?"

"We just have too many pelts, and word is there's no market in Philadelphia."

"Why is that?" Peggy already knew the answer but waited to hear what he knew about the fledgling pelt market.

"I don't know for sure." The shopkeeper shrugged. "Mrs. Ingles had me put the sign up a few days ago and told me not to take any more pelts until we found a buyer for what we have."

"Goodness, that must hurt your trade," Peggy said.

"Sure does. Pelts is all these folks have to trade. No one has any money, and they need salt and supplies."

"How many pelts does Mrs. Ingles have?"

"More than any one wagon around here can carry."

Peggy stepped outside the store. She walked around to the back and, using her sense of smell, found the pelts stored in a small limestone outbuilding. It was built into the east side of a hill, which kept the afternoon sun off the structure. The long narrow openings along the roof eaves allowed the noxious fumes of the pelts to escape. Additional rows of the narrow openings enabled air to circulate. All the openings had thin bars close together to keep varmints out, but allow the cool air in. Peggy could see the pelts stacked floor to ceiling. A large Conestoga wagon or two small freight wagons could haul that load of pelts.

Peggy walked back around to the front of the store where Jake was making room for the two kegs of rock salt he had purchased.

"I don't think we'll get on to the ferry today. Too many wagons waiting to cross the river—teamsters getting impatient and fighting each other for position." Jake shook his head, embarrassed at his fellow teamsters' lack of courtesy toward one another.

"Did you see any teamsters that are headed east with an empty load?" Peggy asked.

"I didn't pay much attention, but I'm sure there are some going back empty. What are you up to?"

"I'm going to see Mrs. Ingles and make her an offer for her pelts."

Jake furrowed his brow. "I thought you said the pelt market was bad."

"It is, and when the market is bad, it's a good time to buy, especially if you control the market." Peggy winked at Jake. "Find us a teamster that you trust with an empty wagon that can leave first thing in the morning."

"They'll want to know what they'll be hauling."

"Tell them either salt or pelts," Peggy said.

She entered the store again and asked the shopkeeper where she might find Mrs. Ingles.

"Mrs. Ingles doesn't like to be bothered."

Peggy stood a little taller. "I didn't ask you about her disposition. I want to know where to find her."

"The big house on the hill, but please don't let her know I told you." The shopkeeper gestured toward a large rock house on a hill overlooking the ferry landing.

"Thank you."

Peggy reached under the pelts on their wagon to find her stash of coins. *No better place to hide something valuable than under a bunch of smelly varmint pelts.* She counted out one hundred ten-dollar coins, looking around to make sure no one was watching. Peggy saddled Mr. Jackson, rode up to Mrs. Ingles's house, and knocked.

A black housekeeper dressed as a woman but with the features of a man opened the door. "Who may I say is calling on Mrs. Ingles?" The housekeeper sounded like a woman.

"Peggy Mitchell is my name."

"Do she know you, Miss Mitchell?" The tall Negress looked down at the visitor.

Even though Peggy was a tall woman herself, she felt tiny under the gaze of the woman, who appeared to be at least six-and-a-half feet tall.

"No, she doesn't, but I'm here to make an offer for all her pelts."

"I know she gonna want to see you! She has a visitor, but I'll tell her you're from . . . ?" The housekeeper waited for an answer.

"Knob Creek, Tennessee."

"I'll tell her." The housekeeper made a sweeping gesture with her long arms. "Please come in and have a seat in the parlor."

Peggy looked around in awe of the fine furnishings in the house, which reminded her of the Cohens' home in Philadelphia.

The servant knocked on a closed door. Peggy could hear voices, but they were too low for her to hear what they saying or even to know if they were male or female.

"Come in, Sara."

"Pardon me, Mrs. Ingles and Sheriff Preston, but there's a lady here from Knobby Creek says she wants to buy your pelts."

Sheriff Preston twisted around in his chair to look toward the door and whispered, "Is her name Peggy Mitchell?"

"That's what she told me."

"You know her?" Mrs. Ingles looked at the sheriff.

"That's the woman I was just telling you about, that trades in pelts."

Mrs. Ingles turned back to Sara. "Well, send her in and bring some tea and biscuits."

Sheriff Preston sat quietly with his back to the door. Peggy didn't know he was in the room when she entered.

"Mrs. Ingles, my name is Peggy Mitchell. I'm from Knob Creek."

"I know all about you," Mrs. Ingles said. "And I've been warned to be leery of you."

Peggy jerked back in surprise. Then she saw Mrs. Ingles glance across the room at a chair in the corner. There sat Robert Preston, the sheriff of Washington County, Virginia. He stood and bowed toward Peggy.

"Mary, this is the lady who saved my life last year and then broke my heart."

"I had no idea you were here, Sheriff, but I'm so glad to see you." Peggy extended her hand.

"I am glad to see you as well." Sheriff Preston shook her outstretched hand.

"Peggy, we've been partaking of the nectar of the grain. Sara will be bringing some tea as well," Mrs. Ingles said.

"Tea would be nice, Mrs. Ingles."

"Please, call me Mary." She turned toward the door and raised her voice. "Sara, please bring Miss Mitchell tea."

Sara carried in a large silver tray with a matching teapot, tiny porcelain tea cups, and an assortment of delicious-looking pastries.

Sherriff Preston asked, "What brings you to Ingles Ferry?"

Peggy picked up the teacup that Sara had filled for her. "Jake Thompson and I are on the way to Philadelphia with a load of pelts and whisky."

"You have a load of pelts? And you want to buy what I have?" Mary asked.

"That's correct. I'm a broker of furs and pelts. Buying and selling them is my business."

"Are you aware that I have a tannery full of pelts?" Mary motioned to Sara that her glass of whisky was almost empty.

Sara picked up the cut glass decanter and filled her mistress's glass.

Peggy took a sip of tea, then put her cup on the small table beside the chair. "Yes, I've seen your inventory and would like to make you an offer."

"You couldn't have inventoried them—the tannery is locked."

"I don't care to inventory those smelly hides," Peggy said. "I just wish to buy your entire inventory."

"My inventory? How would you pay, my dear?"

"Gold coins."

"Well, let's hear your offer." Mary took another swig of whisky.

Peggy leaned back in her chair. "One thousand dollars in gold coins for the lot."

"That's the best you can do?"

"You're as aware as I of the market for pelts, Mary."

Mary nodded. "You're talking about a year's worth of ferry tolls and salt sales that I have invested in pelts."

"I know." Peggy tried to show her some empathy.

"They're fine mountain pelts. How about fifteen hundred?" Mary countered.

"Sorry, one thousand for the lot is my offer."

"I told you she was tough to do business with. Just like you, Mary." Sheriff Preston laughed.

"You have whisky, you say?" Mary winked at the sheriff.

Besides being Mary's drinking partner, the sheriff had been a close friend of her late husband William for many years. William and Mary were like the parents he never had.

"It's good, Mary. The best Tennessee whisky I ever tasted," Sheriff Preston said.

Mary took a deep breath and nodded. "Throw in a gallon of whisky and you've got a deal."

"On one condition—that the gallon of whisky pays the ferry toll for my wagons and that we be placed first in line to go across in the morning."

"Damn, you drive a hard bargain. Let's see your money." Mary impatiently motioned with her hand.

Peggy opened her leather saddlebag and counted out the ten-dollar gold pieces into Mary's hand. Mary then stacked them neatly on her side table, ten stacks of ten coins per stack.

Mary wrote a bill of sale and a note to her shopkeeper and handed both to Peggy. "You better start loading, only a few hours of daylight left."

Peggy took the papers and stood. "It was a pleasure doing business with you. Sheriff, you can come with me, and I'll give you Mary's whisky."

"Watch him and make sure he doesn't head south with it." Mary laughed.

When Peggy and Sheriff Preston caught up with Jake at their camp, Peggy pulled out one of the gallon jugs of whisky and handed it to the Sheriff. "I want you to take this to Mary as I promised her you would."

"I think I'll have to partake of a dram or two to be sure the quality of the Mitchell family recipe hasn't slipped since I last had the pleasure of tasting it."

Peggy placed her hand on his that was already on the cork of the jug. "Please, just take it to Mary and don't drink anymore tonight. I must talk to you, and it's important to me that you are stone sober when I do."

"You sound so serious."

"I am, and you must promise me you will be back at sunup." Peggy gave him a stern look. "Sober."

"Good night then, my beautiful Peggy." The sheriff bowed to her, mounted his horse, and rode off with jug in hand. Peggy shook her head. He was such a gentleman, even when he had been drinking.

***

The storekeeper, a pleasant, middle-aged, and serious man named Daniel Talbot, was Mary Ingles's most trusted employee. He closed the store to open what they called the salt house pelt storage for Peggy and Jake.

"When you get this one emptied out, let me know and I'll open the other one for you."

"The other one? Where is the other one?" Peggy tried to hide her surprise.

"The one by the toll booth. These pelts were from salt sales," Mr. Talbot said. "The toll booth takes in more pelts than the salt house, a lot more. We call that the toll house pelt storage."

"Jake, I think we'll need another large freight wagon." Peggy rolled her eyes.

"I'll take care of it."

He left to secure another wagon and driver as the two Negro teamsters he hired finished loading the salt house pelts.

After they loaded the second wagon at the toll house storage, there were still pelts left over. The two large freight wagons were filled to the top of the side boards. Jake instructed the men to stack the remaining pelts on his wagon, extending the load about a foot higher and making the wagon considerably overloaded.

It was late by the time the wagons were loaded. Jake and Peggy spread out their bedrolls, surrounded by three wagons full of foul-smelling pelts.

"You got more than you bargained for, didn't you?" Jake rested on his elbow on his bedroll and waited for Peggy's reaction.

"Yes, I did. But it will be for naught if I can't find a buyer for such a large lot."

Jake lay down and wiggled around to get comfortable. "I know you'll find a way to turn a good profit."

"I hope so." Peggy turned over on her bedroll. "Goodnight, Jake."

Peggy felt like she had just shut her eyes, but even without opening them, she knew that daybreak had come. She sensed the presence of a man standing over her. She opened one eye that was not yet in focus. "What are you looking at?"

"The fairest maiden of them all, my dear Peggy," Sheriff Preston said.

"It's so early," Peggy moaned.

"I'm here as you instructed, before sunup and sober."

Jake had been up long enough to make coffee and started breakfast. The Negro teamsters were up and checking their loads. Brothers Sam and Billy had helped load last night, and Nathan, the owner of the second wagon that Jake hired, was a good friend of theirs.

Sheriff Preston smiled down at Peggy. "I'm under orders from the mayor to get you across the river safely on the first ferry this morning."

"The mayor?"

"Yes, your new friend Mary Ingles is the mayor of Ingles Ferry. She thinks you're just grand even though you took advantage of her last night."

"I like Mary. She reminds me of my grandmother."

"She does look like your grandmother."

Peggy looked at him with a blank stare, and then said, "Excuse me, Sheriff—I forget that you and Grandmother met long before you and I did."

The sheriff's smiling face turned serious. "If we hadn't, I doubt that I would be here talking to her granddaughter this morning."

Two well-armed riders rode up. "Sheriff, we got to get them on the ferry."

"What's going on? Is there a problem?" Peggy asked.

"Let me introduce the town's marshals—Doc Puryear and Lon Swartz," Sheriff Preston said. "We can discuss it later. Just get your gear together and let's go."

"But I wanna—"

"Not now, Peggy. Please, just do as I tell you. Jake, let's move."

Jake helped Peggy onto the wagon.

The sheriff mounted up and motioned for them to start moving. "Follow me and don't stop unless I tell you to."

"Yes sir." Doc Puryear turned his horse.

They started down the road toward the ferry, a distance of about two hundred yards. People in the crowd lined up for the ferry started hollering and calling them names.

"Are they upset about us going across the river first?" Peggy looked at Jake sitting beside her.

He didn't answer her question, just kept driving.

Teamsters gathered along the roadway, shouting and shaking their fists at the three mounted lawmen and the wagons headed for the river's edge.

At the ferry, the sheriff encountered a group of about twenty men. Peggy and Jake were in the first wagon and could see the confrontation. The unruly men crowded the sheriff's horse. The horse and the sheriff, uncomfortable with the crowd so close, made a unique maneuver to disperse the rowdy crowd. The sheriff spurred the horse while turning its head, making sharp little circles, clearing them out of the way, knocking a few men down as his horse spun first one way and then the other. The maneuver worked, and the crowd quickly dispersed away from the ferry ramp.

The ferryman directed the drivers to park the three wagons across the deck of the ferry. The lawmen were keeping the unruly men back as the donkeys on the other side of the river started to tighten the slack lines for the pull across the river.

Sheriff Preston turned to the marshals. "Can you two hold them back?"

"If I can't, I guess I'll just have to shoot the one that comes the closest to the ferry," Doc Puryear said loud enough for the crowd to hear.

The line moved back a chain's length from the ferry ramp, and the sheriff rode his horse up the ramp onto the ferry just as it began to move forward. He waved his hat at the marshals and tied his horse to the railing. Peggy climbed off Jake's wagon and approached the sheriff from behind with a riding crop clutched tightly in her hand.

"When are you going to tell me why these people are so upset with us? It has to be more than us cutting in line at the ferry." Peggy waved the crop in his face.

Sheriff Preston took a step backward. "I see that you get riled up when you don't get your breakfast."

Jake had climbed down to intervene on the sheriff's behalf. "Peggy, this is my fault. The sheriff is here to protect us. Let me explain."

"I wish someone would. That mob was ready to lynch us."

"We're just about at the landing. You have to get in your wagon and get going. We can talk about this later," Sheriff Preston said.

The ramp was lowered. Jake whistled and called "get up." His team was off the ferry, followed by Sam and Billy coaxing on their team. Then Nathan's wagon came bouncing along, with the sheriff right behind riding hard to catch up with them. The sheriff drew alongside Jake at the top of the first hill. Peggy held onto her bonnet with one hand and the sideboard with the other.

"You can slow down now," Sheriff Preston said. "I told the ferrymen to wait at least an hour before going back across. That will give us a good lead if they choose to pursue us."

"Are you saying that crazy mob may come after us?" Peggy turned sideways on the bench to face Jake. "You better tell me what this is all about."

"The whole thing is about Nathan. On his last trip through Big Lick, a runaway slave of a wealthy plantation owner hid in Nathan's wagon and made it all the way to Lancaster. Someone saw the slave get out of Nathan's wagon there. They told the slave owner, who put up a reward for the slave and a bounty on Nathan's head. The sheriff came along yesterday as the out-of-control mob was trying to lynch Nathan. They accused him of helping other slaves escape and they say Nathan violated the Federal Fugitive Slave Act."

"Is that what all this fuss is about?" Peggy asked.

"That's what it's about. I'm sorry I caused this problem," Jake said.

"Don't be. It's not your fault that happenstance put us in the middle of this unfortunate situation," Peggy said.

They rode along, not saying another word, each contemplating what the consequence of their unintentional actions could be.

After several minutes of silence, Peggy said, "Stop the wagon."

"Are you sure? That mob may be across the river heading our way by now."

"I want to ride with Nathan and get his take on all this," Peggy said.

Jake raised his hand to signal the wagons behind him that they were coming to a stop. Peggy climbed down and motioned for Jake to keep going, waved Sam and Billy on, and put her hand up for Nathan to stop. When he did, she pulled herself up onto the buckboard and sat down next to the white-haired teamster. The rope burn around his neck was still red and blistered from yesterday's near-hanging.

"Nathan, I haven't had the pleasure of meeting you. My name is Peggy Mitchell."

"Glad to meet you, Miss Mitchell." Nathan tipped his hat.

"My friends call me Peggy. I wish you would call me Peggy."

"I appreciate that, but I will feel much more comfortable calling you Miss Mitchell, if you don't mind."

"I don't mind."

"I am sorry for the trouble I have caused you, Miss Mitchell."

"What is done is done." She shrugged. "Nathan, I want to hear your side of the story."

"I was born a freeman in the Conestoga region of Pennsylvania. My father was a blacksmith. His name was Nathan Brown, Sr. and he worked for Mr. Hoffman, who started the Conestoga Wagon Yard. I learned the trade of a wainwright. Mr. Hoffman sent me to school and bought me books." Nathan slowed to work his way around a gully in the road.

"You can read and write?"

Nathan looked around as if fearing someone could hear their conversation over the noise of rattling wagons and cantering horses. "I would appreciate your not mentioning that. It has caused me trouble when white people find out that I can read."

"I won't say anything," Peggy promised. "So how did you become a teamster?"

"I hired out for large wagon trains headed west. My blacksmithing and wheelwright work kept them moving. If need be, I could rebuild a busted wagon on the road. This one ran off into a canyon many years ago. I salvaged what was left of it and rebuilt it by hand. Once I had a wagon, I became a teamster and been hauling freight ever since."

"Are you guilty of what you have been accused of?" Peggy asked.

"I found a man in the back of my wagon, beaten black and blue and hungry. I fed him, doctored him as best I could, and gave him a ride to where he wanted to go. If that is against the law, then, yes, Miss Mitchell, I am guilty." Nathan shook the leather reins, the horses picked their step.

Peggy and Nathan rode along in deep thought, neither saying anything.

Sheriff Preston had been scouting behind them some distance, trying to determine if they were being followed. He rode past them and caught up with Jake. Soon they were pulling off into a meadow.

"It looks clear behind us for now," the sheriff said. "Let's take a break. There's a creek that runs along that line of trees. Good place to water the horses and let them graze a bit."

"Thank you. I'm hungry and I'm sure the men are as well. Can we take time to cook something?" Peggy tilted her head and looked at the sheriff.

"I'm afraid not. We're only ten miles from the James River. We must get across it before dark. I know a place to camp on the other side that would be difficult for anyone to approach without us seeing them first."

Peggy cut the remaining pieces of deer jerky and divided it amongst the six of them. "This will have to do until we reach the James."

"The James River is the halfway point from Big Lick to Lexington," Jake said.

"We won't be safe until we reach Pennsylvania, where the slave laws are seldom enforced," Sheriff Preston said.

Peggy nodded her understanding. "It had to have been a bad political move, your going against the slave owners in Washington County."

"Yes, it was."

"Why did you take up for Nathan?" she asked.

"Remember how close we came to hanging Joshua Coffee back in Abingdon last year for the murder of Mr. Thigpen?"

"You were the only one that believed him," Peggy said.

"Joshua is probably the gentlest soul I have ever met. He could never hurt anyone."

"Did you think Nathan was innocent?" Peggy looked at the sheriff, waiting for his answer.

"No, but I think under the circumstances, he did the right thing." Sheriff Preston looked around at the men preparing to leave. "What we have done is the right thing, but if we're caught with him we'll all be arrested."

"Could that happen?" Peggy asked.

The sheriff nodded as Nathan, Billy, Sam, and Jake led the teams to the wagons. "I have a plan we can talk about once we're across the James."

The three drivers led the wagons north, gradually climbing out of the valley to higher ground. Once the ground was level, the road was greatly improved and they could increase the pace of the teams to a fast canter. Sheriff Preston continued scouting the rear, watching for their pursuers.

# Chapter Eight
## Best Laid Plans

It was the eve of the first Sunday of the month. Reverend Jimmy Witherspoon nervously paced the floor of the Hebron Presbyterian Church and School, preaching to himself.

Since its founding, the small congregation had made the monthly trip to Salem Presbyterian Church, on the grounds of Washington College, for church and an afternoon potluck dinner. The tradition started because the Hebron church didn't have a minister and their worship services were basically Bible study led by an elder.

Now, the Hebron Church had an ordained minister of its own, a minister who had preached at Philadelphia's Pine Street Church, which was considered the National Church of the Presbytery. President John Adams and his wife Abigail worshipped there.

Tomorrow, the Hebron congregation would travel to Salem, but instead of hearing Reverend Samuel Doak preach, Reverend Witherspoon would be speaking. Members of Greeneville Presbyterian Church were also coming with their minister, Hezekiah Balch, to hear Jimmy preach.

Jimmy was excited to be speaking to three congregations, but his lack of confidence was eating away at him. He had memorized the sermon but still fretted about his delivery of the message.

Ibby knocked on the door. "May I come in?"

Jimmy opened the rickety door. "Certainly, Ibby, please come in."

Ibby shut the door behind her using both hands and a foot. "What are you doing in the classroom on Saturday afternoon?"

"Practicing tomorrow's sermon," Jimmy said.

"How is it going?"

"Would you listen and tell me what you think?"

"I'd be honored." Ibby sat down with her hands clasped together like she was in church and listened to Jimmy recite his sermon.

\*\*\*

The travelers made it across the James with daylight to spare. They made camp, and Jake started a pot of beans as Peggy and Sheriff Preston took a walk.

"What should we do?" Peggy asked.

"We should surrender Nathan to the authorities." Sheriff Preston shook his head. "But that would be too simple, and neither of us is good at taking the easy way out."

"If we're caught with him, what will they do to us?"

"If US Marshals find us, we could be arrested and indicted. The matter would be up to a federal judge. That's why we must get to Pennsylvania where things are much different than here in Virginia."

Peggy stopped and looked at him. "You said you had a plan?"

The sheriff stopped alongside her. "As long as Nathan is with us, we're his accomplices and will be treated as such under the law."

"Are you suggesting we throw Nathan to the wolves?"

"No, but if you gave him your horse and some money for his team and wagon, your problem would be solved and Nathan would be safe in Pennsylvania before noon tomorrow." Sheriff Preston started walking again.

"Do you think he'd be willing to do that?"

"I don't know, but let's ask him." The sheriff pointed. "He's under his wagon over there."

They quickly explained the situation to Nathan. He had been thinking of a similar plan, but liked the sheriff's idea better, because he would have some money to make good his escape. Nathan would eat, get some rest, and sneak off during the night while everyone else was asleep. To protect the others, they would not be told of the scheme. Jake, Billy, and Sam would think he stole Peggy's horse and made a run for it.

"Thank you for saving my life yesterday, Sheriff. That was the closest I ever came to being hung." Nathan rubbed his rope-burned neck.

Sheriff Preston nodded.

Peggy handed Nathan ten coins, each worth ten dollars. He put them in a leather pouch attached to his leather belt.

"I'll leave your team and wagon at the Cohen's Stable on Front Street near the Delaware River wharfs. Do you know where it is?" Peggy asked.

"I know it well. Your horse and saddle will be there waiting for you." Nathan bowed his head slightly. "Thank you, Miss Mitchell, for your help."

"Go safely, Nathan." Peggy touched his arm.

The sheriff and Peggy turned and walked away from Nathan and his wagon. She led the way toward the horses.

"I have to say goodbye to a dear friend," Peggy said.

The sheriff stayed back to allow Peggy time alone with her horse.

As Peggy approached, Mr. Jackson threw his head back and whinnied, shaking his long mane in excitement over seeing the only master he had ever known. She held his long nose and petted his strong neck, talking softly into his ear. Sheriff Preston watched from a distance, knowing how difficult it had to be for Peggy to give up the horse she had raised from a foal. He admired the conformation of her horse, a product of decades of selective breeding. Peggy took several deep breaths and walked away, knowing she most likely would never see Mr. Jackson again.

"Now that I have said goodbye to my horse and Nathan's situation is settled, I must talk to you about a matter that troubles me greatly." Peggy started toward the river.

"What have I done that troubles you so?" The sheriff walked beside Peggy, gazing toward the sparkling waters of the river.

"It's what you're not doing that troubles me."

"What might that be?"

"When was the last time you saw your family?" Peggy asked.

"Let me think about that a minute. What is the date?"

"The third day of June, 1797."

The sheriff wrinkled his forehead and looked up at the sky. "I had to be in Philadelphia on May the eighth."

"You've been away from your wife and children for a month."

"About a month, that's right. I was headed home when I met up with you."

"I appreciate your looking out after us, Sheriff, but in the morning you need to head home. And no stopping at Mrs. Ingles'." Peggy shook her finger at him.

Sheriff Preston turned to Peggy with a frown. "Was everyone all right when you went through Abingdon?"

"Yes, everything was fine, except your wife and children miss you very much when you're away."

"I miss them when I'm away." He gazed off in the direction of Abingdon.

"Have you ever told Molly that?" Peggy asked.

"I don't recall."

"Why don't you tell her when you get home and take her a little gift? You have a wonderful wife who adores you."

He smiled and started walking faster. "I'll do that."

"Don't tell her I told you." Peggy smiled.

The Sherriff said, "Thank you for caring. I'll be gone when you awake in the morning."

Peggy said, "Oh!"

"It's a two-day ride if I leave early."

"I'll pray for your safe passage." Peggy waved goodbye and walked alone back to camp.

*****

Jimmy had received the positive reinforcement from Ibby that he usually received from Peggy. He had eaten with the Mitchell family and was feeling good about tomorrow's sermon. Taking his usual walk along Knob Creek, he stopped beside what Adam had told him was a one-hundred-year-old cypress tree with its roots deep in the clear water. The top of the tree was fifty feet high, and two grown men couldn't reach their arms around its trunk. Robert and John had tried and came up short.

"Are you going to climb that tree?" Ibby had come up behind Jimmy, startling him.

"No, I was just thinking about how long it had been here providing shade." Jimmy looked upward at its branches, then turned to face Ibby.

"Are you ready for your big day tomorrow?"

"Thanks to you, I am."

"That's good." Ibby stepped a little closer. "I know the family and your congregation are anxious to hear you preach tomorrow."

"It's strange how I'm nervous talking to people I know, yet in Philadelphia at the Pine Street Church or the Buffalo Church in Martinsville, I'm not."

"That's not strange—we all want to do our best in front of friends and family. I'm proud of you, Jimmy."

"That means a lot to me. And I'm proud to have your friendship." Jimmy looked into her eyes.

They moved closer until their lips touched, at first awkwardly and then passionately. They embraced one another tightly. Desire that he had never known overwhelmed Jimmy. He pulled away, gasping for air.

"Are you all right?" Ibby asked.

He looked down at the ground. "I can't do this, Ibby. It's not right."

"What's not right about loving you? I love you, Jimmy. I have for a long time."

"You have?" He looked into her eyes. "I wasn't aware. No one has ever said that to me."

They embraced, overcome with passion, unwilling or unable to stop.

***

Jake woke Peggy, shaking her shoulder. "Peggy, wake up. Mr. Jackson is gone, and so are Nathan and the sheriff."

"They are? Where did they go?" Peggy tried to sound surprised.

"Don't know, but the tracks show one of them went west and the other east. I don't think Nathan would have headed back toward the mob that tried to lynch him."

Peggy yawned and stretched. "I told Sheriff Preston he needed to go home. He's been gone for a month. For once, he heeded my words."

Jake looked back where the horses were tied. "I'd never have expected Nathan to steal your horse."

"It's probably best that he left. We'd be in some serious trouble if the federal marshals found him with us."

"I feel bad about this," Jake said. "Do you want me to go after him and get your horse?"

"No, I want you to catch your breath and then start a campfire for breakfast. We've got a long day ahead of us to make Lexington before dark. If there's an inn, I want to get a room and—"

"I know—a warm bath. There's a small way station. Don't know about a bath, but they'll have a bed for you." Jake laughed.

"Why are you laughing?"

"You might have to share it with everyone there."

"Then we'll just camp wherever you suggest."

"Things are a little different in Lexington than in Abingdon. If we camp on Cedar Creek, I can show you this big bridge that God made. It's the most unusual thing

120

I've ever seen. Just off the road. I'd like to show it to you." Jake knelt with the kindling to start the fire.

"I'd like to see it." Peggy rolled her bedroll, tying it tight to keep the trail dust out.

Sam and Billy walked up and looked suspiciously at Jake and Peggy.

"Where are Nathan and the sheriff?" Sam asked.

"They both left before daylight," Jake said. "Nathan stole Miss Mitchell's horse."

"No, he didn't." Sam shook his head and tightened his lips. "Nathan could never steal. I know him too well. And he'd never leave without his wagon and those four fine horses. Something's wrong. Did the sheriff take him in for the reward money?"

"No, the sheriff headed for home alone. Tracks show Nathan rode Miss Mitchell's horse east."

Sam faced Jake with a frown on his face. "Nathan is our friend—we been teaming with him for years. Something's wrong. What have you and Miss Mitchell done with him? We will not move another inch without knowing the truth about our friend and what happened to him."

"Are you accusing me of lying to you?" Jake backed away from the smoke of the kindling that had finally ignited.

Sam continued, "Look at Miss Mitchell. Does she act like a woman that just lost a horse that she raised from a foal and spent years training? She loved that Mr. Jackson, I could tell. And Nathan would never leave without saying goodbye to Billy and me." Sam looked at the ground and shook his head.

Billy nodded in agreement.

Jake looked at Peggy. "I know they're right. What's going on?"

"Damn it to hell!" Peggy stomped her foot. "I never could tell a lie."

The men glared at her without saying a word.

"Sheriff Preston, Nathan, and I wanted to protect you."

"Protect us by turning our friend in?" Sam said.

"We did not turn Nathan in!" Peggy glared back at the men. "Yesterday, the sheriff and I had a long talk with him and agreed on a plan. Nathan would take my horse and some money for the use of his team and wagon. We would exchange them at Cohen's Stable in Philadelphia."

"Why didn't you just tell us that?" Sam asked.

"Because now that you know what we've done, you are accomplices to what the sheriff and I did."

Sam said, "From what I understand, all Nathan did was help a man who was severely beaten by his master and needed some caring for. If I'd been there, I would have done the same thing."

Billy nodded in agreement.

"I'm sorry. I should have told you. I thought I was doing the right thing," Peggy said.

"Just like Nathan's situation. Sometimes the right thing is the wrong thing," Sam said.

Billy shook his head.

"Billy, Sam, if you'll get the teams hooked up, I'll have breakfast ready for us by the time you get finished," Jake said. "We'll eat and be ready to hit the trail."

They nodded in agreement and headed toward Nathan's wagon to harness his team.

"I was a fool to think I could tell that story to the three of you." Peggy put away her bedroll.

Loaded and ready to roll, with Jake and Peggy in the first wagon, Sam in the next, and Billy bringing up the rear in Nathan's wagon, the small caravan pulled out onto the Old Wagon Road for Lexington.

Peggy drove so Jake could get back to learning to read and write.

"Do you know what today is?" Peggy shook the reins.

"No."

"Today is the first Sunday in June. What happens on the first Sunday of every month, Jake?"

"We go to Salem Church instead of Hebron."

"The day of the month is . . . ?" Peggy asked.

"It is the fourth day of June."

"How did you get that so fast?" Peggy asked.

"I've been counting each day since the first."

"That's good. Now let's write the days of the week," Peggy said.

They stopped at the natural bridge that Jake had told her about. Peggy was so impressed with it that she took the time to draw a picture in her journal. She made her observations of it as to height and width and the large arches underneath this limestone marvel.

When she'd finished writing in her journal, Peggy looked up at Jake. "You're right. This bridge was not made by man. God created it thousands of years ago with a tremendous flow of water. Thank you for showing it to me. It's more interesting than I had ever imagined."

Jake beamed, knowing that he had shown his teacher something that she had never seen or even known about.

\*\*\*

Services were over at Salem Presbyterian Church. Reverends Witherspoon, Doak, and Balch stood outside the door of the log cabin church. They shook hands with the worshippers as they exited, most praising Jimmy for a fine sermon. When Ibby came through, she gave Jimmy a hug and whispered in his ear, causing his fair skin to turn the color of a ripe peach.

Standing next to him, Reverend Doak noticed the blush. He leaned toward Jimmy and whispered, "Reverend Witherspoon, you will in time learn not to let the admiring young maidens make you blush."

"Especially after you become a married preacher," Reverend Balch quipped.

Next in line, Jimmy's mother, Anna Witherspoon, embarrassed him further by feeling his head with her hand. "Goodness, you feel flushed. I hope you're not catching a cold."

After everyone was outside and headed to tables of food set up under the trees, Jimmy asked for a private meeting with Reverend Doak. They agreed to meet in Reverend Doak's study after the potluck meal.

When they finished eating, Jimmy's teacher and benefactor led the way to the nearby parsonage. The members of the Salem congregation had built the large, two-story house for Reverend and Sister Doak to accommodate the many guests they entertained.

"That was a good sermon you gave this morning. I could tell you reached the congregation with the powerful message of the Lord." Reverend Doak opened the door to his office. "Now, what can I do for you, Jimmy?"

"I seek your advice about a member of my congregation."

Reverend Doak motioned his guest toward a chair. "What is the problem?"

Jimmy took a deep breath. "She has professed her love for me."

"As an unmarried minister, that could be a problem for your church." Reverend Doak sat across from his protégé. "When I was younger, that happened to me on several occasions. I always made my wife aware of the situation, and that was usually the end of it."

"I have no desire to end it."

"Do you have the same feelings for her?" Reverend Doak asked.

"Oh, yes I do." Jimmy nodded.

Reverend Doak asked, "Is she an eligible maiden that would make an appropriate wife for a minister?"

Jimmy leaned forward in his chair and nodded. "Yes, she is."

"Then, I don't understand your problem."

"It is Ibby Mitchell," Jimmy said.

"Peggy's younger sister?"

"Yes, sir."

"I think I see your concern." Reverend Doak looked out his window at the gathering. "Where is Peggy? I didn't see her with the family this morning."

"She's on her way to Philadelphia with her pelts."

Reverend Doak turned his gaze to Jimmy. "Is Peggy aware that you have such deep feelings for her sister?"

"Ibby and I only became aware of our feelings for one another yesterday."

"Yesterday?" Reverend Doak asked. "What is your commitment to Peggy?"

"We have no commitment, and I don't think Peggy will ever marry."

"I know that Adam is anxious for you and Peggy to get married," Reverend Doak said.

Jimmy answered, "He's told me many times that he plans for us to marry, but Peggy has no interest in marriage."

"You are in a conundrum," his mentor said. "For sure, that could cause a rift in the Mitchell family and a schism in your congregation if this is not handled delicately."

"I know, and that's why I've come to you." Jimmy looked out the window and saw Ibby.

She waved at him, and both ministers returned the gesture. They sat looking at her through the window for a moment.

"She has become a beautiful woman," Reverend Doak said. "I can tell you this. Adam Mitchell loves all his children, and I know he loves you as he does his own sons. He has told me that. If I were you and Ibby, I would go to him together. Profess your love for one another. I believe he'll give you his blessing. Tell him that you have my approval." Reverend Doak stood and put his arm around his young protégé.

Jimmy said, "Thank you, Reverend, for all that you have done for me."

They returned to the gathering.

# Chapter Nine
## New Friends

Each morning, Peggy walked the wharfs on the Delaware River looking for Captain McDuffy and his ship, the *Lady Ann*. Peggy had been in Philadelphia a week since arriving on Monday, the nineteenth of June. The nation's capital bustled with activity as the merchants and the federal government prepared for the twenty-first anniversary of independence, which this year would be called the Fourth of July celebration.

Peggy had stored the pelts at Cohen's stables until she could find a buyer. She had called on the local brokers and found they were holding inventory that they couldn't sell. Last year, Captain McDuffy had paid a fair price for her entire lot of pelts and furs at auction. He was now her only hope. She put a sign up at the stables and passed out business cards around the wharf, careful not to recreate last year's fiasco which led many to believe she and her sisters were selling something other than pelts.

Now she was alone in a large city. Her only friends were the Cohens, who owned the stables and boarding house. Last year was different, as she'd had her entourage of family and friends to keep her company.

Peggy attended the Pine Street Presbyterian Church on Sunday. Reverend Annan, the minister, had retired to his country estate. The congregation appeared to fear a woman with no male escort attending church. The ladies seemed to think she was there to steal their man and run away to Tennessee.

A cantankerous widow by the name of Elizabeth Yarde was also a guest in the Cohen house. She and her husband Edward had immigrated to Philadelphia prior to the war from the port city of Plymouth in southwest England. Her family, the Whiddons of Devonshire, had farmed in Devon for centuries. Mr. Yarde had been a silversmith of some notoriety in Philadelphia. He'd died the previous winter after an extended illness.

Lisa, as she liked to be called, was waiting for her nephew to escort her back to Devonshire to spend her remaining years with her sister's family at Whiddon, the family estate. Lisa was not amicable. Peggy thought Mrs. Yarde somewhat uppity and was sure the elderly lady thought of her as just a mountain girl who enjoyed skinning the critters for the hides that she brought to Philadelphia. Mrs. Cohen assured Peggy that Lisa was a good person. She was just out of her element in America, living among commoners rather than the English gentry of Devon.

Peggy frequented the stables to check on Nathan's horses and wagon. The horses needed to be worked, not stabled. Hopefully, Nathan was safe and would arrive soon. Then she would have Mr. Jackson back.

Turning the corner at Pine Street, Peggy saw a hired carriage drop off a new boarder for the Cohen House. He carried a large seaman's bag and was dressed in a sea captain's uniform, with a gold-trimmed, black tri-cornered hat and matching waist-length, sleeveless jacket that revealed ruffled, white sleeves. A wide, leather belt held his tailored trousers in place.

The reddish-purple plume in his hat band reminded Peggy of the peacock that ran about the school yard at home. As she approached, he removed his hat and bowed. "After you, Madame."

"Thank you." Peggy tipped her head in acknowledgement. "It is Miss. If you are looking for the Cohen House, you may follow me."

"It would be my pleasure, Miss . . . " He placed his hat on his head with one hand and picked up his bag with the other.

"I am Peggy Mitchell." Peggy extended her hand. "Are you here for Mrs. Yarde?"

"That I am. My name is William Whiddon. I am her nephew, whom she has never met." He took Peggy's hand and held it for a few seconds before shaking it.

Peggy nodded, and they turned and began walking.

"Do you live at the Cohen House, Miss Mitchell?"

Peggy walked to the porch. "Only when I come to Philadelphia on business."

She was impressed with the long blonde curls that were revealed when he removed his hat. He was about her age and had green eyes and pearly white teeth that produced a seductive smile. Many days at sea had given him a bronze tan that accentuated his handsome features and broad shoulders.

At the door, he opened it and held it for Peggy. "After you, Miss Mitchell."

"Please call me Peggy," she said as she stepped into the foyer.

"You may call me Willy." He removed his hat and tucked it under his arm. "May I ask your business?"

"I am a fur and pelt broker, among other things."

"Really?" Willy raised his eyebrows. "Do you kill the animals yourself?"

"Heavens, no. I just procure them from the trappers and find markets to hopefully sell at a profit."

Lisa's voice from the parlor interrupted the conversation. "Is that you, Willy?"

"Yes, it is. You must be Aunt Lisa."

"Come in here and let me see you."

Willy turned to Peggy. "Please excuse me."

As she watched him enter the parlor, Peggy thought, *Such a handsome man must be married.* She headed up the narrow stairs to her room, hearing the greetings of the family who'd never met. She undressed and pulled the covers back on the feather bed for an afternoon nap, something she rarely had time to do at home.

Later, the chambermaid knocked and spoke through the closed door. "Miss Mitchell, tea will be served in half an hour in the downstairs parlor."

"Thank you."

*It must be 3:30 — tea is at 4:00. Time to get up; I look forward to Mrs. Cohen's afternoon teas.*

When she entered, Peggy heard Mrs. Yarde speaking to their hostess.

"It is nice of you, Mrs. Cohen, to have high tea in honor of your visiting British guests."

*I can let that go. Everyone knows that high tea has been a part of the Cohen House since before Mrs. Cohen started taking in boarders. God forgive me. I can't stand that woman. Poor Willy.*

"Peggy, have you met my nephew, William Whiddon the Third?" Lisa asked.

"Yes, we met on his arrival. It is good to see you again, Willy."

"Willy?" Lisa looked at her nephew with surprise.

He nodded to his aunt and grinned at Peggy.

Lisa and her nephew occupied the settee, while Peggy and Mrs. Cohen sat in matching arm chairs facing them. The tea service and crumpets were nicely arranged on a knee-high table between them.

"Was your trip over a pleasant one, Captain Whiddon?" Mrs. Cohen asked.

"Yes, it was. The prevailing winds were such that we made it from Plymouth in only twenty-one days."

"It took me that long to get here from Knob Creek, and the distance is much less." Peggy picked up her teacup.

"That's the wonderful thing about traveling by sea. As long as you have wind, the ship is in motion," Willy said.

"I never thought of it that way," Peggy said.

Willy leaned forward. "Have you ever been aboard a seagoing vessel?"

"Only to tend business with Captain Duffy last year," Peggy said. "I boarded his ship, the *Lady Ann*. I've always dreamed of taking a voyage on a ship."

"You should do it then, if it is your dream. While I'm here, you'll have to come aboard and see *Devon's Hope*. I will give you a captain's tour."

"I would like that."

Willy said, "Well, it will have to be tonight or tomorrow night as Aunt Lisa and I must get underway on Wednesday morning."

"I always take a stroll after dinner. Could we do it, perhaps, tonight?" Peggy was excited at the thought of touring the ship but did not want to seem unladylike.

"That would be grand!" Willy's face lit up. "I need to check on things with my first mate on watch tonight."

Lisa turned to Willy, ignoring the others in the room. The Cohens and Peggy couldn't help but see that she wished to be alone with her nephew. They excused themselves.

Peggy turned in the doorway to look at Willy. "I look forward to seeing you and Lisa at dinner."

"Dress comfortably," he said.

Peggy nodded and headed up to her room at the top of the stairs. With time to spare before dinner and enough daylight to write, she made entries in her journal regarding today's events. From her room she could see the Delaware River and the boats at anchor. *I wonder which one I'll be boarding tonight.*

The door opened in the adjoining room, and a man's heavy steps hurried down the squeaky staircase. Peggy realized that Willy was occupying the next room, as he was the only man other than Mr. Cohen staying at the Cohen House.

Peggy began to dress for dinner. She put her hair up into a stylish bun held by an antique comb that had belonged to her Grandmother McMachen. Struggling into her undergarments, she wondered how anyone could be comfortable wearing a corset.

As she planned, Peggy was the last to appear in the parlor. Mr. Cohen and Willy were in a conversation that seemed to be about her.

"Peggy, would you mind if Captain Whiddon borrowed your freight wagon and team to move Lisa's piano and a few items to his ship tomorrow?" Mr. Cohen asked.

"A team of horses? Are my aunt's furnishings that extensive?"

Mr. Cohen nodded his head. "I hope, Captain, you have a good-size ship."

"I think *Devon's Hope* will be sufficient. It's her living quarters at Whiddon that concerns me, for they are already well-furnished." Willy looked across the room at his aunt, in conversation with Mrs. Cohen.

"They must be her life's treasures, and she couldn't bear to leave without them." Peggy said.

"We'll take whatever she desires and worry about where to put her belongings once we're at Whiddon."

"You're welcome to use my wagon whenever you want," Peggy said.

"I'm not sure I'd know how to harness a team of horses."

"Four horses is easy," Peggy said. "Six gets to be pretty tricky."

The captain looked at her in surprise. "You needed a wagon that large to haul your pelts?"

Peggy held up three fingers.

"Three wagons? With teams?" He looked at Mr. Cohen for confirmation.

Mr. Cohen nodded.

Willy smiled at Peggy. "That must be some load of pelts."

Peggy and Mr. Cohen nodded in unison.

Mrs. Cohen announced, "Dinner is ready."

On Monday nights, the Cohen House always served chicken and dumplings, one of Mrs. Cohen's specialties. They had green beans and squash from her garden. Dessert was apple tarts. The food was served on plates of fine china and wine was poured into cut glass stemware. The evening meals were quite grand compared to those to which Peggy was accustomed.

Willy entertained them with magnificent stories of the sea and of Devonshire, where he grew up. His aunt told a story about his mother and father that Willy never knew. Peggy learned that Willy was the sixth generation to have been born at Whiddon. His father, William Whiddon II, now deceased, was Lisa's older brother. His mother and Lisa's sister, also a widow, lived on the estate.

Willy looked around the table. "They should call it 'Widowton' rather than Whiddon."

His dinner companions chuckled at his humor.

Willy said, "Aunt Lisa, I promised Peggy a tour of *Devon's Hope* after dinner. Would you like to go with us? Mr. and Mrs. Cohen, you're welcome to come."

His aunt shook her head. "I saw plenty of that ship coming over in 1766 when your father ferried Edward and me across the Atlantic to Philadelphia."

"You two go without us. We'll stay and keep Lisa company," Mr. Cohen said.

Peggy and Willy stopped by the stables to check on the horses. She explained the unusual trade she had made with Nathan for the wagon and team. It has been two weeks since they parted ways. "I'm glad you have a job for the horses tomorrow. They need to be worked. I hate the thought of horses just penned in a stable with no room to run."

Peggy showed Willy his aunt's possessions stored under an oilcloth next to her pile of pelts.

"I say. Those skins do have a bit of a smell. How do you stand it?"

Peggy shrugged. "You get used to it. Besides, I'm only around pelts when I bring them to market."

They walked down a narrow alley to the wharf and made a left turn. *Devon's Hope* was moored to the wharf, its huge hemp bowlines wrapped securely around the wharf pylons.

Peggy stopped and stared. "It's the most beautiful ship I've ever seen."

"Ahoy, mate!" Willy called.

"That you, Captain?"

"Yes, it is. And I have a lady guest. Please alert the crew."

"Now hear this! Now hear this!" the first mate bellowed. "Captain is coming aboard with a lady guest. Crew will maintain W.O.B. protocol until further notice. Aft deck, I await your signal."

The captain stood by with Peggy at his side. Seamen scampered about, raising two small flags. Peggy, not understanding the customs, didn't realize that all this bustling activity was on her account.

A shrill voice called out, "All clear from aft deck, sir."

"Secure below, Mate."

The first mate blew his whistle a series of times.

"After you, Peggy." Willy motioned with his hand and said, "Once on board, if the crew is near, I would appreciate your calling me Captain."

"I understand, Captain."

They walked across the gangway as the first mate blew a strange-looking little silver instrument that hung from his neck. The first mate saluted the captain and his guest.

"As you were," Captain Whiddon said.

"Welcome aboard *Devon's Hope*. May I introduce my first mate, Mr. Denham." Turning toward Denham, the captain said, "Please meet a friend of my Aunt Lisa's, Miss Peggy Mitchell from Tennessee."

*Friend of his Aunt? If he only knew how much I dislike that woman.*

"Pleasure to meet you, Miss Mitchell." Mr. Denham removed his sailor's cap.

"Likewise, Mr. Denham," Peggy said.

"This way to the quarterdeck, where I do my work."

Captain Whiddon explained how his grandfather, William Whiddon I, commissioned the ship to be built in 1765 at the Chatham shipyards in London. The three-masted ship was 226 feet long with a 52-foot beam.

"I don't recognize the two flags raised before we came aboard. What do they represent?" Peggy asked.

"The one on top signifies the captain is aboard ship. The other signifies W.O.B., which is to advise the crew on shore and on board that a woman is on board the vessel," Captain Whiddon said.

"Why is it necessary that they know I'm aboard?" Peggy asked.

"It is about chivalry aboard ship. These seamen spend months at sea without seeing a woman. They get pretty salty in their ways, especially in port and with the required ration of grog I must provide. I am sure you know what I mean," Captain Whiddon said.

"So the lower flag means you have a woman aboard, and the only woman is me?" Peggy asked.

"Yes, that is correct."

Peggy shook her head. "I saw a young woman on the aft deck while you were talking to your first mate."

"Are you sure?

"As a teacher, I can assure you I know a young female when I see one."

"A fur broker and a teacher? I am impressed," Captain Whiddon said.

Peggy opened her mouth as if to speak, then closed it and looked toward the place where she had seen the young woman.

"Let's keep this to ourselves until I can find out where and who she is. This is a big ship. She could be a stowaway," Captain Whiddon said. Peggy shook her head. "Don't think so."

"Why do you say that?" Captain Whiddon asked.

"She waved like she was happy to see me, definitely not trying to hide."

"Really? That's interesting. With this breeze it is a bit chilly on the quarterdeck. Let's go below where we might find a little something to warm us up. I need to speak to my first mate, if you will excuse me for a moment. Feel free to turn the wheel if you like." Captain Whiddon pointed to the helm, then turned and motioned to his first mate.

When they were a few steps away from Peggy, Captain Whiddon asked, "Have you been on watch all evening, Mr. Denham?"

"Aye aye, sir."

"Then how did a woman get on board my ship?"

"You brought her, sir," Mr. Denham said.

"I am not referring to Miss Mitchell, but the woman she saw on the aft deck who waved to her," Captain Whiddon said.

"I will investigate and get back to you, Captain."

"We will be in my wardroom awaiting your report." Captain Whiddon escorted Peggy below.

"We should know shortly about this woman you saw. May I offer you a glass of my favorite Madeira?" The captain reached for the ship's decanter, which had a wide base and long, narrow neck that prevented spillage when the ship rocked.

"Yes, I would. I have never had the opportunity to try it. Please just pour me a small amount. I wouldn't want to waste a drop if I don't care for it."

He handed Peggy the small port wine glass that held the golden amber liquid. The illumination of the wardroom candle onto the hand-cut glass radiated tiny twinkling stars on the wooden walls.

"May all your dreams come true." Captain Whiddon raised his glass.

Peggy followed suit. "Thank you."

They both tasted the famous wine produced on the Madeira Islands in the Atlantic Ocean far from Tennessee. It was a magical moment that Peggy would never forget.

"Have you been to the Portuguese islands?" Peggy asked.

"We sail to Oporto each fall to pick up port and Madeira, then to Valencia for sherry, and deliver the wines to Berry Brothers and Company in London," he said

Peggy smiled at the captain. "That's quite a trip."

He waved his glass under his nose and inhaled the fragrance of the wine. "For three generations, the Whiddons and Berry Brothers have been business associates. You and I are enjoying one of the benefits of that relationship." Captain Whiddon took another sip from his glass.

"Being captain of your own ship, sailing around the world sounds so exciting." Peggy's smile faded.

"It is, but it can be lonely." Captain Whiddon picked up the decanter and poured Peggy another glass of wine, then one for himself.

He motioned for her to sit in the captain's chair. By force of habit, she tried to move it and was surprised it was affixed to the floor.

"You would have to go to sea to appreciate furnishings that do not move."

When Captain Whiddon smiled, Peggy realized she already adored that seductive smile.

Peggy looked around and sighed. "I've always dreamed of sailing on a ship like this.

"Why don't you sail with us to Plymouth? I have no passengers other than Aunt Lisa. I am sure she would enjoy the comfort of another woman on board. You would have your own stateroom, which has a porthole on the starboard side," Captain Willy said.

*Twenty-one days at sea with Lisa Yarde? But what an opportunity for me this is! Surely I could handle being with her that long.*

"You are serious—aren't you?" Peggy said.

"I wouldn't have offered if I wasn't."

"I need to find a buyer for my furs first."

"It will be easier to find a buyer in Europe, and they will pay more for your furs and pelts on the continent, because they will incur no transportation cost," Captain Whiddon suggested.

"Getting them loaded will be a laborious task," Peggy said.

"You have a wagon, and I have men to load them," Captain Whiddon said.

"Until I find a buyer in England, what would I do with the pelts?"

"I have warehousing on our pier in the port of Plymouth," Captain Whiddon replied.

"I don't know what to say."

"*Yes* will do for now. We can start loading pelts in the morning."

Peggy started to pace, but the wardroom was so small that she had to turn around after only a few steps. "Yes, I want to go to England with you, but how would I get back?"

"Whiddon Shipping sends ships to Philadelphia several times a year. I will make sure you get back, when you are ready," Captain Whiddon said.

They heard the sounds of at least three men coming down the stairs toward the captain's quarters. A woman screamed, "Let go of me, you bastard!"

Mr. Denham knocked and said, "Captain Whiddon, we have searched the vessel and located the woman Miss Mitchell saw on the aft deck."

"Would you bring her in for Miss Mitchell to identify?" Captain Whiddon said.

"Aye, aye, Captain."

The young woman was brought in with a deckhand holding her on each side by the wrist.

"Let go of me." She struggled to pull away.

The captain shook his head when he saw the rough way the men were holding the woman. "Please, let her go.".

Once she was released, the woman went after the deckhands, kicking and screaming obscenities. The sailors grabbed her and subdued her again. Peggy identified her as the girl she saw.

"Could you tell me how you got on my ship, and what you are doing here?" Captain Whiddon asked.

"These two met me at the city tavern and we had a bit much to drink. I passed out and the next thing I know, I'm in the rack, below decks, with the both of them."

"Are you saying you were brought on board against your will?" Captain Whiddon asked.

The young woman took a deep breath. "I don't remember how I got here."

"Young lady, where do you live?"

"Let me go and I'll tell you." She tried to break free of the seamen's grip.

"If you will promise not to attack—and to be a lady, I will ask my men to let you go." Captain Whiddon paused for a few seconds and looked into the woman's eyes. When he spoke again, his voice was soft and gentle. "No one will hurt you, I promise. We just need some answers, and then you can go about your business."

She nodded.

"Why are you so mad at my men?"

"They promised me two dollars to come aboard your ship and make merry. One of them had his way with me and didn't pay me."

"I thought you didn't remember how you got on my ship."

"I don't, but before I passed out, I remember the short one promised me two dollars, and I only have one dollar." She held it up.

"Here are three dollars—that makes four dollars for your trouble, twice what you bargained for." The captain handed her the money. "We will say nothing to the wharf-master—if you don't—about this incident."

"Thank you, Captain." The young lady nodded at the captain. "May I have a word with the lady?"

The captain looked at Peggy, who indicated she was willing to hear what the other woman wanted to say. Captain Whiddon went into the passageway to confer with his first mate.

"You are a very classy lady. I've been working the wharf for a long time and never seen a prettier woman than you. I see you got the captain's attention—you can get a lot more money."

Peggy smiled at the girl standing before her. "I know coming from you that is a real compliment. Thank you."

The first mate and captain returned.

The captain nodded toward the woman. "Mr. Denham, make sure she gets safely off the ship and doesn't return. Then confine these two to their quarters until we sail, and forfeit their ration of grog for two days."

"Aye, aye, Captain."

"Do you know where the stables are up the alleyway?" Captain Whiddon asked.

"I haven't been off the ship, sir, but when the breeze is just right I get a good whiff of them horse apples. I am certain I can follow my nose to it."

"Bring four strong men with you for loading the cargo."

"Yes, Captain."

\*\*\*

*I have so much to do; must write the family and tell them I am going to England; arrange for boarding Nathan's horses . . .*

Peggy had worked herself into a dither. She stayed up late trying to explain to her family and Jimmy in a letter how she had suddenly decided to go to England. She chose to simply say, "There are no buyers for my furs here; I will be sailing for Plymouth, England aboard *Devon's Hope*, Wednesday morning, 28th of June. I will write again when I get there."

Lisa's belongings and Peggy's pelts were loaded, and the ship's provisions purchased for the trip and stored. Lisa wasn't excited about Peggy and her animal skins going with her to England. Peggy didn't care—she was going to make the best of this opportunity, which might be her only chance to see Europe.

Lisa insisted on staying at the Cohen House the night before departure. She wanted to spend the last moments on dry land with her friends. Peggy was anxious to get on board, but would feel awkward being on the ship without Lisa.

Wednesday morning, the captain arrived as the sun was beginning to rise over the Delaware. He used Mr. Cohen's carriage to pick up Lisa and Peggy. Efforts were underway to cast off as soon as everyone was on board. Peggy noticed for the first time how frail Lisa was. The widow was always seated when they were together at the Cohen House. She did not do well walking on land; on a rocking ship her mobility would be worse.

It took some effort to get Lisa in the carriage. The strong captain was just able lift her out, once they reached the ship. Lisa stood and looked at the vessel as if it were an old friend and said, "It's been thirty years since I last saw this naughty girl, with her bare breasts exposed for the world to see. She brought us across the Atlantic to the British colony of the Quakers. Now she will take me home where I belong."

"Would you like me to carry you on board, Aunt Lisa?"

"No, thank you, I can walk," she answered.

With her cane, she slowly made her way across the gangway. She turned and blew a kiss. Peggy noticed tears rolling down her cheek.

"Will you miss Philadelphia?"

"Not at all. Edward wanted to come here. I was very happy at Whiddon with my family. My husband didn't have family; he was an adventurer and wanted to make a name for himself in Philadelphia. I came as his dutiful wife. I was never happy here— my heart was always in Devon. Sometimes you have to make sacrifices for the man you love."

"So the kiss you blew . . . "

"The kiss was for Edward, who I miss dearly. He grew up with no family and died with no heirs, as we never had children. He is buried in our churchyard amongst his few friends over that hill. I wish to be buried in my family cemetery at Whiddon." Lisa turned and went to the same stateroom that the newlyweds shared three decades ago.

Peggy and the captain followed her and helped her into the rope bed. She lay back, looked up at the rough hewn ceiling and smiled. She pointed at the words neatly carved into an oak plank over the bed: "I love you Lisa, Edward 1766."

All but one bowline had been pulled in and neatly coiled. The jib was up; the ship was at a 45-degree angle from the wharf.

"Cast off!" Captain Whiddon called to the wharfmaster.

The wharfmaster pulled the hemp loop over the piling, allowing it to fall into the water. Two crewmen pulled the heavy, wet line into the ship, neatly coiling it to dry on the deck. Peggy could see all the activity from the port railing; it was an event to behold.

The first of the three sails was unfurled. They were underway. A sailor in the crow's nest was calling out, "Four fathoms, five fathoms . . . ." He was visually estimating the depth of water and advising the captain as to where the water was safe. In the river's shallow channel, there were places with only a few feet between the keel and the river bottom. All hands were anxiously standing by in the event they hit bottom.

*I wonder what they do if that happens? I hope I never find out. Everyone, including the captain, is so tense.*

"Blue water dead ahead, Captain" was called from the crow's nest.

"Drop all sails," the captain bellowed for the crew to hear.

Peggy watched the mammoth sail cloths unfurl—the sound of the wind catching the canvas took her breath away. She felt as if she were watching a play. Every crewman was an actor with a part in the performance. This crew knew their lines well. The captain motioned for Peggy to come to him at the wheel.

"Did you turn the wheel the other night when I told you? It was all right to do so."

"Yes, I did."

"Now just hold the wheel. You feel the vibration?"

"Yes, what a difference. Why is that?" Peggy asked.

"It's the wind and the water's resistance you feel."

Peggy looked out over the water. "Are we in the Atlantic?"

"We just entered the Bay of Delaware. When the water turns deep blue, we will be in the Atlantic Ocean, about another hour or two from now." Captain Whiddon looked at his pocket watch, then back to Peggy. "Would you be so kind to check on Aunt Lisa for me? The waves will be increasing in intensity as we get further out to sea. It may be the last chance for her to walk about."

"Aye, aye, Captain."

Willy grinned at Peggy as she walked away.

Peggy knocked on Lisa's stateroom door.

"Come in."

Peggy stepped in and looked around the small room. "How are you doing so far?"

Lisa was sitting in the stateroom's only chair and pointed for Peggy to sit on the rope bed. The room was identical to Peggy's stateroom except in reverse since it was on the opposite side of the ship.

Lisa saw Peggy look at the Bible open on the small bed stand built into the wall. "I'm having trouble reading the Bible with only the light from that little porthole."

"If you like, I could take you topside and make you a comfortable place to read in the light," Peggy suggested.

Lisa took a deep breath. "How would you do that? I could never climb those steps."

"I can find two deckhands and put you on a stretcher and they can carry you to the main deck."

Lisa shook her head. "That's too much trouble."

"Not for me it isn't," Peggy answered. "I'll be back shortly."

In a few minutes, Peggy returned with the deckhands, a stretcher, and the captain.

"We have made a comfortable place for you to sit on my quarterdeck, so we can talk, Aunt Lisa," Captain Whiddon said.

"That's too much—"

"Captain's orders, Aunt Lisa."

Once outside in the fresh air, she stopped protesting and seemed to enjoy the scenery and being around people. Peggy began to see the good side of Lisa that Mrs. Cohen knew.

Peggy smiled, thinking of the prostitute who tried to give her a sincere compliment by saying she was worth more. Peggy hoped the girl would someday realize that *she* was worth more and stop selling herself on the Philadelphia wharf.

# Chapter Ten
## The Voyage

Peggy watched the summer sun set slowly, behind the last visible shadow of her homeland. The aft deck on *Devon's Hope* gave her a vantage point to celebrate the passing of each day of her journey across the Atlantic.

She remembered the captivating stories of her grandparents' journey to the colonies. This voyage was the fulfillment of a lifelong dream. She was enjoying every moment, even when the seas were rough.

Captain Whiddon taught Peggy to use the sextant, chronometer, and compass for navigation. Fortunately, the ship had a substantial library so travelers could pass the days at sea reading Daniel Defoe's *Robinson Crusoe* and the great works of Shakespeare and Voltaire. Peggy read aloud to Lisa every day. They were becoming fond of each other, telling stories and laughing at the humor they found in life.

Lisa confided in Peggy that Willy had two children, William IV, who was twelve, and Elizabeth, who was ten. His wife Elizabeth died in childbirth ten years ago. Lisa said that Willy hadn't been the same since, according to her sister's letters.

The evening meals were shared in the wardroom, then the captain entertained Peggy and his aunt with stories of his travels. After dinner, Lisa retired to her stateroom and Peggy and Willy walked the decks, talked, and gazed at the stars.

The captain spotted a lightning storm in the far distance, to the southeast. He ordered the helmsman to correct his heading to the north, three degrees.

Peggy was impressed with Willie's knowledge of navigation and the universe. He could point out and name all the constellations in the sky.

"Where did you acquire this vast knowledge of astronomy?" Peggy asked.

"From my father, who was taught by his father. I knew the constellations before the alphabet or the numbers."

Peggy turned from looking at stars and faced Willy. "Did you learn astronomy in a classroom?"

Captain Whiddon looked up at the stars as he spoke. "This is the classroom of a seafarer; the deck of a ship is the only place to learn about the seas and the stars."

"When did you take your first sea voyage?"

"When I was seven, my grandfather and my father ferried the family, friends, and neighbors from Plymouth to London for the knighting of Sir Joshua Reynolds by King George III."

"Who is Sir Joshua Reynolds?"

"He was a cousin on my Grandmother Reynolds' side of the family. Joshua's father was my grandmother's brother, and the village schoolmaster in Plympton, near Whiddon. He taught my grandfather." The captain motioned for Peggy to sit. "The investiture at St. James Palace was a magnificent event that I shall never forget."

Peggy patted the bench seat. "What did your cousin do to be knighted by the King?"

"He was a famous painter, born in our little village of Plympton in Devon. Grandfather named this ship in his honor, as he was 'Devon's Hope.' He studied under the great masters in London, Paris, and Rome. He made his home in London and was one of the founders of the Royal Academy and its first president. My cousin was the most famous person from Devon."

"Your cousin is a knight?"

"Yes, that is my claim to fame. Now, what is yours?"

Peggy laughed and said, "I won the First Beaver Pelt horse race in Jonesborough, Tennessee. When they discovered a sixteen-year-old girl beat them, they changed the rule the next year and excluded women from the race."

"I could tell by the way you harnessed the four-horse team that you are very much the equestrian."

"Grandfather gave me my first pony when I was twelve. My love has been horses ever since," Peggy said.

"We have a stable of horses that father bred for racing. I have been too busy with other matters to properly oversee them and get them to the track. I am afraid I just turned my father's well-bred steeds into hay burners."

Peggy said, "Sounds like you need a good trainer."

"You do know your horses. Perhaps when we get to Whiddon, you would look at my stable and advise me what you think of my horses' racing potential."

Peggy turned and said, "Willy, we've talked about your horses, the estate, and your ship. But not once have you mentioned your children to me." She leaned over and asked, "Why is that?"

Willy shifted nervously, "I love my son and daughter very much. Talking about them reminds me of their mother, Elizabeth, whom I loved dearly. It has been ten years and I still can't talk about her death. I think about my loss constantly." Captain Whiddon turned to look over the ship's rail.

"You should talk about your loss to those who care about you. The more you do, the easier it will be on you and your children. They have had a great loss, also."

Willy looked down. "I know."

"Lisa has been talking about Edward, sharing the stories of their times together. She says our daily talks helped her immensely."

"I have never been one to speak of such things. I assume it is one of those Whiddon male traits that I am cursed with."

"When you are ready, I am here to listen." Peggy put her hand on his arm.

"Thank you, Peggy. I could use a glass of Madeira. How about you?"

"I could partake of a glass of wine," Peggy answered.

He rose and took her hand to assist her from the bench. Peggy followed Willy as he started toward his cabin. After a couple of glasses of Madeira, they shared their feelings about many things and, for the first time, got to know each other better. There was a timid knock on the captain's door.

"Come in," Captain Whiddon said.

The sailor nodded at Peggy, then turned to Willy. His face was bright red and he stuttered, "Pardon the interruption, Captain. I have been instructed to inform you that the first mate has spotted lightning dead ahead and the air smells of rain."

"I will be right up."

"Aye, aye, sir."

"Peggy, I must get to the quarterdeck. Please check on Aunt Lisa, make sure she stays on the rope bed until I announce all clear." Willy hurried out the door without waiting for an answer.

"All hands on deck to batten the hatches!" The captain bellowed the order from the deck.

Peggy and Lisa huddled together in Lisa's stateroom to wait out the storm. Lisa showed Peggy how to reach under the feather mattress and hold the ropes of the bed. Doing this prevented them from being thrown about the cabin in a storm.

"You have been through a storm at sea before?" Peggy asked.

"Yes and it isn't fun being whipped about."

They could hear the crew above running about securing things on deck. The captain could be heard giving orders to his crew. They closed the porthole of Lisa's room as water was blowing in. Peggy realized her porthole was open and made her way to her stateroom and closed it. She started back to Lisa's room when she heard "loose cannon on the starboard deck!" and a horrendous roar across the deck and then a short, morbid scream of agony.

She struggled back to her room for her medical bag, knowing that it was needed.

Peggy managed to get topside. She ignored the captain when he motioned for her to go below. She saw what had happened—a cannon on wheels had pinned a crewman against the railing near a gun port. Four mates were trying to free him, but the weight of the armament and the angle of the listing ship prevented it.

A sailor came from the bridge and said, "The captain has asked me to take you below."

"I am going to stay here and tend to this wounded man once he is freed from that cannon," Peggy said.

"Coming about!" Captain Whiddon yelled.

The sailor pointed at the cannon. "Then please move aside, as that cannon is going to go the other way as soon as we are about."

The ship listed to the opposite side and the cannon rolled off the wounded crewman. Three men secured it to the deck. The injured man was carried below. The ship was coming about again to get back on course. Four men stood by to keep the injured man from falling when it listed to the other side.

The young sailor was in severe pain and delirious at times. The ship was tossing about so much that they would have to wait to get his clothes cut off for an evaluation of his injury. Peggy tried to comfort him with soothing words, and she held his hand when it began to tremble. In spite of the agony, he smiled at her soothing touch. He was in such immense pain and his wounds so great from the crushing blow of the cannon that it was a blessing he did not suffer long.

"Is he gone?" a shipmate asked.

"I am afraid so. Do you know his name?" Peggy said.

"Charles Robertson—we all called him Charlie. He liked us to call him that."

The sailors removed their caps.

"Goodbye, Charlie." Peggy closed his eyes; the smile was still on his face.

"Come on men; the captain needs us topside. Nothing we can do for him now," the oldest sailor of the four said.

Peggy found a wool blanket to cover Charlie's body.

The seas had calmed. Peggy went to check on Lisa, who was still lying spread-eagled, holding tightly to the ropes of the bed.

"Seems as if we are out of the storm," Peggy said.

Lisa answered, "Lord, I hope so. I've recited every prayer I know."

The captain entered the open door. "Everyone all right here?"

"We are fine," Peggy said.

"Quite a ride you gave us," Lisa said.

The Captain looked at Peggy and asked, "Charlie, the boson's mate?"

Peggy shook her head.

"I was afraid of that. Did he suffer?"

"He was in pain and delirious, but he was so severely wounded that he didn't suffer for long," Peggy said.

"With the weight of the cannon, I am amazed he wasn't killed instantly." Captain Whiddon tried to shake the vision of the accident from his mind.

"Someone was killed?" Lisa asked.

"One of my men. He was the youngest son of the Robertson family up the road from Whiddon. I dread delivering the news to them."

"Did he have family?" Peggy asked.

"No wife or children, just a sweetheart that worked at the local pub. I must get back to the quarterdeck."

"Can I help?" Peggy asked.

"No,"Willy answered. "But I appreciate what you have done. I saw you risk your life trying to save Charlie."

The captain called for muster; everyone was accounted for except Boson's Mate Charlie Robertson. The captain said, "Charlie died trying to stop a loose cannon on the main deck. The armament fatally crushed him against the deck railing. He died a hero trying to protect his shipmates. During morning watch at two bells, weather permitting, he will be buried at sea. Crew members not on watch are dismissed. Everyone else back to your duty."

It was well past midnight when the captain and Peggy were both drawn to the crew's quarters where they found Charlie's shipmates holding a wake. They were telling stories of the young man's escapades on land and at sea. Captain Whiddon asked the quartermaster to furnish his men an extra ration of rum, which was greatly appreciated.

The four men who carried Charlie belowdecks told the others how he smiled when Peggy held his hand. They were convinced that his pain went away when she touched him. She was now known as the "healer." Peggy was greatly respected by the crew for her efforts to save Charlie.

The captain made a toast to the departed seaman and excused Peggy and himself in order that the crew could be alone with their shipmate. As they made their way to the captain's quarters, Willy said, "Charlie Robertson is the only man I have ever lost at sea. I have had men die from illness, but never lost one due to my lack of action."

Peggy stopped walking and touched Willy's arm. "What do you mean? You couldn't have stopped the loose cannon, either."

"If I had inspected the ropes securing it, I would have found that they were badly frayed and should have been replaced while we were in port. As captain, I alone am responsible for Charlie Robertson's death."

# Chapter Eleven

## Whiddon Estates

*Devon's Hope* made good time. The ship glided in to Plymouth harbor on the fourth Sunday of July and was assisted to the pier by smaller boats. Crewmen swiftly wrapped the heavy lines around the pier's large pilings. Peggy saw the large sign for Whiddon Shipping on top of the weathered, gray limestone building.

Willy and his Aunt Lisa insisted that Peggy accompany them to Whiddon Estates. During twenty-six days at sea, they had become great friends.

Deckhands quickly unloaded Peggy's pelts and Lisa's household goods, storing them in the spacious warehouse. Willy summoned a carriage and wagon to take them the twelve miles to Whiddon, just north of the village of Plympton. While they were loading the hired carriage and wagon, a small one-horse buggy approached. It was George Fox, a bachelor friend of Willy's, the working partner of the Fox and Williamson Limited Partnership. The firm had become a large client of Whiddon Shipping since it received a contract to provide gin to the Royal Navy. The men had known each other since childhood and their families had been friends for generations.

"Welcome home, Willy, my boy! I hope you had a pleasant trip to Philadelphia." Mr. Fox remained in the buggy, holding the reins tightly.

"Thank you, George. *Devon's Hope* made good time. Unfortunately, we lost a crew member during a storm at sea."

"I'm sorry about that, Willy—who was it?" Mr. Fox asked.

"It was Charlie Robertson who lived near Whiddon." Willy shook his head. "Excuse my manners, please meet my Aunt Lisa Yarde and Miss Mitchell, who will be our guests at Whiddon," Willy said.

"Welcome home, Mrs. Yarde. Willy has told me much about you. Nice meeting you, Miss Mitchell, and welcome to Devon. I hope you enjoy your stay." Mr. Fox nodded toward the women and turned toward Willy. "I am sorry about the loss of your crewman."

"A tragic accident." Willy shook his head. "I will tell you about it when time permits." He turned and assisted Aunt Lisa into the carriage beside Peggy.

Willy continued, "George, What brings you to the docks today?"

"It's such a beautiful day; I attended church then decided to take a ride along the coastline, trying to train this filly for the buggy. I saw *Devon's Hope* coming in and wanted to say hello and remind you of next Saturday's fox hunt at Foxboro."

"Sounds like fun. I haven't been on a hunt in a while. I must check with the family first. I will commit by midweek, Thank you for the invitation."

"Please bring the family and Miss Mitchell." Mr. Fox smiled toward the ladies and shook the reins, and the young filly was off like she was on the race track.

On the way to Whiddon, the carriage passed through the ancient village of Plympton. Willy explained to Peggy the name meant Plum Tree Town in Old English, for the famous Devon Plums that grow wild there. Plymouth was named for the mouth of the Plymp River which runs through the town.

"Even the rocks grow green in Devon," Peggy said, looking at the lush growth of the countryside from their carriage.

Willy asked the driver to stop at the home of Charlie Robertson. When he opened the carriage door, they could hear Mrs. Robertson inside the house scream. "It's Captain Whiddon from Charlie's ship. Oh, no! Something has happened to my boy."

Willy reached for Charlie's sea bag and hesitated. Peggy placed a hand on his arm and said, "You can do this . . . for Charlie."

The captain nodded to Peggy, pulled the bag out, and started toward the door.

The mother, seeing her son's bag in the captain's hand, came out of the house saying, "What's happened to my son? Where is my Charlie?"

The captain moved the bag to the other shoulder and put an arm around Mrs. Robertson. They walked slowly into the house. Mr. Robertson heard the commotion from his fields where he and his dog had been tending their sheep. He came running, the dog behind him. He stopped to look at the occupants of the carriage, knowing something was terribly wrong, then went inside. The black-and-white collie stayed on the porch awaiting its master.

Mr. Robertson said, "Captain Whiddon, tell me what happened to my son."

"Poor Willy." Aunt Lisa shook her head, hearing the anguished parents' questions.

"Willy needs to do this . . . he needs a resolution of Charlie's death, like he never had after his wife's death." Peggy said.

Lisa looked at Peggy in a strange way, "How can you always be so strong, Peggy?"

"I don't know." Peggy stared at Drake Island far in the distance, trying to understand her strength during such difficult moments as Charlie's accident.

Captain Whiddon explained the circumstances of the accident, gave the grieving parents their son's belongings and his pay for the voyage, plus a gratuitous stipend for his heroism. Hopefully it would help them cope with their loss.

Charlie Robertson's parents walked the captain out to his waiting carriage. "I have heard tales of loose cannons on ships before, but I have never heard of anyone being killed by one. Have you ever lost a man to a loose cannon before?" Mr. Robertson said.

"Never has it ever happened on a Whiddon ship."

"But, why my boy—why our Charlie?"

"I don't know how to answer you. I wish I could, but I can't explain why such terrible things happen. Your Charlie was a good man and died a hero in the eyes of his shipmates. We will miss him." The captain climbed into the carriage, the couple stood holding each other, watching the carriage disappear from sight.

Willy, Lisa, and Peggy rode the short distance to Whiddon in silence.

As they made a curve in the country lane, Lisa broke the silence. "There it is . . . Whiddon Estate, my home." She put a gloved hand to her face as a tear rolled down her weathered cheek.

"It's beautiful." Peggy gazed at the well-groomed fields of clover. The grazing sheep, cows, and horses looked content. One well-bred horse ran up and down along the rock fence that separated the pasture from the lane, nickering and shaking its long, red mane.

"Is that horse yours?" Peggy asked.

"They all are mine, but that one seems to claim me," Willy jested.

"They are fine looking animals." Peggy spoke loudly to be heard over the rumbling wagon and carriage.

Aunt Lisa was having a nostalgic ride, her mind going back in time to when she was a young girl at Whiddon. She was taking in the familiar scenery, not saying a word, grateful to be home.

The hills looked like the mountains of Tennessee to Peggy, but without the bluish smoke color on the vistas. The slopes of the valleys of Devon were more abrupt than the gentle flow of the hills and dales of her home on Knob Creek.

As the carriage and the wagon bearing their luggage turned onto Whiddon Lane, they passed a well-groomed orchard with a variety of fruit trees. It was the largest orchard that Peggy had ever seen. In the orchard were a dozen strange-looking wagons, the tops covered in boards and canvas. The occupants appeared to be living in the wagons.

Once through the large groves of the orchard, they could see Whiddon Castle, a huge limestone complex of buildings that looked like a palace to Peggy. In front of the main entrance, the uniformed service staff and members of the Whiddon family waited in their Sunday best. A neighbor returning from Plymouth on horseback had alerted them that he had seen *Devon's Hope* coming into port.

William and Elizabeth came running to the carriage as soon as Willy opened the door.

"Welcome home, Father," the children called as they ran to their father, who knelt to hug them.

Grandmother Whiddon hugged her son, then her childhood friend and sister-in-law. She stepped back but kept her hands on Lisa's shoulders. "Welcome home, Lisa."

"Attention everyone! This is Miss Margaret Mitchell from Tennessee." Willy gestured toward Peggy.

Peggy smiled at each person. "My name is Margaret, but my family and friends call me Peggy."

"Then I shall call you *Margaret*," William IV announced.

"*I* will call you Peggy," Elizabeth said, looking disapprovingly at her older brother.

"Margaret or Peggy—either will be fine," Peggy said.

Aunt Hanna McAllister, Lisa's sister, waited until the introductions had been made to greet her. They hugged and kissed, looking each other over, reunited after thirty years. The large extended family, friends, and staff of Whiddon were introduced to Lisa and Peggy.

Aunt Hanna motioned toward the front door. "Let's go inside for tea and crumpets. I know you world travelers must be famished."

The upstairs garden room assigned to Peggy overlooked a beautiful display of every color and variety of rose. She had read of such places, and actually being a guest in one felt like a dream.

Peggy's room had a long, copper tub for bathing, similar to the tub in the Abingdon Inn, but this one was a permanent fixture. She took a long, soaking bath in the warm water, using scented lavender soap. Peggy was glad to be off the forever-rocking ship, hoping that the sensation of the seas in her legs would soon stop. She adored her new surroundings and new friends.

When the Whiddon family was together for dinner—which wasn't often—the meal was a special occasion. That night, they were served pheasant, rib of lamb, baked new potatoes, fresh asparagus, and an assortment of breads and pies. After dinner, Elizabeth played the piano and William recited the words of Shakespeare. Both gave competent performances for their father's return. The children loved the adulation and applause from the adults.

Peggy excused herself early to write letters to family and Dr. Chester back home. Hopefully, Willy would be able to locate a ship that would take her posts directly to Philadelphia. Her first nephew would be born before her letter could make it to Tennessee. She knew the family was anxious to hear of her safe arrival in England.

Breakfast was a hectic affair, with Aunt Hanna hurrying about giving the staff orders for the day. William and his father were in the stable, harnessing two hackney horses to an open carriage for an outing.

Elizabeth sat next to Peggy, excited to have her father home, to meet her Aunt Lisa, and to have an American guest who had survived a great battle of the American Revolution.

The inquisitive Elizabeth, like many girls her age, asked some embarrassing questions of Peggy. "Why aren't you married? How old are you? Why did the American's rebel against Britain?"

Peggy was told that today was the start of the plum harvest that would last several weeks. *That explained the caravan circled in the grove.* They were pickers who harvested fruit from the trees, carting the crop to the kitchen of Chateau Whiddon. Aunt Hanna would oversee the making of plum preserves from her secret recipe that had won many awards and honors. It was her grandmother who originated the recipe and passed it down to her. The various fruits grown in the orchards were made into jams and jellies, packaged in small crocks, and sold under the Chateau Whiddon brand wherever *Devon's Hope* sailed.

The Whiddons were proud of their long association with Berry Brothers of St. James Street in London, the official purveyors to St. James Palace, which provided Whiddon Preserves to England's royal table. The endorsement created demand that was sometimes difficult to fill.

Peggy remembered helping her grandmother harvest apples. She volunteered to help pick the luscious plums, but Aunt Hanna advised her that Willy and the children wanted her to accompany them on a tour of the farm. Hanna had prepared a picnic basket for the outing.

"So much for Willy's surprise," Aunt Hanna said.

"What's this I hear about your dashing my hopes of a surprise?" Willy looked at Aunt Hanna, and gave her a kiss on the cheek as he and William entered the kitchen from the back door.

"I am still excited to hear all about it." Peggy smiled at Willy.

"Then, I shall let the children tell you what we planned after you went to bed last night."

"We have put feed in the stables and penned the horses up. Father said you wanted to take stock of them," William said.

Elizabeth bounced up and down in excitement. "Then we will have a picnic with the pickers. It's fun! They sing and dance in their native tongue."

"What is their native tongue?" Peggy smiled at the excited girl.

"They are Spanish gypsies and call themselves 'Gitanos.' The same family comes every spring. They shear the sheep, bundle the wool for shipment, and spend the summer harvesting the fruit. They leave in the fall and we don't see them again till next spring." Elizabeth spoke rapidly in her excitement, but both children had admirable diction and enunciation for their young age.

"You know so much about these people. I am impressed. Where do they go in the fall?" Peggy asked.

Elizabeth wrinkled her forehead. "I don't know. Home, I guess. I've never thought about that."

"They don't have a home, they just wander around." William looked at his sister with an air of superiority. "Those rickety, old wagons are their only home. That's why they call them gypsies."

"I look forward to meeting these gypsies." Peggy smiled at the children.

*** 

The stable was made of limestone and had individual stalls for each of the eight brood mares. *Mr. Jackson would love a home like this.* Peggy had not thought about her horse since leaving Philadelphia. She had come to terms with the fact that she might never see him again.

The first stall held the chestnut horse with the long red mane that welcomed Willy home yesterday along the rock fence. Peggy entered slowly. The horse took an immediate dislike to her. The children came in and petted her. The mare allowed Willy to pet her, and he wasn't even a horse person. Each time Peggy approached, the horse would get excited, nickering and throwing her head about.

"She doesn't like me for some reason, but she is a beautiful mare." Peggy was able to look at her teeth with

Willy holding her. As Peggy slowly caressed her flanks, the mare allowed her to lift its hooves and examine them carefully. "Does she have a name?"

"I call her Foxy."

After examining the mare a little more, Peggy looked at Willy. "She's about six years old and never been bred. Do you intend to have a foal from this mare?"

Willy thought a minute. "You are exactly right—she is six years old, and yes, I would like a foal from her."

"Unless you have a stallion in waiting, you're fixing to miss that opportunity," Peggy said.

"Really?"

"She is in heat, and I don't know when she started."

Willy shrugged. "I guess she'll have to wait until the next opportunity."

They heard a pack of hounds. The howling got louder and louder, then they heard the hooves of horses. Stepping out of the stables, they saw a small trail of dust, then six hounds chasing the dust trail, and then three horses. It was neighbor George Fox on a fox hunt.

"Carry on!" Mr. Fox hollered at the two horsemen and rode up to the stables. "How are Miss Mitchell and the Whiddon family today?" Mr. Fox climbed off his lathered chestnut stallion.

"Hello, George. Who's winning—the fox or the hounds?" Willy jested.

"It has been so long since my hounds sniffed a fox; they're a little out of shape. Trying to get ready for Saturday's hunt, which I hope you can make."

"I know for sure I'll be there with William. I haven't asked the others yet." He turned to face Peggy and Elizabeth. "Would you like to go to Foxboro on Saturday for the hunt?"

"Sounds like fun. I would love to go, Mr. Fox." Peggy thought, *it doesn't have the red mane, but the horse is a solid chestnut except for the stocking feet. They would produce a good-looking foal.* "May I borrow your stallion, please?"

She took the reins from Mr. Fox, who gave her a bewildered look. She walked the stallion into the stables, removed his saddle, and turned him loose with the mare.

When Peggy returned, everyone was laughing, including the children.

"What's so funny? Peggy asked.

"It's just that I told my horse we were going on a fox hunt." Mr. Fox laughed so hard he had to hold his sides. "I'm afraid from now on when the bugle blows, he will be expecting much more."

Peggy thought about it and starting laughing, then Willy joined in. William and Elizabeth didn't understand the humor of the moment, but they laughed at the adults for being silly.

Willy stopped laughing and turned to George. "Seeing as your steed is busy, would you like to join us for a picnic in the plum grove? The gypsies will entertain us. There's room for you in the carriage."

"Are you sure I wouldn't be intruding? I do need your ear."

"Not at all, George; your company will be enjoyed. We'll take you home afterwards and deliver your horse tomorrow." Willy put a hand on his friend's shoulder.

Mr. Fox smiled at Willy and nodded. "Being entertained by gypsies would be enjoyable."

They arrived just as the pickers were finishing their meal. The gypsies greeted Sir Willy, a name their chieftain gave him. They hugged and greeted each other as gypsies do. Peggy spread a quilt as William and Mr. Fox grabbed the lunch basket from the carriage.

One of the gypsy men started playing an accordion. Another sang, while others appeared to chant. The guests did not recognize the words. Elizabeth just called it happy music, which it was.

Three olive-skinned girls, with long, black hair and dark eyes started to dance and shake tambourines. One danced with cymbals in her hands to the beat of the music. Everyone enjoyed the music and the dancers' performance.

Mr. Fox leaned closer to the captain and spoke just loud enough to be heard over the music. "Willy, I know you have just arrived back home. I hesitate to discuss business during a family outing, but I must."

"This sounds serious." Willy traded his smile for a thoughtful look.

"It is. The economy of Devon depends on you and me and the decisions we make together."

Peggy, William, and Elizabeth were watching the entertainment, not paying much attention to the men's discussion.

"This sounds important. Can we discuss it on the ride to Foxboro?" Willy asked.

"Of course we can."

The gypsy men joined the women dancers and the music and dancing became intense. Everyone was so involved in the music that no one noticed horses coming at full gallop, led by foxhounds still chasing an evasive red fox. The frightened varmint ran through the plum trees into the camp of the fruit pickers. It jumped over the blanket they were sitting on so fast that neither Peggy nor the children knew what was happening. The dancing gypsies saw the chaos and ran off in all directions. Willy and Mr. Fox jumped up just in time to wave the riders off.

Mr. Fox hollered, "Call off the hounds!"

The bugler stopped his horse in the middle of the country lane, placed the brass horn to his lips, and called the foxhounds. The hounds stopped baying and slowly came to the mounted dog handler.

"Well, at least they came to the call of the hounds." Mr. Fox looked disappointed.

"That they did." Willy tried not to show his amusement.

The frightened gypsies who ran away during the melee were coming out of the orchard. Those that took refuge in their wagons were climbing down or peering out, confused about what just happened.

The tribal chief asked, "Sir Willy, what happened?"

"In the effort to outwit the hounds, the smart old fox took a short cut through your camp. Please tell your family we apologize."

The chief translated what Willy said. The gypsies looked at Willy with frowns, raised eyebrows, and quizzical expressions.

"Is something wrong? They are looking at me so oddly."

The chief asked his tribesmen why they seemed so confused.

One of the elders said, "Why is Sir Willy apologizing for something a fox did?"

Willy laughed, and then Peggy and Mr. Fox, the children and the gypsies joined in.

The bugler and dog handler rode up to the group. They didn't understand the hilarity of what just transpired.

"It looks like the fox won today," the bugler said.

Mr. Fox and Willy started laughing so hard they held their sides.

Peggy thought they acted so much like her older brothers. William and Elizabeth enjoyed watching the adults acting silly.

"I think the hounds did well, being their first outing in some time," the dog handler said.

That started another round of laughs. The bugler and dog handler looked at everyone laughing and couldn't understand why no one cared that the fox won.

# Chapter Twelve

## Tally Ho!

Willy, the children, Peggy, and George were in great spirits as they left the plum grove at Whiddon. An afternoon shower was approaching from Plymouth Sound, and Willy pushed the horses to make it to Foxboro before the storm. They stopped at a roadside tavern just before the bottom of the sky fell out.

George looked out the door and shook his head. "Looks like we are in for a goose drowner."

"Mr. Fox, what is a goose drowner?" Peggy squinched her nose.

"It's what we call a downpour in Devon. They don't last long—this will be over quickly." He looked into Peggy's eyes. "Peggy, would you please call me George?"

"George it is, then."

The barmaid served the only two patrons who sat at the bar.

Willy picked a table by one of the stained glass windows. "Here we'll be able to see when the rain stops."

The men ordered gin. Peggy and the children enjoyed a pot of tea and shared a sweet biscuit.

"May I speak to you now about that business matter?" George looked at Peggy, then back to Willy.

Peggy recognized the men wanted some privacy. "William and Elizabeth, let me tell you about my horse Mr. Jackson."

William made a funny face. "What kind of name is that for a horse?"

"I'll tell you all about it." Peggy smiled.

Once the children had left for another table, George said, "I have received a proposal from the Purser of the Royal Navy to provide all the ships at sea and British ports with navy proof gin."

"Well, that's good, but I thought you had that business."

"We've provided navy proof gin for the ships that come into Plymouth, Portsmouth, and London. The proposal for the Royal Warrant that has been offered is for exclusivity on all ships and ports of the Royal Navy."

"That's wonderful news for the distillery," Willy said.

"And your business and the community," George said.

"How is that?"

"I will need to hire two more shifts to fill the needs of the navy and also buy more grain from the farmers." George replaced his serious, business-like demeanor with a big grin. "Whiddon Shipping will be needed to ship gin to the fleet in the Mediterranean at Valencia and Trinidad."

"Trinidad?"

"We captured Trinidad. You were at sea and would have had no way of knowing."

"That had to be some battle to take Trinidad."

"It was. Spain lost fourteen ships and four of our vessels were seriously damaged." George shook his head.

"At least our ships can be repaired. They can, can't they?"

After George responded affirmatively, Willy asked, "How did you manage to secure all the business of the navy?"

"It's what I didn't do and my competitors did. In their haste to supply the growing needs of our fleet, they watered down their gin. It was first discovered during this spring's mutinies at Spithead and the Nore."

Willy shifted in his seat. "Mutinies?"

"You didn't know? asked George.

"Remember, I've been at sea."

"That's right: you were on your way to Philadelphia."

Willy shook his head. "Mutiny over bad grog. What's our navy come to?"

"Much more to it, but Parliament is doing everything it can in this time of war to keep the seamen content," George said.

"I had hoped to spend more time at Whiddon." Willy sighed.

George glanced at Peggy at the corner table. "Could Miss Mitchell be the reason you are not as anxious to sail as you once were?"

"I am very interested in her—she's the only woman I've been attracted to since Elizabeth died. Peggy is so much like Elizabeth. Peggy is here on business and will be heading back to Tennessee once her furs are sold."

"Furs? Peggy has furs to sell here in England?"

"Yes, she is a broker of furs and pelts and brought over the largest inventory I've ever seen. They are stored in my warehouse—beaver skins that glisten shiny white in the sun." Willie gazed off in the distance as if he could see the shiny pelts in his mind's eye. "They call them silver bellies."

"I might know a buyer," George said.

"Be sure to tell Peggy."

"I'll tell her as soon as we finish here so she can contact him before he does business with another broker." George grinned and added, "Or maybe you should tell her. That should impress her."

"No, you go ahead and tell her. Now, how can I help you?"

"The Royal Warrant states that I must have a local agent and maintain sufficient inventory in specified ports. I would like you to be that agent in Plymouth and to be the director of shipping, which Whiddon has done most admirably for us."

"Before I commit, I must know more on the quantities and shipping points. Then I can plan the logistics for shipping."

"Let's meet tomorrow at my office. I will have Catherine Parker, my billing clerk, put everything together. You might start thinking about another ship." George looked through one of the amber stained pieces of the multicolored cut glass window. "It appears the rain has stopped for the moment."

"We best make a dash for Foxboro." Willy stood and hurriedly counted out coins, placing them on the table.

"You should let me pay as I am the one begging a ride."

"Let's just say the drinks make us even on the stud fee." Willy laughed, poking George on the arm like when they were school boys.

***

They dropped George off at Foxboro Estates. He asked them to bring the stallion when they returned for the fox hunt. It was late afternoon when the carriage pulled onto Whiddon Lane. The gypsy pickers were busy working in the plum grove.

"We should check on the mare and her stable mate while we still have daylight," Peggy said over the noise of the carriage.

"I'll unhitch the team at the stables and feed them while you visit the honeymooners." Willy grinned.

Peggy looked for signs that the stud had topped the mare and just couldn't tell. *The mare seems comfortable with the stallion being there.* She fed them rolled oats and pitched them some hay.

Willy entered the stables and Peggy said, "I'm going to leave them together in the stall until tomorrow for good measure."

"Might as well leave them till Saturday morning." Willy held open the stable door for Peggy.

They walked down the path toward the chateau. The children were already in Aunt Hanna's kitchen, telling her all about the day's adventures.

"I enjoyed the picnic and the preview of a fox hunt." Peggy laughed as she thought about the fun day.

"You will enjoy the hunt on Saturday. It's the social event of Devonshire. George and his mother have been hosting it for years. I had forgotten how much I enjoyed George's companionship until today."

"You and George remind me of my brothers, who are always joking or pulling pranks on each other."

"First time I've heard you mention family."

Peggy looked down. "When I talk of my family, I become homesick."

Willy gently placed his hands on her shoulders. "I am sorry."

"Please don't be. I love my family and am very proud of them and what they have accomplished in the few years since independence was won."

"Aunt Lisa told me that your home was destroyed during one of the battles of the revolution and that you were there."

Peggy nodded. "All the children, my mother, and my grandmother were in the family spring house during the battle."

"The family stayed, knowing the enemy was coming?" Willy motioned for her to sit on a bench carved from a large limestone boulder.

"Father thought the militia would be able to stop your troops, and he had no idea that once the first line was breached, they would head straight for our farm." Peggy looked at Willy. "We did just fine in that little spring house."

"It's a shame that our countries had to part." Willy stood, giving Peggy a hand.

Peggy took Willy's hand but stared straight ahead. "Someday, I hope I can understand why that war had to be fought."

"Let me know when you do," Willy said.

\*\*\*

Saturday morning, everyone at Whiddon was up early getting ready for the fox hunt. Two carriages were harnessed for the trip. Peggy asked to ride Foxy.

When Willy went to put a sidesaddle on the chestnut mare, Peggy asked, "Would you mind if I sit astraddle on her in a regular saddle? That way, I can get a feel of her racing ability."

"Not at all" Willy looked at her long skirt. "What about your dress?"

"Would you have a pair of riding britches I could wear?"

"I do. I will try to find you a pair." Willy took a long look at her from head to toe.

The chambermaid brought in several riding suits and laid them on Peggy's bed. They appeared to have never been worn. The label read *Made Exclusively for Lady Elizabeth Whiddon by John Weston of 38 Old Bond Street, London.* Peggy stroked the quality woolen material, choosing a brown tweed riding suit. It had an apron that buttoned in front giving the appearance of a long dress while the wearer was standing. The buttons could be unfastened as needed for sitting comfortably in a chair or unbuttoned completely for straddling a horse. Looking in the long mirror of the inside door of the armoire, Peggy liked the way it looked on her.

As she came down the stairs to the waiting room, Willy said, "Look at you."

Peggy acknowledged his compliment with a nod. "I am impressed at the choices you had. Thank you, as I can ride in comfort and not offend anyone."

"Make them jealous perhaps, but you would never offend."

"Thank you for allowing me to wear it."

"I am so glad you could. Elizabeth never saw them. I had brought them from my tailor in London as a gift for her birthday." His voice had a little catch when he said, "She died before I could give them to her."

"I know that she would have been impressed."

William came sliding down the long banister, his sister Elizabeth running down behind him. "It's not fair! I can't slide down in my dress and petticoats. Boys have all the fun."

The Whiddon ladies, Aunts Hanna and Lisa and Willy's mother, came in their long gowns to join them.

Willy looked at the assembled women and children. "Are we all ready to go?"

"Yes, we're ready," Aunt Hanna said.

Willy's mother nodded.

"Then, tally ho!" Willy exclaimed.

"Tally ho!" William mimicked his father.

"What's tally ho?" Peggy looked at Willy.

"You will hear that a lot today. It means 'I see the fox.'"

Two carriages pulled around the circular drive in front of the chateau, each with a uniformed coachman and groomsman. William rode with his father, sitting behind Willy on the horse. Elizabeth rode in a carriage with her aunts and grandmother.

"Why the extra carriage? Peggy asked.

"After a day of fox hunting and frolic, you will be anxious to sit in the carriage on the way home," Willy said.

Peggy was in her element riding straddle the chestnut mare. The stallion was tied to the extra carriage. She and Willy led the way down the road to Foxboro, which was a small village near the Fox estate.

"Is the village named for the Fox family?" Peggy asked.

"Yes, it was named for the proximity to the estate. Many of the servants at the estate live there," Willy said.

"What about the fox?"

"What do you mean?"

"Was the fox named for the family?"

"I don't know; I'll ask George. It's like the chicken or the egg. Which came first?" Willy laughed. "Never thought about it."

They came up on a group of wagons and riders headed for the fox hunt—everyone dressed like they were going to the opera.

"How many will be there?" Peggy asked.

"Nearly everyone in Devon comes to the annual outing. George's father started it long before I was born. It was originally a rivalry between the Whiddon and Foxboro estates."

Peggy looked at Willy with a big smile on her face. "Oh, a rivalry—like a horse race."

"Back then, they set two foxes off in separate directions and the winner would be the first one back with a fox carcass. I remember Father losing one year and having to forfeit the Whiddon silverware for a year. We had to eat on pewter until someone told Father Mr. Fox cheated as he already had a dead fox in his saddlebags before the hunt started."

"Mr. Fox cheated?"

"Father went to Foxboro and demanded the silverware back. They almost got into fisticuffs until they realized how silly it was."

"Really?"

"After nearly falling out over a fox hunt, they agreed to making it a social event. Where everyone chases the same fox. It's great fun for everyone that way."

"Except the fox." Peggy laughed.

When they reached the village, wagons and horses were in the lane, in places two or four side by side. Peggy had never seen such a crowd of horses and humanity going to the same place. Willy seemed to know everyone; he waved and they waved back. It was like the Beaver Run in Jonesborough, only larger. A stable boy recognized the stallion from Foxboro and took him to the stables in preparation for the hunt. George, a gracious host, greeted everyone as they came in the courtyard. Waiters poured beverages and carried trays of food. The crowd had grown to several hundred people.

The hunters were introduced—there were three dozen hunters, everyone else came as a spectator to enjoy the festivities. Ten foxhounds were to be released at the bugler's call. Peggy was introduced as a special guest from America and one of two women hunters.

"What do you think of all of this?" George asked.

"Goodness, it would be embarrassing if the fox got away," Peggy said.

Everyone who heard her remark laughed, except the yellow-haired woman who was also going to be on the hunt. Catherine Parker was about Peggy's age, unmarried, with an eye on both George and Willy. She was a billing clerk at the distillery and reported to George Fox. She had heard that a young American girl had caught the eye of both of the most eligible bachelors in Devon. She was quite jealous and was not going to let a backwoods American girl outshine her.

The bugler played a short tune.

"That's the call to saddle and mount. The hunt will start shortly, are you ready?" Willy helped Peggy up onto Foxy.

Peggy settled into the saddle. "Now may be a little late to ask, but what am I supposed to do?"

"The dogs and the horses do the hunting. All you have to do is sit tall and look pretty. This is not the first hunt for Foxy. Give her the reins and you will see how she got her name."

Catherine was riding sidesaddle in a beautiful, green silk dress and matching hat with long plumes. She was having trouble holding her mount in place. The young bay was biting at the bit, snickering, and stomping about. A stable boy was trying to help her steady the horse.

The fox crate was brought out into the middle of an open meadow, about fifty meters in front of the hounds' cage. It was important that they see the fox and get the scent. The gloved fox handler pulled him out by the tail for all to see. The dogs went wild and started their monotone baying.

The horses sensed the excitement as did Peggy, who still couldn't understand all this effort for one little fox that could easily be snared in a fox trap with a piece of salt pork.

The bugler played "Release the Hounds." The fox handler pitched the fox out in the meadow and it took off with its red tail waving in the air. The dog cage opened and ten hounds were off after the prey. The bugler played "The Fox Is Loose" and the horses were off. Catherine's horse raised straight up, dismounting her in the dirt and fresh horse dung.

"Tally ho, tally ho!" the hunters shouted.

Peggy followed Willy through the meadow across a stream, topping a knoll that had a magnificent view of the bay in the distance.

"Come, Peggy!" Willy waved for her to follow.

She caught up with Willy, who said, "There is a small hedge at the bottom of the hill. Foxy is a jumper. Give her the reins and she will take it easily. Follow me."

They charged down the hill, a group of six riders behind them. The dogs were baying loudly on the other side of the hedge, as Willy's horse went over the hedge. He could be heard saying, "Tally ho!"

Then the dogs that had been baying after the fox started yelping. Peggy knew something was amiss and went around the hedge rather than jumping over it. There was Willy flat on his back, his best jumping horse nickering. The dogs had cornered the fox in the hedge, just prior to Willy's jump. The horse and rider were spooked by ten baying foxhounds on the ground below. The horse diverted his jump to avoid the dogs and landed safely on all four legs, but Willy took a spill, and somehow a dog was injured.

Peggy dismounted and ran to Willy's side. "Are you hurt?"

He just lay there and moaned as others gathered. She looked him over and didn't see any signs of serious injury.

He began to move slowly. She loosened his jacket to make breathing easier. Again she said, "Are you all right?"

Willy tried to speak but couldn't. His eyes were open, and he tried to sit up.

"Just stay there." Peggy turned to the crowd. "Has anyone something to drink?"

Someone handed her a flask. She opened it and put it to his lips. Willy took a sip, coughed, and nodded that he was all right.

"What was in that flask?" Peggy asked.

"Peach brandy," someone replied.

"It worked." Peggy gave him another sip.

Willy began to move about slowly.

"What happened?" Peggy asked.

Shaking his head and trying to get his voice, he said, "I-I-I'm not sure."

She gave him another sip of the peach brandy.

"That's goo-ood."

"You're feeling better?" she asked.

"No, I meant the brandy was good."

"Let's see if you can get up." Peggy put her left arm under Willy's right arm.

George got on Willy's other side, and they got him on his feet. The hunters let out a cheer. "That's our Willy!"

He waved feebly. A small wagon was summoned, and Willy was helped up on the tailgate. He sat on the end of the wagon as Peggy looked him over.

"You're a doctor, also?" Willy asked.

"No, but I have tended to many a victim of a horse tumble." Peggy looked in his eyes, then his ears for any sign of blood.

"Could I have a little more brandy?" Willy reached for the flask and took another sip.

They took Willy back to the house, where everyone gave a hearty cheer when he managed to slowly walk from the wagon to the house. His mother insisted he be put in bed to wait for Dr. Thornton, who was still out on the hunt. George gave Willy his own flask of brandy, which he consumed and fell asleep. Everyone left the room, except for Willy and his mother, who stayed by his side.

***

Peggy walked out on the second floor veranda. "May I join you?" she asked the other casualty of the hunt.

"Was Willy hurt badly?" Catherine motioned for her to sit.

"Mostly his pride, taking such a fall in front of everyone."

"Yes, I know," Catherine said.

"Well, that sly ole fox has taken his toll. I think he should be declared the winner before anyone else is hurt," Peggy said.

They looked down and saw four men carrying another casualty on a stretcher. His right pants leg was bloody and torn, and Peggy could tell from a distance he could be seriously injured.

"Excuse me." Peggy went back inside and saw the men carry the stretcher to the same room Willy rested in.

*Looks like they are turning this room into an infirmary.*

A woman, whom Peggy took to be his wife, vigorously hugged the injured man, trying to wake him.

One of the men said, "What can we do? Dr. Thornton is the only doctor we have! The nearest doctor is in Tavistock."

"She's the one who doctored Willy," someone said, pointing toward Peggy.

The woman who had been hugging Dr. Thornton stood up and turned to Peggy. "Are you a doctor?"

"No, Mrs. Thornton, but I have been trained in medicine. I will be glad to try and help the doctor if I can."

"You are an American. Where would you have studied medicine?" Mrs. Thornton asked.

"Jonesborough, Tennessee—in the backwoods of the Appalachian Mountains, where I was the only healer and midwife for many years. If you would like me to help your husband, just let me know." Peggy turned toward the door.

"I'm sorry. Don't go—please see what you can do for him."

The room had gotten crowded. Peggy asked everyone but the doctor's wife to leave. She began to examine him from the top of his head, finding a large bump over his right ear. She could see no blood in his eyes or ears.

"Did he bring his medicine bag?" Peggy asked.

"Yes, it's in our buggy."

"We need to have someone bring his medicine bag and a pot of warm water and some clean linens."

While Mrs. Thornton spoke briefly to someone in the hallway, Peggy began to loosen his clothing, putting an ear to his chest, noting his breathing and heartbeat. The bump appeared to be the only injury on his upper body. She dreaded looking at the bloody leg. Dr. Thornton was beginning to make some verbal utterance, which was a good sign. Two chambermaids arrived, one with Dr. Thornton's medicine bag and one with hot water and linens.

Peggy removed a pair of scissors from his medical bag. "Talk to him, Mrs. Thornton. Ask him simple questions. We need to know if he knows where he is and who you are."

Peggy started cutting the trouser leg. The doctor knew his wife was there and where he was. The leg was not broken, but had a severe laceration that would need stitches. Peggy breathed easy knowing they would not have to set a broken leg.

"Dr. Thornton, my name is Peggy Mitchell. Do you remember what happened?"

"Thrown from my horse." Those few words seemed to use all his energy.

Peggy finished stitching the wound, then checked on Willy, who could now sit up with some difficulty.

"Oh, I'm sore." Willy tried to move.

"You should be. You took a bad fall from your horse. Try to rest—I'll be back shortly." Peggy found Willy's mother and the children sitting on the veranda.

"You can go back and see Willy. He is awake, but he is pretty sore from the fall."

A well-dressed gentleman wearing a top hat approached Peggy, who was sitting with Aunts Hanna and Lisa. "Miss Mitchell, my name is John Hetherington. I am a hatter from London. Mr. Fox, our host, planned to introduce us, but you both have been quite busy tending to the wounded fox hunters."

"Yes, the fox has taken its toll on the hunters."

"Mr. Fox, the host—not the hunted," he laughed and then continued, "mentioned to me that you have beaver pelts for sale."

Peggy smiled. "Yes, I have furs and pelts for sale, consisting of every type of critter that ever prowled the woods of Tennessee."

Lisa said, "Hanna, let's go back inside and let these folks talk business."

After the widows left, Mr. Hetherington took a seat.

"Are there any beaver pelts?" he asked. "What they call silver bellies?"

"Silver bellies is what I call them. They can only be found around Knob Creek." Peggy looked at him in a questioning way. "How would you know about a silver-bellied beaver?".

Mr. Hetherington smiled. "I'm wearing one." He tapped the brim of his hat. "I bought the pelt last year, didn't know what it was."

Peggy looked at the hat. "It sure looks like a silver belly."

"The person I bought it from said he acquired it in Philadelphia. I made it into this top hat that I wear everywhere. I could have sold many a hat like it, had I been able to locate a source for the pelts."

"Was the person you bought the pelt from Patrick McDuffy, Captain of the *Lady Ann*?"

Mr. Hetherington looked surprised. "Yes, it was him. You know him?"

"He bought my inventory last year, and I'm certain he purchased the beaver pelt you're wearing from me." Peggy took a closer look at his hat and asked, "Was the pelt marked with five X's?"

"Yes, it was. I often wondered what the marks meant."

"That proves it's my pelt. No one else marks the quality of pelts the way I do—five X is top grade. Now I know Captain Duffy was in London. Do you know if he's still there?"

"I don't know." Mr. Hetherington counted on his fingers. "It would have been several months after last year's foxhunt, which is always the fourth Saturday in July, when I saw him last. Around the first of November."

"How was he?" Peggy asked.

"He had a bit of bad luck coming across."

"How's that?"

"Privateers boarded the *Lady Ann*, killed a crewman, and would have killed the captain if he hadn't given them all his money. The only thing they didn't steal was the pelts." Mr. Hetherington recalled, "Poor chap. He'd ordered a hat—short on money, all he had to pay me with was this beaver pelt."

"Will he be coming back to London?" Peggy asked.

"Don't think so. The captain told me his wife said to sell the *Lady Ann* and come home. Said he was going to become a pig farmer." Mr. Hetherington stood. "Seems like he said her family had a farm near Amsterdam."

Peggy shook her head. "I can't imagine Captain McDuffy a pig farmer."

The hatter asked in a serious tone, "Could I see your pelts while I'm here?"

Peggy said, "I plan to sell them as a lot, rather than piecemeal."

Mr. Hetherington said, "I will be glad to make you an offer after I see them."

"They can be seen at Whiddon's Shipping on Tuesday. I'll be there all day."

"I know where it is and I look forward to the opportunity of doing business with you, Miss Mitchell."

Willy's mother came in. "Excuse me, Peggy for interrupting, but Willy is doing much better and would like to go home now."

"If he is up to it, then let's leave while there is plenty of daylight." Peggy turned toward Mr. Hetherington. "I look forward to seeing you Tuesday."

Willy's mother looked around amongst the crowd. "I will find our coachmen to harness the teams—Willy wants to talk to you."

Peggy found Willy standing by Dr. Thornton's bed. "Things are looking up in the infirmary."

"Thanks to you, Miss Mitchell. That was a very good job you did with the catgut on my laceration. It stopped the bleeding and I shouldn't have much of a scar, thanks to your fine needle work," Dr. Thornton said.

"Thank you, Doctor." Peggy looked at Willy. "Are you up to a three-hour carriage ride?"

"Dr. Thornton says I will hurt more tomorrow. He has provided me some laudanum for the journey. The seats are well padded. I will be all right," Willy said.

The carriages for the Whiddon entourage were out front. A group of well-wishers and long-time friends were waiting for the send-off.

"Take care of yourself, Willy," George said.

"Who won?" Willy's speech was slurred.

George whispered in Willy's ear, "The damn fox won again."

"Next year, we will get him!" A slightly tipsy Willy slowly climbed into the second carriage, Peggy behind him.

"Please try to avoid ruts in the road," Peggy told the coachman.

The coachman nodded, shook his reins, and they were on their way home.

"Thank you for telling George that I had pelts to sell. He referred Mr. Hetherington to me. Do you know him?" Peggy asked.

"Yes, he is London's best-known hatter," Willy slurred. "John comes to Plymouth for the hunt every year, selling his wares at the distillery and taking orders for next year. He made my captain's hat, you know."

"The one with the long plume cock feathers?" She tried not to laugh.

"Are you making fun at me?"

"I can't help it." She snickered, "When I saw you wearing it the first time, you reminded me of the big peacock that struts about in the schoolyard." Suddenly Peggy gasped. "Goodness—that's it! Now I know why Catherine's horse threw her. Those feathers frightened the poor horse. I'm sorry, Willy, I'm off the subject. That is why Catherine was thrown from her horse."

"I will remember to only wear this captain's hat on *Devon's Hope*," Willy mumbled.

"Please tell me more about this London hatter," Peggy said.

"He was just another hatter on a back street in London, selling one hat at a time," Willy said, waving his arms about. "Then he gets himself arrested for wearing this outrageous top hat!"

Peggy asked, "Arrested for wearing a top hat?"

"Yes, now it's his trademark."

"The top hat is his trademark?"

"Yes, and he was fined fifty pounds for wearing it. Then, the lucky bastard gets written up by *The Times* in an editorial saying a man should be able to wear a hat of his choice, regardless of how ridiculous it looks. Mr. Hetherington became famous because of a hat!"

"Arrested and fined for wearing a top hat, made from one of my pelts." Peggy laughed with Willy.

"Now he's famous, and his hats are in great demand." Willy grimaced as the carriage hit a rut.

"Sorry, Mr. Whiddon, I didn't see that one coming," the coachman said.

"Carry on!" Willy waved at the driver. "I think the medicine is wearing off."

"I think Mr. Hetherington wants to make an offer on just the beaver pelts, but I wish to sell them all to one party. I don't want to be haggling over every pelt," Peggy said.

"He can buy them all. Just make him think another London hatter wants them." Willy closed his eyes.

Peggy rode along thinking about what Willy had just said. *What price should I ask of the hatter?* She had paid about $500 for the load from Tennessee, $1,000 for the purchase at Ingles Ferry, expenses of about $300 including the $100 she gave Nathan. *The loss of Mr. Jackson makes it about $2,000 total that I have invested. Mr. Deaderick says you should at least double your investment to make a profit. I got a good deal on the purchase of Mrs. Ingles's pelts, and the buyer has no freight cost. I will ask £3,000; with two and a half dollars to the pound, that's $7,500 for three wagon loads of smelly old pelts.*

# Chapter Thirteen
## Tending to Business

Willy and Peggy took the carriage to Whiddon Shipping on Monday morning. Willy was still sore from his horse fall on Saturday. He had much work to do and decisions to make about shipping Plymouth Gin to the navy.

Peggy needed an inventory of the furs, as a serious buyer paying top dollar would insist on that. She needed to know what she had if she must piecemeal the inventory. Peggy had dressed to do the task herself, but fortunately, a hungry vagabond came on the dock looking for a day's work.

"Peggy, this is Harry, who was passing through and will work for a little grub money. No need in you touching those pelts." Willy waved at the stacks of animal skins.

"Good, I need some help. Harry if you can dig into that pile, I want to sort them by type into smaller piles. This is a beaver pelt we call a silver belly. See the difference in it than just an ordinary beaver pelt? I am most anxious to find all the silver bellies first." Peggy laid the pelt down to start the first pile.

Harry picked up a large bear skin rather timidly.

"Don't worry; that black bear can't hurt you now. Just start a pile for black, and you'll find some brown bears. Keep them separate," Peggy said.

Willy said, "I'll be in my office if you need me. We can have a bite at the pub up the way around noon."

"That sounds good. Dealing with these pelts curbs the appetite a bit. Maybe I will be hungry by noon," Peggy said.

"What's this?" Harry asked.

"A grey wolf." Peggy pointed to a spot to start another stack.

"A pack of wolves like these tried to run me out of my cave one night."

"You live in a cave?" Peggy asked.

He nodded and went about sorting without needing any direction. Peggy thought, *What is such a hard-working and fairly intelligent man doing living in a cave?*

By noon Harry and Peggy were almost finished listing the inventory.

Willy came out of his office and said, "I'm hungry! Let's go to the pub for something to eat."

"I'll keep your inventory going as I work," Harry said.

Peggy raised her eyebrows. "You can read and write?"

"Yes, I count and subtract. Graduated from Plymouth Academy, with honors," Harry said.

"We'll be back shortly. You want your usual?" Willy asked.

"That would be good of you, Captain," Harry said.

"He calls you 'Captain'?" Peggy asked as they walked out onto the dock.

"I've known Harry all his life. A sad case, it is." Willy shook his head.

"Why is that?"

"Harry can be just as normal as anyone, and then—poof! He goes into fits like he's drunk. His eyes roll back in his head, and his body shakes—it's awful."

Peggy asked, "You've seen these fits, as you call them?"

"Yes, unfortunately I have," Willy said, opening the pub door.

"Welcome, Captain," said the attractive pub maid.

"I hope you will be serving us," Willy said.

"If you wish, I will tell the owner you requested me to serve you and your lady friend."

"I'm sorry about Charlie," Willy said.

"You did all you could, Captain. The crew came and told me all about it. You must be Peggy that tried to save my Charlie?"

"Everyone tried. I am sorry for your loss," Peggy said.

"Thank you." The pub maid showed them their table.

"Why didn't you introduce her?" Peggy asked.

"I was caught off guard, I know her only as Charlie's sweetheart. I don't know her name. I've only seen her a few times and no one has ever introduced us," Willy said.

"Oh," Peggy said as the girl approached.

"The owner says I can wait on you, and we have shepherd's pie today."

"Pardon me," Peggy said, " but I didn't get your name."

"It's Rosie. I was born Rosemary—everyone calls me Rosie."

"I am honored to meet you, Rosie. I would like to have the shepherd's pie and tea."

"I will take the shepherd's pie, a pint of ale, and a sandwich to take to Harry." Willy said.

Willy tried to get comfortable in the tight wooden booth, then turned toward Peggy. "Once you sell your pelts, what are your plans?"

"I've just been taking one thing at a time and haven't thought much about what is next. You've kept me so entertained since I arrived—thank you again for making it all possible. I do wish to see London while I am in England."

"Good, because I have an opportunity to take you there. I promised to take William and Elizabeth to London before school starts. I have cargo to deliver, then sail to Trinidad, Valencia, and Oporto and back to London. It will take at least three weeks for the round trip. That would give you and the children enough time to see the city, shop, and enjoy some entertainment. You would be paid for being the children's nanny and all your expenses," Willy said.

"I couldn't accept pay, after all you've done for me," Peggy said.

"You must. Otherwise I will not allow you to take on the responsibility of my children."

Peggy asked, "Where would we stay in London?"

"My cousin has a boarding house near St. James Palace, where we usually stay. You'll like Cousin Agnes, who is a great cook and knows her way around London."

Rosie brought their meal and Harry's sandwich. "Is there anything else you might need?"

"Not at the moment," Willy said.

Peggy broke the crust on her shepherd's pie. The steam smelled like lamb. She blew on a spoonful of stew and carefully took a bite. "This is very tasty."

"Well, what do you think?" Willy asked.

"I said it was tasty."

"I mean about London," Willy said.

Peggy smiled at Willy. "How could I turn down such an opportunity?"

He was excited that Peggy accepted the offer. She would be a positive influence on the children, who had spent most of their lives living with older women. Their grandmother and grandaunts did not see life as a younger woman like Peggy did. With her commitment to care for his children, she would have to stay at least till he returned from the Mediterranean.

"Will that be all, Captain Whiddon?" Rosie handed him the ticket.

"Yes, Rosie, it was wonderful." Willy handed her coin for the meal and placed several notes in her hand. "This is a little something from me to you. May it help you in your loss."

She opened the bills and her eyes widened. "You don't need to do that."

"I want you to have this, in remembrance of Charlie." Willy closed her hands around the money.

She started to cry and Willy gave her a hug.

"Thank you," Rosie said.

Willy waved goodbye to Rosie as he opened the door for Peggy. They walked down the cobblestone road to the docks and Whiddon Shipping.

"You were telling me about Harry on the way to the pub," Peggy said.

"Harry started having fits when he was a young boy. When Dr. Thornton couldn't help him, Father sailed Harry and his parents to London to a doctor who specialized in his type of ailment. The doctor at the institute said Harry would have to be committed. His parents refused to leave Harry in an institution. They brought him home and learned to deal with his problem. They died years ago—Harry had no relatives to care for him. He worked odd jobs no one else would take around Plymouth. When he had a spell, the local constable would shackle him in the jail until the demons left his body. Over time, Harry learned that if no one saw him having a fit he wouldn't be arrested. That's why he lives alone in a cave in the woods," Willy explained.

"What should I do if it happens while we are working together?" Peggy asked.

"It hasn't happened in a long time, and apparently Harry has learned the early warning signs. He told me when the shakes begin, he heads to the cave and when he wakes he isn't shackled. He has never hurt anyone, so don't worry."

"Poor Harry." Peggy sighed.

When they arrived, Harry was not in the warehouse. He had all the pelts neatly separated and inventoried on the list she'd started. The first entries were written in fine penmanship, then the entries became erratic until the final entry could hardly be read. As Peggy and Willy looked closer they saw that the shaky scribble read, "must go."

"Do you think he went back to his cave?" Peggy said.

"From his handwriting, I don't think he could have made it. We would have seen him on the roadway if he headed for the woods. I believe he's still here."

They started searching the warehouse, but they couldn't find Harry. Next, they searched *Devon's Hope.* Willy went straight to the hold of the ship and there was Harry, his color pale, his body sweaty to the touch, unconscious but with a steady heartbeat.

"Willy, bring me the sandwich."

"You think he can eat in his condition?"

"I don't know, but I'll bet he didn't have breakfast, and he needs something."

"I'll get it."

"Better yet, do you have some of your Aunt Hanna's jelly?"

"Jelly?"

"Yes, please hurry. Harry is in a bad way."

Willy brought the jelly and the roast beef sandwich. Peggy put some plum jelly on her finger. Harry swallowed it with no difficulty. She did this several times. Harry began to move and his eyes fluttered. When he saw Peggy, he tried to pull away from her.

"You're going to be all right Harry. No one is going to take you away—you're safe with us. Just try to eat this." Peggy tore a piece of the sandwich off and put it in his mouth.

Harry slowly ate the sandwich. His color began to return and the symptoms went away. He was coherent and speaking normally. Willy gave Harry a cup of water. He gulped it down and asked for more.

"How do you feel?" Peggy asked.

"Better—thank you," Harry said.

They got him up and out of the ship's hold. Once in the warehouse, Peggy sat him down and handed him the inventory sheet. "Is this your writing, Harry? Did you write, 'must go' on my ledger?"

"That doesn't look like my writing, but I do remember writing it before I left."

"Would you write 'must go' again underneath it?" Peggy asked.

They watched him write the two words. The writing looked like that of another person.

Peggy asked, "When did you eat last?"

"Yesterday about this time."

"Willy, is there an ant bed near the docks?" Peggy asked.

"Yes, in my stables just off the dock. Pesky little devils they are. Why do you ask?"

"I want to do an experiment, and I'll need your assistance. I need three liquid containers. Your Aunt Hanna's jelly containers would be the perfect size," Peggy said.

They heard someone calling from the front office. "Hello, anyone here?"

Willy recognized his friend's voice. "We're doing a medical experiment, George, come on back."

"That sounds interesting." George entered the large warehouse to find Willy and Peggy pulling pint-sized crock bottles off the shelves and Harry sitting on a mound of bear skins.

"May I watch?" George asked.

Peggy reached for the last container. "I'd like you to participate."

"Sounds like fun." George rubbed his hands together.

Peggy handed a crock to each of the men, placing a small pigeon feather in the bottom of the one she gave to Harry.

"Now, I am going to turn my back, and I want you to do your business in the crock, filling it about half way," Peggy said.

Willy almost dropped the crock he was holding. "You want us to do what?"

"Just relieve yourselves in the bottle, like you do in your bedpan. I can leave the room if you wish.".

"I'm very uncomfortable with this," George said.

"I will leave and come back, if it makes it easier for you. By doing this, we may be able to find the cause of Harry's erratic behavior." Peggy started for the door.

"Just stay where you are, Peggy, if this is for Harry," Willy said.

"For Harry." George raised his crock.

They filled the crocks and handed them to Peggy, who put them all in a small shipping carton. "Now, will you show me the way to the ant bed at the stables?"

They all started for the door, anxious to see what Peggy was going to do next. Once at the ant bed, Peggy poured each crock near the ant hole, and waited. The ants scurried into the urine with the pigeon feather and avoided the other two samples.

"Harry, do you see that the ants went to your urine?" Peggy said.

Harry blushed. "What does that mean?"

"Your urine is high in sugar, while Willy and George's urine is normal. I suspect you have a condition called diabetes mellitus."

"Where did you learn of this medical condition?" Willy asked.

"I had a student, who was sick with similar symptoms. Using Doctor Chester's medical books, I researched the works of a scientist who first used the ant test. I have used it twice and it has worked both times," Peggy said.

"Can you cure me?" Harry asked.

"There is no cure at this time. Doctors have reported a significant improvement in patients who eat something every three to four hours. Have you noticed that when you go long periods without eating is when you have these episodes?"

Harry wrinkled his forehead. "I never thought about it, but when I'm hungry is when the shakes start."

"Never wait to eat until you are hungry. Always, carry a little bread and dried beef with you and drink lots of water. If you do this, you'll feel better and eliminate these episodes." Peggy looked at George and Willy. "And they are *not* fits."

# *Chapter Fourteen*
## London

Peggy stood by the starboard railing of *Devon's Hope*, watching her lifetime dream of seeing London unfold before her. William was an infant when he came to London last, and it was Elizabeth's first trip. The siblings ran up and down the deck pointing to things, asking Peggy what they were. From pictures she had seen and books she had read, Peggy was able to tell the children they were on the River Thames, which runs through the heart of London, now the largest port in the world.

"Please stay beside me, children. Your father shouldn't be distracted, and we must stay out of the crew's way as they maneuver the ship into its berth," Peggy said.

The captain had a dinghy lowered with four oarsmen to row toward the north bank to Billingsgate Dock. The lookout in the crow's nest used the eyeglass to spot his shipmates, now on the dock signaling instructions to *Devon's Hope*.

"Permission has been granted to advance to the dock, Captain."

"Raise the jib slowly."

"Aye, aye, Captain," said the first mate.

A light wind filled the jib, pushing the ship toward the docks. *Devon's Hope* moved quietly between ships at anchor. Peggy and the children watched the crew skillfully backing and filling the large sails, maneuvering the 212 feet of the ship into place alongside the dock. Lines were thrown to the crewmen waiting to tie her off. Peggy had arrived in London on the first day of September of 1797.

It would take most of the day to unload 9,000 gallons of Plymouth Gin in 300 bulky oak casks, each filled with 30 gallons of navy proof gin.

A courier was sent to Mr. Hetherington's shop to inform the hatter the pelts he purchased from Peggy had arrived. Berry Brothers had their empty oak barrels stored on the dock, awaiting shipment to Spain.

The most important product, bat guano, would be unloaded last. Thousands of limestone caves in the forests of Devon provided natural habitat for the native horseshoe bat. Their guano, one of the ingredients of saltpeter, was used to make gunpowder. Tonight, it would be picked up by the Birmingham Munitions Factory in nearby Birmingham.

A large cache of cannonballs and black powder would be loaded. The munitions would be stored in the hold with the gin. The reason for navy proof had more to do with integrity of gunpowder than approval by the seamen. Should the barrels leak on the gunpowder, it would not compromise the firing ability of the powder.

Rum had been the choice of sailors for their daily ration of grog for many years. Unfortunately, it could be obtained only in the West Indies where sugarcane was abundant. The war with Spain had impeded shipments of rum. Domestically produced gin, distilled from native grain, was much easier for the navy to procure.

A carriage was ordered for Peggy, the children, and their baggage for the twelve-mile trip to the boarding house in Leicester Fields owned by Willy's cousin, Agnes Reynolds.

Willy placed a basket on the seat of the carriage. "Don't forget the gift for Cousin Agnes."

"I must stop at the bank on Threadneedle Street. Do you know where that is?" Peggy asked the carriage driver.

"Yes, Madam, I do. I stop there often."

"When will we see you again?" Peggy asked Willy, who had Elizabeth in his arms.

"Once things are unloaded and the cargo I am commissioned to transport is aboard ship, I will come to say my goodbyes. It most likely will be in the morning for breakfast. For now, enjoy your carriage ride through the city." Willy kissed his children, patted Peggy's hand, and waved goodbye as the carriage moved off the dock.

They arrived at the bank just before closing. When the teller realized that she wanted £250 in currency out of the large check she was depositing, he turned her over to an officer of the bank.

"Miss Mitchell, this check is on the account of one of our well-known merchants and the funds are available. However, I don't feel comfortable issuing a woman alone in London with that much cash," the banker said.

Peggy glared at the bank officer. "I can take care of myself as well as any man. Besides, I need cash as I doubt my drafts would be accepted because no one knows me."

"They know me, and I'll be glad to write you a letter of introduction."

"Are you sure that's all I'll need?" Peggy looked at the banker for assurance.

"Yes, and let me get you £50 in notes. That's a year's pay for most Londoners. The bank will be open again Monday morning should you need additional currency."

They arrived at the Reynolds House just as Agnes Reynolds was setting the table for her three resident boarders. Agnes was a middle-aged spinster who obviously enjoyed her own cooking. She was a jovial redhead with the ruddy complexion of her Scots heritage.

"You must be Miss Mitchell, and I remember William, even though he was just a baby when I saw him last. This pretty girl must be Elizabeth." Agnes gave the children a hug.

"I'm glad to meet you," Peggy said.

Agnes wiped her hands on her apron before shaking Peggy's hand.

Peggy gave the children her schoolmarm look. Elizabeth curtsied, and William bowed and handed Agnes the basket of Whiddon preserves.

"Thank you, William." Agnes turned and looked at Peggy. "I've heard good things about you, Miss Mitchell, from Willy."

"Agnes, would you please call me Peggy?"

"Yes, I'll call you Peggy, and thank all of you for this lovely basket. I look forward to the Whiddons coming to London as they always bring their delicious jams and jellies for my kitchen. Peggy, your room is upstairs at the end of the hall—the door is open. Elizabeth's adjoins yours and William's is just across the hall. You get settled, and I'll fix you something to eat."

The driver made several trips in with the baggage and a large trunk full of clothes that had belonged to Willy's wife. Most of the garments fit Peggy, down to her shoes. The rest needed only minor alterations.

As Peggy looked around at the Reynolds House, she was impressed that it was decorated like a castle with coats of arms and portraits of royalty. The home was very masculine, with huge exposed beams like a cathedral. Peggy admired the large, masonry fireplace. Over it hung a large portrait of a distinguished-looking man on one knee being knighted by the king. A small, brass plaque read "Investiture of Sir Joshua Reynolds."

Agnes entered the room. "Oh, this is where you wandered off to." When she noticed Peggy looking at the portrait Agnes said proudly, "That is my Uncle Joshua Reynolds in the painting being knighted by the King of England."

"Willy told me about his cousin from Devon being knighted and all of the Whiddons sailing on *Devon's Hope* to be here for the ceremony," Peggy said.

"Yes, I was at St. James Palace for the ceremony. We lived in London. I was just about Elizabeth's age. That's when I met Willy. I thought he was the most gorgeous boy I ever saw, with those long, yellow, curly locks of hair. He's the favorite of all my cousins. When will he be coming?" Agnes asked.

"As soon as his cargo is secure. Most likely in the morning at the earliest he told me."

"I look forward to making him his special breakfast. May I ask you a personal question, are you and Willy . . . ?"

"No, we are just friends, and I am presently the nanny to his children," Peggy said.

"The reason I asked is you remind me so much of his wife, Elizabeth. He loved her so."

"I know." Peggy turned and gently touched the shiny mahogany wood finish of a desk. "What a beautiful piece."

"I watched Sir Edmund Burke sit at that desk, just after Uncle Joshua died, and write his best friend's eulogy," Agnes said.

Peggy's eyes widened. "Edmund Burke, the writer?"

"That was him," Agnes said.

"Sir Joshua Reynolds lived in this house?" Peggy asked.

"Your room was his bedroom." Agnes nodded. "Mr. Burke sat with him and held him in his arms as my uncle drew his last breath."

"Sir Edmund Burke was in this home?"

"He stayed all night consoling mother and me. We loved him dearly. He passed shortly after mother." Agnes took a deep breath. "Come, the children are at the dining table. I told them to start and I would find you." Agnes waddled down the hall as Peggy followed.

Agnes explained as she walked how she and her mother took care of her uncle up to the end. His last days were not pleasant—he had gone deaf and blind. He left the house to his sister, Agnes's mother, who died two years ago and left the famous property to Agnes.

When they reached the dining room, Agnes motioned for Peggy to sit at the head of the long table. The children were enjoying the second helping of bread pudding with thick, rich cream on top. Food on *Devon's Hope* was nothing like food at the Reynolds House.

***

The night constable had just made his last rounds of the evening, and the village pub was closed. The crew of *Devon's Hope* had eaten and were enjoying their daily ration of grog.

They heard in the distance the sound of a large group of horses slowly moving along the deserted cobblestone streets of Billingsgate, then the cadence of soldiers, marching slowly to the voice commands of a mounted officer. They saw the first team of four draft horses pulling sturdy army wagons on the street above the docks. A column of armed soldiers were on each side, two army teamsters sat on the buckboard, and two armed soldiers stood on a rear platform. The second and third wagons appeared, identical to the first.

The heavily laden wagons crunched the cobblestones with wide-rimmed metal wheels. The first wagon creaked as it slowly descended the freightway to the water level of the docks. Once the first wagon was safely on the level dock, the others slowly followed. Foot soldiers established a perimeter of guards around the docks, with orders that no one be allowed in or out of the area.

A mounted officer called out, "Permission to come aboard, Sir."

"Who goes there?" Captain Whiddon said.

"Ordnance Officer Lieutenant O'Day of the Royal Navy."

"Permission granted to come aboard," Captain Whiddon said.

The lieutenant dismounted, handed the reins to a foot soldier, and threw his black leather saddlebags over his shoulder. At the end of the ship's gangway, he saluted the Union Jack. As he looked up, he saw crew members smoking on the aft deck. "Captain, I have your ship's orders and have been instructed to advise you there is to be no smoking whatsoever on your ship during the loading of munitions."

"My crew knows the regulations."

"You have men on the aft deck smoking at this very moment."

Captain Whiddon said, "When the munitions start to come aboard, my men will quit smoking."

"I have been assigned to your ship, with eighteen gunnery men familiar with your armaments. Should your vessel come under enemy fire, I, as the ordnance officer, will assume command of your ship. Is that understood, Captain Whiddon?"

"Who has given these obtrusive orders?" Captain Whiddon asked.

"The Master of Ordnance, Sir Charles Cornwallis."

"If I don't agree to these orders?"

"Should you not agree, I have been authorized to commandeer your ship under the articles of war."

"I have never sailed under such orders before, and Whiddon Shipping has been hauling cargo for the navy for three generations."

"We are at war; security is tight. I didn't make the rules of war, Captain, I just follow them. You may wish to read this as my men load the munitions." The lieutenant handed him a packet with the ship's orders and told his men to unload the wagons.

It took several hours to move the heavy, wooden flats of cannonballs that ranged in size from six to eighteen pounds per ball and to store them in the ship's hold. Hundreds of small, oak munitions barrels, full of gunpowder, were stacked neatly between the rows of cannonballs.

"Captain, as soon as my men have secured the munitions hold, we will need to be underway," Lieutenant O'Day said.

"I had planned to leave in the morning after having breakfast with my family in Leicester Fields. They are expecting me and will be worried if I don't appear," Captain Whiddon said.

"That will not be possible; you need to prepare your men to get underway. Two frigates await beyond the harbor to escort you to your destination."

"I must let my family know that I am safe."

"Write a letter, and I'll have it delivered for you. Be careful not to divulge anything about our activity."

The captain called all hands on deck to explain that they would immediately prepare to cast off while it was still dark. Fortunately, the night was clear with a full moon and a high tide.

"Now, hear this. There will be no smoking on this ship or dock until further notice. We'll burn only the port and starboard lamps leaving port. All eyes must be alert to the hazards of the night."

The crew showed their displeasure on their faces but understood that they were sitting ducks for enemy saboteurs. The combination of gunpowder, cannonballs, and high proof gin could provide a pyrotechnic event that could destroy Billingsgate Dock.

"We will have nineteen guests of the Royal Navy aboard our floating powder keg for the next leg of our trip. I expect you to show them the same courtesies that you would your shipmates. Should we be fired upon, I will be giving command of the ship to Lieutenant O'Day, and you are to follow his orders."

***

A rooster could be heard crowing in the backyard of the Reynolds House. The hens cackled as Agnes gathered their eggs from the nests. She had planned a special breakfast for her boarders and guests from Devon.

The neighborhood dogs were barking at the three strange-looking freight wagons circling the block of Leicester Square Park. Stopping in front of the house, the driver scurried down the high steps of the first wagon. Peggy had been looking out her window at the beautifully manicured estates around the square. Seeing the official-looking government wagons, she quickly dressed to see what they were doing so early on a Saturday morning. She heard the soldier ask Agnes for Miss Peggy Mitchell.

"Are you looking for me?" Peggy asked.

"Yes, I have a letter for you from Captain Whiddon."

She looked at it suspiciously. "The envelope has been opened."

"Yes, it has."

Peggy put her hands on her hips and demanded. "Who opened it?"

"My superior officer, Lieutenant O'Day," he said.

"Why would he open a personal letter addressed to me and sealed?"

"Matters of military intelligence. If you read the letter you will understand."

Peggy read the letter that explained what had happened. Willy hinted that his letter would be read by others. The last line read, *"Remember, never divulge my ship's whereabouts."*

The soldier climbed back upon his wagon, and the caravan circled the square.

Agnes had been hovering in the backgound until the soldiers left, then she came forward and asked, "What did Willy say?"

"That he has already sailed and will not be coming this morning." Peggy folded the letter and slipped it into her pocket.

"Where is he going?" Agnes asked.

"He didn't say." Peggy turned to see William and Elizabeth, who'd overheard the conversation.

William, upset that his father wasn't coming to say goodbye, stormed back up the stairs to his room and slammed the door.

"Come, Elizabeth, let's see what Agnes has in her kitchen that smells so good."

Agnes asked, "Can I do anything?"

"Give him time. For now, I just need a cup of coffee."

Agnes made breakfast as Peggy and Elizabeth discussed all the fun things they wanted to do in London. First on the list was new clothes for the children.

"I expect Mr. Hetherington will be coming for breakfast, as I sent word that Willy would be here this morning." Agnes bustled into the dining room with a tray of fresh-baked crumpets.

"I look forward to seeing him again. Elizabeth, let's go get dressed for breakfast." She knocked on William's door and said, "Agnes has just made some fresh crumpets. You may want to get them while they are hot."

While they were getting ready, she heard Agnes welcoming Mr. Hetherington and telling him that Willy would not be there for breakfast.

Peggy heard William go out the door and down the stairs. *Poor boy. I don't blame him for being upset.*

When Peggy and Elizabeth entered the dining room, Mr. Hetherington stood and said, "Welcome to London, Miss Mitchell. It is a great pleasure to see you again, and Elizabeth. Young William and I have been catching up on things."

"I'm glad to see you again, Mr. Hetherington. I hope you received your pelts in good order." Peggy sat next to William and gently touched his shoulder. "Good morning."

He nodded and seemed to be over the disappointment of not seeing his father.

"The pelts arrived in good order, Miss Mitchell," Mr. Hetherington said. "Could you please call me John?"

"If you wish, I will call you John, if you call me Peggy."

"Fair enough," John said.

"John, being a hatter, you should know a good tailor," Peggy said.

John puffed his chest out. "You're talking to London's best tailor."

"I thought you were a hatter."

"All hatters are tailors, but not all tailors are hatters. What can I do for you?"

"I'd like to have a suit of clothes made for William, Elizabeth, and myself. I also have some garments that need alterations," Peggy said.

William pointed at the top hat resting on a nearby hat rail. "Can I have a hat like his?"

"You like Mr. Hetherington's hat?" Peggy asked.

"Yes, I do." William reached for the last crumpet.

"Then you shall have one."

"Good, I have a small beaver pelt that would be just his size." John placed his tape measure around the boy's head.

Agnes brought in the breakfast. "I hope everyone is hungry. We have lots of food."

After breakfast, Peggy tried on the clothes that needed to be altered, and the hatter marked them for the seamstress. Peggy and the children were measured for their clothing. They would ride with John to his shop to pick the pattern and materials for their garments, and then they would take him up on his offer to treat them to lunch and a tour of London afterwards.

William was excited about getting his top hat made from a beaver pelt that Peggy had brought from Tennessee.

After Peggy and the children selected their patterns and materials, John took them to the establishment of Thomas Rule in Covent Garden next to the Royal Opera House. The small restaurant specialized in serving raw oysters, at which the children turned up their noses, but they were impressed with the porter pies. Mr. Rule was honored to have a guest from America. When he found Peggy was interested in the opera, Mr. Rule offered his personal box for next Saturday's performance.

Peggy was pleasantly surprised to find the British so friendly toward her, only fourteen years since the end of a bitter war.

Mr. Rule looked at John and asked, "Will you have my top hats by opening day?"

"Thanks to Peggy, who brought the pelts with her from Tennessee."

"What a beautiful-sounding name, Tennessee. Mr. Rule said. "That is the name of one of the newer colonies, isn't it?"

"Yes, it was originally the western part of North Carolina. It is named for a river that meanders through the state," Peggy said.

Looking back to John, Mr. Rule said, "I plan to be open for New Year's Eve— that's less than three months away. Will they be ready?"

"I plan to have them to you by Christmas."

After their meal, they walked through the market and along a few of the nearby streets. John showed Peggy the old building that Thomas Rule was renovating for a restaurant at 35 Maiden Lane.

"I hope Thomas knows what he is doing, opening such a grand restaurant in such austere times." John pointed toward a large, ornate building. "There is the Royal Opera House."

William asked, "Is that where we're going Saturday?"

"Yes, I look forward to going." Peggy stopped and turned to John. "Would you be able to go with us?"

"It would be my pleasure. I will pick you up in my carriage about seven, as the first curtain call is at eight."

# Chapter Fifteen
## Letter from London

The westbound stage from Philadelphia made its scheduled stop in Jonesborough on the way to Nashville. The driver left the mail and Dr. Chester's newspaper at the Chester Inn. The town's only doctor looked forward to reading the *Philadelphia Gazette*. He prided himself on reading every word before passing it on to his friend David Deaderick at the General Store.

In addition to the usual mail, Dr. Chester saw two weathered envelopes from Plymouth, England, one addressed to him and the other to the Adam Mitchell family. He pushed the *Gazette* aside and eagerly tore his letter open and read what Peggy had written. Then he headed to the stables and asked Jake Thompson to harness his horse and buggy.

"Someone must be sick, you in such a hurry." Jake said.

"No, but Peggy sent her parents a letter from Plymouth, England and I am taking it to them. Adam and Elizabeth have been anxious to hear from her," Dr. Chester said.

"Plymouth, England?" Jake put a halter on Dr. Chester's white horse. "Where is that?"

"I've never been to England." The doctor put his medicine bag in the buggy. "I think it is south of London. I know it is where the Pilgrims sailed from to the new world."

"And our Peggy is there?" Jake said proudly.

"That's right, and she took her load of pelts with her, and got a good price." Dr. Chester climbed up into the buggy. "If anyone needs a doctor, tell them I will be back this afternoon."

Adam Mitchell Jr. was born the year independence was declared. Now he was a stout young man of twenty-one years, wielding a double-sided axe, splitting logs that his eleven-year-old brother Samuel brought from the wood shed. The shirtless Mitchell siblings stopped their work to watch the strange-looking buggy coming up the lane.

"Who could that be?" Samuel asked.

"Never seen a buggy like that before, but it looks like Dr. Chester's horse," Adam Jr. said.

"Hello, Adam, Samuel." The doctor looked at Samuel. "Your brother trying to teach you to split wood?"

"I know how, Adam just doesn't trust me with his axe," Samuel said.

"In good time, Samuel. Adam, your parents home?" Dr. Chester asked.

"They have been in bed sick all week." Adam buried his axe in the large tree stump they used to split firewood on. "Nice buggy."

"Thank you, it's called a doctor's buggy." Dr. Chester handed Adam the leather reins. "Why didn't you let me know they were sick?"

"I just told you," Adam said.

"I mean, why didn't you come to town and tell me?" Dr. Chester said.

"I was going to as soon as I got some wood split for Ibby to cook with."

The doctor grabbed his medicine bag from his shiny new buggy and said, "Will you take care of my horse while I check on your folks?"

He entered the rustic log cabin to find Ibby and Rebeckah tending to Adam Sr. and Elizabeth who were in a bad way. According to Ibby, they had been running a high fever for several days. He gave them a quick examination, looking into their eyes, felt for their pulse. "When did they eat last?" Dr. Chester looked at Ibby.

"Yesterday, but they couldn't hold anything down," Ibby said.

"I am awfully sick, thanks for coming over doctor," Adam Sr. said.

"You're welcome, I wasn't aware you were sick. I came to bring you a letter from your daughter Peggy, from Plymouth, England," Dr. Chester said.

Adam tried to sit up, but was just too weak. "Plymouth, England! How did she get there?"

"Here is her letter, maybe she will tell you." Dr. Chester handed the letter to Adam, who was so weak he couldn't open it.

"Did you say Peggy sent a letter from England?" Elizabeth tried to sit up and couldn't. "How is she?"

"Would you like me to read it for you?" Dr. Chester asked.

"Please," Elizabeth said and Adam nodded.

Rebeckah opened the door and said to her brothers, "Doctor is going to read Peggy's letter. She is in England."

"Don't let the boys come in. They are well and I want to keep them that way," Dr. Chester said.

"Dr. Chester wants you stay outside."

He read the letter loud enough that those outside could hear. Hearing Peggy's written words seemed to perk Adam and Elizabeth some, they went back to sleep with a smile on their face. "Where are the youngsters?" Dr. Chester looked around.

"David, James, and Hezekiah are down at the creek playing. Jennett went with them," Ibby said.

"I hope they aren't in that creek water. Ibby, you and Rebeckah are already exposed, nothing we can do about that . . . I am afraid."

"Exposed?" Ibby looked at the doctor. "Exposed to what?"

"It could be cholera."

"That's contagious!" Ibby asked.

"Afraid so." He opened the small wooden door. "I want you, Samuel, to bring your brothers and sister from the creek and don't you get in that water going after them." Dr. Chester said.

"What can we do?" Rebeckah near tears, "I don't want to die."

"You will be fine, if you do what I say. When everyone is here I will tell you, all at the same time, what we are going to do to stop this from making anyone else sick. What about your neighbors? Any of them been ill?"

"Not that I know of," Ibby said.

"That's good, maybe we can contain it . . . Where are the reverend and William?" Dr. Chester asked.

"They went to Limestone for a meeting with the trustees of Washington College," Ibby said.

Dr. Chester opened the windows and door for fresh air. Once everyone was gathered around the door of the cabin, he began his instructions by telling the children to stay out of the creek, explaining contaminated water was the most likely cause of cholera. All water should be boiled before drinking. He instructed the boys to keep soap and water on the porch and everyone should wash their hands often, and always after using the privy.

"Ibby, you and Rebeckah remain with your father and mother in the main cabin. Everyone else stays in the bunkhouse. You need to change the bed linens and wash everything with soap and boiling water. Bathe the sick ones with a mixture of boiled water and vinegar." Looking at Ibby and Rebeckah, the doctor said, "I will help you with your parents."

They heard horses coming. It was Reverend Witherspoon and William riding hard. William was the first off his horse; seeing everyone gathered outside and the doctor's horse and buggy, he thought the worst.

"Are they gone?" William looked at his brothers.

"They have cholera." Adam Jr. stood between the door and his older brother William. "Doctor says if you're well, not to go in."

"What can I do?" Reverend Witherspoon looked in at the doctor.

"Pray and stay away from them, while I make up a mixture of medicine from my bag," Dr. Chester spoke from the doorway.

The family gathered around the reverend and started to pray. Rebeckah started out the door to be with them. The doctor put his arm out and stopped her. "No, you must stay away from those that have not been exposed. You and Ibby can help me."

As the doctor mixed the powders of jalap and calomel, he asked Ibby, "What have your mother and father done that the rest of the family hasn't in the last week? Gone somewhere without the family or eaten something no one else has eaten?"

"Last Saturday, they went to visit the widow Sutherland at Walnut Grove near the head waters of Knob Creek." Ibby said.

"That's it! Adam, can you hear me? Nod your head if you can," Dr. Chester said.

He nodded and opened his eyes.

"Adam, how was Mrs. Sutherland when you saw her last Saturday?"

"She was sick. Elizabeth and I stayed for a while, fixed her something to eat. She seemed better, we came on home." Adam said with much difficulty, then was out again.

"Boys, how far to the Sutherland woman's place at Walnut Grove?" Dr. Chester looked at William, Adam, and the reverend.

"About two miles," William said.

"I think the widow is our source of this illness. Would you go see how she is? If she is still sick don't go in.

Come and get me. I need to get some food and medicine down your folks, before I can go," Dr. Chester said.

"Reverend and I will go, Adam can stay and help you." William and Reverend Witherspoon rode off toward Walnut Grove.

"Adam, start a fire outside, get the biggest pot you have boiling with hot water, we have some work to do." Dr. Chester started a fire in the fireplace to boil water for the contaminated cabin.

Rebeckah and Ibby stripped the soiled linens from their parents' beds and replaced them with clean ones. They boiled the dirty laundry with lye soap over the hot fire, then scrubbed the floor and walls with hot water and lye soap.

William came riding back alone. Dr. Chester met him at the door. "Well?"

"She's dead." William slapped his dusty hat against his britches.

"I told you not to go in."

"I didn't."

"Then how do you know she was dead?"

"Her bed was next to the window," William said.

"You got a good look at her, then? Nothing we can do for her but pray."

"That's what the reverend is doing," William said.

"William, you and Adam Jr. get everyone bathed in clean, hot water. Use lots of lye soap and elbow grease, don't reuse the bath water," Dr. Chester said.

"We will all be ready for church tomorrow," William said.

"No church until we know this cholera is under control," Dr. Chester said.

Once things were disinfected at the Mitchell compound, they had to take care of the widow Sutherland's body. As there was no next of kin, they discussed just burning the house, with her and everything in it. Instead, they buried her in a deep grave, her body covered in lye. It was risky to move her body, but Reverend Witherspoon insisted that she have a proper burial. He performed a short ceremony, witnessed by William and the doctor. The house and its contents were burned.

They rode down the two-mile meandering creek, advising those who lived near it to stay out of the creek and to boil their drinking water.

It was dark by the time Dr. Chester made it home to his family who resided on the top floor of the Chester Inn. Hopefully, a cholera epidemic had been avoided in Jonesborough, thanks to a letter from England.

# Chapter Sixteen
## Master-General

Peggy enjoyed reading the London *Times* with her morning coffee. She thought it was grand reading the paper the same day it was printed. The resident boarders at the Reynolds House didn't understand the American woman preferring coffee to tea. They were appalled at how strong Peggy took her coffee, without any cream or sugar.

"Oh my!" Peggy pulled the paper close to her face. "Mary Wollstonecraft has died from complications of childbirth!" She asked Agnes, "Did you know her?"

"I knew of her. I am proud to say I never met her."

"You sound as if you didn't approve of her," Peggy said.

"She was a tart. I feel sorry for the child that now has no mother." Agnes bent over to see the headlines. "Sir Edmund thought she was an evil woman and so did my uncle. How would you know her?" Agnes looked at Peggy.

"I didn't, but I always wanted to meet her; she is one of the reasons I came to London. I have read everything she wrote. She gave me hope. Now she is dead!" Peggy left the dining room and hurried upstairs to her room, collapsed on the unmade bed, and burst into tears.

Elizabeth heard Peggy sobbing, came into her room and climbed up on the bed. "Why are you crying?" Elizabeth gently caressed her nanny's hair.

"I just learned that someone I wanted so much to meet has died."

"Who?"

"Mary Wollstonecraft, a writer who lived here in London. She gave me inspiration, taught me through her books that women should aspire to higher education, and learn a craft."

"You'll get to meet her when you get to heaven. Father told me that when I go to heaven I will meet my mother there," Elizabeth said.

Peggy wrapped her arms around Elizabeth. "Your father is right. You will meet the mother you never knew in heaven."

"Grandmother and Aunt Hanna said she was just like you," Elizabeth said.

"They said that?" Peggy stood and picked Elizabeth up and hugged her tightly. "Your father should be home any day now."

Two more weeks passed and Willy had not returned. He said the voyage would take three weeks and it was now the fifth week since he'd left rather suddenly from Billingsgate Docks. Peggy left the children with Agnes and hired a hack to take her to the docks. No one had seen or heard anything about *Devon's Hope*. At her wits' end, she visited Berry Brothers' office on St. James Street. No one there knew of the ship's location and they were just as concerned, as their keg wine and brandy inventory was low. The wine and spirits purveyor had started rationing sales to the local pubs that depended on the firm to supply the popular beverages.

She asked the driver to take her to Hetherington Hatters, then dismissed him and his hack for the day, knowing she could easily summon another. Peggy entered the hat shop unannounced in hopes that London's influential hatter might have some information of Willy's whereabouts.

John Hetherington and his seamstress were busy measuring a portly gentleman. Peggy had caught them by surprise, as they worked only by appointment.

John said, "Good day, Miss Mitchell. Please have a seat and I will be with you as soon I am finished with Marquis Cornwallis." He stretched to hand the measuring tape to his seamstress, who was kneeling on the other side of the rotund client.

Peggy chose a high back, wooden chair near the fitting room. From it, she could see the gray-haired man behind the parted purple drapes. The elevated pedestal he stood on made him appear much taller than he actually was. *Could it be possible that this is the general that destroyed our home and took my father prisoner?*

She tried to steal a glance at him when he wasn't looking. She had seen a painting of General Cornwallis many years ago as a young man. He looked to be the right age to have led the British forces during the revolution. Her grandmother Margaret Mitchell described General Cornwallis often and she remembered her saying he was a large man.

Marquis Cornwallis said, "John, I want one of your top hats that have become so popular about town."

The hatter winked at Peggy, making sure she heard the comment. "The importer of the beaver pelts that I use in making the top hat is here."

"Where is he? We're the only men here," Marquis Cornwallis said.

"Miss Mitchell, from Tennessee, is the importer of our pelts from America," John revealed.

"This lovely lady is a fur trader?" Marquis Cornwallis looked at Peggy.

"It is an honor to meet you after all these years, General Cornwallis." Peggy stood, made a few steps toward the pedestal and curtsied to his lordship.

"It's been many a year since anyone called me General."

"Marquis Cornwallis is now Master-General of Ordnances for His Majesty's military forces throughout the world." John looked at Peggy. "Your Lordship, may

I introduce you to Miss Peggy Mitchell of Jonesborough, Tennessee?"

*Interesting that Willy had mentioned in his letter that he was operating under the orders of the Master-General of Ordnance!*

"It is an honor to meet you, as my grandmother has told me so much about you. You are as handsome as she told me you were." Peggy managed a pleasing smile, trying to forget the pain he had caused her family.

"Where would I have met your grandmother? If she was as attractive as her granddaughter, I am sure that I would remember her," Marquis Cornwallis said.

"I was named for my Grandmother Margaret Mitchell. It was her farm where your army was victorious during the Battle of Guilford Courthouse, fought on the fifteenth day of March during the fifth year of the Revolution in America."

"I will remember that fateful day forever." Marquis Cornwallis shook his head. "Bloodiest battle I ever saw."

"My grandmother—" Peggy started to say.

"My aide-de-camp introduced her to me the second day after the battle. I was told she stayed on the field for two days and nights tending to the wounded soldiers of both armies. I am so honored to meet her granddaughter."

"The honor is mine, Your Lordship," Peggy said.

"Please, call me Charles." He stepped off the pedestal, almost knocking the demure seamstress over, as she attempted to measure his large calf.

They were surprised at His Lordship's sudden move and stood with open mouths, watching the friendly banter, not knowing whether to continue the fitting as he talked to Peggy.

Peggy extended her hand; he held it ever so gently, as he gazed into her eyes. "I do see the resemblance to your grandmother. Is she well?"

"We lost her about ten years ago," Peggy said.

"I am sorry for your loss," Marquis Cornwallis said.

"Thank you."

"She was a feisty woman. I remember she brought whisky your father had made. She used it to barter for the release of the captured. It was the best whisky I ever tasted."

"My father is a good distiller, he uses an old family recipe that goes back hundreds of years, to when the Mitchell clan lived in Scotland," Peggy said.

The hatter cleared his throat and Marquis Cornwallis nodded to him. "Sorry about that. It's not every day that I meet someone from a war that I lost."

"I am also the nanny to William Whiddon's children. He owns Whiddon Shipping. I would like to seek your guidance in a matter of importance to his family," Peggy said.

"I know well of the Whiddons of Devon. I would be glad to help you, if I can. Would you dine with me, when John is finished? We can discuss your matter in detail." He looked at the hatter as if to say, *Are we done yet?*

"I only need one more measurement, Your Lordship," John said.

"Then let's get on with it." Marquis Cornwallis climbed back on the round pedestal.

Peggy sat down and anxiously waited for the one man in London who could possibly know where Willy was.

*\*\**

Marquis Cornwallis assisted Peggy into the impressive government carriage as the groomsman held the door. She noticed a sign on the door of the carriage that read *Master-General of the Ordnance* above a red shield with three gold cannons and three cannon balls across the top of the shield. The soldier that delivered Willy's letter and the uniformed groomsman and driver wore the same red shield on their right arms.

"Peggy, I would like to take you to my favorite dining establishment in London, near Covent Garden."

"Would that be Thomas Rule's?" Peggy asked.

"You have been to Rules then! Were you pleased with the food and service?" Marquis Cornwallis sat in the front seat of the carriage facing Peggy.

"Very much so, and I was hoping to have a chance to go again before returning to Devon," Peggy said.

Marquis Cornwallis gave the order. "Tell Ransom to take us to Rules,"

"Yes, Your Lordship." The groomsman shut the door.

The stately carriage pulled by four well-bred, dapple grey, draft horses cantered briskly through the busy streets of London. Other carriages stopped to make way for them, as if they were royalty.

"Could you please tell me what the Master-General of the Ordnance does?" Peggy asked.

"Being from America, I can understand your not knowing of my position. I am in charge of the King's army and navy. Some call me his War Lord. It is a cabinet level position. I report only to the King."

"Oh my! That would make you like our Secretary of War, John Knox," Peggy said.

"That is correct, but the British military is much larger than the colonies'," Cornwallis boasted.

"We call them states now." Peggy smiled.

"Yes, that is correct and Tennessee is the newest state."

"We became the sixteenth state last year," Peggy said.

The carriage stopped at Covent Garden near Rules; people gathered to see who was in the ornate government conveyance.

When they entered, Mr. Rule met them at the door. "Welcome, Your Lordship. I have your usual table waiting." He looked at Peggy and recognized her immediately, but using discretion, did not to let on to his Lordship they were acquainted.

"Let me introduce Miss Mitch—"

"Good to see you again, Mr. Rule, and I want to thank you personally for the loan of your box for the opera," Peggy said.

"I see no introduction is needed." Marquis Cornwallis waited for Peggy to be seated.

"Thank you." Peggy slipped into her banquet seat.

"Is there anyone in London you don't know?" Marquis Cornwallis maneuvered into a red velvet chair.

"It might seem that way, but you apparently know the only people I have met in London."

They talked about the opera, how she had met Mr. Rule through Mr. Hetherington. her pelt business and her connection to the Whiddon family. He suddenly asked, "Miss Mitchell, how can I help you?"

She explained that *Devon's Hope* should have returned weeks ago. That she was William Whiddon's nanny, and had the responsibility of his two young children and must make plans for their schooling. "Their father made arrangements for us to stay three weeks at his Cousin Agnes's boarding house. I don't know what to do . . . Should I stay or should I take them to Devon? I hope you know where the captain is and when he might return." Peggy shed a tear.

"Why would you think I should know where Captain Whiddon is?" Cornwallis asked.

Peggy reached into her bag, pulling out a white silk handkerchief and the captain's letter. She handed Willy's folded letter to Corwallis, and gently touched her moist eyes with the hanky. The marquis opened it and read the short note, folded it and handed it back to Peggy. Looking to see if anyone was listening, he murmured, "I see."

A small man with a pencil moustache and goatee sat alone at the next table, engrossed in the *London Gazette*. No one noticed as he read a week's old edition.

The waiter delivered their food. They sat quietly until they were alone again.

"I have figured out he is on a secret mission of some type. I know you can't divulge details, but I need to make plans for his children, and for my own welfare." Peggy started to cry again.

"Please, don't cry. I will be glad to inquire about his ship's activity from my Admiral of the Fleet and provide you with any information that is not confidential. For now, let's enjoy the wonderful meal that Mr. Rule's chef has prepared," Marquis Cornwallis said.

Peggy told him how the site of the Battle of Guilford Courthouse was still in the Mitchell family, and that his soldiers buried there would never be disturbed. That seemed to please him immensely. He laughed when she told him that there were people around the battlefield that thought her grandmother came back as a mongrel dog that guarded the soldier's graves.

"How old were you when that battle was fought on your grandmother's farm?" Marquis Cornwallis asked.

"I was almost ten," Peggy said.

"I am sorry you and your family had to endure the horrors of war. I have fought many battles, but I never saw such fighting as the Battle of Guilford Courthouse." Marquis Cornwallis shook his head. "I lost many good men that day."

"You won the battle," Peggy said.

"Yes—but because of it, the British lost the war."

They both sat quietly for some time, remembering the sight of the dead and wounded in the cornfields of a farm that adjoined the Courthouse of Guilford County, North Carolina.

Mr. Rule, seeing them looking gloomy, approached the table and said, "Did you enjoy your meal, Miss Mitchell and Your Lordship?"

The little man at the next table turned a page of the *Gazette* and folded it. He wrote on the folded paper in pencil. Peggy noticed the man's eyes blinked often as he read. *The poor fellow may have an eye disease,* she thought to herself.

Peggy nodded, but did not speak. Mr. Rule could tell they were both troubled. Before he left he asked Peggy, "Could I have an address to mail you an invitation for my Grand Opening of the new Rules on New Year's Eve? Marquis Cornwallis is an honored guest as it is his birthday."

"If I am still in the city. I will be here to toast your restaurant's opening and His Lordship's birthday. You may send the invitation to the Reynolds House," Peggy said.

They went directly to the waiting carriage. His Lordship had a meeting with the Admiral of the Fleet and Field Marshal of the Army. "If I can attain any information that will help you, I will deliver it to you in person." He looked out the windows suspiciously. "I fear we have created much attention, the Master-General dining with an attractive young woman half his age. I am being dropped off at the Tower. I will put you in an unmarked carriage for the ride to the Reynolds House. Our meeting and talks must be kept in the strictest confidence."

"You can trust me. Please, just get me enough information to make an intelligent decision, that's all I ask," Peggy said.

"News from a ship at sea is slow." Marquis Cornwallis climbed backwards out of the carriage. "My staff will get you home safely to your wards." He turned and spoke to his driver. Peggy could not hear their conversation.

The driver asked her to remain in the carriage while another was harnessed. Peggy realized she was waiting in the carriage barn of the Tower of London. John Hetherington told her that those who opposed the King were beheaded here. That is why Londoners call it The Bloody Tower.

His Lordship's driver appeared in civilian clothes. "We shall go now. My name is Ransom and I will be your driver to take you to the Reynolds House. If you will allow me to assist you to your carriage." Ransom helped her down onto a wooden platform to protect her from stepping in the dung of royal horses.

Once in the carriage, they proceeded out of the barn, down a lane toward the Thames, and into the woods where another carriage was waiting. Peggy was asked to get into it and wrap an army blanket around her and put on a wig of an old woman.

"Must I?" she protested.

"Miss Mitchell, we are doing this for your safety."

As they were getting in the other carriage, the Master-General's carriage pulled up with a young woman, and a large man who was not Marquis Cornwallis, a driver and a groomsman. They all exited the back gate of the palace; the lordship's carriage went one way and the two unmarked carriages turned the other. At the next crossroad, Lieutenant Ransom went straight and the other carriage quickly turned off.

"What was that all about?" Peggy asked.

"All for your safety, Miss Mitchell."

"My safety—why is my safety suddenly a concern of the military?"

"You would have to ask the Master-General that question, I am just following his orders, to get you home safely and to make sure we are not followed."

They reached the Reynolds House as a beautiful autumn sun made its final curtain call. Ransom tied off the leather reins and started to climb down to assist Peggy.

"Please don't get down—I can get out on my own, but thank you for getting me home." Peggy started to pull the blanket off.

"Please wear them into the house for me and walk like an old woman if you can," Ransom said.

"If I am an old woman, you best help me off this buggy," Peggy said.

He jumped down and took Peggy's hand and assisted her. The lieutenant waited as she made it to the front door of Reynolds House.

# Chapter Seventeen

## A Star is Born

Peggy heard the voice of a very accomplished soprano singing a cappella in the upstairs parlor. *Whoever it is must be a visiting performer of the Royal Opera,* who often stayed at the Reynolds House. Excited at the thought of meeting a well-known vocalist, Peggy opened the front door quietly, removed the wig and army blanket and placed them over the first banister post. Drawn toward the beautiful, female voice singing "Ava Maria" in Latin, she slowly ascended the stairs, trying not to disturb the performance, but anxious to see who was singing.

The singer stopped just as Peggy topped the stairs. The small audience clapped excitedly. She carefully entered the parlor, joining them in their applause. William was exclaiming, "Bravo!" in his high-pitched voice—as he had heard men at the Royal Opera do. Peggy was proud that he recognized a great operatic singer when he heard one. The singer took a long bow to catch her breath. When she raised her beautiful head of red hair, it was Agnes. The audience consisted of William, Elizabeth, and residents of the house. Agnes turned red in the face with all the adulation.

"I didn't realize you were an opera singer. You are wonderful!" Peggy gave her a hug. The children, seeing Peggy for the first time, hugged their nanny and Peggy held them tight.

"I only sing for my church and friends, I have always loved to sing," Agnes managed to say between long breaths.

"More—more!" The small gathering said.

"I must fix something for Peggy to eat," Agnes said.

"I'm not hungry. Please sing some more?"

"Let me catch my breath first," Agnes said.

She sang two more songs. The audience gave Agnes a rousing ovation, said good night and meandered toward their rooms.

Agnes said, "The children were worried about their father. I know that music is the best remedy for sadness. My mother sang to me when I was unhappy, then one day I began singing for her." Agnes watched the children going down the hall. "Let's have some tea. We need to talk."

"That sounds good. Do you have any crumpets?" Peggy asked.

"I think I can find something for your sweet tooth." Agnes noticed the blanket on the banister and picked it up. "Whose is this?" She asked, as she held up the wool army blanket.

"I was cold, the driver loaned it to me," Peggy said.

"And this?" Agnes held up the hairpiece, looking at Peggy for an explanation that didn't come.

The women sat at the dining table not saying a word — just sipping tea and eating crumpets each in their own thoughts, but sharing the same worries.

Peggy broke the silence. "Agnes, no one knows where Willy is. I know he was to unload cargo first in Trinidad. I have someone working on getting a report from there about whether he arrived or not."

"Hopefully, we will know soon." Agnes poured more tea. "I received a letter from Aunt Hanna, and a postscript from Willy's mother. They are expecting the children home, as the school year will be starting. From her letter, they assume you are en route to Plymouth as we speak," Agnes said.

"Agnes, can we stay here until we know what's happened to *Devon's Hope*? I know Willy arranged for just three weeks. I have money and can pay our room and board," Peggy said.

"I am not worried about that." Agnes looked beyond Peggy. "Look who is still up."

William and Elizabeth came in, dressed for bed. Elizabeth sidled up against Peggy. William hugged Agnes and said, "can I *please* have a crumpet?"

"There is one for each of you and a glass of milk. It will help you sleep." Agnes passed the crumpet tray and got up to get them each a glass of milk.

"Did you find out anything about father?" William looked at Peggy.

"No, but I found someone that is going to find out and let us know." Peggy put her arm around the boy's waist. "We will know soon."

Agnes came in with milk and more crumpets and said, "These are for you."

The children took their crumpets and milk and each took a place at the large table.

"I must make a decision and I would like you, William and Elizabeth, to help me make that decision. Your father said he would be back in three weeks. It will soon be six weeks since he left. Should we go back to Devon or stay and wait for him here in London?" Peggy looked at them for an answer.

The children looked at each other, not uttering a word but obviously in deep thought.

Agnes looked at the children and said, "I think Peggy wants to know what you think your father would want us to do?"

"I think father would want us to stay put, until he returns," William said.

"Really?" Peggy looked at Elizabeth.

"Stay put," Elizabeth said.

"Then that is settled, we will stay put in London until we hear from your father otherwise . . . is that agreed?"

They both nodded yes.

"Then, we start school Monday morning." Peggy felt relieved that Agnes and the children helped make the decision.

Agnes offered Sir Joshua's library and study for a classroom. All the teacher needed was a blackboard and chalk. During the inventory of the books in the large collection of Sir Joshua's library, Peggy found copies of all of Mary Wollstonecraft's works, including her first, *The Vindication of the Rights of Man,* which had been well read and had many interesting comments written in the margins. None of the comments were negative in any way toward the author. Agnes and her housekeeper were busy giving the already-clean room a proper dusting for the opening of school. Agnes fussed about excitedly, proud of being a part of her young cousins' education.

"Agnes, would you recognize your Uncle Joshua's handwriting if you saw it?" Peggy showed the book to her.

"Of course—why do you ask?" Agnes wiped her hands on her apron, looked at the open book. "That's my uncle's handwriting for sure. You will find his thoughts scribbled in many of his books." She took it from Peggy, looked at her and asked, "This is the Wollstonecraft woman's book?"

"Yes, and your uncle has all of her works," Peggy said.

Agnes looked up from the book and said, "You don't mean it?"

Peggy pointed to them on the shelf and said, "Here they are."

"Oh, but he and Sir Edmond spoke of her so harshly." Agnes shook her head.

"Sometimes men, out of fear, speak unkindly of the writings of those who challenge their dominance, especially when written by a woman. I think you owe it to yourself to read her works." Peggy closed the book and handed it to Agnes.

Agnes opened it and started reading as she walked down the hall, not to be seen again until shortly before the midday meal.

Peggy made a shopping list of supplies and created a curriculum that included outings, as weather permitted, to the many museums and art galleries. London was a wonderful place to study the arts and history. Agnes agreed to teach music six hours per week and give individual instruction on the piano in the parlor.

Weeks passed. Peggy and Agnes read every word of every paper seeking news of the war. Details of the Royal Navy mutinies were becoming public knowledge, and it appeared Fleet Admiral Howe had his share of rebellious officers and seamen. The London papers reported that Captain Pigot of HMS *Hermione* was killed and thrown overboard and the crew sailed the ship to La Guaira, surrendering it to the Spanish Navy. They thought that *Devon's Hope* was somewhere in Spanish waters, but were careful to never discuss such things in front of the children.

As Peggy worked with the children on penmanship, an unmarked carriage, its cabin enclosed, pulled into the circular drive. Lieutenant Ransom was driving and not in uniform, but Peggy recognized him. He climbed down from the high seat above the cab of the carriage. She noticed him looking toward the park and Peggy saw what he was looking for. Two cavalrymen were at the corner of each street into the block square park. William said, "Look, soldiers on horseback."

"Yes, I see them . . . You both continue practicing your penmanship." Peggy went downstairs. Agnes was at the door, tears in her eyes, looking at the dark carriage, afraid of the news that it might bring. "Will you stay with the children? They are practicing their cursive letters in ink." Peggy felt anguish as she watched Lieutenant Ransom approaching the front door.

"I hope you have brought good news." Peggy looked for any emotion and there was none.

"Miss Mitchell, His Lordship would like to talk to you."

"It's about time." Peggy started for the carriage and turned, "I need my wrap."

"No you don't, please just get in the carriage quickly." Ransom opened the door, almost pushing her into the dark cab, the leather window curtains down and tightly secured at the bottom.

"Good day, Miss Mitchell. Word on Captain Whiddon has come." Marquis Cornwallis handed her a letter and motioned for her to set on the leather padded bench facing him.

"He is alive!" Peggy held the letter to her bosom. "Thank God, he is alive."

"If all goes well, Captain Whiddon will be back by Christmas."

"How can I ever thank you?" Peggy leaned toward his Lordship.

"Find it in your heart to forgive me for the pain and suffering my army inflicted upon your family at the Battle of Guilford Courthouse," Marquis Cornwallis said.

"I already have."

"Thank you, Peggy." He touched her arm. "I must go. No one is to know we talked or I delivered this letter," Cornwallis said.

Peggy climbed out backwards as Ransom assisted her down.

"Thank you, Ransom."

"The honor of knowing you will always be mine," Ransom said.

Peggy walked into the house. Fortunately, the residents were at their work. It was just Agnes, Peggy, and the children at home. She opened the letter and read it as she walked.

"Is everything all right?" Agnes asked.

"Yes, Willy is alive and will be home before Christmas."

"Such good news! Let's tell the children!" Agnes said.

"Tell us what?" William looked over the railing down into the foyer.

"We received word from your father and he will be home by Christmas." Peggy said.

The children ran down the stairs. William said, "I want to read father's letter!"

"Me, too," Elizabeth said.

There was no way to get the excited children back to their studies. Peggy decided to cancel today's lesson and take them shopping. First stop was the hat shop to check on William's top hat and to order another for Willy as a Christmas present.

"Good day, Peggy," John said as he finished blocking a felt derby. "What can I do for you?"

"How much is a top hat?" she asked.

"One like I am making for William, from Tennessee beaver pelts?"

"Yes, I want them to match."

"Five pounds," John said.

"And for three top hats?"

"I could make you a deal of twelve pounds on three hats."

Peggy gave the hatter fifteen pounds and said, "I want one for Willy in time for Christmas."

"Mr. Whiddon is coming home for Christmas then?" John said.

"We . . . hope so, and if he does I wish to have a gift for him." Peggy knew she should not have said anything about Willy or his travels. In her excitement she let it slip. It was too late. The children looked at her as if she betrayed their father. She hoped they didn't mention the letter and they didn't.

"Would you know the size of hat he takes?"

Peggy, mad at herself and agitated said, "You should have his size as you made that ridiculous captain's hat he wears."

"Ridiculous!? No captain has ever been arrested for wearing one of my beaver captain's hats." He donned his top hat and tapped its top and said. "It was the top hat I was arrested for wearing and now is so popular."

John grinned from ear to ear. "Now, who is the other lucky fellow getting a Hetherington top hat for Christmas?"

"I wish to pay for Marquis Cornwallis's top hat he has on order, and when you deliver it, please enclose this card. Now, can you promise me all three will be ready by Christmas?"

"That is a handsome gift for His Lordship."

"Yes, it is. But for the warrior that spared my family, it is an appropriate gift, don't you think?"

"It certainly is."

"We must go now, much to do." Peggy rushed to avoid any more questions from this hatter.

Once outside the hat shop, Peggy said, "Thank you, William and Elizabeth for not saying anything about your father's letter. We should not reveal anything about your father until he is safely home."

"We know," William said and Elizabeth nodded in agreement.

"How would you know that?"

"Never divulge the ship's whereabouts." William put his forefinger to his lips. "That's what father taught us."

Peggy looked at them, smiling an approving smile, impressed that they had learned so early in life to keep secrets that concerned the family's safety or business. How different from the children of Knob Creek, where there were no secrets, and everyone knew their neighbor's affairs.

*** 

Jimmy Witherspoon looked out the window of the one-room log cabin that housed the Hebron Church and School, watching the babbling waters of Knob Creek, pondering his options. He missed not having Peggy to discuss important decisions that concerned his career as a minister. He could write, but couldn't wait for an answer to make the decision. He promised the elders of the Mount Bethel Congregation in Greeneville an answer by the first of December. They had offered him the minister's position.

He knew most of the congregation from preaching there in the absence of their minister. It would pay much better and he would be provided a very comfortable parsonage that was built for the previous pastor and his wife. Hebron only provided a bunk and meals in the Mitchell's bunk house, which was adequate for his needs.

Jimmy was concerned whether seventeen-year-old Ibby and her fifteen-year-old sister Rebeckah could give the children of Knob Creek a proper education. They knew the curriculum and had helped him and Peggy instruct the basics of reading, writing, and arithmetic. The reverend feared the Mitchell sisters wouldn't be able to maintain discipline. Several of the students were their age, and five their siblings; the others were either cousins or neighbor children they had grown up with. Not a good situation for a one-room school.

"Working on your next sermon, Reverend?" Adam Sr. asked from the open window.

"No, just trying to make a decision," Jimmy said.

"You want to talk about it?" Adam asked.

"Yes, I do."

"Come let's take a walk and we can talk."

"I will be right out." Jimmy pulled the window in and latched it as Adam struggled to close the door behind them.

"Tomorrow, I am going to fix that door, now that I am feeling better."

"I am glad you are getting back on your feet. You're looking like the old Adam Mitchell. How is Elizabeth?"

"She is better, but just doesn't have any strength yet. Hasn't been out of the house since we were sick," Adam said.

"You're lucky that Dr. Chester happened by when he did. I saw what cholera did to the poor widow Sutherland." Jimmy shook his head.

"I wish I could have done more for her. I didn't realize what she had. I thought she had a cold," Adam said.

"You and Elizabeth are the only people that I have ever known to survive it."

"God just wasn't ready for us, I guess." Adam bent down to pet his dog, who came for a little attention. "Now, what is bothering you, Jimmy?" He threw a stick in the water and the dog went in after it.

Jimmy explained the offer and was surprised that Adam knew of it and had used his influence with friends at Mount Bethel to ensure he got the job.

"Then you want me to take it?" Jimmy asked.

"Not unless you want to, but it could be a long while before another pulpit comes available around this part of the state." He threw the stick again for the dog. "The elders expressed concern that you were not married." They stopped under the large cypress tree. "I told them you and Ibby were courting."

"You did? Do you approve of my courting Ibby?" Jimmy looked at Adam.

"I had hoped that you and Peggy would marry, but now that she is so far away, I don't think that will ever happen. If you and Ibby were to marry, I would be proud. I have watched you grow into a man and now a fine preacher. You are a part of this family, whether you marry into it or not."

"I am honored you feel that way," Jimmy said.

"Are you going to take the position?" Adam looked for an answer.

"What about the students of Hebron? Do you think Ibby and Rebeckah can handle them alone?" Jimmy asked.

"I have thought about that and William and I will be available to keep order, if needed," Adam said.

"That was my only concern. Yes I am going to take it."

"That's good." Adam put his arm around Jimmy "Come, dinner should be ready and this old man is hungry as a bear."

During dinner, Jimmy announced he would be accepting the position as pastor of the Mount Bethel Church.

Everyone was happy except Ibby who said nothing, but her face displayed her displeasure.

Jimmy waited for Ibby, who usually joined him at the flat rock after the dinner table was clean and the dishes put away.

Ibby came and sat down next to Jimmy, both hands on the rock and her arms rigid. Neither said a word, they just stared at the pond as if they thought it may suddenly disappear. Ibby bent down, picked up a rock, threw it into the water and then said, "So, you'll be moving to Greeneville?"

"Yes, it was not an easy decision to make. I will miss you and your family."

Ibby threw another rock in the pond but much harder. "I can't believe you just accepted the position without asking me!"

"I can understand your being upset."

"Upset! I can't remember being this mad—at anyone!" Ibby said.

"I am sorry that I didn't confide in you. I only made the decision this afternoon after discussing it with your father."

"You and father made this decision without saying a word to me?"

"It just happened. Adam brought it up. He thought it was a great opportunity for me. A larger church and living quarters. Greeneville is only a day's ride away. I will be back often to visit."

"Visit? I thought we were a couple. Couples should be together, not a day's ride away from one another."

"Ibby, don't you understand? This is my chance to establish myself in a church with living quarters and a salary that will support a family. This is what Reverend Doak and Hezekiah Balch prepared me for. Once I have proven myself worthy, I can start thinking about getting married and starting a family."

"You go to Greeneville and prove yourself, I may not be waiting for you when you are ready." Ibby rose to her feet and hastily took the trail toward her quarters.

Jimmy laid back and gazed at the stars and wondered if Peggy saw the same stars and moon in London that reflected on the pond at Knob Creek.

## Chapter Eighteen
### Home from War

As his family and Peggy worshipped at the nearby Anglican church, a hack delivered Willy and his baggage to the Reynolds House. He was welcomed into the empty house by the smells of his cousin Agnes's culinary delights. He found a tray of scones on the buffet and chose an apple and cinnamon tart. Willy left his sea bag in the foyer, not knowing which room he would be staying in.

\*\*\*

This was the first church that Peggy had ever attended that wasn't Presbyterian. She had attended every Sunday with Agnes and the children since arriving in London. Through Agnes she had made friends with many Anglicans and enjoyed worshipping with them. The seven-hundred-year-old greystone cathedral built during Roman times impressed her. She marveled at the elevated choir loft, and the raised pulpit that gave the appearance that the minister was preaching from heaven. Agnes, the church choir director, led the children's choir in a medley of Christmas carols. Then she sang, "The Virgin Mary had a Baby Boy" in her beautiful soprano voice. That concluded the music portion of the service.

Anxious to see Peggy, Agnes and his children, Willy made the short walk to the church of his mother's family where he had often worshipped as a boy. Seeing the church brought back memories of his childhood, but they were like cloudy dreams with very little detail and no color.

The end of services near, Willy anxiously took a position in front of the gothic cathedral, still in uniform. When the large wooden doors laden with Christmas holly were pushed open, worshippers exited into the rays of sunlight onto a large courtyard of cobblestone and well-manicured grass.

He saw Peggy and the children waiting for Agnes near the door and he worked his way through the worshippers, who were happily sharing fellowship. Peggy recognized the obtrusive purple plume on Willy's hat bobbing through the crowd. Seeing him coming up the steps, she alerted the children and everyone near. "There is your father!" Peggy pointed toward the feathered hat moving toward them.

William and Elizabeth ran screaming to Willy who scooped them up, one in each arm. He stumbled and nearly fell, not realizing how much they had grown. Their father wore a black patch over his right eye.

"What's wrong with your eye, Father?" William asked.

"I lost it during a battle at sea."

"Did it hurt?" Elizabeth touched the patch gently.

"At first, it did."

Peggy heard the comment and, touched Willy's shoulder, "I'm sorry you lost an eye, but I'm happy you're home." She noticed a blank stare from Willy—a look she had seen before, long ago in the eyes of a soldier injured in the Battle of Guilford County.

Willy put the children down and gave Peggy a hug. "I missed you, Peggy."

She pulled Willy toward her, kissing him passionately, without any thought to those around them.

She pulled back when she realized Willy was not as demonstrative in his greetings.

"I missed you, and we've all been worried about you."

The congregation applauded, recognizing that a family had been reunited with a wounded officer of the Royal Navy.

Agnes heard the commotion, and seeing her cousin, she hurried to him and they embraced. "We've been so worried. W—what happened to your eye?"

"It's a long story, I'll tell you all about it when we get home." Willy looked toward the Reynolds House. The crowd, realizing it was Agnes's cousin, the sea captain they had been praying for, made way for her family.

The children skipped along, occasionally grabbing their father's hand to hurry him up, chattering all the way about the adventures they had encountered in London. Their father didn't seem to be listening, his thoughts elsewhere.

***

Agnes and Peggy set the table for the traditional dinner of shepherd's pie.

William asked, "Why is it a tradition to have shepherd's pie on the Sunday before Christmas Eve?"

Agnes smoothed a wrinkle out of the Christmas tablecloth. "Mother always said it warmed the cockles of your heart and gets us in the spirit for singing Christmas carols, which we'll do tonight."

Willy looked at Agnes. "I seem to remember the caroling we did as children. Yes, we had fun, didn't we?"

Agnes saw something in his blank expression and the odd way he looked at her—as if he was afraid. *His question was like he wanted her to validate that they did have fun caroling as children.*

Agnes, talking over her shoulder, headed for the kitchen. "Mother so loved caroling, I've made it a tradition at Reynolds House to host the carolers afterwards."

Peggy looked at Willy. "I'm really glad that you brought us here. I like your cousin and enjoy being around her."

Agnes returned with the steaming hot cast iron pot from the hearth of the kitchen fireplace and placed it on a trivet.

"It looks wonderful and smells scrumptious." Peggy inhaled its aroma.

"I can't wait to taste it." Willy rubbed his hands eagerly. "The shepherd's pie must have been what I smelled when I arrived."

"Well, take a seat and let's eat." Agnes pointed toward the dining table.

Peggy heard a knock at the front door. "I'll get the door, please start without me."

John, the hatter, was at the door with Peggy's order. "Please come in."

John handed her two hat boxes.

"While I take these to my room, why don't you say hello to Willy, who just arrived this morning?" She whispered, "He lost his right eye at sea. I don't know any details."

When Peggy returned to the dining room, John sat at the table eating and telling the story of Willy's fall from his horse. She noticed that Agnes seemed to be enthralled with John Hetherington's story, or was it John? Peggy had never seen Agnes show interest toward any man before, and the hatter seemed equally interested in her.

As the hatter told the story of Willy's accident last summer, Willy didn't seem to remember much about it, asking questions that he should have known. In fact, he seemed surprised to hear about his horse throwing him.

After John finished his story, he turned toward Peggy. "I made a delivery to Mr. Rule earlier, and he asked if you would be attending his grand opening on New Year's Eve."

"If Willy is up to it," she looked from Agnes to John, "and Agnes is invited, I plan to go."

"Agnes could come as my guest, and we could make it a grand evening." John looked at Agnes.

Her freckled face had turned the color of a ripe peach.

"Who is this Rule fellow having a party?" Willy asked.

Everyone looked at Willy with expressions of surprise.

"You remember Thomas Rule. We've eaten at his restaurant many times. He's opening a new restaurant on New Year's Eve."

William bounced in his chair. "What about us?"

"I don't think children would enjoy an evening in a public house." Willy said.

William looked disappointed. Peggy knew he wished to go to the party and wear his new top hat.

She whispered, "I'll talk to your father."

The children seemed excited about the possibility of going to the grand opening of the new Rule's.

"It is going to be quite a party." John looked at Agnes. "You will go with me, won't you?"

"I would love to go with you, on one condition."

"What condition would that be?"

"That you stay and go caroling with us around the square this evening."

"I'd love to go caroling with you, Agnes."

She picked up the tray of crumpets. "Would you care for an apple tart?"

The others excused themselves, but John and Agnes, engrossed in conversation, hardly noticed.

"Come, Father, we have a surprise for you. Aunt Agnes has taught us to accompany each other on the piano. We have prepared a special piano recital for your homecoming."

"You play the piano now?" Willy asked.

Elizabeth turned her head sideways. "Father,we've been taking lessons for years. You know that." Willy's face turned pink, and he looked down at the floor.

As his children played a duet, striking the keys with near perfection, Willy's chest swelled with pride. Peggy, sitting beside him, noticed a small teardrop developing in his good eye. She moved her arm under his and gave him a pat with the other hand. He put his free hand on hers. They sat quietly listening, the only audience to the children's performance.

A group of carolers gathered around the open wooden gazebo in the middle of Leicester Square Park. They were dressed warmly for the clear, cold night that was fast spreading its winter solstice shadow over the Village of Leicester.

Newly-elected Lord Mayor William Bellamy took advantage of the opportunity to meet his constituents. The annual caroling event had grown from a small group of Sir Joshua's friends to a dozen teams of six to eight carolers. They would stroll the square singing hymns and carols of Christmas. The neighbors looked forward to the musical parade that made its way through the park and around the square.

Afterwards, everyone would gather at the Reynolds House for tea and crumpets and socializing. Willy would just as soon be alone with his family, but knew the children would enjoy the caroling and party afterwards. It seemed to him London had so much more to offer his children than Devon.

John Hetherington was the last guest to leave. Peggy had put the children to bed earlier. She now sat next to Willy on the settee in the downstairs parlor. Agnes joined them, sitting in an arm chair.

"Agnes, you and John seem to have much in common," Peggy said.

"Not really, but I enjoyed his company very much. I asked him to join us Christmas Eve. I hope you don't mind?"

"I like John—he's a gentleman, like Willy." She nudged Willy.

"He and Willy have been good friends for years.

"Then we should have a wonderful Christmas together," Peggy said.

Agnes leaned forward. "Willy, I'm so thankful you're home. I could stay up all night talking to you, but it's been a long day, and I must get my rest. I'll see you and Peggy at breakfast. For tonight, just take the extra bed in William's room." She put her hands on the arms of the chair and slowly pulled herself up.

"Thank you, Agnes, for everything you've done for us." Willy rose and kissed her cheek.

"You're family. Family takes care of one another."

"That's right. Go now and get some rest. I'll visit with Peggy a while before retiring."

Peggy rose from the velvet settee and hugged Agnes. "Thank you for being such a good friend."

"You're family, too, Peggy."

"Good night, Agnes."

"Good night, Peggy. Willy, it's so good to have you here for Christmas." Agnes waved, walking slowly toward her room.

Willy returned her wave.

"When is Christmas?" Willy motioned for Peggy to sit beside him.

"Next Sunday is Christmas Eve." Peggy moved close to Willy.

"When is Christmas day?"

"The next day, which is next Monday."

"I can't thank you enough for staying with my children. I had no idea I would be gone so long." Willy held her hand as they sat on the settee deep in their own thoughts.

Peggy laid her head on his shoulder. "What happened?"

"About what?"

"Your trip taking so long."

"My ship and I were pressed into service by the Royal Navy."

"What do you mean, 'pressed?'"

"The ship and crew were commandeered by the Royal Navy to support the war effort. We were told that we were sailing to Trinidad. Once underway, I was ordered to the North Sea."

"Why?" Peggy asked.

"My ship's mission all along was to provision the north fleet. The manifest to Trinidad was just a ploy."

"That explains all the secrecy," Peggy said.

"We sailed to the Texel, where we off-loaded the gin and munitions on the waiting warships. When our cargo holds were empty, we sailed to Great Yarmouth, a fishing village on the coast of Norfolk and the home port for the North Sea Fleet." Willy grew silent and stared off into space.

Peggy snuggled a little closer. After giving him several seconds to continue, she asked, "Then what happened?"

"*Devon's Hope* was accompanied by two frigates and three ships of the line. The crew quickly collected what food and supplies were available in the small village. Mostly smelly herring, which I shall never eat again." Willy scrunched up his face as if he smelled the worst smell in the world.

"What were you going to do with this smelly herring?"

"The sailors maintaining the blockade of the Dutch fleet since early September were anxiously awaiting anything edible. Luckily, our argosy reached them just as the last of their rations were depleted. It was our fifth week at sea since sailing from London," Willy said.

"The fifth week." Peggy sat up and looked at Willy. "That's when I met Marquis Cornwallis and asked for his help. I knew something had happened to you." Peggy put her head back on Willy's shoulder.

"You asked the Master-General for help?" Willy turned to face Peggy, and she looked up at him. "You actually met Marquis Cornwallis?"

"Yes, but please finish telling me about the battle and how you were injured," She turned her head back to his shoulder. "Then I will tell you how I met him."

The children heard Peggy and their father discussing the battle and came to the parlor in their long, woolen sleep shirts and sat on the floor in front of the settee. Agnes heard everyone up and came to hear Willy tell the story of the battle that cost him an eye.

Agnes placed a log on the smoldering embers of the fireplace. "It's bad luck to let the yule fire burn out, you know."

After Agnes was seated, Willy continued his story. "Then on the morning of the eleventh of October, the warships escorting us had sailed to within 100 meters of several Dutch frigates that we thought were British."

"How could you mistake Dutch flags for British?" Peggy asked.

"The weather was miserable, visibility so low we couldn't see their flags. Our ships were at the rear of the enemy fleet before we knew it."

William stood in front of his father holding his hands out palm up. "Tell me what happened to your eye, Father."

"Sit down, and I'll tell you." William sat down but leaned forward, looking at his father intently.

"We had unknowingly surrounded the enemy in the Gulf of Texel. They opened fire around midmorning, and by noon British and Dutch ships were within twenty meters of each other, going at one another with their cannons." Willy took a deep breath and reached for Peggy's hand. "The smoke was so thick that at times I couldn't see the pulpit rail or the crow's nest just above my head. The navy signalman assigned to my ship was in the crow's nest trying to see signals from the flagship far to the front of the battle—a distance of 500 meters." Willy paused and looked around the room as if he were seeing something very different.

Peggy squeezed his hand in encouragement.

"Our cannons were firing away at a Dutch ship when I heard an incoming cannon ball. I looked up and the last thing I remember was the foremast coming down on me." Willy's voice cracked. "I was taken to my quarters where I lay unconscious for three days. In addition to my injuries, three of my crew were killed and eight injured."

Peggy shuddered and moved closer to Willy. In her mind's eye, she saw soldiers lying dead in a cornfield rather than seamen dead on a ship.

"Ordnance Officer Lieutenant O'Day, who the Royal Navy sent to commandeer my ship, was killed standing beside me and two of his eighteen gunnery men killed and six wounded." Willy looked up at the ceiling.

After a silence that seemed to go on forever, William asked, "Father, what about *Devon's Hope?*"

"Fortunately, the hull received no major damage. The foremast was completely destroyed, and she was towed to the Yarmouth shipyard for repairs, which could take up to a year."

Peggy shook herself as if trying to shake off a bad memory. "What was this battle about?"

Willy looked at Peggy as if he couldn't believe she asked such a question. "Honor and British control of the seas."

Peggy sat quietly, contemplating Willy's answer. *Ships destroyed, men killed and wounded . . . for honor and control! I don't understand.*

"How did you get back to London?" Agnes asked.

"On a confiscated Dutch ship fitted out for transporting the wounded."

"Did you know we were in London waiting for you?" Peggy asked.

"No, but I knew the letter I wrote you was going to London first by dispatch. I am surprised you stayed. I would have thought that William and Elizabeth would have wanted to go home," Willy said.

"They made the decision to stay put. I gave them the option of going back to Devon or staying. William and Elizabeth chose to stay until you returned."

"I am glad, because I will be staying in London for a while."

"Then we can finish our school year here." Peggy looked for the children's reaction, but they were asleep on the floor.

"I will get William. Can you manage Elizabeth?" Willy asked.

"Yes, and I think it's time for us all to get some rest." Peggy looked at Agnes, who was about to fall asleep in her chair.

*** 

Agnes and her housekeeper were up early and had already milked the cow and gathered eggs. Having tended the fireplaces, they were preparing breakfast for the family. The permanent boarders were away from the city for the Christmas holidays, which gave her family the run of the house. Agnes had not had the company of family in many years. This year, Christmas would be extra special; she not only had her family, but an interested suitor as well. She was happy and it showed as Agnes hurried about her chores smiling and laughing, sometimes breaking out in a favorite song.

Willy had business at the war department. He needed to file a claim for damage to *Devon's Hope* and invoice the Royal Navy for his ship's service. Then he hoped to see a doctor about a prosthetic eye made of porcelain. A naval doctor at the hospital in Great Yarmouth had recommended he consider one for aesthetic purposes. He mentioned it to Peggy, who asked to accompany him to learn more about this modern medical miracle. Concerned about his frequent lapses of memory, she thought someone should go with him.

# Chapter Nineteen
## Appalachian Winter

Adam Mitchell sat at the teacher's desk of the one-room schoolhouse, watching the fire as it began to smoke, then flicker. He had placed a wad of kindling on the hot coals, taken from the family fireplace. Carrying the burning embers to the schoolhouse in the rusty coal bucket was easier than starting a fire from scratch. Orange flames began to lick at the hickory logs, meticulously arranged to ignite into a roaring fire. Adam, headmaster and church elder, had already shoveled mounds of snow from the door.

The small, glass panes in the windows were coated with thick ice. Snow drifts threatened to block the little daylight they provided. Adam lit lamps to augment the natural light.

Knob Creek had frozen over and chunks of ice broken from it were thawing in wooden buckets next to the fireplace. Water was kept handy in the event the fireplace got out of control and to provide drinking water for the school. It had been snowing since school let out on Friday. The students who braved the blowing wind and ice, including his five youngest children, would have a warm fire to greet them. Smoke from the chimney sent a signal to all that school would be open as usual.

Before Adam's daughters Ibby and Rebeckah rang the school bell, he would try to answer Peggy's letter. The heat now sufficient in the log structure to melt ink, Adam took a quill he made from the feather of a peacock, dabbed the point gently in the cut-glass ink well, and wrote.

*Miss Peggy Mitchell*
*Care Of Whiddon Estates*
*Plympton, England*


*My Dearest Peg,*
*We received your letter and are most disheartened that you will not be with us for Christmas. This will be the first Christmas without our loving daughter since her birth.*

*I don't dare tell your mother, but as much as I miss you, I am proud of you and a bit envious that you have sailed the Atlantic to England. I always dreamed of the adventure of my grandparents when they risked all to venture to Pennsylvania from Ireland.*

*A negro man, named Nathan, brought Mr. Jackson home. He had delivered your horse to Philadelphia as you had asked. When Mr. Cohen said you were in England he decided to deliver the horse to Jake's stable in Jonesborough.*

*To make sure you received him, Jake brought him to me. Mr. Jackson looks healthy and happy to be home.*

*Jimmy has accepted the position of pastor of the Bethel Church in Greeneville starting next month. We are proud of him.*

*Reverends Witherspoon, Doak, Balch, and I will tend to the faithful at Hebron Church, in the absence of a full-time pastor. Your sisters Ibby and Rebeckah continue to teach the children.*

*Dr. Chester donated enough glass (surplus from the inn) that I could add five more windows to the one we had. This lets in much more light for studying and worshipping.*

*As it is one week till Christmas, it might be Spring before you receive this letter. Know that you are loved and missed by all.*


*Your Father,*
*Adam Mitchell*

*Knob Creek, Tennessee*
*18-December-1797*

\*\*\*

Peggy sat on a wooden bench in the busy hallway of the war office, fascinated by all the comings and goings of uniformed men. They seemed to be in such a hurry, like the farmers of Knob Creek trying to gather their crops before a rain. She patiently waited while Willy dealt with a naval disbursement officer.

Lieutenant Ransom, walking down the hall, recognized Peggy. "Good morning Miss Mitchell."

"Ransom, it is good to see you again."

"Are you here to see the Marquis?" the lieutenant asked.

"No, I am here with Captain Whiddon, who is here on business," she answered.

"I just assumed . . . since you are sitting right outside his office."

"I had no idea. I knew his office was somewhere in the Tower of London. I didn't know where."

Willy came out of the disbursement office and seeing the uniformed officer talking to Peggy asked, "Is everything all right?"

Peggy stood to introduce the two. "Everything is fine. Captain Whiddon, meet Lieutenant Ransom, aide-de-camp to Master-General Cornwallis."

"It is an honor to meet you, Captain Whiddon, after all I have heard about you."

"Really?" Willy said.

"Peggy, would you and the captain like to say hello to the Master-General? I know he wishes to speak to you, as he mentioned calling on you this morning." Ransom looked at Peggy and said, "Please wait just a moment for me to get him."

"Certainly, we can wait." Peggy looked at Willy, who looked confused.

Ransom went in the office and came out with the Master-General of the Ordnance. Marquis Cornwallis, elegantly dressed in civilian clothes, wore a navy blue woolen coat and top hat. He held his leather gloves clenched in his left fist as if he would be going out in the cold. Ransom now held a leather attaché embossed in the familiar MGO emblem. It was attached to Ransom's wrist by a chain and lock. *Must be some important business in that case*, Peggy thought.

"Peggy Mitchell, I am so happy you are here, so that I might thank you in person for this magnificent top hat that was delivered this morning by its maker, John Hetherington." Cornwallis gently tapped its top and bowed toward Peggy.

"You are welcome." Peggy curtsied. "A top hat is very becoming on you. I am honored that you will be wearing a hat made from one of my beaver pelts."

"I will think of you every time I put it on my head. And, by the way, I will be wearing it to Rules New Year's Eve. I understand from John that you will be there."

"Yes, we will . . . Marquis Cornwallis, may I introduce Captain William Whiddon?"

The Master-General grasped Willy's hand and shook it vigorously. "So glad to meet you, Captain Whiddon. I know well of your family and Whiddon Shipping."

"The pleasure is mine, Your Lordship," Willy said.

"You have served your country well. I am aware of your sacrifices and injuries suffered during the Battle of Camperdown, and my condolences on the loss of your men."

"I appreciate your concerns, sir."

"You realize this was a most significant victory for the Royal Navy." Cornwallis said.

"I was told that at North Sea Headquarters, sir," Willy replied.

"King George is preparing a special ceremony at St. Paul's Cathedral this Saturday to honor the ship captains in the battle." The marquis continued, "You are a war hero, young man, and will be receiving a gold medal presented by the Prime Minister at a joint session of both houses of Parliament when the Battle of Camperdown medals are struck."

"I am honored to have served my country, Your Lordship, and look forward to receiving the medal."

"What brings you to the war department today, Captain?"

"I have claims for my ship's service and the damages it sustained in the battle." Willy explained.

"Ransom, please see what you can do to help expedite Captain Whiddon's claims in this quagmire of bureaucracy."

"Will do, Sir." Ransom nodded.

"We have a meeting with His Majesty to plan Saturday's event. Ransom will contact you about the details." Marquis Cornwallis pointed toward the door, where two armed escorts awaited them.

Willy stood looking at Peggy, trying to take in all that had happened in the last five minutes. "What was that all about?"

"I think you were just assigned a solicitor, who just happens to be the aide-de-camp of the highest ranking military officer in the United Kingdom, and that you will be honored as a hero by your government." Peggy grabbed Willy's arm and led him out of the offices of war.

Willy stopped and looked at Peggy. "You gave him a top hat?"

She beamed back at him. "Yes, I did . . . Did you like it?"

"I did but . . . you gave the Marquis a—Why?"

"He personally delivered your letter to me."

"Really?"

"Yes, he did . . . For helping me, I wanted to give him a proper gift. Please don't tell anyone."

"They found the office of the eye doctor who was recommended to Willy. The sign out front read "Ocularist." The doctor assured them he could produce a porcelain eye piece that would match his good eye. The process would take several weeks with an artist who painted porcelain vases, as well as eyes. The doctor would sculpt the eyepiece to fit over his blind eye and under the eyelid. An appointment was made with the artist for the first sitting, a week after Christmas.

Peggy, seeing for the first time the wound, which was still a nasty mess, realized how serious the blow to Willy's head was. He had not wanted her to see the damage, but she insisted, reminding him she was a medical practitioner, and had seen many wounds before. *No wonder Willy is having memory lapses.*

Peggy had finished her Christmas shopping. Pressed into war, Willy had not had the opportunity to shop for Christmas presents. First stop was Hatchard's on Piccadilly for books, then The Curiosity Shop for a porcelain doll, and finally, Fortnum and Mason for epicurean delights. Willy was surprised to learn Peggy knew of all the quality shops in London.

After an afternoon of shopping, they arrived to find the three widows of Whiddon had arrived by carriage. His mother and Aunts Lisa and Hanna were unloading the many Christmas presents they brought from Devon.

"How did you know I was here?" Willy asked his mother.

"We didn't, but we knew the children and Peggy were and we were not going to have Christmas without them." His mother hugged Willy. "Agnes told me about your injury. I am sorry," she sobbed.

"Don't worry mum, Peggy and I went shopping and ordered another just like it," he joked.

"Be serious." His mother playfully slapped at him with her leather glove.

"We did, I swear. Didn't we, Peggy?"

"We did indeed and I think you will like it, once it is finished." Peggy hugged Mrs. Whiddon.

"Thank you for writing me, Peggy. We looked forward to receiving your letters and hearing of the children's progress in school. I was at first a little upset at your keeping the children in London, but you and the children apparently made the right decision," Mrs. Whiddon said.

Willy was getting hugs and questioned about his injury from his Aunts Hanna and Lisa as they all entered the house arm in arm.

\*\*\*

Lieutenant Ransom sent two carriages to the Reynolds House on Saturday morning for Captain Whiddon's family. The "Widows of Whiddon," as Willy liked to call his widowed mother and aunts, had not expected such a tribute for their Willy. The honor was totally unexpected, and Willy's being in London made attendance mandatory at the ceremony. Many of the captains were still in the North Sea or on their way to Yarmouth or London.

St. Paul's Cathedral's 3,000 seats were assigned by the Master-General's office. Another 1,000 attendees could stand in the halls of the "church of the people." The *London Gazette* had predicted a record turnout for this triumphant event.

As the closed carriages of the ordnance department pulled up in front of the west entranceway of Sir Christopher Wren's greatest work, Peggy sat and gawked out the small carriage window at the dome that reached 365 feet toward the heavens. St. Paul's was consecrated in 1708, after thirty years of construction. Peggy had often seen the cathedral towers from a distance and was anxious to see the inside.

A small man with a goatee and pencil moustache was at the entrance, leaning against the wall. He was writing in his little notebook. Peggy looked at the man and wondered, *Where have I seen him before?*

Two uniformed naval officers escorted the family of eight to their seats near the choir altar. Peggy sat looking at the magnificence of this structure. Nowhere in her home country was there anything to compare—house of worship or government building.

Everyone had worshipped in St. Paul's Cathedral except Peggy and the children. All but Willy were in awe of the ceiling frescos hundreds of feet overhead and the multitude of wide arches, curved like rainbows in the sky. Willy just sat and stared straight ahead.

The sound of the grand pipe organ announced that the procession of dignitaries had started from the west door. The ceremonial entrance was into the nave, where most of the congregation was seated, then the procession passed down the great hall toward the altar. King George III made his grand entrance and the congregation rose, then bowed or curtsied as he was escorted toward the royal box of the cathedral.

The name of every sailor and marine killed in the battle was read aloud by the prime minister. Loved ones in the nave occasionally cried out at the sound of a name. The Bishop led a prayer for them and all the wounded. He asked all who had been wounded to stand. It took a while for some who had been severely wounded to rise. As he stood, Willy looked at them and realized how lucky he was. Then all who participated in the battle were asked to rise. All received a triumphant applause.

Willy was stoical on the ride home, lost in his thoughts about the events that led to the battle, the loss of men and his injury.

# Chapter Twenty
## Holidays in London

Christmas this year at the Reynolds House was an especially happy time, with Willy now home from war. It had been many years since the Whiddon and Reynolds families had been together for anything other than funerals. It was like old times for the three widows, Willy and his cousin Agnes.

Peggy watched William and Elizabeth on their hands and knees, scooting around on the wooden floor underneath the Christmas tree. The children were giddy over the neatly-wrapped gifts, many that were for them.

The fourteen-foot-tall pine tree was cut from nearby Spinney Hill Farm, a dairy goat farm well known in Leicester for its dairy products made from goat's milk. The Whiddon family had picked this pine tree out of the hundreds in the thick forest. The owner cut and delivered it with the live goose and goat cheese Agnes ordered for the Christmas feast at Reynolds House.

They chose this tree because of its height and just the right tip for Agnes's German-made ceramic angel. William had the honor of placing it atop the tree, by leaning over the balcony from the second floor of the open foyer with his father holding on to him. The women anxiously watched the tree topping from the foyer below. Once it was positioned just right, Peggy said, "Great job, William." The others gave the happy boy a round of applause.

Agnes was relieved the family heirloom survived another placement. Sir Joshua brought the angel from Germany to her mother, which started the tradition of the Reynolds House Christmas tree.

Peggy thought Christmas was so different in England, compared to Knob Creek. No one would consider bringing a tree inside a house, let along such a large one. The fact was, no home in Knob Creek would hold one! In Tennessee, a daughter's doll had a head that was lovingly carved and painted by their father's hands—whittled from a piece of wood or a corn cob with their jack knife, then wrapped in sun-dried corn shucks for clothes. Here, they are purchased from a fancy store, a china doll crafted by an artisan in a porcelain shop, dressed in fine silk garments and with hair on its head.

Peggy remembered her mother painstakingly making her siblings' and her clothes from bolts of either blue or buff linsey-woolsey, the only two colors available from Mr. Deaderick's dry goods store, the only place to buy broadcloth in Jonesborough. In London, they had shops with large selections of ready-to-wear clothes in the colors of the rainbow.

As she watched this happy family, a part of her yearned for the simple life of her large family and of friend Jimmy Witherspoon. Peggy wondered how her students at Hebron school were doing. Most had never known another teacher. Hopefully, they were accepting Ibby and Rebeckah and obeying them. This would be her first Christmas away from home in her twenty-five years. Peggy tried not to think of her loved ones, now so far away. She prayed that they were well and would soon be together again.

John Hetherington arrived with more presents, hand warmers he made from scraps of fox fur and matching ear muffs for the women, deer skin gloves for Willy and William. The family would enjoy the warmth of his gifts on the walk to church for Christmas Eve services. It was a tradition at candlelight services that each member of the congregation brought candles for their family to light from the unity candle as they entered Leicester Anglican Church. The candles provided just enough light to read the hymnal and were the only heat source inside the cold stone walls of the centuries old cathedral.

This was the first Christmas that John Hetherington had been with any family. Having lost both parents to cholera at an early age, he spent a lonely childhood in a London orphanage. He'd been indentured in his teens to an elderly bachelor, a hatter, gone mad from inhaling the noxious fumes of his trade. John cared for his benefactor, who taught him to be a hatter, until the old man's death. The only heir, he inherited the hat shop and the man's few possessions. Never having a family, he enjoyed being with one that was so loving and caring. Agnes explained to John the Christmas customs and traditions of the Reynolds-Whiddon family.

Willy and William loved the top hats. William liked the idea of having a grown-up hat, like his father. Elizabeth loved the porcelain doll; it had curly blonde hair and looked so life-like. Elizabeth cradled it in her arms like a baby, talking to it and even trying to feed it. Willy had purchased a hand-painted whalebone brooch in Big Yarmouth for Peggy. He received a warm kiss, which did not go unnoticed by the three widows or Agnes. William and Elizabeth had grown accustomed to Peggy and their father's intimate moments. The children had bonded well with their nanny and hoped that Peggy would be the mother they never had.

Agnes's and John's romance continued to blossom. The couple spent every available moment together. They talked about John boarding at Reynolds House, moving from the small room he lived in over his shop. But Agnes was concerned the permanent boarders and her neighbors might make gossip about such an arrangement.

With no school during the holidays, Willy had the opportunity to spend time with his children and Peggy. There was no improvement in his memory and Willy became increasingly frustrated about it, but also very adept at covering up his lapses of memory.

After a ten-day stay in London, Willy's mother and aunts were on their way back to Whiddon Estates. Aunt Hanna had hired an arborist who was coming to prune the fruit trees, a job that would take weeks in the sprawling Whiddon orchards while the trees were still dormant. According to Aunt Hanna, only she could properly oversee the trimming of her precious trees that produced her award-winning fruits.

***

One hour after the sun had set in the distance on the far side of the River Thames, carriages began lining up at 35 Maiden Lane. Well-dressed gentlemen and ladies were assisted from their carriages by doormen in tails and top hats. They escorted guests from their conveyances to the front door, where the maître d' welcomed them to Rules and confirmed their reservations. A valet took their outerwear and hung the bulky garments neatly in the cloakroom. The host gave them a tour of the new facilities before showing the party to their assigned table.

With shovels in hand, stable boys were busy cleaning up after the waiting horses. Once the guests were inside, the coachmen drove their rigs to the nearby Covent Garden fruit and vegetable market, leased for the evening to accommodate the carriages in waiting.

At the closed market, the coachmen pitched horse-shoes, told stories and ate their ploughman's box lunch compliments of Rules. They sat on large logs in a circle around the roaring fire built for their comfort, sharing a nip of fruit-flavored brandy to warm that part of the body the fire couldn't reach. Each waited patiently for a summons from the doorman that their charges were ready to leave.

Thomas Rule knew how to cater to the gentry of London. His long-time friend John Hetherington was learning from the soon-to-be-famous restaurant owner how to market his hat business. It was Thomas Rule who suggested John parade up and down the streets of London in the new hat he designed. Neither thought that the hat would create such a disturbance that the hatter would be arrested for disturbing the peace. Then the *London Gazette* fortunately learned of John's arrest and fine of fifty pounds. The editor published the story, and opined that a man should be able to wear any hat that he so desires, making a celebrity of the hat maker and his strange-looking hat.

John hired a driver and a special carriage never seen before on the streets of London. Its exterior was made from the precious white limousine oak found only in the forest of central France. The special wood grain was so ornate that it wasn't painted, but buffed instead to a polished natural shine with linseed oil. The owner referred to the unpainted carriage as his "woody." It carried the four adults and two children comfortably from the Reynolds House.

The carriage attracted much attention pulling up in front of Rules, its coachman and two groomsmen in matching beaver top hats and silk tails. The woody received more attention in front of Rules than the Marquis's ornate, gold carriage. Mr. Rule requested the coachmen of both to leave their carriages in front of his restaurant to attract attention to the gathering.

It worked. New Year's revelers admiring the carriages saw the new restaurant and gawked at the elegantly-dressed patrons inside.

The attendees at Rules were not only celebrating New Year's Eve but also First Marquis Charles Cornwallis's birthday. He was born on this date fifty-nine years ago. The Marquis lost his wife Jemima Jones nineteen years ago and never remarried, but showed much admiration to many beautiful women, all of whom adored the English nobleman. He attended the opening with his son Charles, daughter Mary and their spouses.

The new Rules seemed the place to be; hundreds without invitations milled about outside the exclusive establishment to see who was there.

Waiters offered hors d'oeuvres and wine on silver trays as guests mingled about the three rooms of the public house. Once the dinner bell rang, the seventy special guests took their seats for a four-course gourmet meal extraordinaire.

Peggy and Elizabeth sat across from Willy and William. Peggy noticed that William was discreetly giving his father instructions on the proper silverware to use with which course. Soup spoon, salad knife, etc. *Willy has forgotten his table etiquette, and his thirteen-year-old son is showing him which utensil to use.*

Peggy said nothing, but watched them intently. When Willy excused himself to go to the water closet, William followed, which she thought odd.

A harpist played beautiful music on a large harp, the largest Peggy had ever seen.

Mr. Rule stopped at their table. "I hope you enjoyed your meal."

Everyone nodded that the food and beverage was wonderful. Willy complimented him on the lamb, the children praised the pudding.

Peggy said, "The music adds so much to the atmosphere of the room."

"Thank you, Miss Mitchell for your kind words. I had hired an opera singer, a regular at the Royal Opera, who was to sing for us tonight. I am so disappointed she canceled at the last moment. Illness, I was told."

Peggy motioned for Mr. Rule to come close. "You know we have an opera singer sitting at the table."

Mr. Rule leaned over and asked, "You are an opera singer?"

"No, but Agnes Reynolds is." Peggy nodded toward Agnes, who was in deep conversation with John.

"Really? Do you think she would sing for us?" Mr. Rule asked.

"Why don't you ask her?" Peggy suggested.

Mr. Rule worked his way around the table and said, "Excuse me John . . . Miss Reynolds, Peggy Mitchell said you might sing for us?"

"You have caught me by surprise Mr. Rule, but the least I can do is sing for you after such a wonderful meal. Is there anything special you would like to hear?" Agnes asked.

"Anything with which the harpist can accompany you would be wonderful, but be sure to wish the Marquis a happy birthday." Mr. Rule gestured toward the harp player. "I will ask him to come and talk to you." He spoke to the harpist and pointed toward Agnes.

The harpist took a break and approached Agnes, "So I have a singer to accompany, after all? My name is Sean O'Reilly."

"I am Agnes Reynolds, Mr. O'Reilly." She introduced the others at the table.

"Nice meeting everyone," Sean said. They discussed the songs that each were comfortable with in their repertoires.

Agnes sang several songs; one was "For He's A Jolly Good Fellow" for the Marquis, receiving participation and great applause from the guests. She closed as the clock struck midnight, leading the revelers in a sing-along of "Auld Lang Syne." The Scottish poet Robert Burns, who had written "Auld Lang Syne," had died the previous year and his song suddenly became popular.

John Hetherington had only heard Agnes sing while caroling. He knew she had a beautiful voice and was musically gifted, but had no idea Agnes was such an accomplished opera singer. The performance over, Willy stood on his chair clapping wildly for his aunt and yelling, "Bravo! Bravo!" His table rose, the next table rose, until everyone gave Agnes a standing ovation. Her opera career had begun.

Marquis Cornwallis came and kissed Agnes's hand, complimenting her on a great performance, and thanking her for singing the song for him. He thought she was the professional opera singer scheduled to perform. Then he realized that she was not the paid performer, but the niece of Sir Joshua Reynolds. Embarrassed, he hugged Agnes, telling her how much he admired her uncle, and what great friends he, Sir Joshua, and Edmund Burke had been, all members of the same social circle simply called "the club."

"He spoke well of you . . . I remember him speaking of the club." Agnes said.

William and his sister Elizabeth were still wide awake, excited about having witnessed their first New Year's Eve festivities. They felt special being the only children at the celebration.

Just an hour into the new year, the six members of the Reynolds House group loaded up in the woody for the thirty-minute ride to Leicester Village. Snow began to fall on the cobblestone streets of the city. A bright, waxing crescent moon illuminated the shiny flakes as they fell to earth. The Tower of London, blocks away, was encased in a bluish tint, giving the "fortress of death" an eerie appearance.

Marquis Cornwallis, on his way out to his carriage, said to the coachman already atop the woody, reins in his hands, "Hold up a moment, I wish to speak to Captain Whiddon."

"Yes, sir." The coachman held the reins tightly, signaling the lead horse not to move.

"Captain Whiddon, Miss Mitchell, I didn't have the opportunity to visit with you and your family, with all the festivities of the evening." Marquis Cornwallis brushed at the snow on his sleeves.

"Yes, it has been a busy night, Your Lordship."

"I will be back in my office next Monday. Could you stop by about ten o'clock? I need to talk to you about your ship, *Devon's Hope*." A mist of fog came out of the Marquis's mouth as he spoke, caused by his warm breath, the humidity and the near-freezing temperature.

"I will be there, sir."

"Good—you will be my first appointment." Marquis Cornwallis tipped his hat and started toward his coachman, who was holding the carriage door open.

"Happy New Year!" Peggy waved a gloved hand out the small window of the carriage.

"And to you." The Marquis waved back.

"That was interesting." Peggy looked at Willy. He didn't respond, as frequently occurred now. *As if he didn't hear me.*

"That's when we start school—next Monday?" William asked.

Peggy nodded, not to disturb the others who had closed their weary eyes. The doormen covered the riders with heavy carriage blankets laid across each of the facing bench seats up to their necks for the chilly ride home. Exhausted from a long night of celebration and the effects of over-indulgence, the family dozed.

Peggy shut her eyes and tried to visualize what her own family might be doing on the banks of Knob Creek in anticipation of the passing of New Year's and the twenty-first year of American Independence. The sounds of a steady cadence of hooves on the cobblestone roadway lured her into a peaceful sleep.

Once the carriage made the turn onto Leicester Square, the sound of the neighbor's dogs woke the tired revelers. Peggy carried Elizabeth in and put her to bed. John and Agnes were still in the carriage as Willy helped William climb out backward.

William had his feet on the first rung of the carriage steps starting to step down, his father behind him for safety. The boy looked sleepily at his aunt and asked, "What's for breakfast?"

Agnes said, "After that meal, you are still hungry?"

"I will be when I wake up." William then climbed down from the carriage.

\*\*\*

Peggy woke to the sounds of someone screaming in the night. She climbed out of bed and rushed out into the dark hallway. The sounds came from William and his father's room. Picking up a solid piece of firewood from the wood box, she made sure she could get a good grip on one end of it. She entered the dark room to find Willy tossing about and uttering words that she couldn't understand. Speaking softly, she assured Willy that he was safe at home in his own bed, everything was secure and to go back to sleep.

She wondered how William could have slept through his father's outbursts. An overhead dormer gave enough light to see the boy's bed but he was not there. His pillow and down cover were also missing.

Once Willy had calmed down and appeared to be sleeping comfortably, Peggy lit a candle to search for William. She found him lying on the settee in the parlor, awake.

"Your father had a bad dream." Peggy set the flickering candlestick on a small table next to the settee. Seeing his tears, she wrapped her arms around the boy.

"Peggy, what's wrong with my father? Nearly every night just as I get to sleep the screams and moans start."

"I am not sure, William. War does strange things to people and your father sustained some serious head injuries in addition to losing his eye. My father and oldest brother were never the same after the Battle of Guilford Courthouse. They had terrible nightmares—and they were not physically injured like your father."

"Your father and brother were in a battle? Who did they fight?" William asked.

"My father fought the army of General Cornwallis in the Revolution for American Independence. He was captured and imprisoned. Robert, my oldest brother, was just a year older than you. He didn't fight, but he witnessed it and saw the death and destruction it left on our farm."

"I remember father talking about that. He said you were also on the battlefield when Cornwallis attacked. The same Cornwallis we sang 'Jolly Good Fellow' for?"

Peggy nodded, holding William for a long time, hoping that he would go to sleep. William finally spoke. "Sometimes, father can't remember my name and it is the same as his. He tries to say it and he can't. Then he acts like he is mad at me, because he can't remember it."

"When did you first notice this?" Peggy asked.

"The first night he was home. Father would start to say something to me, then he would forget what he was talking about. He asked me several times, whose house this was. I said it was Agnes's. He got mad—said no, it was his uncle's house. He was trying to remember the name of Sir Joshua . . . but couldn't," William said.

"Tonight at Rules, you were helping your father with his silverware at dinner, weren't you?" Peggy used a corner of the cover to wipe his tears.

"He couldn't remember in what order the utensils were supposed to be used, and father taught me left to right when I was a child."

"William, why did you follow your father to the water closet at Rules?"

"To make sure he buttoned his trousers. I didn't want him to come back to the table with his fly open."

Peggy nodded, "You and I are the only ones that have noticed these strange things and we shouldn't embarrass your father about it."

Agnes had been listening from the hallway and now said, "I am aware that something is amiss with Willy." She groped in the dark for the high back chair. Finding it, she sat facing Peggy and William on the settee. "My poor Willy."

"We mustn't feel that way. He is a proud man. We must help him find what has been erased from his memory." Peggy, seeing William's eyes flutter, then close, laid his head gently down on the settee and covered him with the heavy, down blanket.

"Would you have a cup of tea and a biscuit with me?" Agnes asked.

"Yes, I would." Peggy followed Agnes down the dark hall to the kitchen. Agnes picked up a log from the log box and placed it on the fire saying, "My mum always told me it was bad luck to let your kitchen fire go out on New Year's Day." They watched it ignite from the still-hot embers of the hearth.

"We are in luck," Peggy said.

"Yes, we are . . . Peggy Mitchell, you are my lucky horseshoe and my best friend. Your dealing with John Hetherington is the best thing that has ever happened to me."

"How is that?" Peggy asked.

"He asked me to marry him! We are going to have a big church wedding and I want you to be my maid of honor."

"I am so happy for you! I would be honored to be in your wedding. When did he propose?" Peggy asked.

"In the carriage after everyone went in the house. John asked me to stay with him awhile, as he wanted to talk to me. I knew what it was." Agnes was aglow with excitement.

"Have you set a date?"

"Not yet. I told John I needed to talk to my maid of honor first, then the church minister, and I would get back to him with a wedding date." Agnes giggled as she poured tea for her and Peggy.

They were up till dawn talking and making wedding plans, picking dates that needed to be checked against the church calendar.

Elizabeth came into the kitchen carrying her new doll and sat between Peggy and Agnes. "What are we having for breakfast?"

"What are you doing up so early, Elizabeth?" Peggy asked.

"The rooster woke me," Elizabeth said.

Peggy pulled her onto her lap and hugged her.

Agnes said, "Then we will have eggs, seeing as the rooster woke you. Bacon and tattie scones. Does that sound good?"

Elizabeth nodded that it did.

"Agnes is getting married, Elizabeth. I am going to be her maid of honor. Would you like to be her flower girl?"

"What's a flower girl?" Elizabeth asked as her father entered the kitchen and poured a cup of tea.

"Sounds like someone is getting married. Anyone I know?" Willy said.

"John asked me to marry him," Agnes said.

"That's wonderful!" Willy said.

"What's a flower girl?" Elizabeth asked again, a little aggravated at being ignored.

"I am sorry, Elizabeth. The flower girl is the first to walk down the aisle before the wedding starts. Don't worry; we will rehearse before the actual ceremony."

William, smelling the bacon, came to the kitchen as if drawn like a hungry bear to honey.

"William, will you be Agnes's page?" Peggy asked.

"What is that?" William sneaked a piece of bacon from the serving tray.

"I saw that!" Agnes shook her long fork at William.

"As the page, you will carry the prayer book and walk behind me down the aisle of the church," Agnes said.

"I think I can do that."

"No more bacon for you, young man, if you can't." Agnes placed a large pewter platter of bacon, eggs, and tattie scones on the table. "Let's eat before my new fiancé arrives."

The children were excited about being in the wedding. William asked, "Can I wear my top hat?"

"I am sure John will wear his. He looks for every opportunity to promote his business, you know." Agnes shook her head, thinking of the men all wearing their top hats at her wedding.

Willy sat down next to his son and asked. "Who is it . . . you said you were going to marry?"

Agnes was caught off guard and said, "You remember—John the hatter, who made you the deer skin gloves for Christmas." Agnes gave Peggy a worried look.

"Yes I know him, a fine chap he is." Willy reached for some bacon and began to fill his plate.

Peggy served herself a full breakfast. She made coffee, being the only coffee drinker in the household. After being up most of the night, she needed some strong stimulation this morning. *How these Brits can start their day on tea, I will never know.*

After everyone had breakfast, she washed the dishes and Agnes came to put them away. Peggy looked at Agnes. "I must have a talk with Willy. This is worse than I thought. We had just told him about John proposing and two minutes later he couldn't remember who you were marrying."

"I know; it is sad." Agnes shook her head.

Handing Agnes the last plate, she asked, "Can you keep the children busy, while I talk to him? I will take him to Sir Joshua's library to show him the children's work."

"Yes, but I must get dressed for my first visitor," Agnes smiled.

"I guess I know who that will be. I best get dressed," Peggy said.

# Chapter Twenty-One
## Confrontation

Peggy dressed as if she were teaching school today, wearing a full-length, indigo dress, high-topped, laced shoes and a buff-colored woolen shawl over her shoulders. She entered the downstairs foyer and found John, Agnes, and the children playing a game of cards. Peggy asked no one in particular, "Where is Willy?"

"He said he wanted to read a book and went up to the library to find one." Agnes took one of the large playing cards from William's hand.

Peggy asked, "Will you help me, Agnes? I need your support. Willy respects your judgment and will listen to you."

"I know, but I don't think I can . . . " Agnes pondered.

"You can, because you know we must. Let's go while he is in the library. I don't want to have to lure him back up there." Peggy offered her hand to pull Agnes off the settee.

"What about the children?" Agnes handed her remaining cards to William.

"We are having fun." William laughingly taunted Mr. Hetherington with his newly-acquired playing cards.

The children were aware that Agnes and Peggy were going to talk to their father about his strange behavior.

"Let's get this over with." Peggy climbed the open staircase, Agnes behind her. Peggy stopped to view the Christmas tree, admiring the ceramic angel. *I will need the help of a special Angel today, maybe baby Joseph.*

Peggy opened the door to the library, which was also her classroom. She found Willy seated at the long, mahogany work table, crying. Surprised, he turned his head away from Peggy and tried to wipe the tears from his cheeks with his hands. *He cries quite often now. Could that be a symptom of the head injury?* There were a set of drawings and some watercolors on the table in front of him, pictures both children had done of *Devon's Hope* with their father at the helm.

Peggy turned to Agnes in the hall and whispered, "Please give us a minute alone." Agnes nodded that she understood, as Peggy shut the large, double doors.

"Nice work for children, isn't it?" Peggy slid into the chair directly across from Willy.

"They are good. You have done well teaching my children. I am impressed with the artwork they have done in class." Willy leaned back admiring the pictures from a distance.

"They did this on their own with no supervision from me. What you see is their natural talent showing. Especially William, he is quite gifted. Elizabeth's art skills are still developing."

Willy suddenly grimaced in pain placing his palms over his ears. "Damn this ringing in my ears! It will not stop!"

Peggy moved around the table and sat in a chair next to him, putting a hand on his shoulder and looking in his good eye. "Did you ever hear those sounds before your injury?"

"The ringing started after I arrived here. It just comes and goes, but it keeps getting worse."

"What you describe sounds like tinnitus, which I have read about. How is the vision in your good eye?"

"Sometimes my vision is a bit blurry."

Peggy held up two fingers in front of his face. "How many fingers do you see?"

"Two," Willy said.

"Now how many?"

"Three."

Agnes knocked on the door. "May I come in?"

"Please join us." Peggy spoke loudly to be heard through the thick doors.

Agnes opened one of the heavy doors and closed it quietly. "Willy, did you find something to read?" She didn't realize Willy was in pain.

"Agnes, I have been so engrossed in my children's artistic works that I haven't looked." Willy said without flinching as Peggy finished looking into his eye.

Agnes picked up William's watercolor, tilting her head to one side then the other, admiring the boy's work then handing it to Willy, saying in a playful way, "I think William has inherited the artistic traits of the Reynolds side of the family."

"William certainly has captured *Devon's Hope* with great accuracy in this piece." Willy handed it back to her, still in pain.

"He had to do it from memory, 'cause the ship was not here to pose in the water."

Willy managed a chuckle. "I was complimenting Peggy on the children's progress and I know you have participated in their scholarly pursuits as well." Willy started to stand up, but sat back down with some difficulty.

"Are you dizzy?" Peggy stood.

"Just a little," Willy said.

"Perhaps we should put you to bed. Come with me." Peggy started to help Willy up.

He raised his hands to keep her from touching him, but not in defiance. "I will be all right . . . just let me be." He put his head in his hands, his elbows on the table.

They both looked at Willy, so obviously in pain. Agnes looked at Peggy as if to say, *What do we do now?* Then at Willy. "Are you certain, Willy, you don't want to go lie down?"

Willy raised his head. "Yes, I am certain, Agnes. I need to discuss some things with Peggy while the children are playing. Would you please excuse us?" He sounded agitated.

Agnes turned red in the face, looked at Peggy, then Willy. "I should be starting my evening meal."

"I am sorry Agnes, I am just having a bad day of it," Willy said.

Peggy nodded toward Agnes, indicating she could handle confronting Willy alone.

"It's all right, Willy, I understand. I hope you feel better soon." Agnes closed the door behind her.

Peggy sat down again at the table, looking at Willy. She waited for him to say what was on his mind.

Willy got up and walked to the window facing the park. He stood looking down on the dormant foliage of Leicester Square Park. Peggy waited for Willy to say something. When he didn't, she began, "I am here for you. Tell me—what is bothering you?"

He turned and looked at Peggy with a worried look. "Do you think I am insane?"

"No, I don't think you are insane," she said calmly. "But you did receive a stout blow to the head that left you unconscious for days. It has caused some loss of memory that has me and your family concerned. I am certain the head injury is what causes the tinnitus."

Willy looked at her. "Tin . . . "

"That's the sound you hear in your ears," she explained. "It may go away in time. Your injury is still fresh, having occurred less than three months ago."

"My children look at me strangely when I can't recall their names. I know their names. I just can't say them sometimes. It is there." Willy sputtered, pointing at his head. "I just can't get the words out of my mouth!"

"I know," Peggy said quietly.

"How do you know about such things?"

"I find the human body fascinating. I have read every book and periodical on medicine that I could find. The extensive records of the sick and injured I have cared for have helped me to figure out what works and what doesn't. Dr. Chester and I have spent hours on the porch of the Chester Inn discussing our patients. My medical experience came mostly from ministering to my large, extended family."

"When did you develop this desire to heal the sick?" Willy asked.

Peggy pondered the question for a moment. *What was it that drove me to be a caregiver?*

She began, "I have never shared this story with anyone. I don't know why, I just haven't. I guess no one has ever asked me before. You made me realize for the first time why I have such a strong desire to make everyone well."

Willy sat back down across from her, and reached for her hands to hold. He could see that whatever it was she was trying to say was important to her.

"I had a little brother named Joseph. I loved him dearly. Each time a male child was born, Father would sit down at the long table board, open the family Bible and place his finger on a page without looking. The closest name of a Biblical man to his finger would become the boy's name. Father said doing it that way allowed God to have a say in naming his nine sons."

"What about the girls?" Willy asked.

"My parents had agreed before they married that father named the boys and mother would name the girls. When Joseph was born, I was six years old, the only girl in the family at the time. My grandmother asked the oldest, Robert, who was twelve, to take the children outside while she and Father assisted mother in birth. They say I had a tantrum and insisted on staying to help. Mother told them to let me stay, if I wanted."

Willy interrupted with, "You stayed for the birth?"

"Yes, Grandmother said I watched intently and wanted to know everything about childbirth. She put me up on the bed with Mother. With Grandmother's help, I cut the umbilical cord of Joseph and the seven siblings that followed. Grandmother died when I was sixteen, and I assumed her role of midwife for the family and had brought forty-eight babies into this world by my eighteenth birthday."

"That's amazing. What happened to your little—to Joseph?" Willy squeezed her hand gently, letting her know that he wanted to hear more.

Peggy took a deep breath. "I took care of baby Joseph. I begged mother to move his cradle to my room. She did when I turned seven. When he cried, I would change him and rock his cradle. I loved him like he was my own child. There was something about witnessing that beautiful baby boy being born that bonded me to him . . . "

"If this is too hard for you—"Willy began.

"It is difficult, but I need to tell you this." Peggy slowly pulled her hands away from Willy's. She took a lace handkerchief from the cuff of her sleeve to wipe tears that rolled down her cheeks. Peggy then folded it neatly and dabbed her eyes with a corner of the cloth, shook her head and continued. "One fall night there was this terrible thunderstorm that came through. It was during the war about a year or so before the British destroyed our home next to the courthouse. A bolt of lightning struck the house. I remember it well; it almost knocked me out of my bed. I felt the energy from the bolt go through my body, I tingled from head to toe for what seemed like a long while. Everyone in the house felt the same weird sensation. Our hair stood straight up for days. The lightning struck the pine logs near my window and started a fire, but the torrential downpour quickly put it out. That part of the house was badly scorched on the outside. Baby Joseph was then just fourteen months old, a beautiful, healthy baby boy. I lit a taper and looked at him resting so peacefully in his cradle, I blew the candle out and told Mother when she asked that he was fine and was sleeping. I went back to sleep." Peggy closed her eyes and grimaced.

"Then what happened?" Willy reached for her hands again, and cradled them in his.

"I woke hearing my mother screaming that baby Joseph was dead . . . She held him to her breast and cried uncontrollably. Father had to pry the baby from her arms."

"I am sorry." Willy held her hands tightly, realizing how painful this tragedy was for Peggy to tell.

"If I had tried to wake baby Joseph, maybe we could have saved him. I felt responsible for his death, and I begged my mother to forgive me. Joseph died and we all survived. Father said God must have needed a little angel and it was not my fault that my baby brother was killed by lightning.

"I became overly protective of my siblings after that. Doctoring their slightest wounds and learning the different medicinal plants for common ailments. Once we moved over the mountain, neighbors started coming to me with their aches and pains. They knew I had no medical training, but natural healing abilities that worked. With no doctor in Washington County, I became the most knowledgeable medical practitioner."

"You taught yourself?" Willy asked.

Peggy nodded. "Until Dr. Chester came to Jonesborough, right after Tennessee became a state. He took me under his wing and tutored me using his books in medicine and apothecary. He is a good doctor, but I had a difficult time getting my patients to go to him."

Willy said, "They would rather come to you than see a doctor?"

"Yes, they knew me and most of the Knob Creek Community is related to me or married into the family. I turned my records over to Dr. Chester before I left. My being away will force the last holdouts to use him."

"Can you help me get my memory back?" Willy looked at her as if he were begging.

"I have doctored many head wounds, but have had no experience with memory loss other than reading about it. I will do what I can, Willy. I would like to inventory your brain first, to discover what memory is lost and what you still remember."

"Inventory my brain? That sounds interesting, but just how do we do that?"

"I know, for instance, that you forgot your formal table etiquette—a simple thing. William showed you and you quickly relearned the order of the silverware."

"You saw William help me last night?" Willy looked embarrassed.

"Yes, and he did very well. William kept it simple rather than go into a long explanation, telling you to use them as they were set up left to right, and you did. I think we can easily teach you what you have lost, once we know what that is," Peggy said.

"When can we start?" Willy sounded excited.

"We can start after dinner, if you are up to it," Peggy said.

"That would be good. I will need to take a nap. Will you apologize to Agnes for my outburst?" Willy asked.

"Agnes understands the pain you are going through," Peggy explained.

Willy was appreciative that someone would try to help him. Peggy was thankful that Willy realized he had a problem. He was not in denial of his memory loss as she first thought. That would make the recovery easier.

After dinner, Peggy and Willy went back to the library. She used the large slate board and chalk to make the letters of the alphabet. Surprisingly, he could pronounce each and every letter. However, he couldn't recite his ABC's from memory and got very frustrated trying.

Numbers were the same; he knew when Peggy held up eight fingers. But when she asked what was five plus three, he had a blank look on his face. *This may be harder to figure out than I thought.* Knowing how important remembering names was to him she asked, "Willy, what's my name?" As she expected, he froze up and couldn't say anything, and was embarrassed. "Don't be ashamed Willy. We are going to fix your brain."

She sat at her desk and made a pen and ink name tag that read Peggy. She pinned it on her dress with a straight pin. Then she erased the board and drew the face of a boy and girl and wrote William and Elizabeth under them. "What is your legal name?" Peggy asked.

"Willy," he answered.

"You were born William Whiddon III. Your father was the second William and your son is William IV. Your family has always called you Willy, but your legal name is William."

Peggy made name tags for everyone in the house, and if she discovered something he couldn't say, like the settee, she made a sign for it that would stay until he mastered that item. She would tell a story and have him repeat it. It was difficult at first, but he got better as they did it more. She used her flash cards with letters and numbers. They worked tirelessly into the night on the first day of 1798.

Peggy made a pot of hot chamomile tea for Willy and William to drink before bedtime, in hopes that it would help them get some sleep. She molded William ear plugs from wet newspaper to wear, should his father have another nightmare.

Every waking moment of the first week of the new year was spent playing parlor games or using flash cards to stimulate his brain. Amazingly, he read well, but had difficulty retaining what he read.

One of Sir Joshua's proudest possessions in the library was a large globe of the world given to him by his friend Sir Edmund Burke. Peggy asked Willy to point out a certain place and he could point right at it. The same with navigational maps that were rolled up in the library. He could teach the children much when they began geography.

Astronomy was another thing that he could recall. Peggy thought he was as knowledgeable now as he was on the voyage over. On clear nights, Peggy would take him and the children across to the park. They would sit for hours as Willy described all the stars and planets in the galaxy. Peggy wondered, *how can a man know all about the universe and can't remember his son's name, which is the same as his?*

The children and Agnes, with the urging of Peggy, were involved in helping Willy regain his lost memory. He still had the ringing in his ears, the headaches, and felt like he was in a fog much of the time. Peggy kept meticulous notes of her inventory of Willy's brain. She complimented him on what he could do and worked to improve what he couldn't.

# Chapter Twenty-Two
## The Men of Devon

They were greeted at the Tower gates by armed marines and escorted to the lobby of Marquis Cornwallis's opulently furnished offices. Uniformed army and navy officers hurried about the headquarters of the British Board of Ordnance. There was much whispering among the corps and a sense that something was amiss. Lots of messengers with shiny leather satchels around their necks were quickly coming and going. Peggy and Willy looked at each other, knowing that something of importance was occurring in the offices of the War Lord of the United Kingdom.

Willy had asked Peggy to accompany him to the meeting while Agnes agreed to work with the children on their artwork while their teacher was away.

Lieutenant Ransom stepped out of his office and glanced around the crowded waiting room. Seeing them, he said, "A good day to you, Captain Whiddon and Miss Mitchell. I am sorry but there was an emergency meeting of the Board. The Master-General will not be able to meet with you today. He sends his apologies and asked that I negotiate your claim. You were on his calendar as his first appointment, but the mutiny of the *Marie Antoinette* has us a bit busy at the moment."

"What about *Marie Antoinette*?" Willy asked.

"*Marie Antoinette* the ship, not the beheaded late Queen of France." Lieutenant Ransom attempted to jest, but failed miserably.

"I know the ship; it is a ten-gun sloop captured by the Royal Navy some years ago. I provisioned her at sea last year in the West Indies before sailing to Philadelphia. What has happened to her?" Willy said.

The officer looked around nervously. "Let's go to my office, Captain, and I will brief you on the situation." Lieutenant Ransom led them to his office adjacent to the Master-General's suite. He invited them to sit in the two chairs in front of his cluttered desk. "We just received word this morning by a packet ship that the *Marie Antoinette* was sailed into the French port of Gonaïves by mutineers. The report said the crew murdered the captain and his executive officer and threw them overboard."

Peggy grimaced at the harshness of what was said.

"Was the captain a Lieutenant Perkins?" Willy asked.

Peggy looked at him, "You knew Captain—"

Lieutenant Ransom interrupted. "No it wasn't Perkins; he was promoted to Commander of the *Drake*, a fourteen-gun brig. The captain they murdered was a Lieutenant McInerheny, assigned his first command last July and then killed by his own crew." Lieutenant Ransom shook his head.

"That is terrible," Peggy said.

"Yes, it is. The Royal Navy has had a series of mutinies this year and these revolts of our seamen must be stopped. That is why we need *Devon's Hope* until this conflict with France is over," Lieutenant Ransom said.

Willy pondered what was just said. He looked intently at the Lieutenant, but did not speak. Peggy looked at Willy, trying to determine if he understood what was said.

"I have been authorized to repair all the damages resulting from the Battle of Camperdown and get *Devon's Hope* in tip-top condition, at no cost to you." Willy still did not speak and Lieutenant Ransom continued. "We will upgrade her cannons from six-pounders to twelve with the best British-made artillery, which will remain with your ship after it is returned to you."

Willy remained stoic. He just looked at Lieutenant Ransom, who became anxious, after not getting a response. "You understand what I just said, Captain Whiddon?"

"Yes, he understands. He wishes to hear the rest of your offer." Peggy spoke up for Willy, as if it was normal for her to do so for the captain, not knowing for certain whether he understood or not.

Lieutenant Ransom turned his attention toward Peggy and continued. "Navy records say *Devon's Hope* was pressed into service the first day of September. We are prepared to pay £40 per month and I have a warrant issued for £160 for the first four months of service."

Peggy said nothing. Willy remained silent. The lieutenant nervously cleared his throat. "Of course, we will give Captain Whiddon full combat pay of a ship's captain since being pressed into military service."

Peggy looked at Willy to see if he had any questions. Seeing none coming, she asked, "How much would that accrue to?"

Lieutenant Ransom looked in a leather-bound ledger that lay open on his desk. "That would be an additional £40 pounds per month or £160 for his service." Now he looked at Willy for some expression of agreement that didn't come. He turned his gaze toward Peggy. "What do you think of our offer, Miss Mitchell?"

Suddenly Willy said, "You haven't mentioned payment for the provisions I delivered here to Billingsgate Docks three months ago."

"Just submit an invoice and we will pay it." Lieutenant Ransom squirmed uncomfortably in his leather chair, not familiar with settling money matters, especially since the ordnance board was in arrears on its payments due to a lack of funds.

Peggy was enjoying the negotiations. Willy reached into his satchel without being asked and pulled out the bills of lading for the provisions delivered on the first of

September at Billingsgate Docks, gin at Yarmouth, and the North Sea operations during the month of October. He handed them to Ransom.

"I will process them for immediate disbursement. Is there anything else?"

Willy asked, "Who will command my ship, and what has happened to my crew?"

Peggy gave Willy a slight nod of encouragement. She now realized he was following the negotiations, apparently not comfortable talking, but when he spoke he chose his words well.

The lieutenant answered, "Once *Devon's Hope* is seaworthy, a commander will be selected from officers of the fleet. Your crew is now aboard other ships, as needed around the fleet of the North Sea."

Willy spoke slowly but clearly. "Is my pay to continue?"

"You were never a commissioned line officer of the fleet, being pressed into service under the impress order of the Royal Navy. I wouldn't think you would be entitled to convalescence pay."

Willy leaned toward the Lieutenant and said, "That is why your navy is in mutiny. Ships and their crews have been pressed by the Royal Navy. Why should they have any loyalty to His Majesty? Had I been asked to serve my country, I would have volunteered the services of my ship and crew to the King, without hesitation. Lieutenant, we were taken away from our families, without the opportunity to say goodbye. My men risked their lives the same as if they had enlisted. We shouldn't be treated any different."

"In your case, I must agree that what you say is correct. I am sure we can negotiate something. Your ship is needed. Please tell us what it will take, Captain, to place *Devon's Hope* in the fleet of the Royal Navy."

"*Devon's Hope* is not a battleship; it was not designed for war." Willy shook his head and looked down in disgust.

"*Devon's Hope* is armed — most merchant ships are not. She can move large stores of ammunition and supplies to our fleets around the world, keeping the rank and file happy. With the upgraded fire power and two frigates to escort her, your ship will be safe."

"Like it was at Camperdown?"

The lieutenant, knowing Willy was right, didn't respond.

"Grandfather armed her for protection from privateers, not a warring nation."

"That's the reason for upgrading her guns." Lieutenant Ransom leaned back in his chair, exasperated at how the negotiations were going and said, "Just please tell me what you want."

"I want the full pay of a captain of the line and when *Devon's Hope* is repaired, I will command her, with the men of Devon. She has never sailed without a Whiddon at the helm. I cannot bear to think of Grandfather's ship commanded by a stranger." Willy showed a cockiness that Peggy had not seen since he returned from the North Sea. It was that Whiddon pride that had attracted her to him. She was proud of her captain.

"I can't put you on full pay while you are convalescing from your injuries," Lieutenant Ransom said.

Willy leaned toward the lieutenant's desk, his palms up, stared into his eyes and said, "I am ready to take command of my ship and crew."

"Are you capable of commanding a ship at sea, Captain?" Lieutenant Ransom rose, not waiting for an answer, and retrieved a folio from the pigeonhole file behind his desk. He untied the string that secured Willy's medical records in the government envelope. Peggy and Willy watched and waited patiently as he read a document intently as if looking for specific information. "As I thought, the doctor that treated your war injuries in Big Yarmouth questions whether you will ever be fit for military duty again."

"Because I lost an eye?" Willy sat back disgusted and said, "I can still see with one good eye."

Peggy said, "I also strongly disagree with your navy doctor's prognosis. Willy has some lingering difficulties that he is learning to deal with. He still has much to offer the navy." She noticed a large globe of the world next to the Lieutenant's desk. "Pardon me, Lieutenant Ransom, what was the name of that French Port in the West Indies that the *Marie Antoinette* was taken to?

"Gonaïves."

"Could you please point to Gonaïves on your globe?" Peggy gestured toward the hand-carved ball that was about a meter in diameter. It rested in an ornate wooden floor stand, a metal rod through its center for easy rotation. The globe was similar to the one in Sir Joshua's library that she used to teach geography.

Lieutenant Ransom rose from his desk and stood looking down on the globe, turning the ball, searching for the West Indies. Peggy looked at Willy. The faint smile on his face revealed to her that he knew where the French port was.

"Would you show Lieutenant Ransom the port of Gonaïves on his globe?" She watched Willy go to the globe and put his finger on the port city.

Lieutenant Ransom smiled approvingly.

"Can you show Ransom the port city of Trinidad?" Peggy asked, looking slyly at the lieutenant, knowing that she had made her point.

Willy turned the globe a few degrees and pointed at the port of Trinidad.

"How many nautical miles is it from London to Trinidad and how long would the voyage take?" Lieutenant Ransom said, giving the globe a spin with his long index finger, before sitting down in his chair.

"Approximately 3,800 nautical miles." Willy answered without hesitation.

"How long, Captain, would it take to sail to Trinidad?"

"Depending on prevailing winds and good weather, three to four weeks." Willy stood looking at Lieutenant Ransom, who seemed impressed with the captain's navigational acumen.

"I have a position as a Quartermaster-General here at headquarters that I know you can fill. Once you have trained your replacement and your ship is ready, I will advise the Admiralty to give you command of *Devon's Hope*."

"With the men of Devon?"

"Yes, with your men, Captain Whiddon." Lieutenant Ransom smiled and shook Willy's hand.

It was a good settlement. Willy knew that the navy could take his ship with no remuneration, if necessary, in the interest of national defense.

As they exited into the lobby, Peggy turned to Ransom, who was showing them out and said, "Thank you for all your help. Please give our regards to the Marquis and let him know we will be praying for his officers who were murdered so brutally."

"Thank you, Miss Mitchell. I will make him aware of your condolences. I know he will be disappointed to have missed the opportunity to see you again."

Lieutenant Ransom went back to his office. A small man in a seedy, tweed suit, who had been seated nearby, stood up and followed them outside. He followed the couple to their waiting carriage and driver hired for the day. As Willy assisted Peggy up into the closed carriage the man said, "Pardon me, Miss Mitchell and Mr. Mitchell." He removed his hat and held it respectfully to his chest. His eyes blinked often like he had problems with his eyesight. His hair was thin and shabby and he had a pencil moustache that did nothing for his appearance.

Peggy recognized him but couldn't remember from where. "I am Peggy Mitchell. Do I know you?" She gestured toward Willy. "This is Captain William Whiddon

III, not Mr. Mitchell. The captain is my employer. I am the nanny to his children."

"Captain Whiddon! The hero of the Battle of Camperdown? What an honor to meet you both. I have seen Miss Mitchell about town, but have never had the opportunity to meet either of you." He extended a hand stained with printer's ink, which Willy reluctantly shook. "I am Horace Graybill, a reporter for the *London Gazette*. I overheard your comment about the officers who were killed. Were they family or friends?"

"No, neither of us knew them. They were murdered by their own men and thrown overboard. Isn't that terrible?" Peggy said.

"Where did this event take place?" Horace Graybill smiled like a weasel.

"Gonaïves," Peggy said.

"Where is that?" Graybill persisted.

"In the West Indies," Willy answered, while motioning for Peggy to climb in to the carriage. "Mr. Graybill, we must be going now; we are running late," Willy said, as the reporter kept asking more questions. "Let's go home," Willy said to the driver.

\*\*\*

The next morning, Agnes gave the paper boy a penny for the *London Gazette* newspaper. The paper was an amenity for guests that could be read at leisure. Agnes kept the back issues for weeks then used the paper for fire starter or to wrap and clean with. Glancing at the front page, Agnes said, "Oh my . . . " She continued reading the front page, walking down the hall to the dining room. She sunk into her chair and read it again saying, "Oh my."

"What's so interesting?" Peggy asked.

Agnes looked at Peggy with a worried look. "It's about the mutiny of a navy ship in the French port of Gonaïves."

"Yes, we just heard about it from Lieutenant Ransom yesterday morning. What the ship's crew did was terrible," Peggy said.

Agnes looked at Peggy. "The reporter says you and Willy are the source of the story. You should read it for yourself." She handed the tabloid to Peggy.

Peggy read the bold headline, "Ship's Officers Murdered" across the front page. The article began, "Captain William Whiddon and his American female companion confirmed the report of the officers' deaths." The story went on to say the Master-General's office refused to verify or deny the story. Peggy sat down and continued reading at the table.

"Oh my . . . " Peggy looked at Agnes.

"It gets worse—read on," Agnes said.

Peggy read, "Who is this Miss Peggy Mitchell? An American woman, who claims to be the nanny of Captain William Whiddon." The story went on to say, "A permanent co-habitant at the Reynolds House in Leicester, the home of the late Sir Joshua Reynolds, who made this grand estate a comfortable nesting place for all sorts of devious people. They called it "the club." Miss Mitchell has the ear of the Master-General and his aide-de-camp. This attractive woman was aware of the murders of the officers of the *Marie Antoinette* before the Royal Palace or the press. This reporter saw her dining with Marquis Cornwallis at Rules restaurant and driven around the city in carriages belonging to the Board of the Ordnance." Peggy shook her head. "What have I done? He makes me sound like a bad person."

There was a knock at the door. "I will get it," Agnes said.

"I am John Walter, owner and editor of *The Times*, and would like to speak to Peggy Mitchell." Mr. Walter was a well dressed, portly gentlemen, with a pleasant personality.

"Just a moment, Mr. Walters, I will see if she is available." Agnes turned and Peggy was behind her.

"Come in, Mr. Walters, out of the cold." Peggy said. Agnes went back to her kitchen to finish making breakfast.

Peggy took the editor to the parlor. She pointed to the high back chair as she sat on the settee. "What can I do for you, Mr. Walters?"

"Maybe there is something I can do for you," he answered.

"How is that?" She looked at him suspiciously.

"Is what I read in my competitor's paper the truth?" Mr. Walters asked.

"It didn't happen the way he wrote the article."

"I am not surprised. One thing he said I know is the truth."

"What would that be?"

"That you are a beautiful woman." He smiled.

"Thank you, I take that as a compliment."

"I could publish a rebuttal for you, if you like," Mr. Walter suggested.

"What he says did happen. The crew of the *Marie Antoinette* killed their captain and executive officer." She looked around, thinking that others might overhear the conversation.

Mr. Walter lowered his voice. "How did you acquire your information on the mutiny of the *Marie Antoinette*, and did you tell Horace Graybill?"

Peggy shook her head. "Lieutenant Ransom apologized for the Marquis not meeting with us as scheduled, and told us why. Horace Graybill from the *Gazette* must have heard our discussion in the lobby. He approached the captain and me outside the Towers and asked if the officers killed were our family. He tricked us . . . I assumed he had been told of the incident. No one told me it was a secret. If they had I would never have said anything."

Walter continued. "That makes sense. You confirmed what he may have overheard from someone else. Fortunately, no names of the officers were mentioned. Hopefully, the navy can get word to their family before the paper names them. That is why Graybill tricked you, it gave him the opportunity to expose the story."

"Expose the story?"

"He found a way to get the story published before any of the other papers, including mine," Mr. Walter said.

"That's why he made me out to be an enemy of England — to expose a story?"

Mr. Walter nodded "I am afraid so. Unfortunately sometimes a reporter puts the penny before his principles for a story." He stood and said, "unless you have anything else to repudiate the *Gazette* story, I need to be on my way as I have a paper to publish."

Peggy walked Mr. Walter to the door. "Thank you for coming and offering to help."

"I was in hopes of dismissing my competitor's story as rubbish, but it is factual, except for how he deceitfully acquired the story. I will try to repudiate how he tricked you into confirming the story. Good day, Miss Mitchell."

Peggy watched from the door as the newspaper man drove off in his buggy.

***

Willy and the children were having breakfast with two of the permanent boarders when Peggy entered the dining room. "How are you this morning?" Willy smiled at Peggy. She looked at Agnes who was behind him with a plate of fresh biscuits. Agnes shook her head to indicate that Willy wasn't aware of the newspaper story.

"I am doing well. How are you and my students this morning?" Peggy sat down.

Agnes served Peggy eggs and bacon as Peggy reached for one of the hot biscuits. Agnes's and Peggy's eyes met, they knew what the other was thinking without saying a word. They both saw the *Gazette* on the end of the table at the same time. Agnes quickly placed it in her apron pocket and went off into the kitchen to hide it in the baker's pantry.

Willy had finished his breakfast and was looking forward to reading the paper that was usually at the end of the table. "Agnes, did the paper boy come this morning?"

Agnes heard his question coming from the dining room. She was dreading his asking for the paper as he did every morning after breakfast. *It's amazing,* she thought, *how he can't remember his children's names, but never forgets to read the Gazette.*

She answered, walking into the dining room. "Yes, he did." She looked at the usual place. "Someone must have taken it to their room."

Peggy said, "Willy, I need to talk to you before our class starts."

"This sounds serious."

"It is. Would you meet me in the library? I will be right up."

When Willy left the room, Peggy asked Agnes, "Where is it?"

Agnes went to the baker's pantry and brought the folded tabloid to Peggy, dusting flour from it with her hand. "Good luck."

"I will need it." Peggy headed for the library with paper in hand.

She paused before the open door and took a deep breath. Stepping in, she turned and closed the door, latching it from the inside. She turned toward Willy and said, "I'm so sorry. I didn't realize that filthy little weasel of a reporter was using us yesterday to expose a story that he couldn't confirm."

"What are you talking about?" Willy asked.

Peggy handed him the paper, and his eye fixated on the bold headline. He sat down at the reference table of the library, reading the article methodically.

"It appears we are about to become a well-known couple around town." Willy folded the paper neatly and placed it on the table.

"What have I done? This makes us look like traitors."

"We were easy fodder for Mr. Graybill's scheme to get someone inside the Towers to confirm a rumor he had heard." Willy opened his arms and Peggy fell into them.

"How will this affect your commission?" Peggy looked up at Willy.

"I don't know, but we can't change what has been done. We have not knowingly done anything wrong." The couple stared out the library window at William and Elizabeth playing in the park.

# Chapter Twenty-Three
## Escape From Traitors' Gate

"AMERICAN SPY IN LONDON?" screamed the headlines of the *London Gazette*. *The Times,* as its editor Mr. Walter promised, tried to trivialize the *Gazette* article about Peggy Mitchell. It didn't work. Both newspapers found their readers salivating for more about this American woman who somehow had worked her way into the highest offices of the world's greatest military.

The citizens of London were in an angry mood. They demanded to know how this could happen. Spurred on by the London Corresponding Society and a general distrust of all foreigners, especially those from America, the hang-and-burn attitude of the citizenry of England brought about "The Treasonable and Seditious Practices Act" which greatly expanded the definition of treason and the punishment for it, which was death—by hanging.

*The Times* followed the *Gazette's* lead in accommodating their readers with information about Peggy Mitchell. Reporters beat a path to the Reynolds House to interview anyone that could tell them more about the mysterious woman. Even the paper boy who had never seen Peggy was interviewed. "It was more like an interrogation than an interview. Those reporters were so rude," he said.

The *Gazette* reported customs officials had no records of Peggy Mitchell ever arriving in England. Having sailed aboard a private vessel, her arrival was only recorded in the ship's log. Willy had failed to register her or his Aunt Lisa with customs as required by the 1793 Alien Act. Lisa Yarde being family and Peggy becoming his children's nanny, he thought it not necessary. Had the *Gazette* story not run, he would have been correct. Peggy also had not signed a loyalty oath to the government, as was required for all private and public teachers in England.

If customs officials investigating Peggy discovered she imported hundreds of undeclared animal pelts and paid no duty, that would further add to her legal difficulties and implicate Willy and his family.

When the *Gazette* broke the story that there were no port of entry records for Peggy, Mr. Walters, who had been the American's ally, started to question her motives and began investigating Peggy Mitchell's activities. He discovered that last September she had opened a bank account, large in comparison to the average Londoner, at the Bank of England on Threadneedle Street. He learned there that Peggy had written a large draft that paid for Master-General Cornwallis's, Captain Whiddon's, and his son William's expensive, custom-made top hats. After the story ran, cries of influence peddling and espionage in the Board of Ordnance escalated into the call from Parliament for a complete investigation of her contacts with the Master-General and his staff.

Peggy became suspicious of everyone except Willy and his family. She stopped attending church and dined alone in her room to avoid the permanent boarders. Fearing the press, she seldom ventured out of the Reynolds House.

For Peggy's security, Agnes didn't accept any new boarders for the time being, even though the inn had rooms to let. Agnes had posted a large no vacancy sign, but curiosity seekers and reporters continued their efforts to sneak a peek at the accused American spy. They claimed to be seeking a room, to try to get inside the Reynolds House at Leicester Square. Not one intruder made it past Agnes's watchful eye. Agnes was determined to protect her best friend.

\*\*\*

While everyone at Reynolds House slept, Willy was in the kitchen preparing a tray to take to Peggy. He discreetly entered the upstairs parlor with a glass carafe of freshly-decanted port, and two port wine glasses, a cut of stilton cheese and a sliced apple. Willy set the silver serving tray down on a round Chippendale table, next to the settee. "I have brought your favorite treat."

"I see you did—and you brought wine and cheese too?" Peggy smiled at Willy.

He turned and quietly slid the bolt shut on the heavy wooden door, insuring there would be no interruptions.

She intently watched him, trying to remember all his remarkable features in the dim light of the room. Peggy wore only a long chemise. A lone, tapered candle flickered, revealing the natural beauty of her body underneath.

Since the allegations against her began, Peggy and Willy made sure not to be seen together, but met only in the seclusion of the upstairs parlor. Their love for one another had blossomed during the adversity and threats of her being a spy. The red velvet settee they lay on served as their private love nest and a sanctuary from the unknown.

This would be the lovers' last night together, a night that both would remember forever. As he slowly unbuttoned her floor length gown, he didn't say a word. Peggy had never known such passion. She treasured his every kiss and caress. Willy knew how to please in so many ways. He was the first that she had been with in this way. Peggy finally had found love and now she must leave Willy in order to save him and herself.

They had learned of her impending arrest and she had no defense. The accusations were without merit, but were factually true and punishable by death.

***

The time had come for Peggy to take her leave. Willy and Peggy had meticulously planned her escape for days, preparing for every eventuality. They had already said their goodbyes, shedding many tears.

She entered Elizabeth's downstairs room, kissed the girl on the forehead, and placed Elizabeth's doll in the child's sleeping arms. Then she entered the room William shared with his father. The moonlight from the dormer above his bed accentuated his curly, blond locks. The boy looked so much like his handsome father. She noted how he had grown in the seven months William had been her ward. He was one of the brightest students she ever taught and he had such artistic ability. Peggy bent down and kissed his cheek.

With Agnes assisting the new nanny, the children would do well in their studies. She would write them when she was safe back in America, and Willy had his ship and commission confirmed. For now, no one was to know she had left the Reynolds House.

Peggy heard the slow clip clop of a horse and buggy making its way around Leicester Square. Soon the dreaded knock at the front door was her signal to move swiftly to the baker's pantry. Agnes and Peggy ran into each other in the hall. They hugged one last time. "I wish you and John much happiness together. Write me when you think it safe. I love you," Peggy said before she scurried off to prepare for her disappearance.

Agnes used her white baker's apron to wipe the tears from her rosy cheeks. Biting her lower lip, she opened the front door. "Good morning, I am Agnes Reynolds, the proprietress. May I help you?" Agnes spoke to be heard by anyone that might be listening.

"Do you have accommodations for a single woman?" The neatly-dressed woman inquired.

"No, I am sorry I don't have any rooms to let, but please come in and let me fix you a cup of hot tea. You look—terribly cold." Agnes took the opportunity to look up and down the street and toward the park. The driver gave her a nod and a wink.

"That would be most kind of you, Miss Reynolds." The woman stepped inside, out of the morning fog that had blanketed Leicester Square this morning.

The first rays of daylight were appearing and the boarders were still in their rooms. Peggy and the woman, of her same size and height, exchanged clothes quickly in the baker's pantry.

Willy kept a close watch from the window of the parlor at one end of the hall and then moved to the library window at the other end for a peek at the street. The waiting driver discreetly kept a watchful eye as well. It seemed no one was lurking about the neighborhood this morning spying on the traitors at the Reynolds House. Everything was going as planned.

The woman said, "Thank you for the hot tea and crumpet, Miss Reynolds," as Agnes slowly opened the front door. The waiting driver assisted the woman into his buggy, climbed into the rig, tipped his hat at Agnes, then headed the one-horse buggy toward the docks of London.

The woman boarded the North Star, a Canadian ship bound for Halifax, Nova Scotia. The first mate stamped her ticket and seeing her tears, asked, "Is everything good with you, Madam?"

"Yes, it's just that goodbyes are hard to say."

"I understand. Your cabin is starboard down one deck, Mrs. Yarde."

"Thank you."

She went to her cabin, stowed her few belongings, and would stay there until the ship was underway.

She fell asleep, exhausted, in the rope bed connected to the fore and aft bulkheads. She was wakened by someone calling, "Mrs. Yarde, last call Mrs. Yarde! Evening meal is being served in the galley, at the end of the passageway to your right." *I must have slept all day.*

"Thank you," Peggy said to whoever was on the other side of the door. She had forgotten she was now the widowed Mrs. Lisa Yarde, an American tourist from Philadelphia on her way back to the states from England after a long visit with family.

From the cabin's starboard portal, she could see the water was now dark blue, not the brown murky water of the Thames, and no land was anywhere in sight. *Thank God! We have made it out to sea.* Peggy worked her way toward the galley holding tight to a bulkhead railing along the lower companion way.

She heard the sounds of the main sails unfurling, felt the wind catch the canvas, and the ship suddenly lurched forward and leaned portside. Peggy detected from the ship's vibration an increase in speed. She estimated the speed at about fifteen knots, something Peggy learned from Willy — the faster and harder the vibrations, the faster the ship's speed. *Good. The more distance from the Traitors' Gate and those that want to hang me, the better.*

As Peggy walked past a large cargo hold, she saw several families eating on the dirty floor, bed pans strewn about. There were some small rope beds for the parents, the children wrestled one another for a little floor space of their own on which to sit. They were eating porridge in their cabin from wooden bowls. *Who are these people being treated so shabbily?* They spoke English, but with a unique dialect that she had heard before.

Peggy found the ship's galley and entered the small compartment. "Welcome Mrs. Yarde, I am Captain Adolph Penner. I hope you have had a pleasant voyage so far and your accommodations are adequate."

"Thank you, Captain Penner. The cabin is sufficient for my needs," Peggy said.

"We have Irish stew this evening with fresh vegetables from a farmer's winter garden." Captain Penner pointed toward the large pot hanging from a hook over the small kitchen hearth. Peggy took a pewter bowl from a galley shelf and spooned out what remained into her bowl.

The sun had began to set and the crew and ship's passengers had eaten. She was the last to eat, due to not hearing the first call for the evening meal. She would be sure to heed the call tomorrow because all that was left was watery broth; the lukewarm liquid reminded her of dishwater.

Peggy took the stairs to the foredeck for some fresh air and to look at the moon and stars. She took comfort in knowing that Willy could see the same stars from Leicester Park.

She overheard a young boy and girl talking and Peggy recognized them from the cramped cabin she saw earlier. They were on the foredeck sitting cross-legged, intently watching the ship buck the waves as the mist from the sea sprayed up into their faces.

"What's that taste?" asked the girl.

"It's the salt from the sea you tasting, sis—don't you know nothing?"

"I know we will never see our home again," the girl, who looked about ten, said.

"How do you know that?" The boy appeared to be about twelve.

"I heard Mother and Father talking."

"When?"

"You were asleep. I heard them talking last night."

"We're never going back to Ulster?" he asked his sister.

"Never, they say we are undesirable and sending us to Canada."

"Why are we un—" the boy started to say.

"I guess cause we are poor." She shrugged her little shoulders and stared at the ocean that lay before them.

Peggy felt sad for the children and fought the urge to comfort them and tell the boy and girl everything would work out, that God loved them and would provide for them in their new home. She couldn't take the chance of saying anything that would give her identity away. She went back to her cabin, only venturing out for meals and a nightly stroll around the decks in the dark, careful not to engage anyone in conversation.

***

The ship arrived in Halifax on the twenty-first day of February. It was a clear but cold winter day. Now Peggy was only about 750 nautical miles from Portsmouth, Virginia, a trip of no more than five days. Portsmouth, according to Willy, would be many miles closer to Jonesborough than Philadelphia. Now all she needed was a ship going to Portsmouth, which would not be easy as it was a small port with less traffic than Philadelphia.

Peggy, anxious to get home, would take the first ship going to America, regardless of the port or destination. Fortuitously, a large cargo ship had been making frequent trips between Nova Scotia and Portsmouth. It was transporting large timbers from the Canadian forest to Portsmouth for a ship being built for the United States Navy. Peggy was surprised to learn America again had a navy. The first ship was being built at Portsmouth and its keel was being laid with Canadian timber shipped on the same vessel that returned Peggy to her homeland. The ship was late in arriving in Halifax due to bad weather. It took several days to load the extra-long Canadian pine timbers, extending her stay at the Halifax Inn to thirteen days.

Peggy arrived in Portsmouth on Sunday afternoon, the eleventh day of March in the twenty-second year of American Independence. She checked into the only public house in Portsmouth, a neat, framed two-story that overlooked the Elizabeth River on North Street in the center of town.

As she lugged her bag up the steep steps of the inn, a young boy came out. "Please Miss, may I carry your bag?"

"You certainly may." Peggy breathed a sigh of relief. "It's a long walk from the wharf."

"Where you coming from?" The boy opened the door and allowed Peggy to enter.

"London, by way of Halifax." Peggy gasped and breathed deeply. "Let me catch my breath."

"Welcome to Portsmouth." The boy set her bag down and called out toward the back of the large home, "Mother, we have a guest."

A large woman struggled out to the front room. "Need a room?" she said with a heavy German accent.

"Yes, please. My name is Peggy Mitchell. I will need accommodations until the next westbound stage departs."

"You might be here a while." The woman leaned against the door frame to support her weight.

"Why is that?" Peggy asked.

"If there were a stage out of here, the boy and I would have taken it years ago."

"How do people get to Tennessee from here?"

"They sail to Philadelphia, then take a westbound stage down the wagon road."

"Is there a livery stable?"

"Next door; it will be open in the morning."

"Good. For now, I would like to take a warm bath, with lavender soap, please," Peggy said.

"My son, Aaron, will take care of getting your bath water. I don't have any lavender soap, just have pine tar. Lavender doesn't grow in the tidelands."

"That will be fine, if the water is good and warm." Peggy looked at Aaron, making sure he understood she wanted a warm bath.

*** 

Peggy lay in the long, copper tub enjoying the warm water and a getting week's worth of shipboard grime off her body. *The pine tar soap did remove the ship's dirt easier than lavender soap, but the essence of the lavender smells better.*

Her thoughts turned to writing a letter to Willy, Agnes, and the children, but decided it would not be wise. The letter could be intercepted by British officials and they could be implicated as accessories to treasonous acts for helping her escape. They hadn't thought to discuss that possibility in preparing for her escape. Perhaps it wasn't discussed because neither she nor Willy could bear the thought of them never communicating again.

She lay back in the tub and enjoyed the warm water, thinking of how lucky she was to have escaped the Traitors' Gate and a hangman's noose.

\*\*\*

The German-born proprietress of the inn prepared a wonderful meal of smoked ham, yams, and greens. Peggy learned Mrs. Guenther was a widow and ran the inn for Mr. Keeling with the help of her young son, Aaron. The inn provided her and her only child food and lodging and a small income. Mr. Keeling owned several businesses in town, and was investing heavily in Portsmouth's future as a ship-building center for the navy. Mrs. Guenther expected him home from Philadelphia, where he had been on business. She told Peggy. "You know, he has his own ship to travel about."

"That's nice. Is Mrs. Keeling with him?" Peggy asked.

"No, she doesn't travel. Aaron, please take what is left of the ham to Mrs. Keeling."

Just as Mrs. Guenther cleared the dishes, Mr. Keeling arrived in a small carriage. What a noise his driver made! Whistling and hollering at the horse as they pulled up in front of the inn, the horse was all lathered up and whinnied excitedly. The mare knew that once it was unharnessed and curried, Aaron would feed her an ample supply of oats, reward for getting Mr. Keeling home.

Not feeling well, Peggy excused herself and went to her room.

\*\*\*

Roosters were crowing when Peggy walked into the livery stable to find Aaron feeding the stabled animals. "You are the stable boy?"

"Yes, Miss Mitchell."

"Why didn't you tell me you were the stable boy last night?"

"You didn't ask me."

"Does the livery stable have a buggy or horse I can purchase?" Peggy asked.

"Mr. Keeling says everything he has is for sale. He will be here shortly and you can dicker with him for anything in the stables, except the sorrel mare. I know he wouldn't part with her."

"Part with what?" Mr. Keeling said, walking into the stables. He removed his hat and said, "You must be Miss Mitchell, our guest staying at the inn."

"Yes, and you must be Mr. Keeling."

"Please, call me Richard."

"Glad to meet you Richard, please call me Peggy."

"Tell me where around the tidewaters you are going, that you think a horse is needed?" Richard asked.

"Knob Creek, just north of Jonesborough, Tennessee," Peggy said.

"I have heard of Jonesborough; It is south of Abingdon."

"Yes, that's where I'm going."

"Then, why did you sail to Portsmouth?" Richard looked at Peggy, waiting for an answer that was slow in coming.

Pegged stammered, "I—was told that Portsmouth was closer to Jonesborough than Philadelphia."

"Well, it is as the crow flies, by about two hundred miles. But, you are not a crow."

"I don't understand." Peggy was beginning to be concerned.

"Peggy, who told you to sail to Portsmouth?"

"A sea captain, who is a friend in London. We looked at a map on a globe that showed Portsmouth to be much closer to Jonesborough than Philadelphia."

Mr. Keeling explained. "Your captain was correct about the distance, but he has no knowledge of the tidelands. As any seaman around these parts worth his salt knows, you can't go south or west through the tidelands from the Chesapeake Bay—to try would be suicidal."

"Then, how do I get to Tennessee?"

"By way of Philadelphia by sea or up the James River, to the falls at Richmond."

"Richmond, isn't that the capital of Virginia?" Peggy asked.

"It is."

Peggy stated hopefully, "Surely, the capital city would have a stage to Abingdon."

"Most likely." Richard nodded.

"Richmond sounds like the fastest way for me to get home."

"If you can find a ship that can navigate it," Richard said.

"How about your ship?" Peggy asked.

"Well, I don't . . . I have thought about establishing a commercial passenger service to Richmond, with connections to Washington when it becomes headquarters for the central government." Richard looked thoughtful.

Peggy put her hand on his arm and said, "I can be your first passenger."

"Let me think about that. I will let you know at dinner. Mrs. Guenther makes her famous German chicken dumplings on Monday nights. You don't want to miss them, people come from all over to eat her dumplings," Mr. Keeling said with a grin.

"Good, I will see you at dinner." Peggy smiled, turning on the charm, knowing if he didn't agree to take her to Richmond, Philadelphia would be the only other option. She waved going out the stable door.

# Chapter Twenty-Four
## Up the James

Richard Keeling rearranged his schedule to ferry Peggy up the James to Richmond. Rescheduling meant getting permission from Mrs. Keeling to make the trip, which would take at least three days. He failed to mention to his wife that the only passenger was an attractive young woman.

Richard's wife, the daughter of a wealthy Virginia plantation owner, had a voracious appetite. Aaron confided to Peggy that Mrs. Keeling was so large that the stable had no carriage large enough to transport her.

Aaron and his mother cared for her in a room upstairs. Mrs. Guenther cooked constantly trying to satisfy Mrs. Keeling's never-ending hunger. Aaron carried huge trays of food to the room and she devoured them like a bear just out of hibernation. She hadn't ventured out of her room in years and seldom got out of bed.

Richard sat on his boat awaiting Cappy—his driver and the ship's captain. Cappy had taken Richard to the ship earlier and was going back for Peggy. A deacon at Trinity Episcopal Church, Richard didn't dare be seen alone with Peggy, concerned about what neighbors and church members might think.

Cappy turned a sharp corner. "Hang on to your bonnet, Miss Mitchell!"

"I already am!" Peggy yelled. As he made the turn heading down the roadway toward the wharf, the outside wheel of the buggy lifted up off the ground for a moment.

"We are about to hit a wee bit of a bump at the bottom of the hill," Cappy said just before the rig went in the air,

305

coming down with a jolt that made Peggy feel sick inside. Peggy wished she had walked to the wharf.

"Why are you in such a hurry?" Peggy asked.

"Mr. Keeling said to get you there as fast as I can." Cappy popped the buggy whip loudly. "I do what I'm told, Miss Mitchell."

"Please, just slow down, you are scaring me and the mare to death."

"We're just about at the *Lady Daisy*." He pulled back hard on the reins to stop the rig—hollering at the top of his lungs, "Whoa, damn it, whoa!"

He grabbed Peggy's bag in one hand, holding the other out to help her down, then they were running up the gangway.

"Welcome aboard, Peggy," Richard said.

"Glad to be aboard. I hope the voyage up the James is not so frightful as the ride from the inn." Peggy looked disapprovingly at Cappy, as she gasped for breath.

"I am sorry Cappy frightened you." He glared at Cappy, then turned back to Peggy. "I can tell that you are comfortable aboard a ship; that will make for a pleasant trip," Richard said.

"After sailing across the Atlantic and back, then from Halifax to Portsmouth, I have found my sea legs," Peggy said proudly.

"You have met our captain." Richard gestured toward Cappy, who expressed a toothless grin.

*Oh my! I pray he is a better captain than a liveryman.* Peggy nodded politely.

"The First Mate is Samuel." He said, pointing toward a scruffy-looking sailor on the short foredeck ready to man the lines. "That's Luther on the aft deck." Luther waved at her and Peggy waved back and turned toward Richard.

"Three, that is the size of your crew?" Peggy asked, sounding concerned.

"I can lend a hand if needed. On a river trip, four should be sufficient. In open waters, I would have a larger crew." He looked up at the halyard to a wind sock and said, "If the wind holds as she is now, we should be at the port of Bermuda Hundred by dark."

"Where would you like me?" Peggy asked.

Richard pointed toward a bench behind the helm. "You may sit with me on deck or go below out of the sun and wind."

"I like the action of getting underway, I would like to stay topside and watch."

"As you wish, please have a seat until our sails are unfurled." He motioned for her to be seated and for Cappy to cast off.

The ship was small compared to the vessels Peggy had been on. It was about forty-five feet in length and fifteen feet in width. The belowdecks were a small hold the size of two enclosed carriages, but with less headroom. Two staterooms, fore and aft, served as living quarters for the crew.

Lines were pulled in and coiled on the deck, and the lone mainsail was unfurled. As the wind filled the jib and caught the sails, the vessel moved forward toward the mouth of the James River.

As the *Lady Daisy* made its way up the river, Peggy realized why a trip by horse would have been difficult. Water was everywhere. The ship cut its way through the now-green waters. Peggy listened to the abundant sounds of swamp life in the tidelands. She felt at home seeing deer and turkey coming to the river's edge; the critters of the James paid the ship little attention. The river made a sharp bend at what Cappy called Hog Island. The river men named the island for the wild hogs that were its only inhabitants.

Peggy went below seeking shade from a blistering sun on the warm spring day. She became nauseous, something that hadn't occurred at sea, but was giving her difficulty in the calm waters of the James.

Richard brought her a cup of water. "Here Peggy, just sip this."

"Thank you." Peggy took a sip.

"Should you need anything, just bang on the deck with this," handing her a wooden mallet, making a motion to beat it on the bulkhead for attention.

Peggy nodded her appreciation as Richard went topside. She felt uncomfortable on the long bench that ran the length of the small cabin. She looked at the bench on the other side and at the ends. It could accommodate twenty to thirty people sitting around it, but they would be knee to knee, with no headroom. *Not very comfortable for paying passengers.*

There were large metal rings above the seat and on the floor below the bench, rusty chains and shackles stowed in a corner under the bench. Visible marks worn into the rough-hewn bench seats, indications of a precious cargo that struggled with the chains that bound them.

Peggy realized the dark stains on the wooden benches were blood. Without warning she suddenly threw up on the floor, taut black faces in agony now embedded in her mind. She wanted out of the hellhole that was built to transport slaves like caged animals. She couldn't move or scream. The slaves reached out to her, chains rattling, begging Peggy to please help them. Nathan and her life-long friend Daniel sat in waiting, watching the slaves begging for their freedom.

"Peggy, are you all right?" Richard asked. Her head was on his knees, a wet cloth on her forehead.

"I must have fainted." Peggy began to slowly sit up.

Richard had a hand on each arm. "Can you stand?"

"I think so—thank you. I need fresh air. Can you help me out of here?" Peggy stood slowly with Richard's help, both hunched over in the small quarters.

Once outside, she took a deep breath and felt much better, but still could not get the thought of shackled slaves out of her mind. *If I confront Richard about his sinfulness, I could be put ashore in the tidelands swamp to fend for myself.*

"I apologize, Peggy, for the condition of the cabin. I just recently purchased this old slave ship for the passenger service I had been planning. The crew and I were in the process of refitting her when your sense of urgency forced us into immediate service," Richard said.

"It was a slave ship—to transport slaves?" Peggy didn't let on that she had figured that out.

"I bought the vessel at auction in Philadelphia, named it after my wife Daisy."

Peggy sat down, slowly. *Named a slave ship for his wife; that's a strange honor.*

"May I?" Richard gestured toward the space on the seat beside her.

"Certainly you may. Does Mrs. Keeling like to sail?" She asked—curious how he would answer.

"She did when we first married. She is not well now. Hasn't left the house in years."

Peggy said, "I am sorry."

"Thank you, Peggy." Richard took the opportunity to change the subject, saying, "

We should be crossing into Prince Charles County within the hour." Richard rose to speak to Samuel, his first mate. Peggy was relieved to learn that Richard was not a slave trader.

Cappy chose to anchor off the port of Bermuda Hundred until morning. The upper James River from this point on narrowed and could quickly become shallow enough to ground a heavy boat.

Peggy chose to sleep on the foredeck, hoping the bay breeze would keep the flying insects away.

Still asleep, Peggy instinctively knew someone was looking at her. She slowly opened one eye, then the other to see Samuel, the first mate standing over her. "Sorry to wake you Miss Mitchell, but Luther and I must bring in the anchor."

"Bring it in then," Peggy snapped.

"We can't with you there—you are over the hold that we stow the anchor in. You best move aft, so as you don't get wet and muddy." Peggy grudgingly moved to an aft bench.

As they pulled in the heavy anchor, the jib opened and the mainsail unfurled and they were moving north into the upper reaches of the James.

They reached the falls of the James at midafternoon. Peggy paid Richard for passage and said, "I wish you luck on your passenger service. I am honored to have been your first passenger."

A young teamster in his late teens was waiting for what he thought was a boat load of slaves to haul to the auction house in Richmond.

"How many you got what needs hauling?" The teamster hollered from a small landing on the bank.

"One passenger coming ashore!" Richard hollered back.

"No slaves for the auction?" The teamster shook his head as he rowed out to the *Lady Daisy*. He thought, *how can I make any money hauling one passenger?*

The teamster reached up to grab Peggy's leg as she climbed over the rail, putting her feet into the rope ladder. She retorted, "I can make it on my own, just take my bag."

"You brung me a feisty one, and pretty." The teamster said, admiring her derrière from below the rope ladder.

"Watch your mouth, sir! Miss Mitchell is a very proper lady returning from London and I demand you show my first passenger the respect she deserves!" Richard shook his fist as he spoke.

"Sorry—I meant no harm in my jest," the young man with blond hair said, helping her into the leaky boat that could accommodate about six adults.

"Would you know when the next stage to Ingles Ferry would be heading west?" Peggy asked.

"Just missed it—left early this morning," he said as he rowed the boat toward shore. "I could take you. I am going empty and bringing back a load of salt."

"What did you say your name was?" Peggy looked into his blue eyes trying to decide if he was trustworthy.

"Matthew Ingles—just call me Matt." He climbed out of the rickety boat, offering Peggy a hand.

"Are you kin to Mary Ingles, the mayor of Ingles Ferry?" Peggy asked.

"She is my grandmother. Where would a nice lady like you have met Mary Draper Ingles?" Matt asked.

"I met her last year buying furs," Peggy said.

"She told me about you." Matt laughed. "Said you were the best fur trader she ever met."

"Really? I look forward to seeing her again, on my way home," Peggy said.

Matt took Peggy's bag and helped her up to the landing.

"How much for the boat ride?" Peggy reached for a leather pouch that hung from her arm.

Matt shook his head. "I couldn't charge a friend of my grandmother's."

His dog barked.

"I just met her once. I don't think that makes us friends. Acquaintances, maybe."

"You're a friend of Sheriff Preston. Grandmother and the sheriff told me how you saved his life."

"They did?"

"That was quite a story—can't take money from someone that saved my friend Sheriff Preston."

"You know him well then?" Peggy said.

Matthew helped Peggy up into his wagon. It was constructed to haul freight, but was easily converted to haul large groups of people by sliding boards through slots that made convenient, but not comfortable, seating. "Sheriff Preston saved my life, your grandmother saved Sheriff Preston during the revolution, you saved him from the infection. I wouldn't be here had it not been for you and your grandmother."

Matt's dog stood on all fours, tail wagging, head on the buckboard waiting for someone to pay him some attention. "His name is Horse," Matt said.

"I don't understand." Peggy petted the dog's head.

"I named him Horse 'cause he is as big as a small horse," Matt explained.

Peggy said, "I meant I don't know how my saving Sheriff Preston saved you?"

"Sheriff Preston saved my life—your saving his life is why I am here today. That is the way fate works. One good deed leads to another." Matthew stepped up into the wagon.

"It's not fate, Matthew—it's God's plan," Peggy said firmly.

Horse put both front feet on the buckboard and his hind legs were in the bed of the wagon. His head was two feet above theirs. She looked up at the dog and said, "Matt, Horse is the biggest dog I have ever seen. What kind of dog is he?"

Matthew looked at Peggy and smiled, shook the leather reins and said, "It sure looked like Sheriff Preston that pulled me out of the river that day." Shaking the reins harder, his horses responded by pulling the freight wagon up the steep hill toward Richmond. "The drummer that gave Horse to me called him an Irish Wolfhound. I don't see any wolf in him, do you?"

Peggy looked the dog over. "I think he meant he was bred to hunt wolves. Wolfhounds are very popular in England."

Matt shook his head and said, "My dog is a wolfhound," and broke out laughing.

Peggy liked his sense of humor.

***

The next morning, Matthew was out front of the ordinary house of his parents, harnessing his rig for the

250-mile trip to Ingles Ferry. His mother handed him a crate of baked breads and pies take to her mother-in-law, Mary Ingles. "Make sure these get to your grandmother." She insinuated he might eat them on the way. "Make sure Horse doesn't get into them, either."

Peggy came out of the house. "Good morning, Mrs. Ingles, Matthew. It looks like a good day to travel." She handed Matthew her bag. He placed it next to the crate of food under the buckboard, where Horse couldn't get to them.

His father came out from the stables. "Good morning, Miss Mitchell." He was holding a crate containing four live chickens. "Where do you want mother's chickens?"

Matthew placed the chicken cage in the bed of the wagon. White feathers flew when they saw the dog and the chickens squawked about in the cage. Horse seemed more afraid of them than they were of him. Then Matt loaded empty salt barrels that customers had left on the front porch, each owner's name marked in chalk on the oak barrels. Matt would bring them back full. Their customers called their inn the Salt House, as it was the town's only source of salt.

Matt said goodbye and hugged his father and kissed his mother. Watching them reminded Peggy of the family she had not seen in nearly a year. She realized Matthew was a good boy, they had just got off on a bad foot yesterday. *I have been overly sensitive lately, I must work on that,* she thought as Matt drove away.

Matthew said, "Hang on Peggy. While the road is good, I will try to make some good time. The road gets pretty treacherous about ten miles out of town."

Peggy nodded, but the bouncing freight wagon was making her nauseous. Just outside of town she said, "Can you please stop the wagon—I am feeling sick." She lost her breakfast before she could get out of the wagon.

"I am sorry this old wagon has no springs and it rides rough without a load. Do you want to get down?" He sat, reins in his hands, waiting patiently for an answer.

"How far is Ingles Ferry?" Peggy took a deep breath.

"Good weather, I can make it in six days."

"The bouncing is upsetting my stomach," Peggy said.

"I will slow the horses' gait if you wish, but it might take an extra day to reach Ingles Ferry."

"If it takes an extra day, so be it," Peggy said.

"I don't mind, I thought you were in a hurry." Matt started the team slowly.

Peggy answered, "That was before that first bump in the road."

"We'll go nice and easy then." Matt gently shook the rein until the horses were in a comfortable gait.

"Thank you," Peggy said.

"How many days since you left England?"

"What is today's date?" Peggy asked.

"Saturday, the seventeenth day of March," Matt said.

Peggy calculated in her head for several moments. "Six weeks since I left London." She added four weeks and said, "Matthew, please stop."

"Again—you sick again?"

"Help me down, please."

Matthew jumped down and helped her gently to the ground. Peggy took off toward a thicket of Mountain Laurel. Matthew watched her disappear into the woods, shaking his head. He reached for the grub box his mother had packed and devoured a few of the sweet treats she had packed.

Peggy leaned against a large oak tree back in the thicket for some time. She again counted the weeks since she and Willy were first intimate. The nausea and vomiting usually in the morning, symptoms of an early pregnancy of ten to twelve weeks. She felt her belly. *Is it possible, could it be?*

Peggy came out of the thicket smiling, to find Matt and the dog asleep under the wagon. Rather than wake them, she pulled out a bedroll and laid it down at the other end under the wagon. Excited at the thought she might be pregnant with Willy's child, Peggy couldn't sleep.

Matthew, bothered by horse flies, began to stir. He swatted at the buzzing insects wildly, which woke his dog. Seeing Peggy laughing at him, he got up, saying, "Damn horse flies." Slightly embarrassed, he brushed at the dirt on his clothes with his hands. "You ready to travel?" Horse jumped in the wagon with little effort; the chickens squawked and feathers flew.

"We best get moving. Daylight's a burning," Peggy said.

"I like that—daylight's a burning." Matt helped Peggy up into the wagon. "You feeling better now?"

"Much better. Thank you for being so patient with me," Peggy said.

Matt shook the reins and they were off again with Horse's front paws firmly placed between them on the seat.

"Six weeks you been traveling?" Matt shook his head.

"Yes, and I am ready to get home." Peggy sighed.

"That's how long it took Grandmother Ingles to get home when she escaped from the Shawnee," Matthew said.

"Mary Draper Ingles was an Indian hostage?" Peggy looked surprised.

"In the summer of 1755, Shawnee Indians attacked Drapers Meadow, a settlement my great-grandparents started. The Indians attacked while the men were in the fields working. They killed my great-grandmother Draper, that's Grandmother Ingles' mother. They captured grandmother, her sons Thomas and George, and her sister-in-law Betty Draper, and they burned the house down. Grandmother escaped somehow and made it back to Virginia from way up on the Ohio River, about 700 miles—barefoot and naked, in wintertime. She survived on the land for forty-two days." Matt shook his head. "She's one tough woman."

"What happened to her sons and sister-in-law?" Peggy asked.

"The oldest, George, died in captivity. Thomas was ransomed when he was seventeen. He had grown up an Indian and couldn't accept the white man's ways. When Grandmother was reunited with Grandfather Ingles, they moved to the New River Valley farm and because they owned land on both sides of the river, started a ferry on the wagon road. My father John, whom you met, was born at Ingles Ferry. My Grandfather Ingles died when I was just a baby, I can't remember him."

"Do you ever see Indians around here?"

"Not very often. Most have moved west with the buffalo. Those that have remained have accepted or married into the white man's world. If you're worried about Indians—don't be. It's the white highway bandits you need to worry about." Matt pointed at his long rifle.

"Yes, I know from experience."

"I heard some of the stories about you from Sheriff Preston." Matthew laughed. "Did you really dig a piece of shrapnel out of his butt?"

"Yes, I did, but it wasn't shrapnel, but grapeshot that General Cornwallis's artillery fired that hit the Sheriff in his behind."

"Well, we know which way the Sheriff was headed," Matt laughed.

"Not so. You would've had to been there, like I was, to understand."

"You were there?"

Peggy nodded and said, "Yes."

"You saw the battle?"

"Much more than I wanted to see." She looked away, indicating she didn't wish to talk about it.

They rode along not saying a word, each in their own thoughts. Horse laid his head in Peggy's lap as she rubbed his ears and shaggy head.

# Chapter Twenty-Five

### Ingles Ferry

They made it to Ingles Ferry on Saturday afternoon, the twenty-fourth day of March. Peggy remembered the anxious moments of the last ferry crossing at the New River. She hoped no one recognized her as the person who helped Nathan Brown evade arrest. *A year has passed, I have put on some weight. Hopefully no one remembers me.*

"Here we are," Matt said, pulling the team and wagon up to his grandmother's home overlooking the New River.

"We need to find me an inn until the stage arrives from Philadelphia," Peggy said.

"I know my grandmother and she will want you to stay in her house," Matt said.

"Are you sure?"

Matt nodded to Peggy as he grabbed her bag.

Sara opened the door and said, "You get in this house, Matt, and who is this good-looking woman you brought with you?"

"This is Peggy Mitchell—"

"From Nobby Creek?" Sara interrupted Matt.

"Knob Creek," Peggy said.

"That's what I said, Nobby Creek." Sara took Peggy's bag.

While joyous greetings were being exchanged, Horse quietly snuck in behind them and went straight to Mary's room.

"I am sure glad to see you both again. Your Grandmother is not doing very well," Sara said.

"What's wrong with Grandmother?"

"She drinking a lot of whisky, sleeps most of the time. I have a hard time getting her to eat. She just wants to drink . . . "

A blood-curdling scream was heard. "What the hell is this ugly critter doing in my bedroom?"

They ran to Mary's room and found Horse, his chin resting on the end of Mary's canopy bed, looking at her like a long lost friend. Mary was curled up in fear looking back at the enormous, shaggy dog.

"That's Horse, Grandmother, the puppy that the whisky drummer gave me on my last trip," Matt said.

"That is the pup you took home on your last trip?" Mary asked.

"Sure is," Matt said.

"Damn sure glad you picked the runt of the litter." Mary gave her grandson a hug, put on her spectacles and saw Peggy. "Where in the world did you find the girl from Knob Creek? Come here, girl." She put out her arms and gave her a hug.

"Good to see you again, Mary." Peggy held her for a moment. Mary was so much like her grandmother in many ways, except for the drinking and swearing.

"Grandmother, I need to take care of my team and unload the salt barrels."

"Take this damn critter with you. What kind of dog is Horse, anyhow?"

"Irish Wolfhound." Matt said as he pulled the door open.

"They don't have wolves in Ireland." Mary turned to sit on the edge of her bed.

"That's 'cause they have wolfhounds." Matt waved, closing the door.

"Get out of here and take care of your business. Peggy and I got some catching up to do," Mary called out to Matt.

Peggy said, "The two of you are hilarious. Do you always—"

"My grandson Matt has a wit about him that can't be equaled." Mary slowly stood up from her bed and moved to the other high back chair in the large bedroom that had a view of the river.

"How are you doing, Mary?" Peggy asked.

"Not bad for a seventy-five-year-old woman."

Peggy grinned and said, "You're just a few years older than my parents."

"That's crock, Peggy, but how are they?"

"I haven't seen them since I saw you last. I am just now on my way home."

Mary looked surprised. "Just now? Where in the hell have you been all this time?

"It's—it's a long story. I want to hear about you and how you are doing. Then I will tell you where I have been."

Mary snorted and said, "They thought I had the cholera last fall. I knew I didn't, but the doctor that comes through insisted I did—wouldn't leave till I bought his damn medicine." She pointed at a quart-sized jug on the mantel. "I didn't take it just to prove a point."

"What was your point?"

"He told me not to drink any more whisky. Take his remedy for two weeks and I would be well at the end of it."

"So, then what happened?"

Mary attempted a laugh but it came out like a cough, "After two weeks of not drinking any more or any less whiskey, I got well without his medicine. I knew it wasn't cholera."

"How so?" Peggy asked.

"You're a healer, how do people catch cholera?"

"Usually from the water."

Mary said, "I don't drink water, haven't in years—just whisky."

Sara came in to the room and asked, "Can I get you anything?" She looked first at Mary and then Peggy.

They both shook their heads. "I best be getting dinner ready for . . . ?"

"Three," Mary said.

"I couldn't impose," Peggy said.

"You are my guest. I don't get much company—not many want to visit a cranky old woman."

Peggy asked, "Would you mind if I took a nap before dinner? I am worn out."

Mary answered, "Certainly not. Sara, will you put Peggy's things in the guest room?"

Sara was heading for the door. "I already have, brought in a pitcher of water and some towels. Your room is ready for you, Peggy. I will take you to it."

Peggy gave Mary another hug. "I'll see you at dinner."

\*\*\*

Sara pulled back the covers on the guest bed, closed the curtains and said, "In your condition, you need lots of rest."

"My condition—Sara, what do you mean?" Peggy looked at her in surprise.

"You know you are with child, don't you?" Sara asked.

"I could be, but I am not certain. How would you know if I am pregnant or not?"

"You are with child," Sara said assuredly, nodding her head.

"How can you say that with such certainty?" Peggy asked. She removed her shoes, sitting on the vanity stool looking up at Sara. She pushed the stool back under the vanity dresser and struggled to get out of her dress.

"Let me help you." Sara unbuttoned the top button on the back of Peggy's dress. "I seen it in your eyes, when you came in the house with Matt."

"You saw it in my eyes? Sara, how can you tell by just looking in someone's eyes if they are pregnant?"

"Like you, Miss Peggy, I have special God-given powers. Since a young girl I have been able to look in the eye of a woman with child, and see the child in the reflection of the mother's eye."

Peggy realized Sara had to have some kind of special powers. How else could she have possibly known?

Peggy asked, now excited, "I am pregnant then. I am definitely with child."

"That's what I said."

"Can you tell if the baby is a boy or a girl?"

"When you are further along, I may be able to tell you." Sara went to the door "You rest now, good for you, good for the baby." Sara slowly closed the door behind her.

Peggy remembered the story Sheriff Preston had told her—how his friend William Ingles had traded a good team of horses for Sara, several years before his death. Her previous owner, during a bout of serious drinking, had led William to believe the slave being bartered was a man. Male slaves were more valuable, especially those of size. The big-boned slave he called Sam was six-and-a-half feet tall, dressed in loose-fitting men's clothes and looked very much like a man. When he found out Sam was a female, he wanted the Sheriff to arrest the plantation owner who he thought had swindled him. Mary thought it was funny, as did the Sherriff.

Before coming to Ingles Ferry, Sara had several owners, all of whom had encountered misfortune after purchasing her. Her Haitian mother and grandmother were black witches who taught Sara the secrets of their craft at an early age.

The slave owners, often cruel to Sara, felt she created hardships by placing curses on them. She was sold and traded often and soon was known throughout the New River Valley for her witchcraft. No one wanted a black witch, capable of putting a curse on her master.

Mary Ingles thought the talk was hogwash at first. After a while, Mary saw enough to know that Sara had special powers that could be a benefit to her and William.

Sara's size and strength were useful after William became an invalid and needed assistance. Sara was now Mary's greatest asset and would be rewarded with her freedom and a place to live after Mary's death.

When Peggy woke, Mary was sitting beside her bed, now dressed and with her silver-handled walking cane. "When you take a nap, you take a nap."

"How long did I sleep?" Peggy saw candles burning on the mantle and realized it was dark.

"Don't worry, you didn't miss much around Ingles Ferry. Are you hungry?" Mary asked.

"I am starved," Peggy said.

"You should be, seeing as you're with child."

"Sara told you?"

"No, a chimney swallow told me." Mary managed a hoarse laugh. "Sara is loyal—she tells me anything that she thinks I need to know." Mary stood up with the help of her cane. "Food's covered up on the table waiting for you. Matt and I have eaten; he's gone to the tavern. I'll head on down to the dining room while you get ready."

*** 

When Peggy entered the dining room, Mary was sitting in a chair next to the end of a long, oak dining table. There was a small fire in the fireplace that gave the room a delightful oak smell.

Mary pointed and said, "Sit across from me, so I can look at you." She took a sip of whisky.

Peggy looked at the food on the table as she sat across from her hostess. "This food looks delicious. Matt and I lived on bread and dried beef the last few days."

"Help yourself, Peggy." Mary raised her glass.

Peggy filled her plate.

Mary watched her from across the table. A candelabra in the middle of the table with six candles burning lit the room. Mary looked into Peggy's eyes and asked, "Is your baby my great-grandchild?"

Peggy was caught off guard by the question and sat back in her chair for a moment. Then said, "*No*, Mary. Matt ferried me from a riverboat when I got to Richmond. He offered to bring me here after I missed the stage. As attractive as I find your grandson, we have never been intimate. I can understand why you might think that—the two of us traveling alone together. You didn't know the circumstances of our chance encounter on the James River last week."

Mary smiled. "That's exactly what he said."

"So now Matt knows?" Peggy asked.

"Yes—I had to ask him. If the child were to be my first great-grandson, I would expect Matt to do the right thing." Mary took another drink. "Matter of fact, I was a little excited about the possibility of you two having a baby."

"I consider that a very nice compliment, Mary."

Mary took another swig and said, "Who is the father?"

"A British Naval officer." Peggy sighed.

"Will he marry you?"

"He would—if he knew," Peggy said, putting down her fork.

"You are going to tell him, aren't you?"

"I can't." Peggy started crying.

"Where is he?" Mary asked.

Peggy began to tell Mary everything that had happened after leaving Ingles Ferry last summer. Mary just listened and drank, until Peggy finished.

"For such a good person, you sure back your butt into to some big bear traps."

Peggy just nodded and they both sat and said nothing, until Matt came in from playing cards at the tavern.

"You sure are quiet," Matt said, looking at Peggy, then his grandmother.

Peggy started to cry. Mary waved toward Matt like he was a fly—as if to go away. Matt had learned at an early age what that meant and he started to back out of the room slowly.

"Tell Sara I won't be needing her any more tonight and I will see her in the morning. Your room is ready for you . . . and that damn dog you have already snuck in."

"How did you know I brought Horse in?" Matt asked.

"You can't sneak anything that big in the house without your grandmother knowing it."

Matt said, clamoring down the stairs, "Good night, Grandmother; good night, Peggy."

The two women both managed a laugh.

"Peggy, you and I have much in common, despite fifty years difference in our age."

"We do . . . how so?"

Mary continued, "When I was about your age a band of savages captured me and my sons, George and Thomas." Peggy didn't let on that Matt had told her about Mary being captured by Indians.

"The bastards brutally murdered my dear mother in front of me and the boys. Raped my sister-in-law and burned our cabin. My husband, William, was in the fields working. He didn't know what was happening. He saw smoke, ran all the way, by the time he got to the house— we were long gone." Mary stopped and poured another glass of whisky.

"Do you really need more whisky, Mary?"

"You sound like Sara . . . No I don't need any more, but I want it," Mary said sarcastically. "It dulls the memory, but some things—no amount of whisky can wash away."

Mary took a sip from the glass. "I lost our baby girl on the way to the Indian's camp. Pregnant and showing when we were captured, that's the only reason I wasn't raped."

"What about the baby?" Peggy asked.

"The Indians put her little stillborn body in the Ohio River. I watched the baby float away."

"I'm sorry, Mary." Peggy sat back in her chair and let out a sigh at the thought of Mary's experience. "What happened to your sons?"

"They kept us separated and eventually gave them to different Indian families. George died in captivity. My husband ransomed Thomas when he was seventeen. Thomas grew up a Shawnee Indian brave. He could never adjust to the white man's way of life—we lost them both."

"Matt mentioned you escaped from the Indians, but it took six weeks to get home."

"Some things I don't talk about . . . It's not that I am ashamed of things I had to do to survive. When I allow myself to think of them, I tend to drink too much." Mary waited for the drinking sermon that didn't come.

Peggy broke the uncomfortable silence. "I am anxious to get back to my family. When is the next westbound stage coming through Ingles Ferry?"

"It came through while you were sleeping," Mary said.

"Has it gone?"

"They just change out the team and drivers and the stage goes on to Abingdon."

Peggy was annoyed. "Why didn't you wake me?"

"You shouldn't be traveling in your condition. You should stay here until after the baby is born. Sara is the best midwife around for miles."

"I want to go home," Peggy moaned.

"I know you do! You have already put your unborn child at great risk just getting to Ingles Ferry," Mary stated.

"I didn't know I was pregnant for sure until Sara told me!" Peggy blurted out. "I didn't have an option. If I hadn't made my escape, the Brits would have hung me." Peggy sobbed.

Mary shook her head. "Damn girl—you sure know how to stir up a pot of trouble."

"It was just like when I tried to help Nathan Brown," Peggy said.

"That page of your life is closed, Peggy. Nathan came through here last fall with your horse. Told me what you did for him, even loaning him your horse and giving him money. He came through taking your horse back to Jonesborough."

"My horse, Mr. Jackson, is home in Jonesborough?" Peggy asked excitedly.

Mary answered, "That's where he said he was taking him."

"I had decided I would never see Mr. Jackson again," Peggy said.

"You must have faith that all things will work out for the best." Mary rose, pushing up with much difficulty on the heavy table. "Good night, Peggy. Just cover the food and blow out the candles. This old lady is going to bed."

Peggy got up from the table. "Please let me help you into bed." She took Mary by the arm and walked her slowly down the hall to her room.

"You finally ready for your bed?" Sara had been sitting in the high back chair waiting for Mary to come to bed.

"I sent Matt to tell you to go to your quarters," Mary said.

"You know I can't go to sleep until you're in your bed," Sara said.

"I'm going to my room. Good night Sara. Good night Mary." Peggy shut the door behind her.

Peggy went back to her room but couldn't sleep. She lay in her bed tossing and turning, trying to get comfortable. Thinking fondly of Willy and his children, Peggy realized that her child may never know his father or siblings. That thought saddened her, but she would have many cousins and young uncles Hezekiah and James, who would be just seven and nine years older. Peggy thought, *how do I know it's a girl? I just referred to my baby as she. That's interesting.*

Peggy smelled something whiffing in the window from outside. It reminded her of the smell in the Chief's lodge years ago when she and her father went to retrieve their dog Lulubelle. The dog had been severely kicked by the Indian Chief's horse and his squaw nursed her back to health.

Thinking fresh air would do her some good, she decided to take a walk, trying not to wake Matt or Mary. Peggy tip-toed down the wooden staircase and slowly lifted the large, metal latch. Once out of the house, she felt something push against her backside in a very inappropriate manner. She stepped out into the moonlight and saw that it was Matt's dog, Horse.

The dog quietly followed her along the path leading toward the river. Horse's presence gave her comfort and his size gave her confidence. Peggy noticed a small log cabin with the door and window open. The aromatic smell was coming from the cabin.

Peggy and Horse stopped on higher ground where there was a large, fallen tree, just the perfect spot to sit. The light of a full moon made the water of the New River glisten. She heard tree frogs singing and the hoarse call of a hoot owl. She listened as it seemed to say, *"Who cooks for you?"* She hooted back and the owl flapped its wings, as if to let Peggy know it was in the tall tree behind her.

Now rested from her travel, Peggy felt content and happy that she was carrying Willy's baby. Sad that Willy would probably never be a part of their life, she thanked God for getting her back this far and prayed for her and the baby's safe return to Jonesborough.

# Chapter Twenty-Six
## A Special Place

Peggy begged Sara to reveal the sex of her child. She reluctantly said the position of the abdomen suggested the child was a girl. Three months had passed since Matt left Peggy with his grandmother at Ingles Ferry. Now, halfway through the pregnancy, her condition was obvious. Peggy was wise to stay at Ingles Ferry. Mary and Sara gave her the care she needed. The pregnancy was troublesome. Peggy suffered severe cramps, at times so painful she was unable to get out of bed. Mary and Sara pampered the mother-to-be, making sure she got ample rest and nourishment. They giggled and laughed, feeling her belly when the baby was actively kicking.

Helping Sara with midwifery was good for Mary; she now had a reason to live. Mary anxiously awaited the birth of Peggy's child, like it was her grandchild. Sara was amazed at how Mary had perked up in anticipation of the birth, but was concerned about the outcome.

Mountain laurel and rhododendron, now in full bloom, painted the hilly landscape along the river in colors of pink, white and purple. From her room, Peggy could watch the activity of the ferry, as it transported people, their teams and wagons across the New River. The river was anything but new. When the first settlers moving west discovered it, they referred to the new-found waterway as the new river. For lack of a better name, they continued to call it the New River.

Peggy had always been told gambling was the sport of the devil and definitely not a game for ladies. Mary said to the contrary, God would never deduct time playing poker with friends from a person's life. Peggy didn't believe her but enjoyed playing cards with Mary and Sara.

"I fold." Peggy laid her cards down.

"Again?" Mary asked.

"Me, too." Sara laid her cards down.

Mary laughed, "You two are the worst poker players I have ever played cards with. One of you should have called my bluff—I had a pair of twos, that's all I had. Both of you had better hands."

Sara laughed. "You beat us again, Mary."

Mary stood up with the help of her cane and a hand on the table. "It's been fun, but it's time for my nap."

"Let me help you," Sara said.

"No, I can make it to bed, Sara. Wake me about an hour before dinner."

"I will; you get some good rest." Sara shuffled the well-used deck of cards.

"Sleep well, Mary," Peggy said, trying to move her large belly to turn toward Mary, but only managing a wave over her shoulder.

"You uncomfortable, aren't you, Peggy?" Sara leaned across the table toward Peggy and said, "I have never been with child, but it must be hard to move, swollen up like you are."

"It is, Sara. I am so uncomfortable and really hurting." Peggy grimaced trying to get comfortable.

"Would you like me to help you to your bed?"

"No, thank you. I am going to try to stay up until dinner." Peggy reached for Sara's folded hands on the table. "Thank you for all you do for me," she said, putting her hands on Sara's large hands, which made her own look small.

"You are a good woman, Peggy Mitchell. You have treated me like a person. Most people fear me or make fun of me because of my size or the color of my skin. Some say I look more like a man than a woman; others think I'm a witch and can put curses on people I don't like." Sara laughed. "I sure wish I could, sometimes."

Peggy tried to laugh, but her pain was too great.

Sara gently turned Peggy's palms up and began to study them.

"I can see you're going to marry a handsome young man. He is going to help you raise a house full of children . . . "

"When, Sara?"

"It will be soon, Peggy."

"How many children will I have, Sara?"

Sara studied the long horizontal line on Peggy's palm intently for some time, her face close to the open hand as if she were reading small print in a book.

Peggy said, "Tell me how many, Sara."

"I can't." Sara looked into Peggy's eyes.

"What did you see Sara?"

"It's getting late, I got to get dinner started." Sara let go of Peggy's hand, rushing out the door.

"Sara—what's wrong?" Peggy called out.

"Got to go now; no time to read palms."

Peggy heard Sara lumbering down the stairs. From the window, she saw Sara hurrying toward her cabin, rather than the kitchen. *What's wrong with her? Why did she leave so abruptly, telling me she is going to prepare dinner? Then go to her cabin?*

Not feeling well, Peggy decided to go to her room. She felt light-headed when she stood, but managed to get to her room and into bed.

In such pain, Peggy couldn't sleep. *I wish Willy was here.*

After several hours, the pain became so intense she couldn't stand it any longer.

Peggy called out, "Sara, please help me . . . come help me . . . please."

Sara came in, took one look at her and said, "Time has come. I am here for you."

Mary also heard Peggy's screams, and came to her room, saying as she entered, "Sara—what can I do?"

"It's getting dark. Will you light the candles?" Sara looked at the candelabra on the mantel.

Sara saw Mary was just too feeble and said, "Here let me." She took the flint fire starter and lit all four candles.

"I want to help!" Mary said firmly.

"Pray for Peggy—cause her baby is already in God's hands. I need you to pray that I can save the momma." Peggy was straining and breathing hard. One push, a scream, and the lifeless baby girl was now cradled in Sara's left palm. She cut the umbilical cord from around the baby's neck with the other hand. Peggy lay motionless, soaked in perspiration on the bloody bed linens. Sara put her head to Peggy's chest. "Her heart still beat . . . " She looked at Mary, who was now standing with a hand on Peggy's head. It was the first time Sara had seen Mary cry. *She never shed a tear at her husband's death, but she is crying over Peggy's stillborn child and the mother, whom she hardly knew.*

"Sara, she has a terribly high fever."

"I know." Sara poured fresh water into a wash basin from a pitcher. She soaked the washcloth and wrung it out with her strong hands—leaving just enough water to do the job. Sara started washing Peggy's ashen face. The cool, wet rag seemed to revive her.

Peggy moved her head slowly, looking at Mary, then Sara and said, "I want my baby."

"Peggy your baby was born dead. I am sorry."

Peggy laid back. "No, please God—don't take my baby; she can't be dead. "

Sara said, "Let me clean you up."

Peggy beat the feather bed with closed fists.

"I want to see her—it was a girl?" Peggy looked at Sara. "Wasn't it?"

"Yes, she was a pretty little girl," Sara said softly.

"I want to hold her."

"Of course you do." Sara looked at Mary and when Mary nodded, she laid the body of the child on Peggy's naked abdomen.

Peggy gently placed both hands on the back of the tiny body, about the size of a baby kitten. Sara hummed a Haitian lullaby while she continued to cleanse Peggy from head to toe.

Mary just sat with her hands in her lap and wept. Sara, as always, pretended not to notice any emotion from Mary.

"Let me have your baby for a moment and I will clean her up and put her in a baby blanket for you, then you can hold her as long as you like."

"Thank you." Peggy smiled at Sara.

Sara carefully cleaned the baby, wrapping her tiny body in a large wash cloth, showed her to Mary and handed the stillborn baby to Peggy, who managed to sit up slightly when Sara tucked pillows behind her. Peggy instinctively held the baby to her bosom.

Sara choked up. "I will leave you alone with your baby now. I will be right outside. Just holler if you need anything."

Mary kissed Peggy's forehead and gently touched her arm. It had been fifty years since Mary lost her baby, on the banks of the Ohio. She understood Peggy's pain. Their eyes met for a second; they understood without a word.

Sara waited at the door for Mary, helping her out the door to the parlor.

"I need a drink of whisky," Mary said as she got situated in her chair.

"Do you mind if I join you?" Sara asked, pouring two drinks from the decanter before Mary could answer.

"I would be honored if you did." Mary stared at Sara. "What happened Sara? Remember we felt the baby kicking last week?" Mary took one of the glasses from Sara and downed it.

"It was destiny, Mary—Peggy will never have children of her own." Sara took a taste of the straight whisky and made a face.

"Why do you say that?" Mary asked.

"Her palm told me, Mary. You know the lifelines, they predict things like that. She will be the mother to many children, but she will never have any of her own."

Mary looked into her empty glass as if she might find guidance. They both sat in silence, each in their own thoughts.

Mary looked up after a while and said "Sara—light the candle in my window. We will need some help." Mary pointed at the candlestick on the windowsill. It was kept there to summon help.

Sara lit the single candle from the flame of the candelabra on the mantle.

By the time Mary finished her second drink, they could hear a horse coming up the hill at full gallop. The rider dismounted and banged on the door.

"Mrs. Ingles! Sara! It's Jesse Tanner; what be wrong? I was heading for home, I seen your signal in the window and came running."

"I am coming as fast as I can, Jesse!" Sara hollered from the top of the stairs. She opened the door for Jesse, who was the proprietor of the Ingles Ferry tavern. "Thank you for coming Jesse—Mrs. Ingles needs you."

He scrambled up the stairs, his lanky legs taking two steps at a time. At the parlor door he said, "May I come in Mrs. Ingles?"

"Yes, please come in."

"What is the problem, Mrs. Ingles?" Jesse asked as he took off his hat.

"The baby was stillborn. I want you to close the tavern tonight out of respect, tie a piece of black ribbon or cloth on the door. Don't reopen till I tell you. I don't want any disturbances tonight or tomorrow. Ingles Ferry is in mourning."

"Consider it done, Mrs. Ingles."

"Jesse, as soon as daylight comes, get two men digging a small grave at the foot of Mr. Ingles's grave," Mary said.

"You mean beside him don't you?"

"No, I am to be buried beside my husband," Mary insisted. "I want the baby at the foot of our graves. Will you make a nice coffin like you did for my William and get it up here first thing in the morning?"

"I will take care of everything, Mary; don't you worry. I am sorry about the baby." Jesse held his hat reverently with both hands. "My wife Anna was looking forward to seeing the newborn. It's been a while since we had a baby born at Ingles Ferry."

"Thank you, Jesse. You know, William would be proud of what you have done with his tavern."

"Thank you, Mrs. Ingles—I appreciate your giving me the opportunity to own it."

Mary nodded her head and said, "William thought kindly of you and wanted you to have it."

Jesse said, "I know—I miss him." He turned and was down the stairs like a herd of buffalo.

Sara went back to Peggy's room and found her still cradling the dead baby, cooing and talking to it like it was alive.

"How are you doing?" Sara touched Peggy's forehead.

"We are doing fine Sara; we're just fine."

"You still got a fever—I want you to keep this wet rag on your brow." Placing the moist linen across her forehead, Sara said, "You understand we must bury the baby, come morning, while it is cool?"

Still in denial, Peggy didn't answer. She continued holding the baby like no one was going to take her away.

Sara went to the kitchen to get Peggy some chicken broth. When she returned, Peggy was asleep and Mary was sitting in the high back chair with a porcelain doll from her collection in her arms.

"What are you doing up so late, Mary?"

"Praying for Peggy like you asked. Can't sleep thinking about Peggy holding her baby's body."

"I understand." *First time I ever knew of Mary praying—she does believe in God, after all.*

Mary said, "If you will take the baby now, while Peggy is sleeping, I will place the doll in her arms. I have heard this helps the mother in her time of bereavement."

Sara picked up the stiff little body and placed it in a woven cane basket and took it out of the room.

Mary placed the doll in Peggy's limp arms and picked up the pewter bowl of chicken broth and spoon that Sara had set on the wash stand. Mary managed to get a few spoonfuls down Peggy's throat.

Sara came back and stayed up through the night as Mary dozed off and on in the chair. Sara tried to get her to go to bed, but Mary insisted on staying in the room with Peggy.

Sara heard a horse and carriage. She looked out the window to see Jesse and his wife, Anna Tanner, both dressed as if they were going to meeting.

Sara touched Mary's arm. "Wake up Mary. It's morning and the Tanners are here. I am going down to let them in."

"Take me with you. I have things I want to take care of." Mary got up, with Sara's assistance.

Sara opened the large, wooden door. Jesse and Anna Tanner were standing there, Jesse with the tiny coffin and Anna with a large bouquet of wildflowers.

"Come in the house." Mary looked at the coffin about the size of a bread box.

"What do you think of it?" Jesse asked.

"Just what I had in mind." Mary opened it and smiled when she saw how Jesse had lined it with white satin linen and used padding to create a bed for the baby to lay.

Sara reached for the coffin. "Let me have it and I will dress the baby and—"

"No, I want to do this, Sara." Mary tried to take the baby's coffin from Jesse. "Where is the baby?"

"In the root cellar, where it's cool. I will bring her," Sara answered.

Jesse said, "I will check on how the digging is going. Sam and Jeremiah from our church volunteered to dig. They have been at it since daybreak." He gently placed the coffin on the foyer table.

"Anna, why don't you take those pretty flowers up to Peggy and stay with her until I get finished?"

Mary felt the finish of the coffin with her hands and opened it again, admiring Jesse's work.

"Here she is, Mary." Sara handed her the baby basket.

"You sure I can't help you?"

"It's something I need to do for myself and Peggy. I wish Peggy were well enough — "

"I'm here." Peggy said from top of the stairs. "I want to dress her for burial."

Sara carried the coffin as Mary followed carefully with the baby in the basket up to Peggy's room. Sara left the two women alone to place the baby in the coffin. Both having lost a child at birth, they understood what needed to be done.

Mary made a burial gown by cutting the toe out of a sock. Sticking a finger through the toe she said, "What do you think?"

"It will just fit my little angel." Peggy took the sock and tucked the baby's head through the hole cut in the toe.

Mary cried as Peggy placed the baby in the coffin.

"Now she is ready," Peggy said.

Mary called out, "Sara, we need you."

The door opened. "You ready?" Sara asked.

Mary and Sara looked at Peggy, who nodded. Sara pulled a blanket over Peggy, then picked up the coffin. Mary opened the door and they walked to the stairs. Mary saw Jesse and Anna Tanner waiting at the foot of the staircase.

"Jesse, can you take the coffin, so I can help Mary and Peggy?" Sara asked.

Jesse bounded up the stairs, took the coffin in one arm, and helped a very weak Peggy down the stairs with the other, as Sara assisted Mary.

Jesse set the coffin back on the foyer table and said, "Are you ready for me to nail the lid on?"

"Just a moment, please." Peggy stood looking at her angel on the soft cloud of satin Jesse had made. Sara stood on one side, and Mary on the other.

"May I?" asked Anna.

They made room for Anna and the women just gazed into the little box.

Jesse looked at Peggy and said, "May I close the casket now?"

Peggy nodded and wiped tears with a corner of the blanket that covered her shoulders as Mary and Sara hugged her.

Jesse placed the wooden lid on the coffin and gently tapped in six tiny nails to hold it in place.

Jesse carried the box outside as the women followed him to the freshly-dug grave. The Quaker grave diggers, Sam and Jeremiah, removed their hats as the group approached. Their wives stood in mourning as Jesse got on his knees to attach a small wooden cross he had carved to the lid.

Brother Jeremiah stepped forward, Bible in hand, and said, "The cross Brother Jesse attached to this baby's coffin is to identify her as a child of God."

He lifted his hands up and said, "Please accept this child to your Kingdom, Father, for she never had the opportunity to sin."

The brethren sang a hymn and the angel's coffin was covered with the sandy loam dirt at the foot of William Ingles's grave.

# Chapter Twenty-Seven
## Home Again

"The stagecoach to Abingdon will be leaving shortly, Miss Mitchell. We best get going." Jesse Tanner reached for Peggy's bag.

"Give me a moment with Mary and Sara, please, Jesse."

Jesse Tanner nodded, holding his hat and her bag, obviously uncomfortable standing in Mary Ingles' foyer, listening to sad goodbyes.

"I will miss you, Mary. You too, Sara. Thank you both for all you have done for me." Peggy said.

Jesse pushed the three-cornered hat down tight on his head and opened the heavy oak door. "The driver is waiting, Miss Mitchell. We must go—now!"

Sara handed Peggy a basket at the door. "You eat this. What I made is good for you—help you get your strength back. A crock full of good water for you, too."

Mary moved toward the open door, looked into Peggy's eyes, and said, "Should you tell anyone about the baby, that's your business. They will never hear about your child from us." Mary looked at Sara and Jesse to make sure they understood.

"I know." Peggy embraced Mary, and turned toward Sara trying to reach up to hug her, but couldn't. Sara bent over awkwardly and Peggy hugged her neck.

Jesse helped Peggy into his two-wheeled carriage for the ride to the livery stable, where the westbound stage waited.

When they arrived, the driver was pacing back and forth and motioned with his hands for Jesse to quickly get Peggy in the coach.

Peggy said, "Thank you Jesse—you're a good man."

"Glad to bring you to the livery stable." Jesse peered in the open window at Peggy, his hand resting on the bottom of the sill.

"Thank you for everything you and the brethren of your church did for my baby." Peggy placed her hand on his.

"God be with you Peggy. We will pray for your safe travels." Jesse stepped out of the way of the impatient driver.

The cab had thick, black cloth on the windows that could be closed and buttoned to keep out the trail dust. The stage was pulled by four sturdy-looking white horses.

"My name is Charles Pirtle, Miss Mitchell. I will be your driver to Abingdon. Should you need me to stop, beat on the roof with this elm club." He showed her the stick kept underneath the bench seat. "We will be stopping about every twenty-five miles. I appreciate your not asking me to stop unless it is an emergency. We are on a tight schedule, already a half hour late. Any questions?" The bearded driver took her bag from Jesse and placed it on the floor next to her feet.

"How long will it take to get to Jonesborough, Mr. Pirtle?"

"Two days, if the weather holds."

"Would you know the date and the day of the week?"

"It was Monday morning some time ago, but it won't be long if we keep blabbering."

"The date?"

"Second day of July." Mr. Pirtle slammed the door shut, grabbed the step stool and shoved it in the stowage compartment just beneath the coach door.

He kept talking to himself as he climbed to the driver's seat. "How in the hell am I supposed to know what hour of the day it is? What am I, a timekeeper? Let's go!" He yelled and popped the whip.

Peggy was amused at his crankiness and decided to not ask him any more unnecessary questions. *Two days and I will be home with my family.* Peggy leaned back into the corner of the coach and fell asleep thinking of her baby, now buried on the banks of the New River.

The first stop was Wytheville, Virginia, the county seat of Wythe County. A recently-built log courthouse and a spring-fed creek to water the horses were was all there was in Wytheville. Peggy followed Mr. Pirtle as he lead the team to the creek.

As the team drank vigorously and playfully splashed about in the shallow water, the driver looked almost cheerful. "We're making good time, Miss Mitchell. We should be at the stage stop before dark."

"That's good." Peggy looked around for a moment.

The driver held out a deerskin bag of water toward her.

"No thank you. I still have water in my jug—that will suffice until the next stop," Peggy said.

"I filled my bag upstream from the team, Miss Mitchell."

"I saw you did. What concerns me is where the last team of horses passing through stood," Peggy said.

"Never thought much about that."

"You should—streams like this spread cholera." Peggy looked around for privacy and saw a clump of thick mountain laurel and headed toward it.

"Take your time. I need to check the rigging and harness the horses." Mr. Pirtle walked the team back to the stage coach, parked on a level portion of the wagon road.

They arrived at the stage stop as the sun set over a distant ridge. The mountains took on a hue of blue. The primitive way station, just recently set up, was maintained by German Quakers at the base of a high mountain that separated the Commonwealth of Virginia from the State of North Carolina. Peggy slept in a limp rope bed with no mattress. Excited about getting home, she didn't care that the stop was just a small room attached to the horse barn.

At daybreak, they were up and off with a new team and driver to Abingdon. Peggy yearned to see her old friends Molly, Sheriff Preston, and Josiah Coffee. *I can't tell them what has happened since I saw them last year. They will want to know where I have been, what has happened. What will I tell them?*

When they arrived in Abingdon at sundown, a black stable boy was out front to greet the stage.

Peggy asked, "Where is Josiah Coffee?"

"Mr. Coffee gone to Ken-tuck with Sheriff Preston's family."

"New owners," the driver said, handing Peggy's bag to the stable boy.

"What about Molly's family?" Peggy asked.

"President Adams appointed Sheriff Preston to the U.S. Marshall's job in Kentucky. He took his whole family and Josiah with him," the driver said as he unharnessed the lathered team of horses.

Peggy was disappointed, but also relieved that she wouldn't have to answer their questions.

The new owners were all business, not friendly like the McDonalds. They were busy with a house full of guests to feed. Every bed was filled; business was good.

The coach was full as Peggy boarded the stage for Jonesborough. She had butterflies in her stomach, anticipating the homecoming that awaited her.

A fellow passenger shared a recent edition of a *Philadelphia Gazette*. It was difficult to read as the coach bounced along the bumpy road. At midday, things began to look familiar. The crossing on the Watauga at the ford revealed the spring rains had been sufficient, for the river was running higher than usual. *Maybe Father will have a good corn crop this year.*

At the last stop before Peggy's destination, she asked the driver to stop at the seven-mile marker just southeast of Knob Creek. The driver, new to eastern Tennessee, advised her to use the club when she wanted him to stop, as he only knew where Jonesborough was.

She beat on the roof with the club as the stage made it across Knob Creek. The driver stopped when the stage got out of the water and onto level ground.

"You sure you don't want to go on into Jonesborough with us?" the driver asked.

"This is where I am going. See that stone?" Peggy pointed.

"Yes, I do."

"It has a seven chiseled into it by my father's hand. It's exactly seven miles from that stone to the Chester Inn. You best get going; your other passengers are waiting."

"Right you are!" The driver said, climbing back onto the driver's bench.

Peggy smiled at the driver and waved as she headed down the narrow lane toward home.

Coming toward her were children throwing rocks as they walked down Mitchell Lane. Getting closer, she saw that it was her youngest brothers Samuel, David, James and Hezekiah. When they saw her they started screaming and hollering, "Peggy is back! Peggy is back!" When they met up, the boys in their excitement to hug her almost knocked her down.

"You have all grown so much—Hezekiah you're so big I don't know if I can lift you." She bent down and gave each a kiss.

Her brothers asked her so many questions she couldn't respond to them before they asked another.

"Please boys, let's get home, and I will tell you all about my travels."

She learned on the way that Ibby had gone to Kentucky with the oldest son of Mr. Young, whom Ibby taught last year. It didn't sound as if either family was happy about it.

Her mother and father stood in the lane near the house with Rebeckah and Jennett, who must have heard the commotion.

Her parents looked weak. They had aged considerably in the year she was gone.

"Welcome home, daughter." Adam hugged her as her mother cried.

"What's the matter, Mother?" Peggy hugged her.

"I'm just so happy." Elizabeth wiped tears from her eyes with her long apron. "I didn't think I would ever see you again."

Peggy held her mother as the family went into the main house out of the hot sun. The familiar smells of a meal in preparation caught Peggy off guard.

"You have company coming?" Peggy asked her mother.

"Everyone is coming this afternoon for the Fourth of—"

"That's right; it's Independence Day. I almost forgot."

"It has been twenty-one years since we declared our Independence. We invited the neighbors for a celebration. It'll be extra special now that you're home." Adam hugged Peggy again as Elizabeth and Rebeckah looked on.

"Reverend Witherspoon will be excited to see you," Rebeckah said.

"Will he be here?"

"Reverend Witherspoon comes every Wednesday afternoon from Greeneville for dinner and stays overnight. During school he stays to teach on Thursdays," Rebeckah said.

"How is Jimmy?" Peggy asked.

"I think that's him on Star coming up the lane." Jennett pointed.

"That's Star for sure, I recognize that special sideways gait of his. Never seen another horse that could prance about like royalty," Peggy said.

"Looks like he brought Thomas for the fireworks," Rebeckah said.

"You would never think that they are not kin." Adam shook his head. "Reverend took the boy and his mother in when he was called to Greeneville."

Nearing the house, Jimmy squinted his eyes. "Is that Peggy?" Jimmy jumped off to give her a hug. "Welcome home! I have missed you."

"And I have missed you. I see you have taken good care of Star." Peggy glanced at the chestnut mare.

"Best horse a man could ever have. You know your Mr. Jackson is here don't you?"

"Mary Ingles told me Nathan brought him home," Peggy said.

"Peggy, didn't you get my letter?" Adam asked.

"No, Father—I never received any mail while I was gone. I want to see him." Peggy headed for the horse pen.

Mr. Jackson must have caught Peggy's scent. He started nickering and running around the pen excitedly. When he saw Peggy, he stopped in his tracks and stood, head held high. His nickering stopped and he pawed the ground gently. Peggy approached him slowly first then broke and ran to him. The horse waited, acknowledging her with a nicker and a gentle shake of his mane. Peggy put her arms around the horse's neck and tears of joy flowed down her cheeks.

# Chapter Twenty-Eight
## Nineteenth Century

"WAR OF 1812 OVER!" read the headline of the week-old *Philadelphia Gazette* dated February 1, 1815. Peggy read every word of Dr. Chester's newspapers left lying about the parlor of the Chester Inn. The inn was now her home and Peggy had a nice room on the second floor that looked out over Jonesborough's Main Street.

This afternoon, she was sitting in the parlor with a shawl wrapped around her shoulders. The wind had shifted and was blowing out of the east. The windows rattled from the wind and the glass panes were foggy, a good indication that the temperature had dropped below freezing. She instinctively got up and put another log on the fire, then returned to her rocker.

She thought back to all the twists and turns her life had taken. She had so many adventures, most of them the results of her own choices. When she married Jimmy Witherspoon, she expected to raise her younger siblings, then spend many years living quietly, helping Jimmy with his ministry, and enjoying their comfortable companionship. But instead she was alone again—Jimmy dead and the children grown and on their own.

A patient stepped out of Dr. Chester's office and the doctor followed, wagging his finger and saying, "Remember to take every last drop of that medicine, even if you think you are well." The local farmer nodded that he would follow doctor's orders.

Dr. Chester opened the outside door for him. "You best get on home before it gets any worse—looks like we are in for a hard winter." He quickly shut the door against the cold wind.

"Mind if I join you, Peggy?" Dr. Chester asked as he sat down in the rocker next to her.

"You know I enjoy your company—why do you always ask me?" Peggy neatly folded the tabloid newspaper in her hands.

"It just seems like the gentlemanly thing to do when a man sits down next to a pretty lady." Dr. Chester settled back into the rocker.

"We've been friends for eighteen years. Besides, this is your inn. What would you do if I said no?" Peggy asked.

Ignoring the question, Dr. Chester continued, "It's been that long since you came barging into my office over Deaderick's Store?" He counted on his fingers.

"I'm a teacher—I can count, you know." Peggy made a face.

"And a fine one you are." Dr. Chester rocked.

"Your flattery is appreciated, but what do you mean I barged in on you?" Peggy looked at the doctor.

"You did." He leaned back, looking up at the ceiling teasingly.

She swatted at the doctor with the folded paper. "I did not, you old goat."

They both chuckled, as the wind howled across the long front porch of the inn, knocking over a chair with a clatter.

"The wind is picking up." Peggy gazed out the window.

"How's your room?" Dr. Chester asked.

"It will be fine once you get that squeaky step on the staircase fixed," Peggy said.

"The carpenter is coming next week." Dr. Chester put his hands on his chubby knees.

They both rocked quietly for a while, just watching the fire.

After several minutes, the doctor asked, "What's bothering you, Peggy? It's not like you to sit around doing nothing."

Peggy looked at Dr. Chester. "Nothing's wrong with me."

"You haven't been out of the inn in weeks, not even to go to church." The doctor got up to put a another log on the fire.

"Are you keeping an eye on me now?" Peggy asked.

"You have friends who are concerned about you, that's all." Dr. Chester warmed his hands by the fire.

"Do you have plenty of firewood? I wouldn't want to be without in this weather." Peggy tried to change the subject.

"I have sufficient wood for the winter." Dr. Chester sat down in his rocker and turned toward Peggy.

"Is it split?" Peggy asked.

Dr. Chester said, "Stop trying to change the subject." He continued somberly, "I am your doctor and I hope also a good friend."

"Yes, you are a dear friend." Peggy pulled her shawl tighter around her.

"Good, then tell me what's bothering you." Dr. Chester clasped his hands and rocked.

"It's this war that's distressing me." Peggy shook her head. "My brother John and Rebeckah's husband Thomas Smith haven't returned from the war that's supposed to be over. I hate war!"

""You have good reason to hate war after experiencing it firsthand when you were just a child. But you shouldn't be worrying about John and Thomas. It's a long way up the Natchez trace from New Orleans. It will take a while for them to get back." Dr. Chester tried to reassure her.

Peggy rocked back in her chair. "They're off fighting a damn war that's over, except for the treaty. They wouldn't have any way of knowing it's over, would they?"

"I am sure by now General Jackson has gotten word that peace negotiations are going on." Dr. Chester leaned forward, reaching for the iron poker to stir the coals of the fire.

Peggy said, "The men of Washington County would follow that warmongering Andrew Jackson off a cliff if he asked them to."

"Careful what you say—your old beau is a hero." Dr. Chester smiled, knowing he hit a nerve.

"Don't call him my beau," Peggy said.

Dr. Chester laid the poker down. "He could have been, if you—"

"Well he's not!" Peggy rocked a bit faster. "Don't you ever forget anything?"

Seeing that Peggy was riled, Dr. Chester chose his words carefully. "We wouldn't have this warm parlor to sit in, if Andrew Jackson hadn't smelled the fire and jumped into action, back in . . . "

Peggy finished his sentence. "It was 1802."

Dr. Chester agreed. "That's right. You are good at recalling dates. How do you do it?"

"I group things with events that I will never forget. The year of your fire was the same year my parents died."

Dr. Chester recalled, "Andrew Jackson was a guest. Smelling smoke, he began to wake everyone in the inn. Then Andrew climbed up on the roof in nothing but his night shirt. He bellowed orders from the roof to the crowd that gathered below to form a bucket brigade from the creek. Everyone worked together in a single line, passing buckets one at a time until the fire was under control. Andrew Jackson saved the inn and the town. That's why men follow him—he's a born leader." Dr. Chester smiled after telling his favorite story about the famous General saving his inn.

"That's what they say." Peggy kept rocking.

"I know you're worried about the boys coming home." Dr. Chester turned toward Peggy, his palms tight on the rocker arms. "I think you're still grieving for Jimmy. This August will only be two years since his death."

"I do miss him. I had planned to grow old with Jimmy, as a minister's wife." She looked into the fire, and then continued. "It wasn't God's plan, and I accept that. But . . . " She started to cry.

The only sound was the fire crackling and the creak of the rockers, until Dr. Chester said, "Are you crying for Jimmy or do your tears have anything to do with that letter you received from London?"

"You saw my mail?" Peggy slapped the arm of the rocking chair in frustration.

"I am the innkeeper who also sorts your mail. It's hard not to notice a letter from London."

Peggy sighed. "I am crying about losing Jimmy and about the letter. The letter brought sad news—a very dear friend has died."

"I am sorry for your loss. Someone you met in London?" Dr. Chester inquired.

"Captain Whiddon, a widower who took me there. I became nanny to his children."

"You've never said much about your time in London. I didn't know you worked over there. But I guess it was natural for you to be a nanny—you've been taking care of children your whole life."

"I didn't consider it work. I loved the children and enjoyed taking care of them."

"What happened to the captain?" Dr. Chester leaned forward.

"The letter didn't say. Only that he had died and bequeathed me two thousand pounds."

"That's about what it cost me to build this inn. The captain thought well of you." Dr. Chester leaned back in his rocker.

Peggy took a deep breath and let it out slowly. "I loved Willy dearly."

"If I may be so bold as to ask, why didn't you stay in London and marry him instead of coming home and marrying Reverend Witherspoon?"

"I had to get out of England. I was at risk of being tried and hanged for treason."

Dr. Chester's eyes widened. "You? Treason?"

Peggy hadn't intended to tell Dr. Chester or anyone, but she was so distraught about Willy's death that she'd already said more than intended. She gave a brief description of her experiences in London. "I never thought I could love anyone the way I loved Willy. Leaving was the hardest thing I've ever done."

"Did Jimmy know?"

"I never told him. My sister Ibby had hurt him enough running off to Kentucky with another man." Peggy glanced out the window. "Jimmy loved Ibby and could never get her out of his mind."

"He told you that?" Dr. Chester stopped rocking.

"He never told me, but some things a woman just knows," Peggy said.

"Did you love Jimmy?" The doctor asked.

"Yes, but it was different. From an early age I was told that we would marry some day. We had a great respect for one another and having known each other since childhood, understood one another's ways. We were always great friends."

"You seemed so compatible."

"We never said a harsh word or argued." Peggy laughed. "I asked him to marry me."

"That doesn't surprise me. When you want something, you go for it." Dr. Chester leaned back and chuckled.

"I needed him. Mother and Father died, leaving me the responsibility of raising Rebeckah and Jennett and our four brothers." Peggy rolled her head on the high back rocker, thinking of the responsibility. "Seven children! No wonder God made sure I didn't have any of my own."

"You and Jimmy made good parents—they've all turned out well. You should be proud. You gave them a good education and a Christian upbringing." Dr. Chester looked at her.

Peggy nodded. "After Father died, Jimmy just assumed the role of their father, as he had done with his step-brother Thomas. You know he bequeathed half of his estate to Thomas and Rebeckah and I received the remainder. With what father and Willy left me, I have enough to live comfortably."

"The men in your life took good care of you. You should be happy." Dr. Chester leaned toward her.

"I always thought I could take care of myself, but I didn't know if I could take care of myself and seven children. But I was happy with our family. I miss being a minister's wife and a mother to seven children. They have their own families now. I'm not their mother or a grandmother to any of them. They just call me Peggy and their children, Aunt Peggy." Her voice cracked.

"They have all told me numerous times how much you and Jimmy did for them after Adam and Elizabeth died. Hezekiah told me he would have been an orphan at the age of nine had you and Jimmy not made a home for him."

"Hezekiah said that?"

"Yes he did and so did the others." Dr. Chester pushed back in his chair.

"My brother John and his family are going to Kentucky. Thomas wrote Rebeckah in his last letter that he wants to claim his bounty in Alabama after the war. Hezekiah is off surveying the Louisiana Purchase and I don't think he is coming back."

Dr. Chester listened and rocked.

"What bothers me is, I am afraid I'll die and be left here all alone . . . like my baby." Peggy's voice cracked.

"Your baby?"

Peggy wiped a tear from her eye and told her friend about her stillborn baby.

"I didn't know, Peggy." Dr. Chester stopped his rocker.

"I never told anyone." Peggy leaned back in her chair. "But the grief got the best of me when I read about Willy's death."

Dr. Chester looked into her teary eyes. "I won't say anything."

Peggy sniffled. "I know — that's why I told you."

Dr. Chester got up, stood behind Peggy's rocker and placed his hands on her shoulders. "Is there anything I can do for you?"

She reached back behind her and gently touched his arm. "You just did."

"How's that?"

"You listened to me." She wiped at her eyes. "I'll be fine, just feeling sorry for myself. I shouldn't burden you with my problems."

"That's what friends are for." Dr. Chester patted her shoulder. "I'll see you at dinner."

"Thank you for being my friend," Peggy said.

As Dr. Chester climbed the stairs to his quarters on the top floor, Peggy wiped fog from a windowpane and looked down Main Street. She reminisced about racing down the same street as a young girl on a horse named Cherokee and winning the first Beaver Run.

She saw the log courthouse across the street and was reminded of the day Andrew Jackson proposed to her. She turned back to the glowing embers of the fire and recalled Christmas at Reynolds House and the passion of those late nights with Willy.

Peggy thought of the men she could have married other than Jimmy: Andrew Jackson, John Hammer, Sheriff Preston, and Willy. She had no interest in marrying any of them except Willy. She would have married him if the circumstances had been different. But in her heart of hearts, she knew that if God intended for her to marry Willy, the circumstances would have been different.

She realized it was God's plan for her to marry Reverend Witherspoon, who agreed to help her raise her young siblings. They were good parents to the children, and with her help and support, Jimmy was an even better minister. Together they had made a difference in the lives of her brothers and sisters and in the lives of Jimmy's congregation.

*I have lived my life as God planned it, and I have no regrets.*

## The End

# Other Books in The Westward Sagas

The Westward Sagas began with **Book 1: *Spring House***
    The Mitchells just wanted to be left alone to farm their land, practice their faith, and raise their family. But their response to the extraordinary circumstances of frontier life, politics, and war made heroes of these ordinary citizens.
    Adam fought the British, while his mother, wife, and children endured deprivation and danger on the family farm in the midst of the battle.
    The story of Adam's two loves – his first wife Jennetta who died bearing their son and his second wife Elizabeth who bore him twelve more children – creates the human backdrop to the historical events of Revolutionary War times. ISBN: 978-0-9777484-0-2

The story continued in **Book 2: *Adam's Daughters***
    Peggy Mitchell, a survivor of the Battle of Guilford Courthouse, grows up in Jonesborough, Tennessee during the tumultuous first twenty years of the nation's existence.
    Though haunted by memories of war, she matures into strong, independent young woman who is courted by Andrew Jackson and who has a freed slave as her best friend. Her younger brothers and sisters become her surrogate children and students.
    Together the children of Adam and Elizabeth take on renegade Indians, highwaymen, and the hardships of an untamed land. ISBN: 978-0-9777484-3-3

Available at www.westwardsagas.com, Amazon.com, SignedByTheAuthor.com, Smashwords.com, BarnesAndNoble.com, Google Books, and at bookstores by special order.

# A Note from the Author

*Children of the Revolution* is the third book in the Westward Sagas Series. Like the two books before it, the editors and I have made every effort to make each book stand on its own for its entertainment value. It is not necessary to read book one or two before three, as enough back story is presented in each book to quickly get the reader acquainted with the characters.

The series will continue to be written and published in chronological order as the westward expansion of our nation continues. I invite you to ride along with me or join me somewhere on the trail. We hope you enjoy the read where ever you start.

If you want to learn more about history and genealogy, I list some resources on the next page that have been invaluable to me in my research.

# RESOURCES

Arthur, John Preston. *Western North Carolina: A History from 1730 to 1913*. Johnson City, TN: Overmountain Press, 1996.

Brands, H.W. *Andrew Jackson: His Life and Times*. New York, NY: Doubleday, 2005.

Bushman, John. Winifred Lois Smith Pearson, compiler and editor. *"I Will Sing"; The Life Story of Lois Angeline Smith Bushman*. Provo, UT: Irvin B. Pearson Family Organization, 1990.

Cox, Joyce and W. Eugene Cox, compilers and editors. *History of Washington County Tennessee*, Washington County Historical Association, Inc. Johnson City, TN: Overmountain Press, 2001.

Cox, Joyce and W. Eugene Cox. *Jonesborough's Historic Churches*. Jonesborough, TN: Heritage Alliance of Northeast Tennessee and Southwest Virginia, n. d.

Fink, Paul M. *Jonesborough: The First Century of Tennessee's First Town*. Johnson City, TN: Overmountain Press, 2002.

Gibson, Jo Chapman. *Salem Presbyterian Church*. Johnson City, TN: Overmountain Press, 1993.

Greensboro Historical Museum, 130 Summit Avenue, Greensboro, NC 27401. www.greensborohistory. org

Guilford County Genealogical Society, P.O. Box 4713, Dept. W, Greensboro, NC 27404-4713. www.rootsweb.ancestry.com/~ncgcgs/

James, Marquis. *The Life of Andrew Jackson*. Indianapolis, IN: Bobbs-Merrill Company, 1938.

Leyburn, James G. A *Social History: The Scotch Irish*. Chapel Hill, NC: The University of North Carolina Press, 1962.

McCullough, David. *John Adams*. New York, NY: Simon and Schuster, 2001.

Meyer, Annie Galbreath. *History of Our Mitchell Ancestors from 1743 to 1959*. Charleston, IL: Dorite Press, 1960.

Miller, John C. *The First Frontier: Life in Colonial America*. New York, NY: Dell Publishing Company, 1966.

Rogers, Shawn. Director of Mendenhall Plantation, 603 W. Main Street, Jamestown, NC 27282. Descendent of Patriot Ansel Fields, also at the Battle of Guilford Courthouse.

Rouse, Jr., Parke. *The Great Wagon Road*. Petersburg, VA: The Dietz Press, 1915. Reprinted 2008.

*Washington County Tennessee Inventories of Estates Volume 00, 1779-1821*. Signal Mountain, TN: Mountain Press, Reprinted 2000.

Williams, Samuel Cole. *History of the Lost State of Franklin*. Johnson City, TN: The Watauga Press, 1924.

# About the Author

David Bowles, a native of Austin, Texas, lives in San Antonio with his best friends and constant companions Lulubelle and Daisy, yellow Labs. He grew up listening to stories of his ancestors told by family members in the generation before him. The stories fascinated David so much that he grew up to become a tale-spinner, spinning tales through the written word in The Westward Sagas and through the spoken word speaking to groups of both adults and children.

David started writing stories of his family to ensure that his children and grandchildren had accurate records of the family history. However, while the original versions, written in narrative textbook style, did maintain the records, they didn't maintain the interest of the readers. So he used his imagination and creativity to fill in the gaps of what might have happened when the details weren't available. He created dialogue and scenes to add true life drama to the story of the Mitchell Family from colonial days to the settlement of the West. He hopes these stories fascinate his readers as much as the stories of his ancestors have always fascinated him.